The first romance stories Stephanie Laurens read were
se   the b   nd these
co   exert   n escape
from   lry world of professional science, Stephanie
started writing Regency romances, and she is now a *New
York Times*, *USA Today* and *Publishers Weekly* bestselling
author.

Stephanie lives in a leafy suburb of Melbourne, Australia,
with her husband and two daughters, along with two cats,
Shakespeare and Marlowe.

Learn more about Stephanie's books from her website at
www.stephanielaurens.com

Praise for Stephanie Laurens:

'This sensual tale of lust and seduction in 19th century
England will leave you weak at the knees'
Now

'Stephanie Laurens' heroines are marvellous tributes to
Georgette Heyer: feisty and strong' Cathy Kelly

'Sinfully sexy and deliciously irresistible'
Booklist

Viscount Breckenridge
to the Rescue

A CYNSTER NOVEL

piatkus

PIATKUS

First published in the US in 2011 by Avon Books,
An imprint of HarperCollins Publishers, New York
First published in Great Britain as a paperback original in 2011 by Piatkus
By arrangement with Avon
Reprinted 2011

Copyright © 2011 by Savdek Management Proprietary Ltd
Excerpt from *In Pursuit of Miss Eliza Cynster* copyright © 2011 by Savdek
Management Proprietary Ltd

The moral right of the author has been asserted.

A CIP catalogue record for this book
is available from the British Library.

ISBN 978-0-7499-5504-5

Printed and bound by CPI Group (UK) Ltd, Croydon, CR0 4YY

Papers used by Piatkus are from well-managed forests
and other responsible sources.

MIX
Paper from
responsible sources
FSC® C104740

The Cynster Family Tree

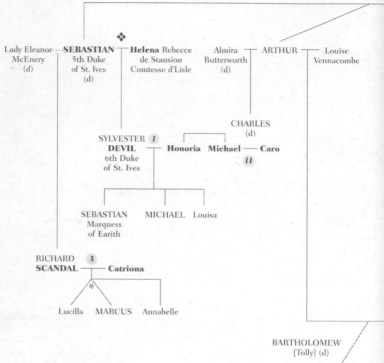

Lady Eleanor···**SEBASTIAN** ─┬─ **Helena** Rebecce   Almira ─┬─ ARTHUR ─┬─ Louise
McEnery   5th Duke   de Stansion   Butterworth   Vennacombe
(d)   of St. Ives   Comtesse d'Lisle   (d)
(d)

CHARLES
(d)

SYLVESTER *1*
DEVIL ─┬─ **Honoria**   Michael ── **Caro**
6th Duke   *11*
of St. Ives

SEBASTIAN   MICHAEL   Louisa
Marquess
of Earith

RICHARD *3*
SCANDAL ─┬─ **Catriona**
  ✳

Lucilla   MARCUS   Annabelle

BARTHOLOMEW
[Tolly] (d)

8
Martin ──── **Amanda**

MALE Cynsters in capitals   ✳ denotes twins
CHILDREN BORN AFTER 1825 NOT SHOWN

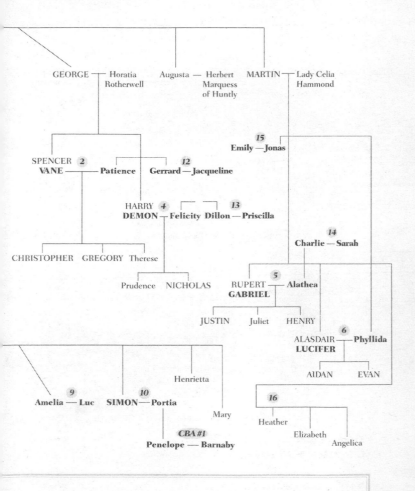

GEORGE — Horatia Rotherwell   Augusta — Herbert Marquess of Huntly   MARTIN — Lady Celia Hammond

15 Emily — Jonas

SPENCER *2* VANE — Patience   *12* Gerrard — Jacqueline

HARRY *4* DEMON — Felicity   Dillon *13* — Priscilla

14 Charlie — Sarah

CHRISTOPHER   GREGORY   Therese

Prudence   NICHOLAS

RUPERT *5* GABRIEL — Alathea

JUSTIN   Juliet   HENRY

ALASDAIR *6* LUCIFER — Phyllida

AIDAN   EVAN

Henrietta

9 Amelia — Luc   *10* SIMON — Portia

16 Heather

Mary

CBA #1 Penelope — Barnaby

Elizabeth   Angelica

---

11. *The Ideal Bride*
12. *The Truth About Love*
13. *What Price Love?*
14. *The Taste of Innocence*

15. *Temptation and Surrender*
16. *This Volume*

Prologue

February, 1829

The castle was silent and still. Outside snow lay heavy on the land, a white blanket smothering hill and vale, loch and forest.

He sat in the armory, one of his retreats. Head bent, he concentrated on cleaning the guns used earlier that day, when a break in the weather had allowed him and a small group of others to venture forth. They'd bagged enough fresh meat to keep the castle supplied for a week, maybe more. He'd taken some small satisfaction in that.

Meat, at least, he could provide.

The sound of determined footsteps reached him. All satisfaction fled. What replaced it . . . he couldn't put a name to the roiling mix of fury, frustration, and dread.

His mother stalked into the room.

He didn't lift his head.

She came to a halt at the end of the central table at which he sat.

He felt her glare, but stoically continued to reassemble the gun he'd been cleaning.

She broke first. Slapping a hand on the table, she leaned forward to hiss, "Swear it! Swear that you'll do it—that you'll go south, seize one of the Cynster sisters, and bring her here so I can have my revenge."

He took his time reacting. Clung to the slowness he habitually used to cloak his true nature and so better control others. However, in this instance, his mother had schemed well enough to put herself beyond his control, indeed to the extent that he now found himself in hers.

That stung.

The *what if*s still resounded in his head. *If* he'd paid more attention to her ramblings, might he have noticed some sign

1

of her scheme earlier? Early enough to step in and put a stop to it? Yet she'd been thus for as long as he'd been old enough to notice, filled with black thoughts, with burning vengeance at her core.

His father had never seen her clearly; to him she'd always put on a sweet face, a mask impenetrable enough to cloak the bitterness beneath. For his part, he'd hoped his father's death would drain the black bile from her heart. Instead, the poison had welled even more corrosively.

He'd grown too accustomed to hearing her ravings; he'd stopped listening long ago.

To, it seemed, his and others' cost now.

But it was too late for regrets, much less recriminations.

Raising his head enough to meet her eyes, letting nothing he felt show in his face, he held her gaze for a moment, then briefly nodded. "Aye, I'll do it." He forced himself to say the words she wanted to hear. "I'll bring one of the Cynster sisters here, so you can have your revenge."

Chapter One

March, 1829
Wadham Gardens, London

Heather Cynster knew her latest plan to find a suitable husband was doomed the instant she set foot in Lady Herford's salon.

In a distant corner, a dark head, perfectly coiffed in the latest rakish style, rose. A pair of sharp hazel eyes pinned her where she stood.

"Damn!" Keeping a smile firmly fixed over her involuntarily clenching teeth, as if she hadn't noticed the most startlingly handsome man in the room staring so intently at her, she let her gaze drift on.

Breckenridge was hemmed in by not one but three dashing ladies, all patently vying for his attention. She sincerely wished them every success and prayed he'd take the sensible course and pretend he hadn't seen her.

She was certainly going to pretend that she hadn't seen him.

Refocusing on the surprisingly large crowd Lady Herford had enticed to her soiree, Heather determinedly banished Breckenridge from her mind and considered her prospects.

Most of the guests were older than she—all the ladies at least. Some she recognized, others she did not, but it would be surprising if any other lady present wasn't married. Or widowed. Or more definitively on the shelf than Heather. Soirees of the style of Lady Herford's were primarily the province of the well-bred but bored matrons, those in search of more convivial company than that provided by their usually much older, more sedate husbands. Such ladies might not be precisely fast, yet neither were they innocent. However, as by common accord said ladies had already presented their husbands with an heir, if not two, the majority had more years in their dish than Heather's twenty-five.

From her brief, initial, assessing sweep, she concluded that most of the gentlemen present were, encouragingly, older than she. Most were in their thirties, and by their style—fashionable, well-turned out, expensively garbed, and thoroughly polished—she'd chosen well in making Lady Herford's soiree her first port of call on this, her first expedition outside the rarefied confines of the ballrooms, drawing rooms, and dining rooms of the upper echelon of the ton.

For years she'd searched through those more refined reception rooms for her hero—the man who would sweep her off her feet and into wedded bliss—only to conclude that he didn't move in such circles. Many gentlemen of the ton, although perfectly eligible in every way, preferred to steer well clear of all the sweet young things, the young ladies paraded on the marriage mart. Instead, they spent their evenings at events such as Lady Herford's, and their nights in various pursuits—gaming and womanizing to name but two.

Her hero—she had to believe he existed somewhere—was most likely a member of that more elusive group of males. Given he was therefore unlikely to come to her, she'd decided—after lengthy and animated discussions with her sisters, Elizabeth and Angelica—that it behooved her to come to him.

To locate him and, if necessary, hunt him down.

Smiling amiably, she descended the shallow steps to the floor of the salon. Lady Herford's villa was a recently built, quite luxurious dwelling located to the north of Primrose Hill—close enough to Mayfair to be easily reached by carriage, a pertinent consideration given Heather had had to come alone. She would have preferred to attend with someone to bear her company, but her sister Eliza, just a year younger and similarly disgusted with the lack of hero-material within their restricted circle, was her most likely coconspirator and they couldn't both develop a headache on the same evening without their mama seeing through the ploy. Eliza, therefore, was presently gracing Lady Montague's ballroom, while Heather was supposedly laid upon her bed, safe and snug in Dover Street.

Giving every appearance of calm confidence, she glided into the crowd. She'd attracted considerable attention; although she pretended obliviousness, she could feel the assessing glances dwelling on the sleek, amber silk gown that clung lovingly to her curves. This particular creation sported a sweetheart neckline and tiny puffed sleeves; as the evening was unseasonably mild and her carriage stood outside, she'd elected to carry only a fine topaz-and-amber Norwich silk shawl, its fringe draping over her bare arms and flirting over the silk of the gown. Her advanced age allowed her greater freedom to wear gowns that, while definitely not as revealing as some others she could see, nevertheless drew male eyes.

One gentleman, suitably drawn and a touch bolder than his fellows, broke from the circle surrounding two ladies and languidly stepped into her path.

Halting, she haughtily arched a brow.

He smiled and bowed, fluidly graceful. "Miss Cynster, I believe?"

"Indeed, sir. And you are?"

"Miles Furlough, my dear." His eyes met hers as he straightened. "Is this your first time here?"

"Yes." She glanced around, determinedly projecting confident assurance. She intended to pick her man, not allow him or any other to pick her. "The company appears quite animated." The noise of untold conversations was steadily rising. Returning her gaze to Miles Furlough, she asked, "Are her ladyship's gatherings customarily so lively?"

Furlough's lips curved in a smile Heather wasn't sure she liked.

"I think you'll discover—" Furlough broke off, his gaze going past her.

She had an instant's warning—a primitive prickling over her nape—then long, steely fingers closed about her elbow.

Heat washed over her, emanating from the contact, supplanted almost instantly by a disorientating giddiness. She caught her breath. She didn't need to look to know that Timothy Danvers, Viscount Breckenridge—her nemesis—had elected not to be sensible.

"Furlough." The deep voice issuing from above her head and to the side had its usual disconcerting effect.

Ignoring the frisson of awareness streaking down her spine—a susceptibility she positively despised—she slowly turned her head and directed a reined glare at its cause. "Breckenridge."

There was nothing in her tone to suggest she welcomed his arrival—quite the opposite.

He ignored her attempt to depress his pretensions; indeed, she wasn't even sure he registered it. His gaze hadn't shifted from Furlough.

"If you'll excuse us, old man, there's a matter I need to discuss with Miss Cynster." Breckenridge held Furlough's gaze. "I'm sure you understand."

Furlough's expression suggested that he did yet wished he didn't feel obliged to give way. But in this milieu, Breckenridge—the hostesses' and the ladies' darling— was well nigh impossible to gainsay. Reluctantly, Furlough inclined his head. "Of course."

Shifting his gaze to Heather, Furlough smiled—more sincerely, a tad ruefully. "Miss Cynster. Would we had met in less crowded surrounds. Perhaps next time." With a parting nod, he sauntered off into the crowd.

Heather let free an exasperated huff. But before she could even gather her arguments and turn them on Breckenridge, he tightened his grip on her elbow and started propelling her through the crowd.

Startled, she tried to halt. "What—"

"If you have the slightest sense of self-preservation you will walk to the front door without any fuss."

He was steering her, surreptitiously pushing her, in that direction, and it wasn't all that far. "Let. Me. Go." She uttered the command, low and delivered with considerable feeling, through clenched teeth.

He urged her up the salon steps. Used the moment when she was on the step above him to bend his head and breathe in her ear, *"What the devil are you doing here?"*

His clenched teeth trumped her clenched teeth. The words, his tone, slid through her, evoking—as he'd no doubt intended—a nebulous, purely instinctive fear.

By the time she shook free of it, he was smoothly, apparently unhurriedly, steering her through the guests thronging the foyer.

"No—don't bother answering." He didn't look down; he had the open front door in his sights. "I don't care what ninnyhammerish notion you've taken into your head. You're leaving. Now."

Hale, whole, virgin intacta. Breckenridge only just bit back the words.

"There is no reason whatever for you to interfere." Her voice vibrated with barely suppressed fury.

He recognized her mood well enough—her customary one whenever he was near. Normally he would respond by giving her a wide berth, but here and now he had no choice. "Do you have any idea what your cousins would do to me—let alone your brothers—if they discovered I'd seen you in this den of iniquity and turned a blind eye?"

She snorted and tried, surreptitiously but unsuccessfully, to free her elbow. "You're as large as any of them—and demonstrably just as much of a bully. You could see them off."

"One, perhaps, but all six? I think not. Let alone Luc and Martin, and Gyles Chillingworth—and what about Michael? No, wait—what about Caro, and your aunts, and . . . the list goes on. Flaying would be preferable—much less pain."

"You're overreacting. Lady Herford's house hardly qualifies as a den of iniquity." She glanced back. "There's nothing the least objectionable going on in that salon."

"Not in the salon, perhaps—at least, not yet. But you didn't go further into the house—trust me, a den of iniquity it most definitely is."

"But—"

"No." Reaching the front porch—thankfully deserted— he halted, released her, and finally let himself look down at her. Let himself look into her face, a perfect oval hosting delicate features and a pair of stormy gray-blue eyes lushly fringed with dark brown lashes. Despite those eyes having turned hard and flinty, even though her luscious lips were presently compressed into a thin line, that face was the sort that had launched armadas and incited wars since the dawn of time. It was a face full of life. Full of sensual promise and barely restrained vitality.

And that was before adding the effect of a slender figure, sleek rather than curvaceous, yet invested with such fluid grace that her every movement evoked thoughts that, at least in his case, were better left unexplored.

The only reason she hadn't been mobbed in the salon was because none but Furlough had shaken free of the arrestation the first sight of her generally caused quickly enough to get to her before he had.

He felt his face harden, fought not to clench his fists and tower over her in a sure-to-be-vain attempt to intimidate her. "You're going home, and that's all there is to it."

Her eyes narrowed to shards. "If you try to force me, I'll scream."

He lost the battle; his fists clenched at his sides. Holding her gaze, he evenly stated, "If you do, I'll tap you under that pretty little chin, knock you unconscious, tell everyone you fainted, toss you in a carriage, and send you home."

Her eyes widened. She considered him but didn't back down. "You wouldn't."

He didn't blink. "Try me."

Heather inwardly dithered. This was the trouble with Breckenridge—one simply couldn't tell what he was thinking. His face, that of a Greek god, all clean planes and sharp angles, lean cheeks below high cheekbones and a strong, square jaw, remained aristocratically impassive and utterly unreadable no matter what was going through his mind. Not even his heavy-lidded hazel eyes gave any clue; his expression was perennially that of an elegantly rakish gentleman who cared for little beyond his immediate pleasure.

Every element of his appearance, from his exquisitely understated attire, the severe cut of his clothes making the lean strength they concealed only more apparent, to the languid drawl he habitually affected, supported that image—one she was fairly certain was a comprehensive façade.

She searched his eyes—and detected not the smallest sign that he wouldn't do precisely as he said. Which would be simply too embarrassing.

"How did you get here?"

Reluctantly, she waved at the line of carriages stretching along the curving pavement of Wadham Gardens as far as they could see. "My parents' carriage—and before you lecture me on the impropriety of traveling across London alone at night, both the coachman and groom have been with my family for decades."

Tight-lipped, he nodded. "I'll walk you to it."

He reached for her elbow again.

She whisked back. "Don't bother." Frustration erupted; she felt sure he would inform her brothers that he'd found her at Lady Herford's, which would spell an end to her plan—one which, until he'd interfered, had held real promise. She gave vent to her temper with an infuriated glare. "I can walk twenty yards by myself."

Even to her ears her words sounded petulant. In reaction, she capped them with, "Just leave me alone!"

Lifting her chin, she swung on her heel and marched

down the steps. Head determinedly high, she turned right along the pavement toward where her parents' town carriage waited in the line.

Inside she was shaking. She felt childish and furious—and helpless. Just as she always felt when she and Breckenridge crossed swords.

Blinking back tears of stifled rage, knowing he was watching, she stiffened her spine and marched steadily on.

From the shadows of Lady Herford's front porch, Breckenridge watched the bane of his life stalk back to safety. Why of all the ladies in the ton it had to be Heather Cynster who so tied him in knots he didn't know; what he did know was that there wasn't a damned thing he could do about it. She was twenty-five, and he was ten years and a million nights older; he was certain she viewed him at best as an interfering much older cousin, at worst as an interfering uncle.

"Wonderful," he muttered as he watched her stride fearlessly along. Once he saw her safely away . . . he was going to walk home. The night air might clear his head of the distraction, of the unsettled, restless feeling dealing with her always left him prey to—a sense of loneliness, and emptiness, and time slipping away.

Of life—his life—being somehow worthless, or rather, worth less—less than it should.

He didn't, truly didn't, want to think about her. There were ladies among the crowd inside who would fight to provide him with diversion, but he'd long ago learned the value of their smiles, their pleasured sighs.

Fleeting, meaningless, illusory connections.

Increasingly they left him feeling cheapened, used. Unfulfilled.

He watched the moonlight glint in Heather's wheat gold hair. He'd first met her four years ago at the wedding of his biological stepmother, Caroline, to Michael Anstruther-Wetherby, brother of Honoria, Duchess of St. Ives and queen of the Cynster clan. Honoria's husband, Devil Cynster, was Heather's oldest cousin.

Although Breckenridge had first met Heather on that day in sunny Hampshire, he'd known the male Cynster cousins for more than a decade—they moved in the same circles, and before the cousins had married, had shared much the same interests.

A carriage to the left of the house pulled out of the line. Breckenridge glanced that way, saw the coachman set his horses plodding, then looked right again to where Heather was still gliding along.

"Twenty yards, my arse." More like fifty. "Where the damn hell is her carriage?"

The words had barely left his lips when the other carriage, a traveling coach, drew level with Heather.

And slowed.

The coach's door swung open and a man shot out. Another leapt down from beside the driver.

Before Breckenridge could haul in a breath, the pair had slipped past the carriages lining the pavement and grabbed Heather. Smothering her shocked cry, they hoisted her up, carried her to the coach, and bundled her inside.

"Hey!" Breckenridge's shout was echoed by a coachman a few carriages down the line.

But the men were already tumbling through the coach door as the coachman whipped up his horses.

Breckenridge was down the steps and racing along the pavement before he'd even formed the thought of giving chase.

The traveling coach disappeared around the curve of the crescent that was Wadham Gardens. From the rattle of the wheels, the coach turned right up the first connecting street.

Reaching the carriage where the coachman who'd yelled now sat stunned and staring after the kidnappers' coach, Breckenridge climbed up and grabbed the reins. "Let me. I'm a friend of the family. We're going after her."

The coachman swallowed his surprise and released the reins.

Breckenridge swiftly tacked and, cursing at the tightness, swung the town carriage into the road. The instant the conveyance was free of the line, he whipped up the horses. "Keep your eyes peeled—I have no idea which way they might go."

"Aye, sir—my lord. . . ."

Briefly meeting the coachman's sideways glance, Breckenridge stated, "Viscount Breckenridge. I know Devil and Gabriel." And the others, but those names would do.

The coachman nodded. "Aye, my lord." Turning, he called back to the groom, hanging on behind. "James—you watch left and I'll watch right. If we miss seeing them, you'll need to hop down at the next corner and look."

Breckenridge concentrated on the horses. Luckily there was little other traffic. He made the turn into the same street the coach had taken. All three of them immediately looked ahead. Light from numerous street flares garishly illuminated an odd-angled four-way intersection ahead.

"There!" came a call from behind. "That's them—turning left into the bigger street."

Breckenridge gave thanks for James's sharp eyes; he'd only just glimpsed the back of the coach himself. Urging the horses on as quickly as he dared, they reached the intersection and made the turn—just in time to see the coach turn right at the next intersection.

"Oh," the coachman said.

Breckenridge flicked a glance his way. "What?"

"That's Avenue Road they've just turned into—it merges into Finchley Road just a bit along."

And Finchley Road became the Great North Road, and the coach was heading north. "They might be heading for some house out that way." Breckenridge told himself that could be the case . . . but they were following a traveling coach, not a town carriage.

He steered the pair of blacks he was managing into Avenue Road. Both the coachman and James peered ahead.

"Yep—that's them," the coachman said. "But they're a way ahead of us now."

Given the blacks were Cynster horses, Breckenridge wasn't worried about how far ahead their quarry got. "Just as long as we keep them in sight."

As it transpired, that was easier said than done. It wasn't the blacks that slowed them but the plodding beasts drawing the seven conveyances that got between them and the traveling coach. While rolling along the narrow carriageways through the outskirts of the sprawling metropolis, past Cricklewood through to Golders Green there was nowhere Breckenridge could pass. They managed to keep the coach in sight long enough to feel certain that it was, indeed, heading up the Great North Road, but by the time they reached High Barnet with the long stretch of Barnet Hill beyond, they'd lost sight of it.

Inwardly cursing, Breckenridge turned into the yard of the Barnet Arms, a major posting inn and one at which he was well known. Halting the carriage, to the coachman and James he said, "Ask up and down the road—see if you can find anyone who saw the coach, if they changed horses, any information."

Both men scrambled down and went. Breckenridge turned to the ostlers who'd come hurrying to hold the horses' heads. "I need a curricle and your best pair—where's your master?"

Half an hour later, he parted from the coachman and James. They'd found several people who'd seen the coach, which had stopped briefly to change horses at the Scepter and Crown. The coach had continued north along the highway.

"Here." Breckenridge handed the coachman a note he'd scribbled while he'd waited for them to return. "Give that to Lord Martin as soon as you can." Lord Martin Cynster was Heather's father. "If for any reason he's not available, get it to one of Miss Cynster's brothers, or, failing them, to St.

Ives." Breckenridge knew Devil was in town, but he was less certain of the others' whereabouts.

"Aye, my lord." The coachman took the note, raised a hand in salute. "And good luck to you, sir. Hope you catch up with those blackguards right quick."

Breckenridge hoped so, too. He watched the pair climb up to the box seat of the town carriage. The instant they'd turned it out of the yard, heading back to London, he strode to the sleek phaeton waiting to one side. A pair of grays the innkeeper rarely allowed to be hired by anyone danced between the shafts. Two nervous ostlers held the horses' heads.

"Right frisky, they are, m'lord." The head ostler followed him over. "They haven't been out in an age. Keep telling the boss he'd be better off letting them out for a run now and then."

"I'll manage." Breckenridge swung up to the phaeton's high box seat. He needed speed, and the combination of phaeton and high-bred horses promised that. Taking the reins, he tensioned them, tested the horses' mouths, then nodded to the ostlers. "Let 'em go."

The ostlers did, leaping back as the horses surged.

Breckenridge reined the pair in only enough to take the turn out of the yard, then he let them have their heads up Barnet Hill and on along the Great North Road.

For a while, managing the horses absorbed all of his attention, but once they'd settled and were bowling along, the steady rhythm of their hooves eating the miles with little other traffic to get in their way, he could spare sufficient attention to think.

To give thanks the night wasn't freezing given he was still in his evening clothes.

To grapple with the realization that if he hadn't insisted Heather leave Lady Herford's villa—hadn't allowed her to walk the twenty-cum-fifty yards along the pavement to her carriage alone—she wouldn't have been in the hands of unknown assailants, wouldn't have been subjected to whatever indignities they'd already visited on her.

They would pay, of course; he'd ensure that. But that in no way mitigated the sense of horror and overwhelming guilt that it was due to his actions that she was now in danger.

He'd intended to protect her. Instead . . .

Jaw clenched, teeth gritted, he kept his eyes on the road and raced on.

Her captors left Heather trussed and gagged until they were some way out of Barnet and bowling along an empty stretch of road.

The instant they'd bundled her into the carriage outside Lady Herford's, they'd wrapped a strip of linen about her face, efficiently gagging her, and had swiftly tied her hands, then her feet when she'd tried to kick them.

There hadn't been just the two men. A woman, large and strong, had been waiting in the carriage with the gag held ready. Once Heather had been silenced and her limbs secured, they'd sat her on the forward-facing seat, next to the woman, and both men had sat opposite. One had told her to calm herself and just wait quietly, and all would soon be revealed.

That promise, and the fact they'd made no attempt whatever to harm her—indeed, they hadn't even threatened her in any way—had given her pause. Enough to realize that she had no real choice, so she might as well do as they'd asked.

That hadn't stopped her thinking. Or imagining. But neither activity had got her very far. She knew so little. Nothing beyond that there were three of them plus the coachman on the box, and they were taking her north out of London. She had glimpsed enough landmarks along the way, recognized enough to be sure they were heading north.

They were on the Great North Road when the thinner of the men, at the taller end of medium height and decidedly wiry, with curly, mousy-brown hair and a sharp-featured face, said, "If you're willing to be reasonable and behave, we'll untie you. We're on a long, lonely stretch and won't be slowing for a good long while—no one about to hear you

15

if you yell and scream, and if you manage to get out of the door, at this speed you'll likely break a leg, if not your neck. So if you're willing to be quiet and just sit and listen, we can untie you and explain what's going on—how things are and how things are going to be. So." He raised his brows at her. "What's it to be?"

In the dimness within the carriage, she couldn't truly see his eyes, but she looked in that direction and nodded.

"Smart girl," the wiry one said. The comment held no sarcasm. "He did say you'd be clever."

He, who? She watched as the wiry man, seated opposite, bent, reaching for her feet, then stopped.

He flicked a glance at the woman beside her. "Best you untie her feet." Straightening, he reached for the cords binding Heather's wrists.

Puzzled, she glanced at the woman, who huffed, then lumbered off the seat and crouched between the benches. She reached beneath Heather's silk skirts to the linen strip wound about her ankles.

While they worked to loosen the bonds, Heather realized they'd been mindful of her modesty—as mindful as she'd allowed them to be. She hadn't imagined kidnappers would be so . . . gentlemanly.

Once her feet were free, the woman settled back beside her. "The gag, too?" the woman asked the wiry one.

His gaze on Heather, he nodded. "We're to allow her as much comfort as possible, so unless she's sillier than we all think, no need to keep it on."

Heather turned her head, allowing the woman access to the knot at the back of her skull. When the linen fell from her face, she moistened her lips, worked her jaw, and felt a great deal better.

She looked at the wiry one. "Who are you, and who sent you?"

He grinned—a flash of white teeth in the shadows. "Ah, now, you're getting a trifle ahead of us there, miss. I think perhaps I'd better first explain that we were sent to fetch one of the Cynster sisters—you or one of the others. We've been watching you all for more than a week, but none of you go anywhere without others about. Not until tonight, that is." Wiry—Heather decided to call him that—half bowed. "We're obliged to you for that. We'd started thinking we'd have to arrange something drastic to get one of you on your lonesome. Howsoever, now we have you, it's best you realize that no attempt to escape us is likely to succeed—no one will help you, because we've a story that accounts for us taking you, and whatever you do or say, whatever protests you make, are only going to make our story seem more real and truthful to others."

"What's this story?" she asked. Wiry had an air of quiet competence about him; he didn't seem the sort to make foolish declarations.

Just her luck to be abducted by kidnappers who could think.

As if to confirm her suspicion, Wiry smiled. His satisfaction resonated in his voice. "It's a simple enough tale. We've been sent by your guardian to fetch you back to him. Ran away to wicked London, you did, escaped from his strict household. So he's sent us to find you and take you back, and"—pausing dramatically, Wiry drew a folded sheet of paper from his pocket and waved it—"this is his authority for us to do whatever we need to do to hold you and transport you back to him."

She frowned at the paper. "My father's my guardian and he gave you no such permission."

"Ah, but you're not Miss Cynster, are you? You're Miss Wallace, and your guardian, Sir Humphrey, is most anxious to get you back home where you belong."

"Where's my home?" She hoped he might say where they were taking her, but Wiry only smiled.

"You know it well, of course—no need for us to tell you."

She fell silent, mentally reviewing their plan, seeking any

17

possible way she might scupper it, but she carried nothing that would prove who she was. Her only hope—one she wasn't about to voice—was a chance meeting with someone who knew her by sight. Unfortunately, the likelihood of that happening in the country in late March, with the Season just starting in London, wasn't all that high.

She glanced at the woman beside her.

As if sensing the question in her mind, Wiry explained, "Martha here"—with his head he indicated the woman—"is, of course, the maid Sir Humphrey sent to lend you countenance on the journey." Wiry's lips curved. "Martha will remain with you at all times. Especially all the times it would be inappropriate for one of us—me or Cobbins here—to be by your side."

Deciding that at the moment it behooved her to, as Wiry had put it, behave, Heather inclined her head, first to the woman alongside her, " Martha," then to the barrel-chested man, shorter than Wiry but of heavier build, who'd remained quietly seated in the far corner of the coach. "Cobbins."

She turned her gaze on Wiry. "And you are?"

He smiled. "You may call me Fletcher, Miss Wallace."

Heather thought of a few other epithets she might call him, but she merely inclined her head. Settling on the seat, she leaned her head back against the squabs and ventured nothing more. She sensed that Fletcher expected her to pro-test, perhaps beg for mercy, or try to subvert him and the others from their goal, but she saw no point in lowering her-self to that.

No point at all.

The more she thought of all Fletcher had let fall, the more she felt certain of that. This had to be the strangest abduc-tion she'd ever heard of . . . well, she hadn't heard the details of any abduction attempts, but it seemed distinctly odd that they were treating her so considerately, so . . . sensibly. So terribly calmly and confidently.

They—Fletcher, Cobbins, and Martha—did not fit the

prescription for run-of-the-mill kidnappers. They might not be genteel, yet they were not of the lowest orders, either. They were neatly and unobtrusively dressed. Although rather large and solid, Martha could indeed pass for a lady's maid, certainly a lady who lived mostly in the country. Cobbins appeared reserved, and in his drab clothes seemed to fade into the background, but he, too, did not seem the sort one would find in a seedy hedge-tavern. Both he and Fletcher looked precisely like the sort of men they were claiming to be—the sort some wealthy country squire might hire to act as his agents.

Whoever had sent them to London had prepared them well. Their plan was both simple and, in the situation in which she now found herself, well nigh impossible to counter. That didn't mean she wouldn't escape—she would somehow—but before she did, she needed to learn more about the most puzzling aspect of this strange kidnapping.

They'd been sent to abduct not her specifically but one of the Cynster sisters—her, Eliza, or Angelica, and possibly her cousins, Henrietta and Mary, also "Cynster sisters."

She couldn't imagine what reason anyone would have for doing so other than a simple demand for ransom, but if that were the case, why take her out of London? Why take her off to some other man? She thought back, reassessed, but couldn't shake the impression that all Fletcher had revealed was true—the trio were fetching her for some employer.

Hiring three people of the trio's ilk, and a coachman and coach-and-four, and they'd been watching her and the others for over a week . . . none of that sounded like a straightforward, opportunistic kidnapping for ransom.

But if not ransom, what was behind this? And if she escaped without learning the answer, would she and the others still remain under threat?

They'd had fresh horses put to in High Barnet, and so rattled on past Welham Green and through Welwyn.

Eventually, the carriage slowed, and they entered a small

town. Fletcher leaned forward and looked out of the window. "Knebworth." Sitting back, he studied Heather. "We're going to stop here for the night. Are you going to be sensible and keep your mouth shut, or do we need to restrain you and tell the landlord our tale?"

If they did . . . if her family came searching for her, as she knew they would—Henry, their old coachman, would have alerted the household by now—then having heard she was a Miss Wallace, the landlord and his staff might not mention her.

Eyes on Fletcher, she lifted her chin. "I'll behave."

He smiled, but encouragingly rather than victoriously. "That's the ticket."

Heather inwardly sighed. Fletcher's lack of smugness proved he was intelligent. Despite his story, if she'd been prepared to throw a screaming tantrum she might have been able to have the local constable summoned—might have been able to convince him to hold her while he checked her story against her captors'. Unfortunately, her reputation wouldn't easily withstand being so publicly found in kidnappers' hands, Martha notwithstanding. Especially after she had that very evening made the unspoken declaration implied by stepping into the racy world of Lady Herford's salon.

But above and beyond all else, while she remained quiet and played the role they'd planned for her, she wasn't, as far as she could see, under any real threat, and wouldn't be until they reached their employer. Until then, she would put her mind to ferreting out what lay behind this very strange kidnapping.

And *then* she'd use her wits and escape.

Chapter Two

Three hours later, Heather lay on her back in a not-so-comfortable bed in a room on the second floor of the Red Garter Inn at Knebworth and stared at the ceiling. Outside, the moon had finally sailed free of the clouds; the shaft of silvery light beaming in through the uncurtained window allowed her to see the ceiling well enough, not that she was actually studying it.

"What the devil am I to do?" She sent the whispered question floating upward, but no answer came.

She'd been right in rejecting the notion of making a scene and trying to bend the innkeeper and his patrons to her cause. Once she'd observed her captors in lamplight, she'd realized her earlier estimation of their competence hadn't done them justice. Fletcher in particular appeared personable enough to raise questions as to whether she'd left London with him willingly or not. Meeting his eyes with light enough to see into them had confirmed beyond doubt that he was not only intelligent but quick-witted and cunning as well. If she tried to persuade others to help her against him, he would use every possible argument to counter hers. And he knew what "every possible argument" encompassed. If she pushed him hard enough, her reputation would be shredded, and she still might not win free.

Bad enough, but any consequent idea that it might perhaps be wiser to escape now, while she was still within reach of London and the protection of her family, even without learning more about the reasons behind her abduction, had been slain shortly after birth.

They'd taken her clothes.

In the carriage, long before they'd untied her, Martha had produced a dark wool cloak and solicitously wrapped it about her. That, indeed, had been the first sign that they intended to take reasonable care of her; she'd been grateful for the warmth as the night had progressed. At Fletcher's instruction, she'd kept the cloak close about her when they'd entered the inn. Once she and Martha had repaired to this room and shut the door, however, Martha had reclaimed the cloak. She'd then suggested Heather remove her gown before getting into bed; Heather had complied without really thinking—she wasn't in the habit of wearing evening gowns to bed.

She was, however, accustomed to wearing something more substantial than a silk chemise, which, barring her even sheerer silk stockings, was all she presently had on.

And there were no other clothes, hers or Martha's, available to her if she took it into her head to pick the lock on the door—Martha had the key in the pocket of the voluminous undergown in which she'd elected to sleep—and sneak downstairs to raise some alarm. In her chemise and silk stockings? Heather inwardly snorted. And glanced again across the room at the other single bed on which Martha lay snoring.

Loudly.

Martha's clothes, all of them including those she'd had packed in a big satchel, along with Heather's evening gown and shawl, and a simple round gown Martha had brought for Heather to wear the next day, resided under Martha's large and heavy figure. The "maid" had laid the garments neatly under the sheet on the bed, and then lain down upon it.

For tonight, Heather was stuck with her captors.

Part of her was definitely inclining toward panic, not least because thus far said captors had proved adept at guessing what she might do and had taken steps to nullify each option before she'd taken it. Against that, another, rather more intrepid part was pointing out that perhaps her current predicament was fate's way of ensuring she stayed with her abductors long enough to learn what lay behind the threat to her and her Cynster sisters.

She was debating—panic versus fatalistic pragmatism—when a skittery scraping on the windowpane sent horrible shivers down her spine.

Frowning, she glanced at the window—and saw a shadow looming beyond it.

A man-sized shadow—head and shoulders. Broad shoulders.

Slipping out of the bed, she grabbed the coverlet, wound it about her, then hurried across the bare floor. Reaching the window, she looked out—

Straight into Breckenridge's face.

For an instant, shock held her immobile. He was quite the last person she'd expected to see. Then again . . .

His exasperated expression as with one hand he brusquely gestured for her to lift the sash window shook her into action. The room was, after all, on the second floor. He seemed to be hanging onto a pipe.

Reaching up, she struggled with the window latch. Perhaps she should have realized he'd appear. He had been watching her walk to her parents' carriage. He must have seen her seized and bundled into Fletcher's coach. Finally forcing the latch free, she eased up the sash, glancing over her shoulder at the lump that was Martha as the wood scraped and slid.

Martha's snoring continued unabated, rhythm undisturbed.

Breckenridge had seen the glance. "Is there someone there?"

The question reached her as the barest whisper. She nodded and leaned on the sill so her head was level with his. "Yes. A large and strong maid, but she's sound asleep. Those are her snores you can hear."

He listened, then nodded. "All right." Then he frowned. "Where did you get her—the maid?"

"My captors—Fletcher and Cobbins—are working for some man who has employed them to bring me to him, but said employer has instructed them to provide me with every comfort along the way. Hence Martha. She was in the carriage when they grabbed me."

No matter what else one might say and think about him, Breckenridge most assuredly was neither stupid nor slow.

"Your abductors have provided you with a maid."

She nodded. "To see to my needs and lend me countenance. Fletcher, the thin, wiry one—he seems to be the leader—actually said so while introducing me and Martha to the innkeeper. They're calling me Miss Wallace."

Breckenridge hesitated, then asked, "Is there some reason you haven't told the innkeeper your real name and demanded his assistance in escaping Fletcher and company?"

She smiled tightly. "Indeed there is." She told him of Fletcher's story, the tale of her guardian, Sir Humphrey, her supposed flight to the wicked streets of London, and the letter of authority Fletcher had, presumably, forged.

When she finished, Breckenridge remained silent for some time.

Heather peered over the sill, confirming that he was indeed clinging to a lead downpipe, one booted foot wedged on a support. Given his size and undoubted weight, gaining that position, let alone maintaining it, had to be counted an impressive feat.

If she'd been in a mood to be impressed.

Which made it even stranger that every last iota of her incipient panic had vanished. Raising her gaze, she met his eyes—found him staring, then he looked deep into hers. Then he blinked, shook his head slightly, then eased a hand from the pipe and beckoned. "Come on—time to leave."

She stared at him, then looked over the sill again—at the ground far below. "You have to be joking."

"I'll keep you before me and steady you down the pipe."

She looked at him. He'd steady her down the pipe by holding her against him, trapping her body between his and the pipe? The notion . . . made her inwardly shiver. "I haven't got any clothes—Martha's lying on them."

His gaze dropped to her throat, bare, then lower, to the

coverlet she'd wrapped about her. "You're naked under that?"

His voice sounded strained. Or was it disbelieving?

"Just my chemise, which, as you no doubt can imagine, is as good as naked."

He briefly closed his eyes, then opened them again. His expression had grown a touch grimmer. "All right. In that case, go out of the door and I'll meet you downstairs—"

"The door's locked, Martha's sleeping with the key, and although I could pick the lock, I suspect I'd wake even her— and even if I didn't, do you really think I should risk bumping into some sleepless bumpkin downstairs *en deshabille*?"

He actually thought about it.

"Besides, I haven't told you all of it."

His eyes narrowed, as if he suspected her of playing some game. "What haven't you mentioned?"

She ignored his look and related the instructions Fletcher had been given. "So he could have seized any one of the three, or perhaps five, of us."

Breckenridge frowned uncomprehendingly. "So? In terms of ransom, any one of you would do."

"Yes, but if this employer was merely seeking to ransom me, why take me out of London? Why go to all this trouble and expense? Why provide me with a maid? None of that makes sense."

Breckenridge hesitated, then said, "The maid makes sense if the reason he's kidnapped you is to force you into marriage and so get his hands on your dowry."

"True. But if that was his aim, then his orders don't make sense—anyone who made even the most superficial inquiries would readily learn that while Eliza and I have inherited considerable wealth, Angelica hasn't. She wasn't born when our great-aunts died, so she missed out on the inheritances." In her eagerness to explain, Heather leaned even further forward over the sill.

Breckenridge, with the knowledge of her all-but-naked state high in his mind, would have liked to ease back, but there was nothing but thin air behind him. He had to mentally grit his teeth, not so figuratively gird his loins, and bear with her naked nearness.

"So you see," the bane of his life continued, utterly oblivious, "that can't be the reason behind the abduction either." Her eyes met his, held them. "Whatever the reason, if there's any chance of learning the truth of it—learning if there's some continued threat against not just me but Eliza and Angelica, perhaps Henrietta and Mary, too—then I have to go along with Fletcher and company, at least while matters continue as they are and I am under no immediate personal threat."

She was presently under more personal threat from him than from her captors. The realization made him wince, an expression she saw and took to signal his understanding.

Reaching out from under the coverlet, extending one slender arm, she briefly touched his hand where it gripped the windowsill. "If you would consent to take a message home for me, let the family know that I'm in no immediate danger, and that I'll send word the instant I get free?"

He looked at her. She actually thought he would . . . "Don't be daft." He glowered at her. "I can't leave you like this, in your captors' hands, and simply drive away."

He studied her, wondered how much she weighed, wondered if he dared risk—

She must have sensed the assessment in his gaze; she straightened, took a step back, and leveled a finger at his nose. "Don't even think of grabbing me and hauling me away—not now, not ever. I'll scream bloody murder if you so much as lay a finger on me."

Wonderful. He narrowed his eyes at her, but he knew her well enough to know her threat was not an idle one.

She seemed to realize he'd accepted that. Her stance softened. "So if you would take a message—"

"I've already sent your coachman back with a message for your father, telling him you're being driven up the Great North Road in a coach, and that I'm following. I suspect that if they don't hear from us within a day, your cousins will start tracking us."

Folding her arms, she frowned at him. After a moment, she inquired, "Does that mean you intend to follow me onward?"

"Yes." He spoke—whispered—through clenched teeth. "Naturally. I could hardly let you be taken God knows where."

"Hmm." Her gaze on him, she seemed to ponder, then offered, "All right. Here's what I'm planning to do. I'll interrogate and extract everything I can about their employer, his orders, and his motives from Fletcher, Cobbins, and Martha, enough at least to determine what the threat to my sisters and cousins might be. Then I'll escape. If you're still close, you can help me."

She paused, her eyes on his, clearly waiting for his response.

He knew what he felt like saying, but . . . she had to come with him willingly, and Stubborn was her middle name. "Very well." The words were an effort. He considered, then said, "I'll send word back to London, then follow the coach onward, staying close." He met her gaze, his own ungiving. "I'll need to meet with you every night." He glanced toward the maid, still snoring in her bed. "Clearly that shouldn't be too difficult, even if we have to meet like this. Once you've learned what you feel you need to—immediately you do—you'll leave with me and I'll escort you back to London. When the time comes, I'll hire a maid, so it'll all be above board."

She considered for a moment, then allowed, "That sounds an excellent plan."

He bit back a sarcastic retort; she never reacted well to such rejoinders from him. He nodded. "Close the window and go back to bed—I'll see you tomorrow."

She stepped forward and slid the sash carefully down. She remained behind the pane for a moment, then turned and glided away.

He looked down—manfully resisting the temptation to

peek when she doffed the coverlet and climbed between the sheets—and started on his journey back to the ground.

Although more or less disgusted, certainly disgruntled with how matters had played out, as he backed down the wall, hand below hand, foot by foot, he had to admit to a lurking but very real respect for her stance.

Family mattered.

Few appreciated that better than he. He who had no true blood kin. His biological father had been the late Camden Sutcliffe, diplomat extraordinaire—womanizer extraordinaire, as well. His mother had been the Countess of Brunswick, who had borne her husband two daughters, but no son. Brunswick had from the first claimed Breckenridge as his own—initially out of relief arising from his desperate need of an heir, but later from true affection.

It was Brunswick who had taught Breckenridge about family. Breckenridge rarely used his given name, Timothy; he'd been Breckenridge from birth and thought of himself by that name, the name carried by the Earl of Brunswick's eldest son. Because that's who he'd always truly been—Brunswick's son.

So he fully comprehended Heather's need to learn what was behind the strange abduction, given that it had been targeted not specifically at her but at her sisters, and possibly her cousins, as well.

He himself had two older sisters, Lady Constance Rafferty and Lady Cordelia Marchmain. He frequently referred to them as his evil ugly sisters, yet he'd slay dragons for either, and despite their frequent lecturing and hounding, they loved him, too. Presumably that was why they lectured and hounded. God knew it wasn't for the results.

Nearing the ground, he swung his legs back from the wall, released the pipe, and dropped to the gravel at the side of the inn. He'd bribed the innkeeper to tell him which room he'd put the pretty lady in; still clad in his evening clothes, it hadn't been hard to assume the persona of a dangerous rake.

Straightening, he stood for a moment in the chill night air, mentally canvassing all he needed to do. He would have to swap the phaeton for something less noticeable, but he'd keep the grays, at least for now. Glancing down at his clothes, he winced. They would have to go, too.

With a sigh, he set out to walk the short distance to the small tavern down the road at which he'd hired a room.

High above, Heather stood peering out of the window. She saw Breckenridge stride away and let out a sigh of relief. She hadn't been able to see him until he'd walked away from the wall; she'd been waiting, watching, worried he might have slipped and fallen.

She might not like him—not at all—and she certainly didn't appreciate his dictatorial ways, but she wouldn't want him hurt, especially not when he'd come to rescue her. She might have decided against being rescued yet, but she wasn't so foolish as to reject his help. His support. Even, if it came to it, his protection—in the perfectly acceptable sense.

His abilities in that regard would be, she suspected, not to be sneezed at.

Still, she found it odd that the instant she'd recognized him outside the window, confidence and certainty had infused her. In that moment, all her earlier trepidation had fled.

Inwardly shrugging, she turned from the window. Assured, more resolute, infinitely more certain the path forward she'd chosen was the right one, she padded back to the bed, flicked the coverlet back over the sheets, slipped beneath, and laid her head on the pillow.

Smiled at the memory of Breckenridge's expression when he'd gestured at her to open the window; he hadn't been his usual impassive self then. Amused, relieved, she closed her eyes and slept.

Chapter Three

The next morning, relatively early, Heather found herself back in the coach and heading north once more.

Martha had woken an hour after dawn and consented to hand Heather the round gown of plain green cambric they'd brought for her to wear. Heather had retrieved her fringed silk shawl, but her amber silk evening gown and her small evening reticule had been packed into Martha's commodious satchel. Martha's planning hadn't extended to footwear. With the woolen cloak about her and her evening slippers on her feet, Heather had been escorted downstairs to a private parlor.

Over breakfast, taken with Fletcher, Cobbins, and the hatchet-faced Martha, Heather had had no chance to even make eye contact with the busy serving girls. If anyone did come asking after her, she doubted that the overworked girls would even remember her.

While she'd eaten, she'd thought back over her behavior in the carriage the previous night. Although she'd asked questions, she hadn't given her captors any reason to believe she was the sort of young lady who might seriously challenge them or disobey their orders. Admittedly she hadn't burst into tears, or wrung her hands and sobbed pitifully, but they'd been warned she was clever, so they shouldn't have expected that.

Although it had gone very much against her grain, by the time they'd risen and she'd been ushered, under close guard, into the waiting coach, she'd decided to play to their apparent perceptions, to appear malleable and relatively helpless despite her supposed intelligence. Her plan, as she'd taken her seat on the forward-facing bench once more, was to lull the trio into viewing her much as a schoolgirl they were escorting home.

In the few minutes while she, Martha, and Cobbins had waited in the coach for Fletcher to finish with the innkeeper and join them, she'd looked out of the coach window and seen an ostler holding a prancing bay gelding, saddled and waiting for its rider.

The temptation to open the coach door, jump down, race the few feet to the horse, grab the reins, mount, and thunder back down the road toward London had flared—and just as quickly had died. Not only would the maneuver have been fraught with risk—with no money or possessions, let alone proper clothes, she might have potentially jumped from frying pan into fire—but, successful or not, it would have ensured she got no chance to learn more about what lay behind her abduction.

She'd decided she would have to rely on Breckenridge, have to count on him following her. She'd wondered if he'd yet risen from his bed. He was one of the foremost rakes of the ton; such gentlemen were assumed to see little of the morning, certainly not during the Season.

Then Fletcher had climbed in, shut the door, and the coach had jerked, rumbled forward, and turned north—and she'd discovered that trusting in Breckenridge wasn't all that hard. Some part of her had already decided to.

She bided her time, lulling her three captors as planned, letting a silent hour pass as the miles slid by. She waited until sufficient time had elapsed to allow her to lean forward, peer out, and somewhat peevishly inquire, "Is it much farther?"

She looked at Fletcher, but he only grinned. The other two, when she glanced questioningly at them, simply closed their eyes.

Looking again at Fletcher, she frowned. "You might at least tell me how long I'll be cooped up in this carriage."

"For some time yet."

She opened her eyes wide. "But won't we be stopping for morning tea?"

"Sorry. That's not on our schedule."

She looked horrified. "But surely we'll be stopping for lunch?"

"Lunch, yes, but that won't be for a while."

Adopting a put-upon expression, she subsided, but "stopping for lunch" suggested they would be heading on afterward. She debated, then asked, "How far north are you taking me?" She made her voice small, as if the thought worried her. Which it did.

Fletcher considered her but volunteered only, "A ways yet."

She let another mile or two slide by before restlessly shifting, then asking, "This employer of yours—do you normally work for him?"

Fletcher shook his head. "We work for hire, me and Cobbins, and as we've known Martha forever, she agreed to assist us."

"So he approached you?"

Fletcher nodded.

"Where did you meet him?"

Fletcher grinned. "Glasgow."

She met Fletcher's eyes, grimaced, and fell silent again. She'd eat her best bonnet if either Fletcher or Cobbins hailed from north of the border, and from her accent, Martha was definitely a Londoner . . . did that mean the man who'd hired them was Glaswegian?

Were they actually imagining taking her over the border?

Heather longed to ask, but Fletcher was watching her with a faintly taunting smile on his face. He knew her questions weren't idle, which meant he'd tell her nothing useful. At least, not intentionally.

Yet from what he'd let fall, she had at least until sometime after lunch to quiz him and the others. Folding her arms, she closed her eyes and decided to lull him some more.

There were really only two answers she needed before she escaped—who had hired them, and why.

She opened her eyes when the houses of St. Neots closed around the coach. They passed a clock tower, the dial of which confirmed it was only midmorning. Stretching, she surveyed the view outside, then settled back and fixed her gaze on Fletcher. "Have you and Cobbins always worked together?"

That wasn't the question he'd been expecting. After a moment, he nodded. "Grew up together, we did."

"In London?"

Fletcher's smile returned. "Nah—up north. But we've been down in London a lot over the years. Lots of jobs there for gentlemen like us."

She wondered, then decided it wouldn't hurt to ask, "I don't suppose you'd consider earning more than your employer is paying you by turning the coach around and taking me home?"

Fletcher shook his head. "No. Much as I wouldn't say no to extra money, double-crossing an employer is never good for business."

She frowned. "Is he—your employer—paying you so well then?"

"He's paying all he needs to get the job done."

"So he's wealthy?"

Fletcher hesitated. "I didn't say that."

No, but you believe he is. She sat forward. "I'm curious—how does a man like your employer go about hiring men like you? You can't possibly put a notice in the news sheets advertising your services."

Fletcher chuckled. Even Cobbins cracked a smile.

"We get business on recommendation," Fletcher explained. "I don't know who mentioned us to him, but he sent word to our contact, and we met him in a tavern. He laid the job before us, and we accepted. Simple enough."

"So you don't know his name?" It was one step too far, but, she judged, worth the gamble.

Fletcher's expression closed, but when she continued to look expectantly at him, his slow, taunting smile returned. "It's no use, Miss Wallace, but if you truly want, I can put my hand on my heart"—he suited action to the words—"and tell you he called himself McKinsey."

She caught the implication. "That's not his name."

"No, it's not. And before you bother asking, I don't know his real name—he's the type wise men don't question about anything they don't want to reveal."

She pulled a face and sat back. And asked nothing more for the moment.

The man who had hired them to kidnap her and deliver her to him was wealthy, lived somewhere in the north, possibly as far north as Glasgow, and was of the caliber to inspire a healthy respect, if not fear, in men like Fletcher.

Despite her curiosity over his identity, she felt increasingly certain she didn't want to actually meet the man.

They halted for lunch a little after noon in the village of Stretton. As they turned into the forecourt of an inn, Heather noted the sign—the Friar and Keys. She'd been this far on the Great North Road on several trips to visit her cousin Richard and his wife Catriona in Scotland, but she couldn't say she recognized the village.

Descending from the coach, she eased her cramped limbs, then looked swiftly around. Would Breckenridge notice that they'd stopped?

Assuming, of course, that he was indeed following and wasn't too far behind.

"Come along." Martha took her arm and propelled her

toward the inn's main door. "Let's order that lunch you were asking after before Fletcher changes his mind."

Heather went docilely enough, but the comment had her glancing back. Fletcher and Cobbins had left the coach, which, thankfully, was being led not deeper into the yard but to one side of the forecourt, where it would be readily visible from the highway. Fletcher and the taciturn Cobbins had walked to the highway's edge and were looking back along the road, talking, possibly arguing, as they watched.

Allowing herself to be led inside, then steered to a wood-paneled booth in the back corner of the taproom, at Martha's nod Heather sat, then scooted along the seat so Martha could sit, too, hemming Heather in against the wall. She looked toward the door. Fletcher and Cobbins had yet to come inside.

A serving girl approached. Martha asked what was available, then ordered shepherd's pie for them all. "And three mugs of ale." Martha glanced at Heather, then added, "And one of cider."

The serving girl nodded and took herself off.

"Thank you," Heather said.

Martha only grunted.

Heather let a moment of silence elapse, then, her gaze still on the open door, asked, "What's Fletcher waiting for?" Could this be where she was to be handed over?

"He's just playing cautious. It's habit with him. He's making sure no one's following us along."

Heather's heart sped up. Keeping her tone even, she ventured, "But how could anyone be following? If they'd seen me snatched off the street, they would have caught up long before now, surely?"

Martha nodded. "So you'd think. But like I said, old Fletcher's a man of caution. No doubt but that's why he's survived for so long."

The serving girl arrived with a tray piled with plates.

Another came up bearing four mugs. The pair blocked Heather's view of the main door. By the time they deposited the plates and mugs and drew back, she was ready to suggest that she or Martha, or even the serving girls, should summon Fletcher and Cobbins before their meals grew cold, but then she glanced at the door and saw Cobbins, followed by Fletcher, enter.

She nearly sighed with relief. Reaching for her cider, she took a calming sip.

Cobbins sat opposite. Fletcher followed him onto the booth's bench seat. He met Martha's eyes. "No one. Looks like we got clean away."

Martha, mouth already full, barely looked up from her plate to nod.

Cobbins lifted his fork and dug into the mound before him. Fletcher followed suit.

Heather picked up her fork, prodded at the meat topped with potato, then lifted a small bite. She tentatively tried it, then went back for more. The dish was surprisingly tasty.

She didn't know what made her look up several minutes later, but glancing at the door she saw Breckenridge standing just inside the room. He was looking at her but immediately shifted his gaze, surveying the tap as if deciding where to sit.

Pretending to look down at her plate, from beneath her lashes she surreptitiously watched as he stirred, then, surprisingly silently for such a large man, tacked through the tables, heading toward their booth.

She blinked and lifted her head when he disappeared behind the high panel at Fletcher's back; he'd slipped into the next booth, behind her male captors.

Which almost certainly meant he would overhear anything they said.

Laying down her fork, fixing her gaze on Fletcher, she took a sip of cider, then cleared her throat. "Where are you taking me?" Looking down, she set her mug back down. Carefully, as if she were nervous and tense.

Fletcher shot her an assessing glance. "We're taking you further north."

She looked up, met his gaze, tried for beseeching. "But how far? Further up the Great North Road? Or somewhere else?" She managed to imbue the last words with an unspecified dread, as if there were something she feared in the north, something other than her abductors' employer.

Fletcher frowned. "Like I said—north."

"But *where* in the north?" Histrionically, she spread her arms. "There's lots of places north of here! Where—" She artistically let her breath catch, swallowed, then went on more quietly, "Where are we stopping for the night?"

Her tone suggested she was close to panic at the idea they might stop too close to that something.

Fletcher frowned harder. Leaning forward, he lowered his voice. "I don't know what bee's got into your bonnet, but we're stopping at Carlton-on-Trent overnight." He searched her face. "Is there any reason we shouldn't?"

Breckenridge might not have heard.

She raised her head, hauled in a breath. "Carlton-on-Trent?" She summoned a weak smile, then shook her head. "No, no . . . there's no reason we can't stop at Carlton-on-Trent."

"Good." Fletcher sat back, still frowning, then he glanced at the other two. "Eat and drink up. Let's get back on the road."

The other two grumbled. Heather quickly ate a few more bites of her nearly cold lunch. The others were still clearing their plates; heads down, none of them noticed the large man who rose from the next booth. Without a single glance in their direction, Breckenridge walked out of the inn.

"Come on." Fletcher pushed back his plate and stood.

The others more slowly followed him out of the booth.

Heather played the obedient abductee and allowed Martha and Cobbins to usher her outside. Stepping into the forecourt, she was just in time to see Breckenridge, in drab, dull clothing quite unlike his usual elegant attire, turn a plain curricle out of the inn yard and set his horses pacing up the highway, heading north.

She surmised he'd decided to go on ahead of them.

Fletcher hadn't taken any notice of the curricle and its driver; he'd gone straight to their own coachman and had started some discussion. She didn't think Cobbins had noticed Breckenridge either, and Martha had emerged from the inn behind her; at best she would have seen his back, and that at a distance.

Fletcher opened the coach door and waved her in. She climbed up and settled on the seat, in her now usual position. While the others climbed in, she prayed Fletcher hadn't realized her ploy, hadn't realized Breckenridge was following, and had therefore told her a lie.

If she lost Breckenridge's protective presence . . .

Even as the thought formed, along with the realization of how very alone she would feel if she didn't know he was close, how very much more afraid and truly panicked she would be, she couldn't help but recognize how ironic it was. How strange that her nemesis—he who she habitually avoided and thoroughly disliked—had somehow transformed into her savior.

Breckenridge, her savior.

She very nearly snorted. Turning her head, she looked out of the window as the coach lurched, and rumbled out of the yard.

Breckenridge swept into Newark-on-Trent in the middle of the afternoon. He'd driven like a demon to get far ahead of the coach carrying Heather, and the pair of grays were flagging. He turned in at the first large posting inn and shouted for the ostlers and stableman.

Despite his unprepossessing attire, they responded to the voice of authority and came running. Stepping to the ground, he tossed the reins to the first ostler, spoke to the stableman. "I need the best pair you have, harnessed and ready to go in . . ." He drew out his fob-watch, checked the time, then snapped it shut. Tucking it back in his pocket, he met the stableman's eyes. "One hour."

"Aye, sir. And the grays?"

He gave the man the direction of the posting house in High Barnet, then strode out of the inn yard and made for Lombard Street.

His first stop was the local branch of Child's Bank; once he replenished his supply of cash, he followed the bank manager's directions to the town's premier bootmaker, and was lucky enough to find an excellent pair of riding boots that fit him. His next stop was the best gentlemen's outfitters, where he created a small furore by demanding they assemble for him outfits suitable for a groom and for a north country laborer.

The head tailor goggled at him and the assistants simply stared; holding onto his temper, he brusquely explained that the outfits were for a country house party where fancy dress was required.

Then they fell to with appropriate zeal.

It still took longer than he would have liked. The tailor fussed with the fitting until Breckenridge declared, "Damn it, man! There's no prize for being the most perfectly dressed groom in the north!"

The tailor jumped. Pins cascaded from between his lips and scattered on the ground. His assistants rushed in to gather them up.

The tailor swallowed. "No, of course not, sir. If Sir will remain still, I will endeavor to remove the pins . . . although really, such shoulders . . . well, I would have thought . . ."

"Never mind about showing off my damned shoulders—just make sure I have room to move." The instant the dapper little tailor stepped back, Breckenridge swung his arms up, then forward. Neither jacket nor shirt ripped. "Good—these will do."

He nodded at the other outfit and the jacket and breeches he'd traded his evening coat for back in the Knebworth tavern. "Just parcel those up. I'll wear what I have on. I have to get back on the road."

The tailor and his assistants scurried to obey.

Breckenridge paid and tipped them well, grateful they hadn't led him to lose his temper, which seemed to be riding on a distinctly frayed rein.

The parcel of clothes under one arm, he strode quickly back to the posting inn. A pair of decent-looking blacks had been harnessed to the curricle he'd hired in Baldock to replace the too-showy phaeton. He inspected both horses, then paid the stableman, stowed his parcel beneath the seat, climbed up, sat, and, after testing the reins, nodded to the ostlers. "Release them."

The ostlers let go. Both horses lunged but immediately felt a firm hand on the reins. They tossed their heads but quickly settled. With a flick of his wrist, Breckenridge sent them pacing neatly to the street, then turned out and headed briskly on, up the Great North Road.

He was in position in the tap of the Old Bell Inn in Carlton-on-Trent when the coach carrying Heather turned in under the inn's arch and drew up in the forecourt. Seated at a table in the front corner of the tap, he sipped a pint of ale and watched the group descend from the coach. As before, Heather was closely guarded and ushered toward the inn's front door, which opened to the inn's foyer.

The foyer, most helpfully, was separated from the tap by a wooden partition. From where he sat, he could hear every word uttered, even muttered, in the foyer, but no one in the foyer could see him. Of course, he couldn't see them either, but he hoped Heather would have noticed that there was only one inn in the small village, and would assume he'd be somewhere near.

He heard the front door open, followed by the usual sounds of arrival, then someone rang the bell on the counter. He sipped and listened as the innkeeper arrived and quickly set about the business of welcoming his guests and getting them settled. Breckenridge paid particular attention to the room allocations, both the women's and Fletcher and Cobbins's. Like the women, the men would share a room, but their room would be in another wing.

Breckenridge listened as Fletcher tried to change the innkeeper's mind and get a room closer to the women's. The innkeeper insisted that he only had the two rooms still available, many others being closed due to rain damage during a recent storm. Fletcher grumbled, but reluctantly conceded that he and his friend would take the offered room.

"Good," Breckenridge murmured. He'd paid the innkeeper to ensure that both Heather's male captors would be far distant from her room that night. He sincerely hoped that by this evening she would be ready to quit their company and return to London. The further they went . . . yet, as attested to by the extra disguises he'd bought, he wasn't placing any wagers on her coming to her senses, especially not because he thought she should.

The abduction party fussed over their luggage, then Heather spoke, her voice carrying clearly into the tap. "I'm unaccustomed to being cooped up all day—I really must insist that you permit me to enjoy a short walk."

"Not on your life," Fletcher growled.

From the sound, Breckenridge realized the group had moved closer to the tap.

"You don't need to think you're going to give us the slip so easily." Fletcher again.

"My dear good man"—Heather with her nose in the air; Breckenridge could tell by her tone—"just where in this landscape of empty fields do you imagine I'm going to slip to?"

Cobbins opined that she might try to steal a horse and ride off.

"Oh, yes—in a round gown and evening slippers," Heather jeered. "But I wasn't suggesting you let me ramble on my own—Martha can come with me."

That was Martha's cue to enter the fray, but Heather stuck to her guns, refusing to back down through the ensuing, increasingly heated verbal stoush.

Until Fletcher intervened, aggravated frustration resonating in his voice. "Look you—we're under strict orders to keep you safe, not to let you wander off to fall prey to the first shiftless rake who rides past and takes a fancy to you."

Silence reigned for half a minute, then Heather audibly sniffed. "I'll have you know that shiftless rakes know better than to take a fancy to me."

Not true, Breckenridge thought, but that wasn't the startling information contained in Fletcher's outburst. "Come on, Heather—follow up."

As if she'd heard his muttered exhortation, she blithely swept on, "But if rather than standing there arguing, you instead treated me like a sensible adult and told me what your so strict orders with respect to me were, I might see my way to complying—or at least to helping you comply with them."

Breckenridge blinked as he sorted through that pronouncement; he could almost feel for Fletcher when he hissed out a sigh.

"All right." Fletcher's frustration had reached breaking point. "If you must know, we're to keep you safe from all harm. We're not to let a bloody pigeon pluck so much as a hair from your head. We're to deliver you up in prime condition, exactly as you were when we grabbed you."

From the change in Fletcher's tone, Breckenridge could visualize him moving closer to tower over Heather to intimidate her into backing down; he could have told him it wouldn't work.

"So *now* you see," Fletcher went on, voice low and forceful, "that it's entirely out of the question for you to go out for any ramble."

"Hmm." Heather's tone was tellingly mild.

Fletcher was about to get floored by an uppercut. For once

not being on the receiving end, Breckenridge grinned and waited for it to land.

"*If*, as you say, your orders are to—do correct me if I'm wrong—keep me in my customary excellent health until you hand me over to your employer, then, my dear Fletcher, that will absolutely necessitate me going for a walk. Being cooped up all day in a carriage has never agreed with me—if you don't wish me to weaken or develop some unhealthy affliction, I will require fresh air and gentle exercise to recoup." She paused, then went on, her tone one of utmost reasonableness, "A short excursion along the river at the rear of the inn, and back, should restore my constitution."

Breckenridge was certain he could hear Fletcher breathing in and out through clenched teeth.

A fraught moment passed, then, "Oh, very well! Martha—go with her. Twenty minutes, do you hear? Not a minute more."

"Thank you, Fletcher. Come, Martha—we don't want to waste the light."

Breckenridge heard Heather, with the rather slower Martha, leave the inn by the main door. He sipped his ale, waited. Eventually, Fletcher and Cobbins climbed the stairs, Cobbins grumbling, Fletcher ominously silent.

The instant they passed out of hearing, Breckenridge stood, stretched, then walked out of the tap and into the foyer. Seconds later, he slipped out of the front door.

The river Trent flowed peacefully along, a mere hundred yards from the rear of the inn. A well-beaten path wended along the bank. Heather ambled down it, genuinely glad to have the chance to stretch her legs, to breathe fresh air, but her principal reason for insisting on the walk was to gain some inkling of whether Breckenridge was there.

Until she saw him, she had no way of knowing if he was—whether he'd arrived ahead of them or was still on his way.

One thing she did feel certain about was that he would

materialize and hover close. He'd said they would have to meet every night. She was under no illusion; if he thought she was in real danger, he would intervene and rescue her, regardless of what he might have to do to accomplish that. By the same token, when they met that night—however they managed it—he would most likely try to bully her into giving up her quest and returning to London with him.

So while she walked, she reviewed all she'd learned—not enough, but a few telling facts, enough to justify persisting, and learning more if she could. She ordered the points in her mind.

She was mentally far away, absentmindedly strolling, when Martha, plodding heavily alongside, said, "You're taking this awfully well."

Heather glanced at her, met Martha's shrewd gaze.

"I'd expected," Martha continued, "to have to deal with hysterics—bouts of weeping and pleading at the very least."

"Yes, well . . ." Heather pulled an expressive face. Looking ahead, she went on, "I have to admit I did feel like panicking at first, but . . . I've been wondering if I shouldn't view this as an adventure." She had to deflect any suspicion, so offered the one explanation that might serve. She gestured dramatically. "A romantical adventure, complete with mysterious villain, who might or might not prove to be devastatingly handsome."

Martha snorted. "So that's the way it is—you're romanticizing this blackguard who's arranged your kidnapping."

"Do you actually know if he's a blackguard?" Heather didn't have to manufacture her concern.

Martha grimaced. "I can't rightly say. I haven't had anything to do with the beggar. Fletcher and Cobbins were the ones that met him. But," she continued, "any blighter who arranges a kidnapping, and one as coolly planned as this, take it from me, handsome or not, you won't want to meet him." Martha glanced at her again. "Sure you don't want to rethink those hysterics?"

Heather arched her brows. "Will they get me any further?"

"Not with me—and Fletcher's more like to slap you than come over all solicitous."

"Well, then." Heather tipped up her face. "I believe I'll just go on romanticizing, at least until I have cause not to. You should be grateful—I'm making your task much easier."

Martha snorted. "Speaking of which." She halted. "This is far enough. You may need the exercise, but I don't—we head back from here."

Heather halted, filled her lungs full, then exhaled on a sigh. "Oh, very well." Swinging around, she fell in beside Martha's large, darkly garbed figure, and they started back toward the inn.

The "maid" was an inch or so taller than Heather, and at least two of her in girth, yet despite her size and usual plodding gait, Martha could move fast enough if she wished, and Heather had seen the size of the arms concealed by her voluminous black sleeves. Martha might be large, but she was mostly muscle. If Heather had to escape the woman, she'd need to ensure Martha was incapacitated first.

They walked slowly back to the inn—Martha because that was the speed at which she walked, Heather because she saw no reason to cut short her time in the crisp, late afternoon air.

Reaching the narrow path they'd taken from the inn to the river, they left the river path and, with the Trent at their backs, climbed the shallow slope toward the inn.

Raising her head, Heather looked at the gray stone building—and saw the tall, broad-shouldered, dark-haired man who'd paused in the shadows by one corner.

Earlier, in Stretton, he'd worn the clothes of a country townsman, the sort who might own a local business. Now he was garbed more like one of his own grooms. Regardless, she recognized him instantly. Her heart lightened considerably; she started to smile, only just remembering to suppress the reaction.

Glancing sideways at Martha, toiling beside her, she was relieved to see that the maid hadn't noticed.

She looked at the inn again . . .

Breckenridge had vanished.

Not that it mattered. Now she knew he was near, they would meet tonight somehow. She turned her mind to rehearsing her report, to listing all she'd learned in the manner most likely to convince him to agree to her continuing on with her captors.

The Old Bell Inn was in truth a very old inn. Its bedchambers possessed latches, with hooks on the doors to secure them, but no locks. Heather blessed the innkeeper for not modernizing; once the inn had settled for the night and every two-legged occupant had retired to their beds, with Martha snoring fit to drown out any creaking boards, Heather lifted the latch on their chamber door and slipped out into the chill darkness of the corridor.

She hadn't dared light a candle, but her eyes had adjusted to the night; she could see well enough to, with one quick glance, confirm the corridor was empty. Once again she'd been deprived of her outer clothes, but she'd complained about the cold and had used the excuse that they wouldn't want her to take a chill to persuade Martha to allow her to keep her silk shawl and to spread her cloak over her bed for extra warmth.

The cloak was wrapped about her now, and cinched at her waist with the silk shawl. Although the makeshift gown left her ankles and lower calves exposed, at least her skin there was screened by silk stocking, and the gown otherwise was a significant improvement over the previous night's coverlet; it didn't rely on her holding it in place to remain decent.

Which was a pertinent consideration given she was off to meet Breckenridge. He'd more or less made it a condition for his agreeing to allow her to continue traveling on with her captors, and she knew him well enough not to call his bluff, because it would be no bluff. Besides, she wanted to share what she'd learned, and see if he might have any further insights. His knowledge of their world, especially beyond the confines of the ton, was significantly greater than hers.

Silently closing the door behind her, carefully easing the latch back into place, she turned in the direction of the stairs. For several moments, she held still, straining her ears for any sound, allowing her vision to better adjust to the deeper darkness of the corridor, and reminding herself of the way.

When she and Martha had risen from the table they'd shared with Fletcher and Cobbins in the tap through the evening, Breckenridge, seated across the room and closer to the door, had anticipated them; he'd risen and left the tap ahead of them. He'd been climbing the stairs when she and Martha had reached the foyer.

They'd followed him up and had seen him open the door of a room not far from the head of the stairs. He hadn't so much as glanced their way but had gone in and shut the door. She'd walked on with Martha, past that door, down the corridor and around a corner to their chamber.

Drawing in a tight—faintly excited—breath, she set out, quietly creeping back to the corner, her evening slippers allowing her to tiptoe along with barely a sound.

Nearing the corner, she paused and glanced back along the corridor. Still empty. Reassured, she started to turn, intending to peek around the corner—

A hard body swung around the corner and plowed into her.

She stumbled back. Hard hands grabbed her, holding her upright.

Her heart leapt to her throat. She looked up, saw only darkness.

She opened her mouth—

A palm slapped over her lips. A steely arm locked around her—locked her against a large, adamantine male body; she couldn't even squirm.

Her senses scrambled. Strength, male heat, muscled hardness engulfed her.

Then a virulent curse singed her ears.

And she realized who'd captured her.

Panic and sheer fright had tensed her every muscle; relief washed both away and she felt limp. The temptation to sag in his arms, to sink gratefully against him, was so nearly overwhelming that it shocked her into tensing again.

He lowered his head so he could look into her face. Through clenched teeth, he hissed, *"What the devil are you doing?"*

His tone very effectively dragged her wits to the fore. He hadn't removed his hand from her lips. She nipped it.

With a muted oath, he pulled the hand away.

She moistened her lips and angrily whispered back, "Coming to see *you,* of course. What are *you* doing here?"

"Coming to fetch you—*of course.*"

"You ridiculous man." Her hands had come to rest on his chest. She snatched them back, waved them. "I'm hardly likely to come to grief over the space of a few yards!"

Even to her ears they sounded like squabbling children.

He didn't reply.

Through the dark, he looked at her.

She couldn't see his eyes, but his gaze was so intent, so intense that she could feel . . .

Her heart started thudding, beating heavier, deeper.

Her senses expanded, alert in a wholly unfamiliar way.

He looked at her . . . looked at her.

Primitive instinct riffled the delicate hairs at her nape.

Abruptly he raised his head, straightened, stepped back. "Come on."

Grabbing her elbow, he bundled her unceremoniously around the corner and on up the corridor before him. Her temper—always close to the surface when he was near—started to simmer. If they hadn't needed to be quiet, she would have told him what she thought of such cavalier treatment.

Breckenridge halted her outside the door to his bedchamber; he would have preferred any other meeting place, but there was no safer place, and regardless of all and every-

48

thing else, he needed to keep her safe. Reaching around her, he raised the latch and set the door swinging. "In here."

He'd left the lamp burning low. As he followed her in, then reached back and shut the door, he took in what she was wearing. He bit back another curse.

She glanced around, but there was nowhere to sit but on the bed. Quickly he strode past her, stripped off the coverlet, then autocratically pointed to the sheet. "Sit there."

With a narrow-eyed glare, she did, with the haughty grace of a reigning monarch.

Immediately she'd sat, he flicked out the coverlet and swathed her in it.

She cast him a faintly puzzled glance but obligingly held the enveloping drape close about her.

He said nothing; if she wanted to think he was concerned about her catching a chill, so be it. At least the coverlet was long enough to screen her distracting ankles and calves.

Which really was ridiculous. Considering how many naked women he'd seen in his life, why the sight of *her* stockinged ankles and calves should so affect him was beyond his ability to explain.

Turning, he sat alongside her, with a good foot of clear space between them. "So what have you learned?"

She studied him for a moment, then said, "Not as much as I would have liked, but they did let fall that their employer hired them in Glasgow, that he's paying for everything, and they seem happy with the financial arrangements, suggesting that he's at least reasonably wealthy, but as yet I haven't been able to drag from them any further detail about where they're taking me." Huddling into the coverlet, she frowned across the room. "The only other thing I dragged from them was more by way of an impression."

When she didn't go on, he prompted, "What impression?"

The line between her brows deepened. "They—Fletcher and Cobbins, at least, they're the ones who met him—view him, their employer, with a certain . . . I suppose you'd say wariness."

"Respect?"

Her lips twisted. "Yes, but more in the physical sense. He might simply be a nasty, dangerous sort."

Breckenridge thought for a moment. "Where in Glasgow did they meet him?"

"In some tavern. Apparently they do work like this for others, for hire. He heard of them from someone else they'd worked for, and approached them through some contact they have in place."

"So they don't necessarily know much about him?"

"I gathered not—they gave me a name, but before you get excited, Fletcher made it clear that they're certain it's not his real name."

"What was it?"

"McKinsey."

"Scottish—so he's most likely a Scot." Still far too aware of her perched on the bed—his bed—beside him, Breckenridge stood. He started to pace back and forth.

Heather looked up at him. "I'm not sure we can assume that. It might be that the reason Fletcher's so certain McKinsey isn't his real name is because he—their employer—is English."

Breckenridge grimaced. "True. And there are Englishmen aplenty in Glasgow."

Beneath the coverlet, she straightened. "Regardless, it's clear I need to learn more."

The dark look Breckenridge slanted her wasn't encouraging. "We're already a long way from London, and we're still on the Great North Road. We have no notion how far north they intend taking you, but every mile takes you further from your family, further from safety."

Her lips tightened, but she held to her composure. So far he'd been reasonable and supportive. For once she'd try reason with him and see where it got her. "As to that, strange though it seems, they have orders—strict orders—to keep me safe. Safe, unharmed, and healthy. I used those orders to insist on being allowed to walk by the river, so it seems they're taking them seriously."

Somewhat reluctantly, Breckenridge nodded. "I was in the tap, on the other side of the partition separating it from the foyer. I heard it all." He kept slowly pacing, his face set in its usual impassive mien, then shot her glance. "I admit that this is decidedly strange."

She nodded. "Indeed. And every mile we go further from London makes the notion of ransom even more unlikely. So we're still no closer to learning what's behind this—neither the who nor the why of it." She waited until he swung around again and caught his eye. "I believe we need to consider the wider implications."

His lips twitched—she was almost certain of it—but he didn't stop pacing. "Meaning you want to continue on with this"—he gestured—"quest of yours."

She tipped up her head. "Of course. I'm here, already kidnapped, but they've provided me with a maid and are under strict orders to see to my health and safety, orders they're clearly committed to obeying. On top of that"—she waved at him—"you're here. If you continue to follow our party, when it comes to the point where escaping becomes necessary, I'll be able to do so and hide behind you. God knows, you're large enough."

He quirked a black brow.

Before he could respond verbally she went on, "Given the threat extends beyond me to my sisters, and possibly even to my cousins, and that as yet we have insufficient information with which to counter or nullify that threat, then while remaining with Fletcher and the other two exposes me to no additional danger, it's patently my duty to stay with them at least until we learn enough to identify who's behind this, and, if possible, his motives."

Fixing her eyes on Breckenridge's, she concluded, "In my

estimation, the reasons against continuing on with my captors are outweighed by the reasons that I should."

Breckenridge studied her as he paced. He wanted to inform her that she was wrong, that in *his* estimation the imperative of keeping her totally and absolutely safe—which to his mind meant taking her back to London and depositing her under her father's roof—by far outweighed every other consideration. And for him, it did. But for her . . . the damned thing was he could understand her stance. And he could hardly accuse her of being a headstrong, willful, heedlessly selfish female when she was driven by such a selfless, family-duty-derived motive.

One he would feel were he in her shoes.

Halting, he raked a hand through his hair, then realized what he was doing and lowered his arm. He glanced at her, sitting on his bed wrapped in his coverlet, her head high, chin tilted upward, but the angle was not yet an outright challenge.

He knew that challenge would come if he didn't agree with her direction and tried to pull her from it. He could, very easily—he was Viscount Breckenridge after all—but she would fight him every step of the way and hate him forever after. All of which he would accept without a qualm if he could only be certain that he was, indeed, acting in the best interests of her and her family.

As things stood . . .

"Very well." Halting, he met her eyes, a darker gray in the lamplight. "If you're stubbornly determined on this?"

Up went her chin. "I am."

"In that case, we'll continue on, more or less as we have been, at least for tomorrow." He frowned. "We'll have to play it by ear." He'd have to trust her to do so. "If you'll give me your promise that the instant you learn either the employer's name or his direction—or even the place where they plan to hand you over—you'll tell me, give me some sign at least so I can arrange to whisk you out of their clutches . . . if you promise that, we'll go on as we have been."

She smiled, pleased. "I promise. As soon as I learn anything useful, I'll give you some sign so we can meet and discuss it."

He noted the difference between what he'd asked and what she'd promised, but that, he suspected, was the best he could hope for. He nodded in acceptance, then waved her to the door.

She rose, slid the coverlet from her shoulders and laid it back on his bed, then walked to the door.

Keeping his gaze on her face, he waved her to a halt. He opened the door and looked out. The corridor was empty. Reaching back, he took her arm and drew her through the door. He escorted her quickly and silently back to her room.

She opened the door, and the sound of robust snoring issued forth. She turned to him, grinned, and mouthed, "Good night."

Slipping through the door, she quietly closed it behind her.

He stepped back, put his back to the corridor wall opposite the door, and waited, listened. After enough time had elapsed for her to have slipped back into bed, and the sonorous snoring hadn't ceased, he pushed away from the wall and headed back to his room.

Inside, he stripped and slid beneath the covers—and was immediately enveloped in a subtle scent he had no difficulty identifying.

It was hers, the scent that clung to her hair and had transferred to the coverlet. The airy, delicate, vibrantly female scent instantly evoked the vision of her stockinged ankles, the way the sheer silk had sheened over the curves . . .

He groaned and closed his eyes. Clearly he wasn't destined to get much sleep.

Accepting that, dampening his reaction as well as he could, he sought distraction in the pragmatic details of the adventure they'd somehow embarked on. He was going to have to devise ways of staying close to her while remaining invisible to her captors. Appearing inconspicuous wasn't a skill he'd had much cause to develop.

No more than he'd had cause to learn the ways of dealing with her on a rational basis.

Keeping her safe on her quest was a task that looked set to tax his ingenuity in ways it had never before been challenged, yet no matter how he turned the puzzle of her kidnapping over in his mind, no matter what perspective he took, in one respect she was incontestably correct.

This was no ordinary, run-of-the-mill abduction.

Chapter Four

At one o'clock the following afternoon, Breckenridge sat at one of the trestles set up outside the White Horse Inn in the small town of Bramham. Leaning his shoulders against the inn's stone wall, he sipped a pint of ale and watched the archway leading into the yard of the Red Lion Inn further up the road.

The coach carrying Heather and her captors had turned into the yard more than an hour ago. After scouting the place and confirming that there was only one exit from the Red Lion's yard, namely under the archway, he'd retreated here to keep watch while simultaneously keeping his distance and, he hoped, staying out of Fletcher and company's sight. He was fairly certain they hadn't yet seen him, or if they had, hadn't noticed him enough to recognize him again, especially given he was varying his disguise.

Today he'd reverted to the outfit he'd acquired in Knebworth. The ill-fitting jacket and loose cloth breeches made him look like a down-on-his-luck salesman; as long as he remembered to modify his posture, he'd pass a cursory inspection.

He took another sip of ale. He increasingly misliked how far north they were heading. They'd traveled all morning further up the Great North Road. Bramham was nearly as far north as York. Yet despite his misgivings, he, too, was finding this abduction and the challenge of learning who and what was behind it increasingly intriguing. Now he'd had time to digest all Heather had learned yesterday, he had to admit it was a most peculiar puzzle.

A pair of horses appeared beneath the Red Lion's arch, followed by a second pair, then the kidnappers' coach. The coach turned ponderously out of the inn yard, still heading north.

Breckenridge watched it lumber on, then drained his pint, set the mug down, rose, and headed for the side yard of the White Horse where he'd left his hired curricle.

Five minutes later, bowling along the highway once more, he glimpsed the coach ahead and slowed the bays he currently had between the shafts. He rolled slowly on in the coach's wake, far enough back that they'd be unlikely to spot him even on a long straight stretch. Not that they'd shown any signs of searching for pursuers. They might have looked back once or twice, but since he'd caught up with them at Knebworth, they'd seemed unconcerned about pursuit.

Of course, as far as they knew there had been no immediate chase given from Lady Herford's house; no doubt they assumed they'd got clean away. And indeed, if he hadn't seen them seize Heather, any pursuit the Cynsters would have mounted would have been days behind. It most likely wouldn't have even started yet, because her family would have had to search extensively to determine in which direction she'd been taken—even that she'd been taken out of London at all. As she'd pointed out, if she'd been kidnapped for ransom, then it would have been assumed her kidnappers would keep her in the metropolis; so much easier to hide a woman among the teeming hordes, in the crowded tenements, where no one would ask awkward questions.

The miles slid by. Initially he kept pace with the coach, but the further north they rolled he gradually closed the distance. Their steady push north was making him increasingly nervous about where they were headed and, especially, why.

Heather forced herself to wait until they'd been traveling north for at least an hour after their luncheon halt before recommencing her interrogation of her captors.

She'd been acquiescent, and had made no fuss through the

morning. Other than casting a quick glance around the inn where they'd stopped for lunch, searching for Breckenridge—but they hadn't known that—she'd played the part of gently bred and, therefore, relatively helpless kidnappee.

Although she hadn't sighted Breckenridge, she felt reasonably confident that he'd be somewhere near. Leaving him to his self-appointed but now gratefully accepted role of watching over her, she'd applied herself to encouraging her captors to relax and, she hoped, grow less careful and more talkative.

By way of introduction, she heaved a huge sigh and glanced out of the window.

Fletcher, seated opposite as usual, looked at her consideringly. Assessingly.

Facing him again, she caught his eye, grimaced. "If you won't tell me where we're going, or your employer's name, can you at least tell me what he looks like? Seeing I'll be meeting him, I presume sometime soon, then you'll hardly be revealing anything vital, and it would certainly help my nerves to know what sort of man you'll be handing me to."

Fletcher's lips curved a little. "Not sure how knowing what he looks like is going to help you, but . . ." He glanced at Cobbins, who shrugged. Looking back at her, Fletcher asked, "What do you want to know?"

Everything you can tell me. She widened her eyes. "Hair color?"

"Black."

"Eyes?"

Fletcher hesitated, then said, "Not sure about the color, but . . . cold."

Black-haired, cold-eyed. "How old, and handsome or not?"

Fletcher pursed his lips. "I'd say in his thirties, but exactly where I couldn't guess. And as for handsome"—Fletcher grinned—"you'd probably think so. Bit rugged for my taste, though, and with a blade of a nose."

She frowned, not entirely liking the image.

Fletcher continued, his tone tending teasing, "One thing I

do remember—he had a black frown. Devilish, it was. Not the sort of man to get on the wrong side of."

"How tall was he?"

"Big bloke. Large all around. Lots of Scottish brawn."

"So he's Scottish?"

Fletcher hesitated, then shrugged. "Like you said, you'll meet him soon enough. We took him for some laird—lord knows, they've plenty of those—but where exactly he hailed from, lowlands or highlands or anywhere in between, we couldn't say."

She was even more puzzled, but she didn't want to waste Fletcher's attack of loquaciousness. "Is there anything physically that sets him apart—a scar, a particular ring, a gammy leg?" Anything to identify him.

Fletcher met her eyes. A moment passed, then he said, "Think I've told you enough to settle your nerves."

She looked at him, then sighed and subsided back against the seat. "Oh, all right." One step at a time.

Contrary to Fletcher's belief, her nerves were distinctly unsettled, indeed, decidedly jangling, when, in the fading light of late afternoon, the coach drew up outside the King's Head Hotel in Barnard Castle.

They were no longer on the Great North Road. They'd turned west off the highway in Darlington, and there'd been no way she'd been able to think of to ensure Breckenridge noted the change in direction.

The possibility that he was no longer there, at her back to save her, had blossomed and burgeoned in her mind. By the time the coach rocked to a halt, trepidation danced along her nerves and her stomach was tied in knots.

Handed down to the pavement by Cobbins, she glanced, inwardly desperate, about.

"Come along." Martha prodded her on. "Let's get inside, out of this chill."

Heather climbed the hotel's front steps slowly. Increasingly reluctantly. Then over the bustle caused by their arrival, the sound of hooves ringing on the cobbles reached her. Gaining the raised porch, she quickly turned and looked—and saw Breckenridge, looking like a lowly traveler, driving a curricle along the main street. He didn't look her way. She quickly turned toward the hotel's door so Martha, toiling up the steps behind her, wouldn't see her relief.

But oh, what relief.

Walking a great deal more calmly into the hotel foyer, she couldn't help but acknowledge it. Couldn't help but admit that her nemesis had indeed lost that hat. While she might not truly view him as her savior, she knew she could rely on him, could have faith that he would in all circumstances do the very best he could to keep her safe.

She trusted him explicitly and implicitly; despite their previous history, that had never been in question.

Raising her head, drawing in a revivifying breath, feeling immeasurably more confident, she swept toward the reception counter where Fletcher was discussing their accommodations. The more she knew of where they'd all be that night, the more readily she'd be able to meet with Breckenridge.

She next saw Breckenridge when, preceded by Fletcher and flanked by Martha, with Cobbins bringing up the rear, she walked into the hotel's dining room that evening.

He was seated at a table in the corner by one window, head down, his attention apparently fixed on a news sheet. He evinced not the slightest interest in their party.

For their part, neither Fletcher nor Cobbins, both of whom surveyed the room, seemed to truly notice him. They saw him but instantly dismissed him.

Heather was frankly amazed. Breckenridge might be wearing yet another disguise, this one making him appear less scruffy and more like a gentleman traveler, yet how anyone could miss the steely strength in those broad shoulders, let alone the arrogance in the set of his head, she had no idea.

To her he always appeared as he truly was. Dangerous and

unpredictable. Not the sort of man one should ever take for granted, let alone dismiss.

Shown to a table for four across the room, she deftly claimed the chair that would allow her to keep Breckenridge in sight from the corner of her eye. Martha, the least observant of her captors, sat alongside her. Fletcher and Cobbins sat opposite, from where they could see the door and through it part of the hotel foyer.

Unbeknown to them, the real danger lay behind them.

Increasingly assured, increasingly buoyed, she set herself to winkle further details that might shed some light on the identity of the mysterious laird from her dinner companions.

"Did you dine with this laird—the one who hired you?" She widened her eyes at Fletcher.

He gave her a look. "We met him in a tavern, and food wasn't on any of our minds. It wasn't a social meeting."

"Hmm . . . how did he arrive at the tavern?"

Fletcher blinked.

Cobbins, frowning, answered. "Don't know—we were there when he walked in the door, and he left before we did." He glanced down as the serving girl placed a plate piled with pie and steamed parsnip before him. "We stayed for a pint, to celebrate like."

Heather held her tongue while they all started to eat.

A minute later, Fletcher looked up from his plate, a frown in his eyes. "I don't know why you want to know more about the man—seems like you'll know all you'll want to once we hand you over to him."

"But when will that be?" When no answer was forthcoming, she pointed the tines of her fork at Fletcher. "See? That's why I'm asking. If you'll simply tell me what to expect, I won't be so curious."

Fletcher grunted. "You'll learn all soon enough. Until then, you'd do best to let it be."

Heather subsided and gave her attention to her plate. To assembling all she'd dragged from her unwilling sources during that day into a cogent report. Breckenridge would want to know all, of course, and she was keen to share her discoveries.

Working her way steadily through her baked fish, she thought of Fletcher's response, his tone. Cobbins's words. She had to wonder just how much they knew of their employer.

From beneath her lashes, she studied Fletcher. His expression was tightly closed, almost pinched. She doubted he'd tell her any more that night. It would, she sensed, be better not to ask. He was more likely to be forthcoming tomorrow if she let the matter slide for now.

Breckenridge was sitting too far away, and the dining room was too noisy, for him to have overhead even the most recent exchange. Indeed, he wasn't making the smallest effort to eavesdrop; he was leaving the interrogation completely to her, trusting that she would report later. So . . . where to meet with him?

Almost as if he'd heard her question, he pushed back his chair and rose. News sheet in hand, he briefly looked her way. Her captors didn't raise their heads, didn't lift their eyes from their plates.

Breckenridge captured her gaze, then turned his head and looked further down the dining room. Heather followed his gaze and saw a pair of glass-paned doors at the rear of the room. From what she could see through the doors, the room beyond was the hotel bar's snug.

Shifting her gaze carefully back, she checked her companions—still oblivious—then briefly raised her eyes to Breckenridge as he walked slowly to the dining room door. She didn't dare nod, but she met his gaze, then he looked back at his news sheet and continued walking. He passed through the door; a second later, she heard his footsteps climbing the stairs.

"I haven't been along this road before." She glanced at Martha and Cobbins. "I noticed there's a ruined castle just down the road, overlooking the bridge. Are there any other particular sights we might pass in the coach tomorrow?"

Martha shook her head but looked curiously at the other two.

Cobbins shrugged. "Couple of old castles not far from the road, and a Roman fort or two, but there's not much left to see of those, not from the road, anyways."

Fletcher scowled at her. "You'll see what you'll see." Setting his napkin beside his plate, he pushed back his chair. "Time for you and Martha to retire, seeing you've another long day in the coach to look forward to."

Heather met his eyes, then inclined her head and rose.

Escorted by the trio, she climbed the stairs and headed toward their rooms.

She crept back down the stairs as the clocks throughout the hotel's reception rooms bonged and chimed with a single peal. One o'clock; she hadn't dared creep out earlier. The room she shared with Martha was this time next door to the one in which Fletcher and Cobbins slept; to get to the stairs, she'd had to pass their door.

Martha might sleep like one dead and snore like a walrus to boot, but Heather was much more wary of Fletcher, and even the taciturn Cobbins.

She descended the stairs close by the wall, careful to avoid squeaks. Gaining the foyer, she hugged the shadows and slipped into the dining room. With no curtains at the windows, there was light, faint but enough to see her way; on slippered feet she padded to the glass-paned doors. She peered through, into a room shrouded in shadows. The snug was L-shaped. The nearer section was dark, but the other arm was softly, a touch eerily, lit by the moon.

Drawing a fortifying breath, she reached for the doorknob, turned it, pushed open one door, and slid through. Eyes wide, trying to pierce the shadows, she eased the door closed, heard it click.

Holding her breath, she stepped out, heading for the better-illuminated section of the room.

Hard hands closed about her upper arms.

She started—very nearly squeaked—then once again wilted with relief as Breckenridge drew her back, closer to his large, warm body; he'd been standing in the dense shadows by the wall.

"Shssh."

The order—despite the sibilant sound, she was quite sure it was an order—shivered across her ear.

Irritated, she glanced up and back. "If you'd stop scaring me witless, I wouldn't make a sound."

For a moment, their eyes met through the dimness. Their faces were close. Then he released her and eased back. "Would you rather I'd tapped you on the shoulder?"

She humphed. "No, but—" She broke off as he swiped up a large document from a nearby table, along with his cloak. "What's that?" She nodded at the document.

"A map. I'm not as familiar with this area as I'd like." He flicked out the cloak and draped it about her shoulders.

It was long enough to pool about her feet.

"Thank you," she murmured, a touch surprised that he'd been so thoughtful. She had been a trifle cold in her makeshift robe, and she'd washed her stockings, so she didn't even have them on.

"Just keep it close." Through the cloak, he grasped her elbow. "We should be safe around the corner."

Assuming his injunction was a warning to keep the cloak, voluminous on her, from tripping her or getting caught in the chairs, she obediently snuggled the folds closer—and felt the warmth still clinging to the material, detected a scent she associated with him—pine and very male.

The scent wreathed through her head and played havoc with her attention. Luckily, he steered her steadily on, tacking between the tables and chairs to round the corner of the bar and reach the more secluded and better-lit area.

Breckenridge released her by a table beneath one window. The moon gave them enough light to see, both each other's faces and the map.

Heather sat, gathering the cloak about her, hiding all the distractions he didn't need to see.

He drew out the chair opposite, placed the map on the table as he sat. "First, tell me what you learned today—I assume you made some headway?"

She nodded. "He—the man who arranged this—is a Scotsman, at least Fletcher and Cobbins believe he is. They describe him as a 'laird,' but on what grounds they decided he's a large landowner, I'm not sure. He's apparently black-haired with cold eyes—neither remember the color—and a particularly devilish black frown. And he's large and apparently not a man they'd willingly cross."

When she paused, he asked, "That's all?"

"Yes." She grimaced. "And I know there must be hundreds if not thousands of Scottish lairds who fit that description. I did try for something more distinctive—a scar, ring, injury—but Fletcher cut me off at that point."

"He cut you off?"

"Hmm. I could be wrong, but I think my asking questions made him realize how little he actually knows about this man they're working for. They don't even know if he came to their meeting in Glasgow in a carriage, or if he rode, and if so, what type of horse."

Leaning both forearms on the table, Breckenridge considered all they'd thus far learned. He debated, but in the end shifted his gaze and met her eyes. "Are you ready to escape them and return to London?"

She held his gaze for a long moment, enough to have him hoping . . . but then she said, evenly and reasonably, "I've given them no hint that I might try to escape, and they have no idea that you even exist, let alone are close by. They're growing more relaxed, and gradually more inclined to answer my questions—even Fletcher. I haven't really had time to work on Martha yet—I've been concentrating on Fletcher, as he seems the one with most knowledge, and he's the most observant, too."

"He's also the most dangerous of the three."

"Yes, I know, but he's also unwaveringly committed to following his orders, so I'm safe from him, at least in that regard. He won't harm me—from all they've said, neither he nor Cobbins are at all eager to get on the wrong side of their employer. So I am making headway, but I still haven't learned enough to identify this laird. And so far Fletcher's resisted telling me—even giving me a hint—about where they're taking me to hand me over. If we learned that, we might have some chance of identifying the laird as someone who comes to that place."

He let a moment elapse, then said, "You're not going to escape yet, are you?"

For a moment, she held his gaze, then her lips twisted. "To be perfectly honest, I don't think I can. If I did, and later Eliza, Angelica, Henrietta, or Mary was kidnapped, and perhaps hurt in the process . . . I don't think I could live with that."

He nodded. "All right." He didn't like it, but he'd expected it, and, indeed, understood.

During the long hours he'd driven behind the lumbering coach, he'd had time enough to assess their situation. He'd already accepted that, given they'd been absent, on the road, alone as far as the ton could ever know, for two full days, then, him being him and her being her, regardless of how this adventure played out, their wedding was now an unavoidable outcome.

The realization . . . hadn't bothered him that much. He had to marry and beget an heir, and his dear evil ugly sisters had been after him for years to make his choice. Heather would fit the bill nicely, at least in all the ways society deemed important.

What, however, had shocked him to his toes was the ease

with which the notion of him and her, man and wife, had so readily slotted into his forward planning, his not-all-that-well-defined vision of his future life. The idea of her as his wife simply slipped into the center of his nebulous universe and clicked into place, acting as a catalyst, allowing associated elements to connect and clarify. Solidify.

They might not like each other, but he, at least, was perfectly well aware of the nature of the spark that had always flared between them, even from their earliest acquaintance. He knew that that spark could be fanned to a flame, one strong enough, powerful enough, to give them some hope of making a shared life work.

Such a union might not be perfect, but it could work.

Of course, he knew ladies, and her in particular, far too well to mention that issue at the present time. He wasn't entirely surprised that she hadn't thought of it herself; given she viewed him in a determinedly cousinly, if not avuncular, light, she wouldn't necessarily see the danger in being—in ton terms—alone with him.

"Good." She relaxed, softly smiled. Her blue-gray eyes shimmered silver in the moonlight. She glanced down at the map. "Given this laird is Scottish, I assume we'll be heading into Scotland. Fletcher let fall that they couldn't tell whether the man was a highlander or a lowlander."

Frowning, Breckenridge spread the map on the table between them. "That's odd. The accents are distinct, and Fletcher and Cobbins had been living in Glasgow."

She shrugged. "We don't know how long they'd been there. They might have just arrived."

"If you get a chance, see if you can learn how long they've spent working north of the border."

"All right." After a moment of studying his face, she asked, "Are you going to tell me why?"

His lips curved despite the grimness he felt. "Not yet. Get me the answer, and I might." He shifted the map, then pointed. "We're here—Barnard Castle."

"As this laird is Scottish, it seems safe to assume that Fletcher and company will carry me over the border at some point." Heather traced their road onward, west across the north of England, just south of the border. There were several smaller connecting roads that led north into Scotland. "Cobbins mentioned that I'd see castles and a Roman fort or two from the coach." She peered more closely at the map. "Is that possible if we remain on this road—or does it suggest we'll turn north somewhere soon?"

They pored over the map, then he grunted. "There's several castles close by the road, and at least two Roman forts. What that tells us—clever miss—is that the coach will remain on this road at least until Penrith."

She smiled at his approbation, then examined his face. "Why are you so satisfied over that?"

He met her gaze. "I want to stop somewhere and get some provisions." A better disguise, one good enough to allow him to get much closer to her and her captors. He also wanted a weapon or two, at least one pistol and a blade. He hesitated, then said, "I'm going to leave early tomorrow—no sense in giving them any unnecessary chance to get to know my face. I'm going to wager on them taking you into Scotland—and yes, I agree Scotland sounds a certainty—via Penrith, and then Carlisle."

She studied the map. "That seems the most likely route." With one finger, she traced the road running north from Carlisle, deeper into Scotland. "Given we were on the Great North Road, heading directly for Edinburgh, but have now turned off and look to be heading for Carlisle, then it seems Glasgow, rather than Edinburgh, might be their destination."

He nodded. "Glasgow, or further north. If this laird met them in Glasgow, perhaps that's where they're to hand you over." He paused, then asked, "Do you know if any of your family have any Scottish enemies?"

She looked up, her gaze arrested. A moment ticked by, then she slowly shook her head. "None that I've ever heard of. And I can't see why that would be—we've never, as far as I know, had any real dealings north of the border. Well, except for Richard and Catriona, of course."

He considered, then shook his head, too. "I can't imagine why, even if Richard had fallen foul of some Scottish laird, that laird would take it into his head to target you and your sisters. The connection's not close enough." He refocused on her face. "Your brothers have never mentioned any problems in Scotland?"

She pulled a face. "I've never heard of any difficulty from either, but"—she lifted one shoulder—"it's possible Rupert's been involved in exposing some fraudulent Scottish scheme. You know how he is. Or Alasdair might have snaffled some precious artifact from under the nose of some avid Scottish collector."

"Hmm—I've a suspicion that if either of your brothers thought there was the least threat to you or your sisters, you'd already know of it."

She smiled. "True. There would have been blood on the floor in Dover Street when they tried to hem us in."

They sat quietly for a moment, both thinking their separate thoughts, then he reached for the map. Refolding it, he stored it in his coat pocket, then rose and held out his hand. "Come on—I'll see you back to your room and the estimable Martha."

She put her hand in his and let him draw her to her feet.

"Tomorrow . . . don't worry," he murmured, as he ushered her back through the darker side of the snug. "I'll be waiting in Carlisle to fall in behind the coach when you go past." Through the dimness he met her eyes. "I won't lose you."

Her lips softly curved. "I didn't imagine you would."

Chapter Five

Heather had spent a restless night. She'd risen before dawn and had stood at the window, looking east over the inn's rear yard. As the sky had softened to a pearly gray streaked with faint streamers of gold and pink, she'd seen Breckenridge come out, get into his curricle, and, with a flourish of his whip, drive away.

Several hours later, she climbed back into the coach in no good mood. As they rumbled out of Barnard Castle, she looked out of the window and acknowledged a trepidatious uncertainty that they might turn north along some other road, and Breckenridge would miss their trail. She couldn't discount the possibility, but, determined not to let it unnerve her more than it already had, she shoved it to the back of her mind and concentrated instead on what more she might learn about her captors' employer—the mysterious laird. Reviewing Fletcher's answers of the day before, she sensed that she was nearing the limit of his knowledge regarding the man. Recalling Breckenridge's question, she considered, then fixed Fletcher—once again sitting opposite—with a direct look.

She openly studied him, until, shifting under her gaze, he arched a grumpy brow.

"What?"

"I was just wondering . . . I presume we're heading over the border, that the place we're to meet this laird will be in Scotland. You said you'd met him in Glasgow. Although I've been to Edinburgh, I've never been to Glasgow before— what's it like?"

Fletcher shrugged. "Much like any other city with a big port." He considered, then said, "More like London—no, more like Liverpool, I'd say."

"I take it you live there."

"On and off." Fletcher met her gaze, then smiled knowingly. "We've moved about over the years, going wherever business was best. We've been quartered in Glasgow for the last several years, but I'm thinking, once we hand you over, it might be time to relocate."

As if his plans were of no interest to her, which they weren't, Heather shrugged and looked out of the window again. She had the answer Breckenridge had wanted, but she'd have to wait until she saw him again to understand its portent.

Cobbins sat forward and drew her attention to a castle on a nearby hill.

She looked, and exchanged observations on the structure with Cobbins and Martha. Sitting back again, she felt rather more confident that they'd interpreted Cobbins's comments of the day before correctly. They were currently on the road to Penrith—the one with several castles and Roman forts flanking it.

What else could she ask? What else might she learn?

Fletcher responded better to short bursts of questions, and to tangential approaches. Yet no matter how she wracked her brains, she couldn't think of any other way to ask, "Where are we to meet this laird? I can't see why you won't tell me."

"Well, now." Fletcher exchanged a glance with Martha, one heavy with some unspoken communication.

From the corner of her eye, Heather saw Martha shake her head.

Fletcher shifted his gaze to Heather. "No need for you to know that I can see. You'll find out when we get there."

"But—"

She pushed, pressed, badgered, and pestered, all to no avail. From Fletcher's thin-lipped smile, she got the distinct impression they were playing with her.

Finding Fletcher immovable, she appealed to Martha. "Surely you understand—knowing would help."

Martha snorted. She resettled her voluminous cloak, then folded her arms and shut her eyes. "No point in carrying on so. You'll learn where we're taking you soon enough. No reason for you to know ahead of time—it won't make any difference to you."

Martha lapsed into silence. When Heather turned her gaze back to Fletcher, she discovered he, too, had closed his eyes.

With every appearance of high dudgeon, she slumped back against the seat, crossed her arms, and settled in her corner.

Cobbins still had his eyes open, idly watching over her. The trio had, she realized, been unobtrusively vigilant; one or more of them was always watching against her escaping, even in moments like this. Only when they believed she was secured, either because she was hemmed in by them at some table, or shut in a room with Martha during the night with no outer clothing to hand, did they take their eyes off her.

They rolled past another two castles, which Cobbins took pains to point out. A few miles later, she saw a sign declaring Penrith to be seven miles on. Relief flooded her, easing some of her building tension. If they were going through Penrith, and intended to take her over the border into Scotland, then they were certain to pass through Carlisle, where Breckenridge would be waiting.

She'd definitely changed how she viewed her "nemesis." Indeed, she doubted she'd ever think of him as that again. To her mind, he now represented safety, security, and regardless of all else he might be, she knew he was a man she could rely on.

Confidence of a sort returned, buoying her.

With nothing else to do, she reviewed all she knew about the lands over the border. It was already late morning, nearing noon. Traveling at this rate, they had to be planning to halt for the night somewhere not too far over the border; there was no chance they could reach Glasgow that day.

That much she knew, but not much else. On all her previous journeys into Scotland she'd veered west soon after Carlisle, turning off the highway at Gretna onto the road to Dumfries and so on to New Galloway, and from there north to the Vale of Casphairn, Richard and Catriona's home. She knew those roads, those towns, that landscape, but beyond that, and Edinburgh, which she'd visited once with Richard and Catriona, Scotland remained a mist-shrouded, mizzle-veiled, damp and cold unknown.

In the circumstances, the prospect of seeing Glasgow, or even traveling further north into the highlands, didn't fill her with eager excitement.

Meeting with a mysterious laird who had arranged to have her kidnapped was, she felt, something she truly didn't need to do.

Learning who he was would be quite sufficient.

The coach rolled into Penrith, turned north onto the main highway toward Carlisle, and rattled on.

She was feeling faintly light-headed, definitely in need of sustenance, when, after several more ponderous miles, the coach rolled into the village of Plumpton Wall and, at last, slowed. The coachman turned into the yard of a small inn and halted his horses.

Descending into the cool sunshine, Heather drew in a deep breath, then glanced around. Martha appeared by her shoulder and urged her on, into the inn. As Heather climbed the shallow steps and followed Fletcher into a tiny taproom, she thought back over their halts, inwardly acknowledging how quietly careful her captors had been.

Believing her to be too lacking in resolution and too inhibited by their well-thought-out charade to attempt any scene in public, they'd treated her reasonably, yet they hadn't taken any chances, either. Everywhere they'd stopped—Knebworth, Stretton, Carlton-on-Trent, Bramham, Barnard Castle, and now Plumpton Wall—had been either a very small town or an out-of-the-way place, the sort where it had been highly unlikely they would have encountered anyone who would have known her well enough to have recognized her. That was the only real weakness in their plan, and they'd taken steps to reduce the threat.

In reality, with the ton busy in London with the Season just commencing, the risk of a chance encounter with anyone she knew was as near to nonexistent as made no odds.

She preserved a tight-lipped silence while they ate; she saw no reason to even try to extract more information, at least not at present.

When, an hour later, she climbed back into the coach and sat in her usual corner, she was conscious of a sharpening edge of tension, of trepidatious expectation welling once more. She waited until they were back on the road, rolling steadily north, then reassessed her captors, only to realize that her sharpening anticipation was merely a reflection of theirs.

Fletcher was no longer slouching, but sitting upright and alert, his gaze trained mostly outside, a frown on his face, as if he were calculating. Cobbins sat with his hands on his thighs, eyes staring across the carriage, but, Heather would swear, not seeing. He was thinking, imagining; until now he'd shown little sign of indulging in either activity.

A sideways glance showed that Martha, too, was wide awake.

Heather tried to imagine what might be causing all three to remain so watchful. The border itself lay beyond Carlisle . . . perhaps it was simply that the border town was by far the largest they'd passed through since London, and was usually awash with soldiers and officials, Customs and Revenue agents, and the like.

Perhaps her captors' vigilance was merely reaching new heights.

She looked away, staring out of the window at the spring fields rolling past. Despite the tension, she felt inwardly settled. Calm and ready to meet whatever lay ahead.

Because, regardless of all else, they were definitely going through Carlisle.

Breckenridge stood in the shadow where the curved outer wall of one of the towers of Carlisle Castle met one of the straight side walls. The red stone at his back, he watched the carriages coming north along the highway from Penrith. To enter Carlisle proper, all conveyances had to pass his position. Cloaked as he was in deepening shadows, no passenger in any of the passing parade of coaches was likely to see him, not unless they peered specifically at him.

He was satisfied with all he'd accomplished by way of preparation for whatever dangers lay beyond the border. His first purchase had been a pair of pistols, short-barreled and silver-mounted, small enough to fit in a coat pocket. The coat and breeches, plain shirt and waistcoat, had come next. He'd had to visit more than one tailor to find garments already made up in his size, especially as he was so adamant on appearing faintly shabby. His latest disguise of a solicitor's clerk, down on his luck and presently unemployed, was expressly designed to allow him to draw closer, openly so, to Heather's three captors.

Although he'd purchased a shaving kit in Newark, he'd omitted to shave that morning. His beard now darkened his cheeks and jaw, making him appear rougher, less polished, more disreputable. With the scarred and well-used writing desk and implements he'd subsequently found in a second-hand shop, with the ink he'd worked into his right middle finger and the pad of his right thumb, he was intent on appearing as one with Fletcher, Cobbins, and Martha—an equal, someone for whom they would feel no instant, instinctive distrust.

If the lack of attention he'd subsequently garnered when, making an effort to suppress his innate, born-to-the-purple arrogance and demeanor, he'd walked through the town was any guide at all, he'd succeeded. He'd been able to purchase a rackety old trap with a close to broken-down horse without having to insist that yes, he really did want that horse, that trap.

If any of his friends could see his new equipage, they'd laugh themselves into stitches.

Shifting against the wall, pleasantly warm with the heat retained from the earlier sunshine, he continued to watch the carriages, outwardly the soul of patience, inwardly increasingly restless.

He'd considered sending another missive south to the Cynsters. Had debated it for more than an hour, but in the end, he hadn't. For a start, if Heather's cousins reacted and charged north, as they were very likely to do, they would almost certainly achieve the opposite of what he'd striven thus far to do, namely keep Heather's presence with her captors a secret.

If the ton ever learned that she'd been in the hands of Fletcher and Cobbins for even one night, her reputation would be irretrievably shredded, Martha's presence notwithstanding. Nothing he could say or do afterward would serve to rectify that, not in the censorious eyes of the ton. Those close to her, and him, would accept the truth; society at large would not.

On top of that, it was too hard to explain the situation simply to someone who didn't know the full story, to convey that Heather was still in the hands of the kidnappers, but that she was safe. That he would ensure she continued to be safe.

It was that last that was most difficult to communicate, especially when placed alongside the information that they were on the brink of crossing into Scotland. No matter what words he devised, what glib explanation, the result read as a thinly veiled acknowledgment that he would marry her.

But what if she refused? Until he knew what direction she would take, making any statement would be unwise.

Of course, given the situation, compounded by his reputation as one of London's most notable rakes, and hers as a well-connected, well-bred, and largely well-protected young lady, there was no other option. Especially as both their families moved within the most rarefied circle of the ton. And while one part of him felt he should rail at such a socially dictated fate, the larger part was surprisingly acquiescent. He suspected that was at least partly due to her being "the devil he knew."

Even as the appellation crossed his mind, he was recalling all the things he hadn't known about her but had learned courtesy of the past days.

She'd proved surprisingly quick-witted. She'd been resolute and loyal. She'd observed and acted where many other ladies would have sunk into a helpless funk. Weak she wasn't, neither in will nor in character.

He could do a lot worse for his bride.

Neither of their families would raise a fuss; while it might not be a love-match, currently all the rage, after the last days he was reasonably certain that, should they agree to, he and she could rub along well enough.

Which was more than he could say of any other lady of his acquaintance.

Love-matches might have currently been the vogue, but he, personally, had given up on love long ago. Fifteen years ago, to be precise. And while he suspected Heather would prefer a love-match, she was twenty-five, and at this Season's close would be formally considered on the shelf. Clearly her Prince Charming hadn't appeared to sweep her off her feet. Given what he'd seen of her pragmatism recently, he suspected that, when he offered for her hand, once she thought the matter through, she would accept.

But if she didn't . . .

He frowned, straightened, then shook aside the notion. She was a sane and sensible woman; she'd accept the necessity.

Yet if she didn't . . . there was that spark that had always flared between them, that he could, if he wished, fan into a compelling blaze, one fierce and fiery enough to raze her objections.

Convincing her might even be fun.

His imagination was engaged in assessing the possibilities when a familiar coach loomed out of the thronging traffic, immediately claiming his attention. Hanging back in the concealing shadows, he waited until the coach rumbled past, watched it ponderously veer away from another large road and continue on, north.

It was midafternoon, and the border was only ten miles up the road. Clearly, her captors intended to carry Heather into Scotland that day.

Straightening from the wall, Breckenridge watched the coach for a moment more, then strode off to retrieve his trap from a nearby stable.

Heather felt a moment of simple panic as the coach rolled slowly across the bridge spanning the river Sark and rumbled into Scotland.

She told herself that Breckenridge would be close behind, that she wasn't alone. That when the time came, he would help her escape. That helped.

Some miles back, the coach had passed a major road that led to Edinburgh via Hawick and Selkirk; they were, it seemed, definitely heading for Glasgow.

For the next few miles, the way was familiar to her. The village of Gretna lay just beyond the border, cottages spread haphazardly to the left of the highway. A minute later, also to the left, they passed the turn into the road she was accustomed to taking to Dumfries and ultimately to the Vale.

Sitting back, resting her head against the squabs, she reflected that she was now, for her, traveling into uncharted territory. She wondered how much further they would go that day. She'd asked multiple times, but all Fletcher or Martha would say was that she "would learn soon enough."

She inwardly humphed and settled back, hugging the

cloak Martha had provided closer; although it was spring, Scotland was distinctly cooler than southern England.

The coach slowed.

Glancing out of the window, she saw the cottages of the hamlet just north of Gretna. Gretna Green was notorious for the runaway marriages performed over the anvil of the blacksmith's forge.

The coach slowed almost to a stop, then turned ponderously left.

Martha, looking out of the other window, said, "Is that it, then? The famous smithy?"

Fletcher flicked a glance that way. "Yes—that's it." He looked back and met Heather's eyes. "We're stopping at a little inn just down this lane."

It was just one of their usual halts. Heather told herself that the proximity to the famous anvil was incidental. While they'd passed a number of inns in Gretna, the small country inn before which the coach pulled up was definitely more Fletcher's style.

The Nutberry Moss Inn was old. Its two storeys looked worn, but also still solid. With walls of whitewashed stone, black window frames and doors, and immense black beams supporting the dark gray slate roof, it seemed sunk and anchored into the earth, as if it had literally put down roots.

Fletcher descended first, then handed Heather down. She paused on the coach step to glance around. There were few trees to impede her view. She didn't see Breckenridge, but she did manage to get her bearings. The lane in which the inn stood continued further west, merging with the larger road to Dumfries a little way along.

Stepping down to the rough gravel of the forecourt, she scanned the front of the inn; it exuded an air of homely comfort. Then Martha joined her; with Cobbins bringing up the rear, they followed Fletcher into the inn.

Inside, it was a great deal warmer. Heather held out her hands to the small blaze in the fireplace built into one wall of the hall, and glanced around curiously. A set of narrow stairs led upward, dividing the front hall into two. The landlord had just come out of a swinging door at the rear of the hall to the left of the staircase; that door presumably led to the kitchens. Wiping his hands on a cloth, he welcomed Fletcher. On being informed they needed rooms, the landlord crossed to a long counter set against the wall to the right of the stairs.

Turning back to the fire, Heather was reviewing potential questions—reviewing what else she might learn from her captors—when she heard Fletcher inform the landlord, "Don't know how many days we'll be here. Two at least, but most likely more. We'll be here until Sir Humphrey Wallace's agent—a Mr. McKinsey—arrives to escort the young lady on."

Swinging around, Heather stared at Fletcher—at his back. He remained engaged with the landlord, haggling over rooms.

Snapping back around, she pinned Martha with a demanding glare. "*This* is where you're to hand me over? We're waiting for this laird of yours here?"

Martha shrugged. "So Fletcher says." Her hatchet face was entirely uncommunicative.

"But he's not here yet?"

"No." Martha resettled her shawl. "Seems it'll take him a few days to reach here, wherever he's coming from."

Fletcher was still engaged with the innkeeper. Heather turned to Cobbins, as always standing near. "When did you send him word that you'd seized me and were bringing me north?"

As she'd hoped, Cobbins answered, "Put a message on the night mail at Knebworth."

Heather calculated; she was losing track of the days, but . . . if McKinsey had been in Edinburgh or Glasgow, he should be here, if not by now then certainly by tomorrow.

Before she could follow that idea further, Fletcher strolled up.

"Two rooms as usual, both in the east wing, but not next to each other." He glanced at the two lads carrying in their bags. "Cobbins and I will take the room nearer the stairs."

Heather straightened, lifted her chin. Narrowed her eyes on Fletcher's face. "Why are we stopping here?"

Unconvincingly mild, Fletcher returned, "This was where McKinsey told us to bring you."

"Why of all the towns in Scotland did he chose Gretna Green?"

Fletcher opened his eyes wide. "I don't know." He exchanged a glance with Martha, then looked back at Heather. "We might guess, but"—he shrugged—"we really don't know. This is where he said, so this is where we've brought you. Far as we know, that's all there is to it."

And they didn't believe that for a moment.

Heather absolutely definitely did not like the implications. She knew that, theoretically, a woman had to be willing to be married, over an anvil or any other way, in Scotland or anywhere else in the British Isles.

What she didn't know was, in a place like Gretna Green, just how agreeable a woman had to be. Did she have to make any statement of agreement? Or could she be drugged or coerced in some way to ensure the deed was done?

One thing she did know was that marriages conducted over the anvil at Gretna Green were legal and binding. Her parents had been married there.

She made no demur when Martha shooed her up the stairs and ushered her to their room. Inside, she'd grown strangely detached. To her mind, the way forward had just become crystal clear. It was obviously time to leave her kidnappers, to cut and run with what she'd already learned. When Breckenridge arrived, she'd tell him she was ready to escape. . . .

Except Fletcher had said they'd be here for at least two more days.

Entering the room ahead of Martha, barely registering the

pair of narrow beds and the single small window, Heather considered, but she didn't think Fletcher had been lying. He wasn't honest, but in general he focused on his route forward; she didn't think he was likely to have invented the tale of having to wait for days.

Why would he? He didn't know Breckenridge was close, her ready route out of their clutches. There was, from their point of view, no reason to lie to her about how long they would remain there, waiting on McKinsey's arrival.

Sinking onto the bed further from the door, she stared at the wall and wondered if there was any way she could exploit the situation for her own ends. Whether with what she now knew, she could pressure Fletcher, Martha, and Cobbins for yet more about McKinsey. And when she ultimately decided to escape, whether that escape might be timed so that she and Breckenridge could remain close enough to watch and see McKinsey arrive.

If she and Breckenridge could get a good look at the man, they'd have a much better chance of identifying him, and subsequently nullifying any threat he might pose, now or later, to her sisters, her cousins, and herself.

Drawing in a deep breath, she put aside such speculations until she could discuss them with Breckenridge, then rose and crossed the room to open negotiations over what clothes her "maid" would allow her to retrieve from the large satchel Martha continued to guard like a terrier.

Breckenridge was in the tap, deep in his guise of a solicitor's clerk, elbow to elbow with three locals, each consuming a serving of the inn's dinner stew, when Heather and her captors walked into the room.

The inn was, fortuitously, too small to boast a separate dining room. Along with the other men, all older and distinctly more grizzled than he, he could look up, apparently distracted from his meal by the sight of a young lady of quality—no matter how Heather dressed, her carriage, her composure, screamed her antecedents—gliding into the room.

Briefly—fleetingly—he met her eyes. Hers had widened only slightly when she'd seen him; otherwise nothing showed in her expression as her gaze moved on, scanning the occupants of the tap, then passing on to the serving girl bustling up to steer her and the other three to a table at the front of the room.

Of all the men present, he was probably the only one who correctly read the upward tilt of her chin. She was putting on a good face, which meant something was troubling her.

Looking down at his plate, he inwardly frowned. She hadn't previously seemed all that concerned with her captivity. Not that she hadn't recognized it for what it was, but she'd seemed to view it as a cross to be borne until she could learn what lay behind it. Now . . . something had changed.

Instinct prodded, more insistently this time. He hadn't been thrilled by Fletcher's choice of inn, not with that far-too-well-known smithy within easy walking distance, but given they'd assumed her captors were taking her to Glasgow, he'd viewed the Nutberry Moss Inn as simply a convenient halt.

Given Heather's sudden concern, perhaps that wasn't so.

Toying with the lumps of mutton swimming in the gravy filling his plate, he turned his mind to considering where, exactly, to meet her that night.

Across the small room, Heather sat on a bench with her back to the wall, wedged into the corner by Martha's stout form. The only useful aspect of her position was that she could see Breckenridge where he sat with three locals at a table near the bar.

Even as she idly, apparently absentmindedly, stared in that direction, he made some comment and the other three laughed. His hair had been roughed up, so it no longer sat as it should, making him look more loutish, especially with his beard shading his cheeks and jaw. A napkin tucked into his collar, he had both elbows on the table, leaning on them as with a fork he scooped up stew—and spoke while he chewed. She'd never met his late mother, but could they see him, his sisters would be appalled.

Still, his disguise definitely worked. Although he wasn't a local, and still clearly stood out as someone different, he nevertheless fitted into the Nutberry Moss's picture. He appeared to belong.

The relief still coursing through her—that had flooded her the instant her eyes had alighted on his dark head—was intense; she must have been more worried than she'd let herself admit.

But now he was there, close, she could set aside said worry and concentrate on extracting every last piece of information she could before McKinsey's pending arrival forced her to escape.

The serving girl arrived with their meals. Heather said nothing but applied herself to consuming the thinly sliced roast lamb, parsnip, and cabbage, while inwardly she compiled a list of all the little telltale snippets Fletcher, Cobbins, and Martha had let fall.

When Breckenridge and she met later, she would need to put forward all she'd learned in support of her contention that, with McKinsey still days away, they need be in no rush to slip away from the Nutberry Moss Inn. They could stay a few days more and see what more she might learn.

Although Fletcher kept looking at her assessingly—she suspected he was waiting for her to have hysterics over the implications of the nearness of the blacksmith's forge—she kept her head down and clung to her passivity. It wasn't at all natural, but her captors didn't know that.

Once she finished mentally cataloguing all she'd learned, she turned her mind to what other questions she might conceivably ask—and her arguments for remaining to ask them.

The meal ended. Martha glanced at her, then humphed.

"Don't know about you, but I want my bed. Come along—upstairs."

With that Martha heaved herself off the bench. Heather glanced at Fletcher, then sighed and slid along the bench to rise and join Martha. Fletcher and Cobbins remained seated; both were still nursing pints of ale.

As she walked up the room, following in Martha's ample wake, Breckenridge glanced at her and she met his eyes.

Immediately he cut his gaze forward—out of the door, across the foyer.

She looked that way, saw the reception counter, and the narrow door behind it that led to what appeared to be a tiny cloakroom.

Glancing back, she found Breckenridge looking at her again. Along with all the other men in the tap.

Tilting her head, she poked at her hair, as if a ticklish lock was the reason for the movement.

Breckenridge looked down, into the ale mug cradled between his hands.

Turning, Heather followed Martha out of the tap and up the stairs.

Satisfied she'd understood him, Breckenridge drained his pint, then offered to refill the mugs of the other three men who'd provided him with such excellent cover through the evening. Friendly souls.

They all drained their mugs and handed them over, but one thought to say, "Here—thought you was out of work."

"I am." Gathering the mugs, Breckenridge stood and grinned down at them. "But it'd be a hard day when a man can't share a drink with like-minded souls—what'd be the point of working at all if you couldn't at least do that?"

They all vociferously agreed. Crossing to the bar, he leaned on it while the barman refilled the mugs. Most of those in the tap appeared to be locals, not inn guests; although he'd assumed he and Heather would be at the inn for only one night, if he needed to, extending his stay wasn't likely to be hard.

Swinging around, he glanced back at his table of ready friends. In the edge of his vision, he could see Fletcher and Cobbins, talking quietly over their beers. He toyed with the idea of approaching them, but if they did remain here for more than one night, then putting in the time to establish his bonafides as a harmless solicitor's clerk—one accepted by the locals—might bear better fruit than a more direct befriending.

"There you be." The barman placed the last of the four refilled mugs on a tray.

"My thanks." Breckenridge remembered just in time to pull out some coins and pay, rather than simply expect the man to put it on his slate. Unemployed solicitor's clerks were unlikely to be afforded credit.

Carrying the tray back to the table, he set it down and sat, then he and the other three all reached for their mugs. Silence reigned as they all sipped. It was in fact a quite palatable brew.

Then one man commenced a tale of a local drover whom the Customs and Revenue men stationed in Gretna had halted before he could cross the border. "He's having to prove all the steers are his."

One of the other men snorted. "I'd like to see him do that—everyone round about knows he 'finds' his stock up in the hills. Just amble along and join his herd, they do—least to hear him tell it."

There was general laughter, and the conversation continued, addressing various aspects of local life.

Trays of ale came and went. After a time, the man sitting next to Breckenridge nodded down the room at Fletcher and Cobbins. "Any notion who they be?"

Along with the others, Breckenridge shook his head.

"Well, then," said his companion, well-flown with ale,

"let's see if they wanna come and join us. Be friendly like." Raising his voice and his mug, he called down the room, "Here—you two over there. Come join us and drink."

Demonstrating, the good fellow drained his mug, then smacked it down onto the table.

Breckenridge watched Fletcher and Cobbins exchange a look, a few words, then both pushed back their chairs, picked up their mugs, and, dragging their chairs over, came to join the table.

Introductions were made. The youngest man of the four already seated, Breckenridge waited. Helpfully, one of his unwitting allies waved at him and said, "And this here's Timms. A solicitor's clerk up from Lunnon, he be, but sadly out of work and headed up Glasgow way to look for a new post."

Breckenridge nodded to Fletcher and Cobbins and shook their proffered hands. Beyond that, however, he made no further overtures, allowing Jim, Cyril, and Henry to carry the conversation. They, naturally enough, were curious as to what had brought Fletcher and Cobbins onto their patch. When they inquired, Fletcher glibly related the tale Heather had told Breckenridge about. If previously he'd harbored any notion that said tale would be easy to contradict, hearing Fletcher smoothly explain it all eradicated any such hope.

Fletcher was totally believable. He presented exactly the right persona for a man acting as hired agent for some ageing lordling.

In his role as Timms, Breckenridge nodded sagely. "Lots of young girls run away when they think their guardians are too strict. Saw it all the time in London. Lots of girls find themselves in trouble there."

He let the conversation swirl on, satisfied with his now established role, with the way Fletcher no longer studied him but now viewed him as one with the others. Not the same, yet indistinguishable, unremarkable.

The barman finally thumped the counter and told them

he was closing up. "Just leave those mugs there—the girls'll fetch them in the morning."

They all exchanged glances, then drained the dregs of their ale. Setting down their mugs, they lumbered to their feet. Breckenridge was grateful for his earlier years of dissipation, of drinking spirits into the small hours; at least he was steady on his pins.

Between him, Fletcher, and Cobbins, they got the other three out of the front door. The landlord thanked them, threw the bolts, and wished them a hearty good night.

Breckenridge headed for the stairs. Fletcher followed, Cobbins laboring in the rear.

At the head of the stairs, Breckenridge paused and glanced back at Fletcher. "I was going to head on to Glasgow, but I've an old wound in m'side"—he pressed a hand to his right side and grimaced painfully—"and it's twingeing something awful. Probably from driving all this way in my rattle-trap of a gig." Raising that hand, he saluted them as he turned away. "So I might see you tomorrow, or I might not. But good luck to you anyway."

"And you," Fletcher called after him.

Without looking back, Breckenridge gave an acknowledging wave and strode on down the corridor. Smiling.

Heather crept down the stairs of the Nutberry Moss Inn, clinging to the balustrade to keep from stumbling. While the upstairs rooms had been darkly dim, the well of the stairs and the foyer below lay in Stygian gloom. Reaching the last stair, she stepped carefully down onto the stone flags of the foyer; turning to where she knew the reception counter to be, she saw with considerable relief that the narrow door behind it stood ajar, outlined in faint, wavering candlelight.

Crossing the floor, she slid around the counter, then eased open the door.

Breckenridge was sitting on a narrow bench that ran along one wall beneath a rack of coat pegs, presently empty. He looked up as the door moved; elbows on his knees, hands clasped with his chin resting on them, he raised his head and nodded at the door. "Close it," he murmured, "and come and sit."

Clad in her customary outfit, this time fashioned from the coverlet off her bed cinched at her waist with her silk shawl, she did as he said.

He rose as she turned from the door, swirled the cloak from his shoulders, and solicitously draped it about her, over-lapping the front edges. Grateful for the additional warmth, holding the voluminous cloak close, she sat. "Thank you. It's rather chillier here."

"Hmm." He resumed his position on the bench, beside her. "So what have you learned?"

He'd spoken in a muted whisper. She did the same, leaning close, nearer his broad and distinctly comforting shoulder. That was one thing she was learning to appreciate that she hadn't previously admired; his size was reassuring. "First, as to the question you asked—whether Fletcher and Cobbins had spent much time in Glasgow. According to Fletcher, they've made it their base for the last two or more years—several, he said." She studied Breckenridge's unshaven and strangely more ruggedly handsome face. "So what does that tell you?"

He hadn't been looking particularly happy—she was start-ing to be able to see through his mask—but on hearing her words, his lips set in an openly grim line. "It suggests that this laird of theirs might well be more than that." He met her gaze. "You know that a laird simply means someone who owns an estate?" When she nodded, he went on, facing for-ward once more. "If their laird had been of the lower gentry, he would have had an accent, and if Fletcher and Cobbins had been in Glasgow for more than a year, they should have been able to pick it as either lowland or highland. Glasgow is the second-largest city in Scotland, and the largest port. Scots from all over the country congregate there. Hearing the different accents and learning to distinguish them, given Fletcher's and Cobbins's trade, would have been something they would have learned to do, almost as second nature."

He paused, then continued, "In fact, if you think about what Fletcher said, he specifically said they *couldn't* pick where the man was from—so they'd tried, had expected to be able to tell, but couldn't."

"Yes, that's true. But what does that mean?"

"It means we're not dealing with a laird who hails from the lower gentry." He glanced at her. "Scotland has excellent schools, in Edinburgh and elsewhere. If this laird was a nobleman's son, he would have been sent to one for his schooling. He would have been schooled in English by Englishmen, and encouraged to lose his accent the better to be regarded as civilized when south of the border. I've brushed shoulders with a few noble Scots in my time, and they speak as if they'd been to Eton."

She grimaced. "So our laird isn't just any old landowner but most likely, if not certainly, a member of the aristocracy?"

He nodded. "That's how I'd interpret that."

She sighed, then said, "He's coming here to collect me, as if I'm some package." Feeling Breckenridge tense beside her, she hurried on. "However, Fletcher and Martha both said that he won't be here for several more days—two more at least." Glancing at Breckenridge, she met his stony gaze. "Apparently it's going to take him that long at least to reach here, even though they sent their message on the night mail from Knebworth. If he's still not here and won't be for at least two more days . . ."

She watched while Breckenridge did the same calculations she had.

Watched as he pulled a very unBreckenridgelike face.

"A highlander. He's got to be a highlander. That message would have reached Edinburgh two days later. Even allowing for it having to be passed on by someone, it's still been too long. I can't imagine this laird, whoever he is, would have set this kidnapping plan in motion, and then gone off on a trip somewhere. He would have been waiting for word, and would surely set out as soon as he'd received it."

After a moment, Breckenridge met her gaze again. "There's no other way to reasonably account for the delay. He must be a highlander." He shook his head; when he spoke, his tone was faintly disgusted. "A highland nobleman. Who knows what ancient bones he might have to pick with the Cynsters?"

She'd heard that her late uncle Sebastian and her long-dead grandfather Sylvester had both acted for the Crown in Scottish affairs at various times. Slowly, she nodded. "That might well be it—I've heard the Scots have long memories, especially about the wars and the clearances."

"Indeed." After a moment, Breckenridge went on, "Regardless of his reasons, the fact he's chosen this place, of all places in Scotland, to have you brought to and held until he arrives can't mean anything good."

He glanced at Heather, drank in her profile, sensed the uncertainty and the instinctive aversion her expression didn't truly show. She simply looked pale, a trifle haunted.

As for him . . . the situation was significantly worse than he'd anticipated. If the laird truly was a Scottish nobleman, then while Breckenridge was in Scotland, even as Breckenridge, heir to the Earl of Brunswick, he would have a hard time countermanding the enemy. The Scots, understandably perhaps, had a habit of paying more attention to their own nobles, and too often taking any opportunity to bring the arrogant sassensachs down a peg or three. As he'd mentioned, he'd crossed a few Scottish lairds in his time; they tended to fight for keeps. The warrior and strategist inside him usually appreciated their tenacity, but not when Heather was in any way involved.

Her safety was, and would continue to be, his paramount concern.

"I think," he said, catching her eyes as she lifted them to his face, "that you should leave with me now and return to London."

Slipping a hand free of his cloak, she laid it on his arm. He fought not to tense, to react in any way; it was almost as if she didn't truly register what she'd done but drew comfort, perhaps reassurance, from the contact.

"I've definitely considered doing just that, but . . ."

He mentally gritted his teeth; of course she would have a "but."

Squeezing his arm lightly, she looked away, then retrieved her hand. Perversely he wanted her to put it back.

"The laird won't arrive tomorrow, and they're not expecting him the next day, either." Glancing up, she met his eyes. "So we have two more days in which to drag something—anything—from Fletcher and Cobbins that will allow us to identify the man, this mystery laird, and . . ." She drew breath, held his gaze. "I thought if we timed my escape to just before he arrives, then we might dally in the vicinity long enough to get a glimpse of him."

When he just looked at her and didn't immediately reply, she put her hand on his arm again and leaned closer. "We've managed to come this far without any real difficulty—neither Fletcher, Cobbins, nor Martha has any inkling you're here to rescue me, and I've been deliberately lulling them into thinking I'm resigned and helpless. With a few more days, who knows what we might learn, especially now we've reached Fletcher's destination, so he might start to relax, at least in respect of what he lets fall?"

All he needed to look at was the set of her chin to know he had no chance of dissuading her. As he also had no right to order her or insist—at least none she would recognize, let alone accept—his options were severely limited. Causing any sort of scene was out of the question. He'd worked out a plan that would allow him to save her with her reputation intact and unblemished, but a public fracas would put an end to that . . . and between them, the damage was already done, the die cast, the matter settled and sealed, and a few more days would alter none of it. Regardless, he put off agreeing, capitulating. Asked instead, "What questions do you think to pursue?"

"I had thought to press them over where they'd sent their message, the one from Knebworth. How they had been instructed to contact this laird. Of course the message would have been sent to someone else to pass on. If this laird is careful enough to give them a false name, then he's certainly not going to give them his address. So." She exhaled, then went on, "My other questions have to do with what the laird knows of my sisters, my cousins, and me—what did he tell Fletcher and Cobbins? He clearly told them enough to allow them to find and follow me, but what else do they know?" She met his gaze. "The answers might shed light on who this laird is—is he someone we meet in London occasionally, who goes about within the ton? Or is all his information of the sort anyone with an interest could have learned, even from a distance?"

He could do nothing else but incline his head. "Not a bad tack. And you're right—it might tell us more."

A moment passed—a moment in which he rapidly reassessed and came to the same conclusion he had earlier. Inwardly grim, he nodded. "All right. We'll use the next few days to see what more we can glean." He met her gaze. "Both of us. In my latest disguise, I'll be able to get closer to Fletcher and Cobbins. If you find me with them, remember you don't know me—behave as you would to a lowly, unemployed clerk."

She grinned. "Is that what you are?"

He fought against returning her smile; he could almost see her thinking what an excellent tale this might be to tell of him later. "But there's one thing you can do that I can't—question Martha."

She frowned. "She wasn't there when they met the laird."

"No, but they'll have told her about the meeting, and about the man. If I know women—and I do—she'll have formed a view of this laird based not just on what Fletcher and Cobbins told her but how they'd felt and reacted. They might well have communicated more to her than they themselves are aware of. Regardless, I'd put more faith in Martha's view of the man than in theirs."

She was nodding slowly. "Yes—I understand." She briefly met his gaze. "Women are more observant in that regard."

He grunted. "Possibly." She might be more observant in that sense, but she hadn't yet realized that courtesy of this adventure of hers, he and she were doomed to wed. The prospect of how she might react when she did realize flitted through his brain. He shifted restlessly. "So you ask your questions, and then see what you can extract from Martha. I'll concentrate on drawing close enough to encourage Fletcher and Cobbins to confide in me man-to-man." He met her gaze. "Even more importantly, however, I'll put my mind to arranging your escape."

She nodded, quite brightly. "All in all, that's a sound plan."

He drank in her approval, the eagerness and agreement investing her face, her eyes, and registered the novelty of her looking at him like that. This adventure of hers had had its beneficial aspects. Quite aside from allowing him to see her in a considerably different light, he'd found himself challenged by the situation in ways that were entirely outside the norm; meeting each new testing of his mettle and his mind left him with a sense of triumph he'd forgotten he enjoyed.

And while his primary objective was to keep her safe, like her, he was increasingly intrigued over who the mystery laird might be and his reasons for such a strange action; he felt increasingly certain that the Cynsters would be grateful for whatever he could learn, just as long as he kept Heather safe.

Heather studied his eyes; the melding colors appeared softer, less crystalline. She realized her hand still rested on his arm; she'd somehow just left it there. Administering a quick pat, she retrieved her hand; facing forward, she tucked it back under the cloak.

His cloak; she could smell the subtle scent of him insidiously wrapping about her.

It was altogether peculiar, this shift in her view of him. She'd always been attracted to him, but then what lady of the ton wasn't? According to the gossipmongers, not even seventy-year-old dowagers were immune to his charms. Yet that didn't explain why she now felt far more attracted than previously.

From beneath her lashes, she glanced at him sidelong, took in the shabby coat, the evolving beard, the much rougher appearance. If, in London, cloaked in sophisticated elegance, he held the power to fascinate, here, now, appearing one step up from a laborer, he exuded a raw masculine appeal that was much more potent. . . .

She looked forward, fighting the impulse to fan herself.

Conscious of the prickly awareness that, as always when he was near, crawled over her skin. She'd managed to ignore it, block it out, until then.

Ridiculous. This was Breckenridge. A point she should strive not to forget. He might be her savior now, but no doubt he would later revert to being her nemesis.

He might be treating her, dealing with her, as if he viewed her, trusted her, as an adult, an equal partner, but when this was all over he would doubtless go back to his usual ways, viewing her and treating her as if she were some silly young girl.

Just because some inner demon was prompting her to thank him with a kiss—to seize the excuse just to see what it would feel like—didn't mean she should surrender to the impulse.

Forcing her limbs to function and take her away from his warmth, his magnetic strength, she rose. "I'd better get back upstairs. Thank you for the cloak."

94

She slipped it off her shoulders and immediately felt its loss.

He'd looked up the instant she'd moved. He got to his feet and took the cloak from her. He met her eyes, hesitated for a moment, then murmured, "Let's meet here tomorrow night."

She nodded. "Yes, all right."

Turning away, she slipped through the door before her demon got the better of her. While creeping up the stairs, she reminded herself of another pertinent consideration. At the moment she was dealing with Breckenridge reasonably well. If she kissed him, and he responded . . . she wasn't at all confident that she would be strong enough to pull back.

The lowering truth was she might not even try.

And then where would they be?

Chapter Six

The next morning, Breckenridge, in his guise of Timms, unemployed solicitor's clerk, was already in the tap, sipping a mug of coffee and reading a news sheet at a table by the window, when Fletcher and Cobbins, followed by Heather and Martha, came in. As he'd expected, Fletcher led his party to the same corner table they'd occupied the previous evening—the table next to his. He looked up as they neared, nodded to Fletcher and Cobbins, then, evincing no interest in Heather or Martha, returned his gaze to the news from Edinburgh.

And listened.

He knew better than to approach Fletcher and Cobbins, to show any further overt interest in them or their business. But it was cloudy and drizzly outside, and if they were waiting for their employer to arrive, it seemed unlikely the pair would venture forth, which meant they'd be seeking entertainment, most likely in the tap.

Most likely with the only fellow guest, namely him. The three other travelers who'd stayed overnight had already breakfasted and gone on their way.

His story of an old wound in his side would account for his continuing presence, especially given the inclement weather; turning over the news sheet, he sipped his coffee, and waited.

The serving girl came bustling out to take their orders. Heather opted for the oatmeal porridge. Martha, Fletcher, and Cobbins gave their selections.

Heather barely waited for the serving girl to leave before

stating, "I need to get some air. A short walk after breakfast, just along the lane and back—"

"Nope." Fletcher cut her off. "Not here."

"Nonsense. Martha can come with me."

"Out in that wet muck?" Martha sounded faintly scandalized. "Thank you, miss, but I'm not stirring out of here."

"Too right," Fletcher stated. "You aren't going out of the inn today, nor yet tomorrow."

"Why?" Heather protested. "It's not as if I'm likely to make a break for the hills."

"Don't know, do we?" Fletcher responded. "But we have to wait here at least for two days, and I can't see any sense in letting you get too acquainted with the lie of the land. I've already hired the private parlor."

Apparently idly, Breckenridge glanced up in time to see Fletcher nod in the direction of the closed door on the other side of the inn's front hall.

He looked down again as Fletcher continued, "You and Martha can just sit tight in there until your guardian's man comes to collect you."

From beneath his lashes, Breckenridge saw Heather lean across the table toward Fletcher. Voice lowered, she hissed, "We both know there's no guardian, and—"

"We also both know that there's nothing you can do." Fletcher's voice had hardened. "If you make a scene, I'll tell the innkeeper our story, and I swear we'll tie you up and sit you in the parlor. Your choice."

Even though he was no longer watching, Breckenridge could sense Heather's fulminating glare.

When silence reigned, heavy but unbroken, he felt a moment's admiration for Fletcher; he'd succeeded in standing fast against Heather's wheedling, which was more than he'd been able to do, and she hadn't even wheedled at him.

The serving girl returned with their breakfasts.

Breckenridge called for more coffee and pretended to read the front page of the news sheet for the third time.

Eventually, breakfasts consumed, Heather, prodded by Martha, rose and, nose in the air, swept huffily out of the tap. He couldn't see her cross the hall, but he tracked her by her footsteps; she marched past the stairs, paused, presumably to open the parlor door, then went on. Martha's heavier, shuffling footsteps followed in her wake. A second later, the parlor door softly shut.

Fletcher and Cobbins resettled in their seats to savor their coffee.

After ten minutes of desultory talk between the pair, Fletcher straightened, glanced around the empty tap, then turned to face Breckenridge.

Breckenridge looked up, met Fletcher's gaze.

"Are you heading off, then?" Fletcher asked.

Breckenridge shook his head. "Not for a few days." He grimaced. "Getting back into that trap of mine would be torture. I'll need a few days at least before the pain eases off." He glanced toward the window. "Not that this weather's helping, but it'd be worse if I was out driving in that."

"So you're at loose ends?" Fletcher asked.

"Until I can drive on again."

Fletcher grinned. "In that case, can I interest you in a game of cards?"

Breckenridge smiled. "Why not?"

They commenced by playing vingt-et-un, progressed to speculation, then as the morning waned, turned to euchre. Breckenridge took care not to win too often. Lunchtime saw several locals amble in. Play was suspended while the three of them chatted with the farmers and two travelers on their way to Glasgow. Then the serving girl came out of the kitchen and announced a simple menu—mutton stew or mutton pie. While the men debated the offering, Fletcher sent the girl to take two servings of the stew to the women in the parlor. The girl complied, then returned to ferry plates of mutton pie out to the hungry males.

Breckenridge bided his time and made sure both Fletcher

and Cobbins had three pints of ale with their meal. When the locals rose and went forth into the increasingly dismal day, and the travelers wrapped themselves in their cloaks and departed, both Fletcher and Cobbins had mellowed.

Settling back at the table near the window, Breckenridge picked up the pack of cards but let them idly drop, one by one, from his fingers. Fletcher, sitting opposite, watched the cards fall, as if mesmerized.

"So," Breckenridge said, "how long do you have to sit in this thrillingly exciting atmosphere and wait?"

Fletcher's grin was a trifle lopsided. "Don't rightly know. Two days at least until the laird—the girl's guardian's man—gets here, but it might be longer than that. Depends."

"Laird, heh?" Breckenridge stifled a fabricated yawn, then blinked sleepily. "A real laird? Or just someone calling himself that?"

"Oh, he's a laird, right enough." Cobbins leaned both elbows on the table and propped his chin in his palms. "Not that he said so, o'course, but you could tell."

"Oh?" Breckenridge frowned as if having trouble focusing. "How?" He looked at Cobbins. "How can you tell a man is a laird just by looking?"

Fletcher chuckled. "Not just by looking, for one thing. His voice, the way he spoke. He was one for giving orders and having them obeyed, right enough. There's that attitude the nobs have about them, as if the world and all in it ought to know well enough to get out of their way."

"And there were signs to see, too." Cobbins slumped lower on the table, cradling his head on one arm. "He's a big bastard." Cobbins squinted across the table at Breckenridge. "You're tall, but he's taller. Broader, too. Heavier. And he doesn't walk—he strides."

Breckenridge snorted. "He could just be full of himself."

"Nah." Fletcher slumped back in his chair, stretched his legs out under the table, and closed his eyes. "Face like hewn rock and eyes like ice." He shivered dramatically. "Like

Cobbins says, there's something about them—the nobs—that you just know."

Breckenridge watched the pair. Both had their eyes closed. Then Cobbins uttered a soft snore.

Fletcher cracked open an eyelid, glanced at his companion, then sighed and closed his eye again. "Think I'll just have a little nap, too. We can play cards later."

Breckenridge stayed where he was until he was sure the pair were both asleep, then, pushing back his chair, he slowly rose, and walked—not strode—silently from the room.

In light of her captors' sudden insistence on keeping her under close guard, Heather felt forced to devote most of the day to shoring up her façade of a typical, and therefore harmless and helpless, young lady of the ton.

By the exercise of considerable willpower, she managed to hold back the need to interrogate Martha until after she'd badgered the older woman into ringing and requesting afternoon tea, and the little serving girl had arrived with the tray and departed again.

Finally quitting her position by the window, where she'd been standing literally for hours gazing out at the dripping day, Heather crossed to sit on the sofa and pour.

Ensconced in an armchair, Martha, fingers flashing with her incessant knitting, watched her, not openly suspicious but as if there was something about her she couldn't quite reconcile.

Heather poured Martha a cup, too, then held it out.

Martha softly grunted, settled her needles in her capacious lap, and accepted the cup.

Heather sipped, sighed, then relaxed back against the sofa. "Tell me—how did you fall in with Fletcher and Cobbins? I know you've known them for years, but this particular time?"

Setting her cup on her saucer, Martha shrugged. "I take jobs nursing most times. I'd just finished with one of my patients—the old biddy upped and died—so I was at home when Fletcher came calling. Hadn't seen him in two years or more, not since he'd headed up north to Glasgow. He told me about this laird who wanted you taken north, with a maid for countenance. Seemed a nice, easy lark—see a bit of the country, all expenses paid, and the money was good."

Heather sipped, let a moment go by, then asked, "What do you know about this laird?" She met Martha's sharpening gaze. "Seeing I'll be meeting him soon, and he's going to take me away, surely there can't be any harm in telling me."

Martha studied her for a moment, then her lips kicked up. "If it'll make you cease your pacing and staring, I can tell you he's definitely handsome—Fletcher wouldn't have thought of the word else. And not that old—younger thirties would be my guess."

Heather looked her interest, looked encouraging.

"I didn't meet him, don't forget." Draining her cup, Martha leaned forward and placed cup and saucer on the low table between them. "But I know Fletcher and Cobbins, so this laird is . . ." Martha pursed her lips, then stated, "Powerful. Fletcher and Cobbins, they don't scare easily. Been around for quite a while, those two, but this laird made quite an impression on them both."

"You make him sound dangerous."

"P'raps, but not simple dangerous—a bully boy might be dangerous, but he wouldn't impress the likes of Fletcher and Cobbins."

Studying Martha's face, Heather tried to divine just what her "maid" was trying to convey. "They . . . what? Found him imposing?"

Lifting her needles, Martha nodded. "That's closer to the mark. Not fright, not exactly awe. They were impressed, and wary. Regardless, they're very sure they don't want to disappoint him, and it's not simple fear driving that."

Heather pondered that unwelcome insight.

"A toff he is, no question." Martha set her needles clicking again.

Heather frowned. "Do they know he is, or is that just"—she waved a hand—"conjecture? A guess?"

Eyes on her knitting, Martha snorted. "No guess." She glanced up, met Heather's eyes. "Stands to reason. Take it from me, only a toff would have thought of hiring a maid as part of his kidnap plans."

That, Heather realized, was perfectly true.

Which meant the man who had ordered her kidnapping was almost certainly one of her own class. Which made him even more dangerous to her.

"You just behave yourself, you hear me?"

Heather glanced in surprise at Fletcher. She and Martha had just walked into the taproom for dinner. Fletcher had seen them; leaving the table of local men he'd been drinking with—which group included a certain viscount who not even his sisters would recognize—he'd come over to join her and Martha as they took their seats at the table in the room's front corner.

Fletcher's diction, normally precise, was a trifle slurred, especially as he'd hissed the words beneath his breath.

Heather frowned. "Why?" Realizing her tone wasn't quite in keeping with her helpless and harmless—gormless—persona, she sniffed and added, "And anyway, when haven't I behaved?" With a flounce, she sat and looked up at Fletcher with petulant irritation, as if he didn't appreciate her as he ought.

Fletcher frowned back. "Just sit there, keep your head down, and eat. Don't think to say anything. He's just an out-of-work solicitor's clerk—don't go imagining he might help you escape."

He looked back at the other table.

Following his gaze, Heather saw Cobbins lumbering to his feet—along with Breckenridge. Deciding her alter ego would inquire, she asked with innocent interest, "Who's he? Is he coming to join us?"

"Yes, he is, but you don't need to know his name." Fletcher turned back to her. "This isn't some society dining room—you're not going to be introduced. Like I said"—he leaned closer, lowered his voice as Cobbins and Breckenridge neared—"just sit and eat, and keep your mouth shut."

Heather glared, but then Martha heaved herself onto the bench alongside her, and Fletcher turned away to greet Breckenridge.

Fletcher waved Breckenridge to the seat he normally occupied, opposite Martha, and drew up another chair to the head of the table, between Martha and Breckenridge. Cobbins settled into the chair opposite Heather.

"This here's Martha." Fletcher waved to Martha, who nodded across the table. "This is our friend, Timms, who's on his way to Glasgow to find himself a new job."

Head dutifully bowed, hands clasped in her lap, through her lashes Heather saw Breckenridge nod to Martha, then look at her, then he arched a brow at Fletcher.

"I think," Fletcher said, "that the less you know about our charge, the better her guardian would like it, if you take my meaning."

"Ah, yes. Of course." Breckenridge amiably turned his gaze from her. He looked past Fletcher at the serving girl hurrying up. "So what's on the menu tonight?"

Haddock and turnips, or mutton again.

When asked, Heather glanced at the girl and whispered, "Haddock. And a glass of water, please." The other four had opted for ale.

As she'd been bid, Heather sat with eyes downcast and listened to the conversation, occasionally glancing up through her lashes at her companions.

Mostly at Breckenridge.

She knew it was him—despite the dark roughness of his beard, his tousled hair, and his less-than-kempt appearance, she could see it was him—but his voice was quite different, which unsettled her. She was used to his fashionable drawl, and equally accustomed to his clipped and incisive, unaffected speech—the voice he used when ordering her about—but listening to him now . . . if she didn't look, she could almost believe he was indeed some clerk one step away from the slums of the capital.

As for his choice of subject matter fit for the dinner table . . .

Pushing pieces of overcooked haddock around her plate, she listened in fascinated horror as he bandied details of cock-fights he'd witnessed with Fletcher and Cobbins. Glancing at Martha, Heather saw that even she was following the often gruesome details. Suppressing a shudder—describing chick-ens decapitated or ripped to shreds by spurs fixed to other chickens' talons wasn't her notion of uplifting discourse—she tried to focus on something else, but the haddock was uninspiring.

Her mind drifted . . . to the peculiar fact that despite Breckenridge not sounding or appearing like himself, she still felt enveloped by the aura of comfort, of security, that she now associated with being near him. And even in his currently rumpled, distinctly unelegant state, she was still aware of the underlying attraction. . . . which was strange. She'd always assumed it was his handsomeness that so ef-fortlessly held her interest. But if not that, then what?

For long moments—in the taproom of a tiny inn at Gretna Green—she tried to puzzle it out, tried to solve the riddle of what it was in Breckenridge that had always commanded that particular, intense, oh-so-feminine awareness.

Then Fletcher grunted and she jerked back to the present.

She hadn't heard how Breckenridge had managed to re-direct the conversation, but Fletcher readily volunteered, "We'll definitely be here all tomorrow, and most likely the day after that, too. I thought I'd counted the days right, but I did another reckoning this morning, and seems I was a day out."

Fletcher focused, rather blearily, on Breckenridge, who was looking increasingly disreputable. "What about you, then? You well enough to drive on tomorrow?"

Staring at the ale mug he held clasped between his hands,

Breckenridge seemed to think, then slowly shook his head from side to side. "Nope. Wound's still aching something fierce." His lips curved in what appeared to be an intoxicated smile. He raised his glass to Fletcher. "But this helps."

"Good excuse." Fletcher lifted the pitcher the girl had left on the table. "Here—never let it be said I denied an injured man his medicine."

Breckenridge grinned in a thoroughly idiotic male way, and when Fletcher filled the mug, raised it and saluted him. "You're a scholar and a gentleman, sir."

Fletcher grinned. Cobbins guffawed.

They were all well-flown. Even Martha's head was nodding, lower and lower.

Fletcher noticed. He poked Martha's arm. "Here—you and the young miss ought to get upstairs."

Martha snorted and shook herself, then glanced at Heather. "You're right. I'm for bed." Hauling her bulk up, she jerked her head, signaling Heather to follow suit.

Stifling a sigh, she slid along the bench and rose. As she did, she glanced at Breckenridge, but he was looking at Martha and nodding a vacuous farewell.

With an inward sniff, she followed her "maid" from the table. Without a backward glance, she left the room in Martha's wake.

The inn quieted early that night. Heather made her way cautiously down the stairs as soon as the silence grew thick; waiting in the tiny cloakroom for Breckenridge to appear was better than listening to Martha's snores.

Her gusty, inebriated snores.

Reaching the hall, she slipped around the counter and cautiously opened the cloakroom door. Inside, the confined space was dark and gloomy, but her eyes were well enough adjusted to the night to be sure there was no one inside.

It wasn't only her eyesight that informed her Breckenridge wasn't there waiting.

Tense, she hesitated, not liking the idea of stepping into the dark alone. He might be another hour; he might be as intoxicated as Martha. They hadn't agreed on any specific time—

A sound cut across her senses; silently whirling, she saw candlelight wavering in the taproom, the bearer still out of her sight, heard heavy footsteps plodding her way.

A dark shadow swooped down the stairs, straight to her.

She opened her lips—

A hard palm slapped over them. A steely arm wrapped around her.

Breckenridge lifted her from her feet and, holding her against him, slipped them both into the cloakroom and nudged the door closed . . . almost shut.

Removing his hand from her lips, he lowered his head and whispered, ghostlike, in her ear, "Be quiet."

She wasn't about to say anything; she wasn't sure she could manage a single word—not a coherent one. From his crisp tone, she surmised he wasn't at all inebriated. He hadn't, however, let her go.

Her heart was thudding; she couldn't see properly, but sensed he was listening intently to movement beyond the door. She swallowed, strained to listen, too. Eventually, over the beating of her heart she heard mumbling grumbles from just beyond the door . . . the innkeeper. He must have come to check something at the counter.

A thin line of light delineated the edge of the almost-closed door.

They waited, silent and still, for the innkeeper to finish his business and leave. She worked on simply breathing, on slowing her racing pulse, on telling herself she was safe— safe. Safe in Breckenridge's arms.

One part of her mind reeled.

The rest was too busy absorbing the warmth, the alluring masculine heat that seeped through the layers of cloth between them and stroked over her skin.

She was wearing her customary nighttime garb, her coverlet wrapped over her filmy chemise and cinched at her waist with her silk shawl. He was wearing his cloak; it had swept about her and now half enveloped her, shielding her from the chill night air.

As her pulse slowed, she struggled to draw air into lungs inexplicably constricted. She'd tensed with terror in the instant before he'd touched her, then had all but slumped, limp with relief, when his touch, his nearness, had impinged on her senses and she'd known who had seized her. Almost immediately, however, her nerves had started to tense again, steadily drawing taut with every second she remained clasped against him—every second his hard, undeniably male body remained flush against her much softer form.

He was protecting her, shielding her. She kept telling herself that, yet her senses remained giddy, distracted.

She'd managed to regain some hold on her composure when the innkeeper uttered a distinct, "Aha!"

The sounds of a drawer shutting reached them. Seconds later, the light seeping past the door flickered, then steadily faded.

"Don't move."

The warning was less than a breath stirring errant wisps of her hair, brushing tantalizingly past her ear.

By main force suppressing a shiver, she told herself he couldn't help it; that was probably how he always whispered to women he held in his arms.

She waited for him to release her.

After several moments, she felt the battle-ready tension that had invested his muscles, his entire frame, slowly, gradually, ease.

But he didn't entirely relax.

He didn't let her go, either. He did rearrange the cloak so it enveloped her completely, cocooning her within the contained warmth.

"We can't risk a light," he murmured.

His deep voice at such close quarters all but frazzled her nerves.

She tipped her face up, trying to make out his features in the gloom. All she could see was a pale outline, cheeks shaded with black beard, eyes too shadowed for her to even glimpse, and the lines of his lips and chin, both presently uncompromisingly grim.

"We'll have to make this quick."

She nodded. They would. Or else she might do something unutterably stupid. She made a mental note never to let him ever again seize her in the dark.

"As you heard, the laird won't arrive until at least the day after tomorrow. That makes it an odds-on certainty that he's a highlander, which means his reasons for kidnapping you or one of the others could well be buried in the mists of time. Worse, both Fletcher and Cobbins are very sure, for multiple reasons, that their employer is someone accustomed to wielding power—to giving orders and expecting to be obeyed." He studied her. "Did you learn anything from Martha?"

She cleared her throat. Breathed back, "A little. From her reading of how Fletcher and Cobbins reacted to the man, she says he, the laird, is, in her words, powerful. Fletcher and Cobbins found him impressive, imposing, and she's also certain he's a toff, because only a toff would have thought of hiring a maid to give me countenance."

Breckenridge's lips twisted in a grimace. "She's right."

After a moment of staring down into her face, he murmured, "We have a problem."

She certainly did; she was finding it difficult to breathe enough not to feel giddy.

"This laird . . . from all Martha, Fletcher, and Cobbins have said, he's a laird with a capital L. Almost certainly a noble. He's not going to be easy to counter, especially not on his home turf."

Face like hewn rock and eyes like ice.

Breckenridge hadn't forgotten Fletcher's description. "By all accounts, he's not the sort of man we want to find ourselves facing. Not here in Scotland, too far from anyone who can vouch for our identities."

He watched a frown overtake Heather's fine features. Until then, they'd been . . . a trifle wide-eyed, a touch arrested. He knew perfectly well why. Her heartbeat . . . he couldn't exactly feel it, but he'd seduced far too many women not to sense it. To know that she was as attracted to him as he was to her.

That wasn't something he'd needed to have proof of, but now he did . . . the knowledge kept circling, prodding and pricking at instincts that, where she was concerned, he'd always kept buried and inflexibly contained.

"But there's no reason to leave yet," she murmured. "They've said the laird won't arrive for days yet, and we haven't yet learned of anything we can use to identify him." Her frown firmed, giving her expression a mulish cast—one with which he was very familiar. "We can't leave yet."

He pressed his lips tight against any unwise utterance. Tried to sort through the contradictory impulses pressing on him from all sides. His deepest instinct was to remove her from all danger, yet while he remained with her, he could and would keep her safe—and he was now convinced that she stood in no danger whatever from Fletcher, Cobbins, or Martha. Indeed, it was in their best interests to protect her from all and any threat, at least until the mysterious laird claimed her. For the moment, she was safe.

And he knew her brothers, her cousins, her father, her uncles. They wouldn't fault him for cutting and running, and hauling her back to London and safety, but at the same time, they, like him, would dearly love to learn just which laird had had the temerity to kidnap one of their darlings.

One couldn't arrange for justice if one didn't know at whom to point the sword.

"All right." The instant he spoke, her expression softened. He hardened his own. "But just for a day. One more day."

Her lips curved. "All right. We'll see what we can learn tomorrow."

Her smile . . . it flirted with the ends of her lips. He blinked, found a frown. "And regardless of whether we learn anything, after tomorrow, we leave. Understood?"

Even whispering, he made the last word a command.

Her smile only deepened. "Yes, of course. But let's see what tomorrow brings."

He looked into her face, and time suspended.

Dangerous, he knew, but he couldn't seem to move, to break the strengthening spell.

Her smile slowly faded; her eyes searched his . . . her breath all but silently caught, hitched. She started to tip closer . . .

Then she dragged in a quick, too-tight breath and rocked back on her heels. "Wound—you said you had a wound."

He seized the unexpected lifeline. "I made that up to excuse me staying put and not traveling on. As a reason, it's open ended, especially in this weather."

"Oh, good. I mean . . . that you're not injured." She finally dropped her gaze, eased back.

He lowered his arms, let her free . . . reluctantly.

Too reluctantly for his peace of mind.

She stepped back and let the folds of his cloak slide from her.

"Go up," he murmured. He tipped his head to the door. "I'll watch you, then follow."

With a nod, she turned. Opening the door, she paused for a moment, then slipped out.

He held the door ajar and from the gloom within the cloakroom watched her slip wraithlike up the stairs.

And wondered why he hadn't kissed her.

She wouldn't have objected. She might have been a touch flustered, but . . . he would, at last, have learned what she tasted like—a question that had haunted him for the last four years.

They were, after all, destined to marry. After this little escapade, there was no other choice, not for either of them.

But if he'd kissed her . . . she would have known he'd been

thinking along the same lines as she, which was something she didn't at that moment know. He felt certain that to that point she'd gained no inkling of his true view of her. And if they were indeed to marry . . .

She was a Cynster to her toes. Much better she never knew just how deep his fascination with her ran. Just how persistent and intense—intensely irritating—that fascination had proved to be. Just how impossible to eradicate.

He'd tried. Hundreds of times.

No other female had ever been able to supplant her in his mind. At the core of his desires, at the heart of his passions.

And that was definitely something she never needed to know.

So . . . no kisses. Not yet. Not until she'd realized that their wedding was a foregone conclusion. Him initiating a kiss then wouldn't be so revealing.

Something within him bucked at the restraint, but he'd long ago learned to keep desire and passion on a very tight leash. No unintended revelations for him.

She had to have reached the room she shared with Martha. He moved out of the shadows, silently climbed the stairs, and headed for his bed.

"You can't be serious?" Heather stood in the middle of the inn's front hall and stared at Fletcher. "I stayed in that room all day yesterday, and you want me to sit quietly and stare at Martha knitting for another whole day?"

Jaw set, Fletcher nodded. "And tomorrow, too. Until the laird comes for you, I want you under Martha's eye at all times. Safer for you, anyway."

Heather narrowed her eyes at him. "I'll sit quietly after I've had a brief walk—just up the lane and back."

"No." Fletcher shifted closer, trying to intimidate.

Martha and Cobbins looked on, neither much interested, both simply waiting on an outcome of which they had no doubt.

The four of them and Breckenridge had been the only

guests down for breakfast that morning; Breckenridge had just ambled into the tap and was currently out of sight. The innkeeper was busy elsewhere; there was no one about to hear their argument.

Glowering down at her, Fletcher raised an arm and pointed to the parlor door. "You are going to walk in there and remain in there for the rest of the day, until dinnertime. If you need exercise, you can pace in there. If you need distraction, you can look out of the window, or help Martha count her stitches for all I care."

Heather opened her mouth.

Fletcher pointed at her nose. "You know our story. If you push me, I swear I'll use it to tie you up and gag you, and sit you in there with Martha."

She frowned, not just at Fletcher but at the realization that although she ought to be at least wary of him, if not outright afraid, she wasn't—simply wasn't. In her mind he featured merely as a hurdle to be overcome—a source of information to be milked, then left behind when she escaped. With Breckenridge.

Was it because he was close that she didn't fear Fletcher?

Regardless, it didn't take much cogitation to see she had no real option at that time. "Oh, very well!" She swung on her heel, marched to the parlor door, shoved it open, and sailed through—reluctantly refraining from slamming the door because Martha would be following.

Sweeping to the window, Heather crossed her arms and stared out at the new day. Spring had already arrived in London, but here it was struggling to break winter's hold. Other than the conifers, all the trees were still bare. The morning was still chill, the wind still a touch raw, but the clouds had thinned and the drizzle had ceased, and somewhere high above the sun was trying to shine through.

Behind her, the parlor door closed. She heard Martha's large bulk ease down into the armchair.

Eyes fixed outside, Heather humphed. "The lane's still

112

muddy, but the verge is drying nicely. It would be perfectly possible to go for a stroll. Perhaps after lunch."

"Forget it," Martha advised. "You heard him. No going outside."

"But why?" Swinging around, Heather spread her arms. "What does he think I'll do—escape into the wilderness? If I was going to escape, I'd have tried that first night." She let her shoulders slump. "I'm a young lady of the ton—I can play the pianoforte and waltz with the best of them, but escaping isn't something I have the vaguest notion how to do!"

Martha eyed her, not without sympathy. After a moment, she said, "Humor him for today. I'll have a word with him tonight, or perhaps tomorrow morning. If it's fine, perhaps he'll let you have your walk then, but mind, I'm making no promises."

Heather met Martha's gaze. She felt compelled to incline her head in acceptance of the olive branch. "Thank you."

Turning back to the window, she grimaced. That still left her with an entire day to waste, with nothing much more she could gain from it. She'd already questioned Martha; she doubted there was any more to learn from her "maid," and further probing might instead raise suspicions in Martha's quite sharp mind.

If there was nothing more she could learn, nothing else she could do . . .

The thought that had been haunting her—that had followed her into her dreams last night and been in her mind when she'd awoken that morning—flared again. Last night, in the cloakroom, she'd almost kissed Breckenridge. It hadn't been an accident, a mistake—she'd known exactly who he was the whole time. But she'd wanted to kiss him, would have, would have welcomed his kiss if he'd been so inclined. If he'd given the slightest sign of welcoming her advance, she would have stretched up and touched her lips to his.

The only thing that had stopped her—that had stopped the

kiss from happening—was that she hadn't been able to read his face, his expression. Hadn't been able to see his eyes.

She'd searched, but there'd been nothing to tell her what he thought—whether he felt any attraction toward her at all, let alone something similar to what she felt for him. It was, she thought, a latent sensual curiosity—something the enforced closeness of their adventure had caused to grow from their previously strained and prickly interaction. Regardless, she'd definitely wanted to kiss him last night, and would have if she hadn't suddenly been assailed not by missish sensibility, let alone modesty, but by the horrible thought that he might not want to kiss her.

Which led her back to her persistent fear, nay, entrenched belief, that he saw her as little more than a schoolgirl. A girl child. A female so young and inexperienced that a man of his ilk could never see her as a woman, let alone ever stoop to taking advantage of her.

Much less anything else, any consensual liaison.

Arms tightly folded, frowning unseeing out at the trees, she had to admit her attitude toward him had changed over the last days. Changed . . . or perhaps clarified. Previously she would have been more likely to use her lips to berate him than kiss him, but now . . .

The thought of kissing him—just seizing the moment and doing it, and getting the madness out of her system and satisfying her curiosity—was rapidly becoming an obsession.

An obsession that, for the next hours, she could do nothing about.

She humphed, inwardly pushed the subject aside.

Determinedly focusing on the trees outside, she turned her mind to the only other thing she might accomplish—evaluating ways in which she and Breckenridge could escape, but then keep watch on the inn and get a look at the mysterious laird when he arrived, sufficient to identify him.

Breckenridge spent the morning outside the inn, taking advantage of the brighter weather to avoid Fletcher and Cob-

114

bins, the better to ensure they didn't suspect him of taking too great an interest in their business. If the laird wasn't expected until at least the following day, then Heather would be safe enough, confined, as she was, to the inn parlor.

After breakfasting late, he strolled to the inn's stable and checked over the old chestnut he'd hired in Carlisle, along with the ancient pony trap. The horse was faring well; it would carry him and Heather far enough to make good an escape.

But in which direction? He spent the rest of the morning ambling around the hamlet of Gretna Green, taking note of the roads and the cover afforded by the landscape in each direction, then he strode the half mile or so back down the highway to the main village of Gretna, with the Customs and Revenue Offices, and the border itself just beyond.

With clouds blowing up and the wind tending bitter, he returned to the inn at lunchtime. Pausing in the front hall, he glanced at the parlor door, but all was quiet inside.

Turning away, he walked into the tap. And fell in once again with Fletcher and Cobbins. They were joined by the usual band of locals during the meal, but once the platters were cleared and the farmers departed for their fields once more, the three of them gathered about the table by the window.

Fletcher had brought the pack of cards but seemed uninterested in any game. He picked up the pack and let it fall an inch to the table, over and over again.

Breckenridge noted it. "Are you worried about this laird of yours showing?"

"Heh?" Fletcher focused, then shook his head. "No—he'll be here. I just wish he'd be here sooner."

"Tomorrow, isn't it?"

Fletcher shrugged. "Tomorrow, or the next day. He'll definitely be here by then." He glanced at Breckenridge. "It's just that I don't like sitting in one place, waiting. Sort of like being a sitting duck—it grates on my nerves."

"Ah. I see." The only men Breckenridge had previously

encountered who chafed at being forced by unavoidable circumstances to remain in one place were felons of one stripe or another. It made them feel trapped. Glancing at Cobbins, more taciturn than Fletcher, he saw a similar edginess growing.

Unless he missed his guess, both men had at some time been very much on the wrong side of the law; they might never have been caught, but both knew what it was like to be hunted.

Which was a fact worth noting, given he intended to filch their latest prize from under their noses. He'd already learned through general conversation that Fletcher was good with knives, and had several on him at any time, while Cobbins was a true bruiser at heart, a heavy man who, once he mowed into something, wasn't likely to stop until he was the last one standing.

"Tell me." Relaxing back in his chair, he projected the air of someone seeking to distract the pair from their angst. "How does this sort of caper work? Seems to me it's a capital lark—you do the job, hand over the package, get paid, and everyone's happy." He frowned, as if thinking it through. "But then you have to stump up the wherewithal to set up the snatch in the first place, and the cost of the travel and all the rest—" He broke off because Fletcher was shaking his head.

Setting aside the cards, Fletcher leaned his arms on the table. "No. It's better than that. Mind you"—Fletcher sent a sharp glance his way—"it takes years and years to work up a reputation like we have. You don't get the arrangements we do straight off, first time."

Cobbins nodded. "Professionals, we are."

"Exactly." Fletcher looked back at Breckenridge. "So the way it works for us, us being professionals and well known in this work, is that we get paid wages up front—proper compensation for our time doing the job—and enough to cover all expenses, like our travel down to London and back, staying in the capital, Martha's wages, and all the rest."

"All up front?" Breckenridge blinked in genuine surprise. Whoever the laird was, he was not only wealthy but also willing to invest serious money for the chance of seizing one of the Cynster girls.

"Cash in hand, at the start," Fletcher confirmed. "We don't take the job without it."

"But . . ." Breckenridge felt a chill as the question formed in his mind. "What guarantee does your employer have that you'll actually do the job?"

Fletcher grinned. "Our bonus, of course. There's two thousand pounds coming our way, along with the laird."

"*Two thousand*?" Breckenridge didn't have to feign his shock.

Smile deepening, Fletcher nodded. "Told you this is a really sweet job." Fletcher hesitated, studying Breckenridge, then looked at Cobbins and exchanged a glance before turning back and adding, "If you ever get tired of being a clerk, you look us up—you'd be useful. If we brushed you up, with your looks you could pass for a gentleman. Useful, that is, in our line of work."

Still coping with the discovery of just how much the mysterious highland laird wanted Heather, Breckenridge managed a nod. "I'll think about it." He stirred, then shook his head and sat up. "Two thousand! That's . . . amazing."

Amazing, and revealing, in the worst possible way.

Chapter Seven

I think it's time for me to make my escape." Heather said the words before she'd even sat beside Breckenridge on the narrow bench beneath the coat pegs in the tiny cloakroom.

She'd waited until it had been so late that there would have been no chance of the innkeeper surprising them, all the time fervently hoping that Breckenridge would not only have been waiting but would have found and lit a candle by the time she arrived.

He had; the wavering light had welcomed her. Slipping inside the confined space, pushing the door closed behind her, she'd taken in the reassuring sight of him as he'd glanced up at her.

He waited as she settled, then flicked out the cloak he'd been holding in his hands and, turning to her, swirled it about her. He hadn't been wearing it, so it didn't hold much of his scent, but she was grateful for the added warmth nonetheless.

"Is that woman ever going to give you back your clothes at night?"

"I doubt it. It seems to be her habitual way of controlling her charges."

He grunted, then, his lips setting in a surprisingly grim line, met her gaze. "Escaping, I regret to say, isn't going to be as easy as we'd thought."

She blinked, studied his face. "Why?"

He looked down at his hands, clasped between his spread

knees. "Fletcher and Cobbins stand to collect two thousand pounds when they hand you over to the laird."

"*Two thousand . . .* good God!"

"My sentiments exactly."

"But . . ." She struggled to take it in. Finally said, "Clearly this laird is no penny-pinching pauper. He's definitely not wanting me for ransom, nor yet to marry."

"At least not to marry for your money."

She glanced at him. "I really don't think I've met this laird, so why else . . . oh, you mean for the connection to the family?"

"Who knows? But regardless of his reasons, we now face a significantly greater problem than we'd foreseen." He met her gray-blue eyes. "Fletcher and Cobbins are no bumbling fools. They're dangerous, and they're not going to let two thousand pounds slip through their grasp without making a determined bid to snatch it—you—back."

She nodded; her expression stated she understood and accepted his argument, yet she didn't seem overly worried. After one blink, she refocused on his face. "So what now?"

Staring into her eyes, lit by the candlelight, the truth hit him like a sledgehammer. She trusted him. Trusted him implicitly to protect her and get her out of this, away from any danger. He would, of course, but he hadn't expected her to be so . . . accepting. Lips twisting, he looked forward. "We're going to have to find some way to distract Fletcher and Cobbins, so that they're too busy to notice you've escaped, if at all possible for a day. They're going to chase us like madmen."

"Madmen motivated by two thousand pounds."

"Precisely. But as well as distracting them to whatever extent we can, we need to make for the nearest safe place."

She grimaced. "We can't just escape and put up at some inn in Gretna, can we?"

He shook his head. "I'd assumed we would head back to London—possibly detour to the Brunswick estates on the way." His father was at Baraclough, the earldom's principal estate in Berkshire. If he and Heather were to marry, he wanted to tell his father first, in person. "But that's the first direction in which Fletcher and Cobbins will look, and there's no safe harbor along that route that we can be sure of reaching before they catch up with us."

He hesitated, then went on, "Admittedly, once back in England, as long as we saw them coming I could use my title to have them taken up. However, if we don't see them closing on us—and given their experience, I'm not confident we would—then that won't save us." Save her. If Fletcher and Cobbins caught up with them, they'd at the very least incapacitate him and steal her back—and then make absolutely certain she was without delay placed directly into the hands of their mysterious laird.

Equally undesirably, however, invoking his title would make their journey together without any acceptable chaperon public, something he would prefer not to do. He was confident the Cynsters would have covered up her absence—she'd be recovering from a hideous chill or something of that nature—and his absence wouldn't have even been noted; if any in the wider ton wondered about him at all, they would assume he was at Baraclough. If at all possible he intended to present their necessary betrothal as something that had been arranged quietly between their families, not as something necessitated by her being kidnapped, and not even by him.

Calling attention to themselves would end all hope of keeping her reputation intact.

He stared at his hands. "And we can't afford to let them catch us in Scotland—not at all. We have to assume this laird's a nobleman, some arrogant and, as it happens, very wealthy highlander. If it comes to his title versus mine—and neither you nor I have anything with us to verify who we are, and there's no one close who can vouch for us—then it's perfectly possible he'll be able to lay claim to you, and take you off God knows where while I protest my innocence and identity from a cell."

That scenario was his worst nightmare.

She was frowning. "Don't you have any cards with you?"

"Yes, but I don't think a silver card case with cards in the name of Viscount Breckenridge will do us much good." He met her gaze. "He'll—they'll—claim I stole it."

She grimaced and looked forward.

Looking back at his hands, he continued, "So we need somewhere safe that's reasonably close—some place we can reach within a day. I've been racking my brains, but I can't think of anywhere."

"Casphairn."

He glanced at her. Her tone had been definite; her expression was confident and assured. "Where?"

"The Vale of Casphairn. It's where Richard—my cousin Richard—and his wife, Catriona, live. It's . . . well, a day's journey in a carriage from Carlisle."

"In which direction?"

"To the west. We pass through Gretna, then go west to Annan and Dumfries. . . ." She grimaced. "I'm not sure of the road after that. I know we go through a town called St. John's of Dalry. That's about an hour from the Vale."

"If I get us a map, could you find it?"

She nodded. "And I know Richard and Catriona are there. They don't come down for the Season, not usually, and they weren't expected in London this year."

"Good." He knew Richard Cynster. He nodded. "We'll make for there."

Heather embraced the notion with relief. The thought of Breckenridge being slung in a cell while she was dragged off by some loutish highlander . . . she gave an inward shudder, then determinedly banished the thought. "So how do I escape?" She turned to look at Breckenridge. "And when?"

He considered, then shook his head. "Not tomorrow. According to Fletcher, he's not really expecting the laird until the following day. That gives us tomorrow to plan."

He glanced at her, then rose.

She rose, too.

He held her gaze for a moment, then murmured, "I'll find us a map, for a start. Meanwhile, both of us should put our minds to thinking of a way to distract Fletcher and Cobbins long enough for us to get safely away."

She nodded, then remembered and slipped his cloak off her shoulders. Once again, she immediately felt the loss. "Martha said that if tomorrow is fine, she'll try to get Fletcher to let us go for a walk, so I might have a chance to learn something useful."

He took the cloak from her, but caught and held her gaze. "Whatever you do, don't jeopardize how they currently view you. We don't need them to realize what you're capable of and decide to keep you under lock, key, and tighter guard."

The acknowledgment that she wasn't some meek and mild—helpless and gormless—fashionable miss had her smiling. "Don't worry, I won't."

He grunted and reached for the door. Paused with his hand on the knob. He caught her gaze, looked at her . . . long enough to have her lungs tightening and thoughts far removed from escape rising in her mind . . . but then he grimaced and looked away. "Regardless of what we find, we'll have to get you out of Fletcher's clutches by the day after tomorrow." His voice was a bare whisper as he added, "That's when the laird is supposed to arrive."

She felt a sudden chill and told herself it was simply the effect of losing the protection of his cloak.

He blew out the candle, then opened the door, looked out, and stepped through and to the side. She slipped out of the cloakroom and, with a last glance his way, headed straight up the stairs.

Lecturing herself that she couldn't at this point give in to the impulse to simply walk into his arms and see what came next.

It hadn't happened that morning, as Heather had hoped, but after lunch Martha finally convinced Fletcher that he needed to allow both her and Heather out for a walk. The day had been sunny since morning, and the grass was no longer wet, just damp. Fletcher hadn't been happy, but he'd grudgingly agreed that they could walk across the fields to a nearby grassy hillock.

Martha had eyed the slight mound, a goodly distance away, then told Fletcher not to expect them back for at least two hours. "We're going to have a sit in the sunshine."

As Martha had become quite belligerent over the whole question of their walk, Fletcher had gritted his teeth and waved them off.

Heather took the opportunity afforded by the walk to get a better sense of the surrounding land. They passed the stables at the side of the inn, to the west of the main building, then tramped southwest. The fields were largely flat; what hedges there were weren't thick or dense. At this time of year, with all the branches bare, there was precious little cover to be found. The faint hope she'd harbored that they might lurk close enough after her escape to glimpse the laird when he arrived died.

The hillock wasn't that far. When she halted on its crest and looked south, she could see the glint of sunlight off the waters of Solway Firth.

Martha looked, then set down her knitting bag and shook out a large rug she'd carried under her arm. Laying it on the grass, she pointed to one end. "Sit you down there, and don't make me regret taking up for you and getting you out in the fresh air."

Remembering Breckenridge's warning not to step out of her assumed character, Heather dutifully subsided. Martha sat, too, and pulled out her knitting.

Although the fresh air was welcome, within ten minutes, Heather was thoroughly bored. The last thing she needed was time to dwell on Breckenridge and the unruly impulses that increasingly came to the fore when he was near.

She definitely didn't need to think about those, and even less about him, and her steadily changing opinion. It had been much easier to deal with him, and her misguided attraction to him, when she'd thought him a too-handsome-for-his-own-good, far-too-experienced-to-look-in-her-direction, arrogant, indolent, and self-indulgent rake of the first order.

Now . . . he might still be all that, but he'd also shown himself to have qualities she knew enough to recognize as admirable. Protective males could be difficult to manage; against that, they were likely to be there when one needed them, and when one was in danger, their presence was comforting. More, he'd shown a—to her—surprising ability to deal with her as a partner. That, she most definitely hadn't expected, especially from him.

The thought reminded her of what they were both supposed to be assessing that day—means of escape. She glanced at Martha. The older woman's head was nodding, but she felt Heather's gaze and looked up.

Heather glanced back at the inn, clearly visible across the fields.

Martha misinterpreted and chuckled. "Oh, don't worry. He won't come charging out to drag us back." Setting down her knitting, Martha, too, looked back at the inn. "Mind you, I'd wager he watched for the first ten minutes or so, but he'll have seen by now that there's no risk to you." Martha waved her arms at the fields around them. "No chance anyone could creep up and steal you away."

Heaving a huge sigh, Martha lay down full length on her end of the rug. "I'm going to have a nice little nap in this sun. Don't think to wander off—I'll know if you move. A very light sleeper, I am."

Heather stared, speechless, at the woman who slept so soundly every night that she'd never heard Heather slip out of their room, or back in. Heather managed not to shake her head in disbelief, just in case Martha was watching through her lashes. Instead, she drew in a deep breath and looked around with more interest.

Considered the firth, not more than a mile away. Could they possibly escape by water? Surely they could find a fisherman who might . . . but no. Travel by small boat at this time of year wouldn't necessarily be fast—faster than going by land—and she was fairly sure there would be no benefit to them in trying to get closer to Casphairn by sea. The Vale lay well inland, that much she knew.

While Martha's snores kept the birds at bay, she wondered what possible distraction they might stage. It had to be something to keep Fletcher and Cobbins occupied—

The soft sound of a footstep had her turning quickly, to see Breckenridge quietly walking up. He looked at Martha, then nodded politely at Heather. "This looked like a good place to get some air. Do you mind if I join you?"

Understanding they were to continue to play their fictitious roles, she inclined her head. "If you wish."

He sat on the grass a little way away. Drawing a map from his pocket, he opened it and spread it out—laying it between them, where she could see it.

Pointing to Gretna, Breckenridge murmured, "I thought I'd work out the best road to Glasgow."

He'd spoken quietly, but distinctly. He waited, but Martha's snores didn't break rhythm.

Looking at Heather, he arched a brow.

Leaning closer, she extended one tapered finger, with it traced the main road from Gretna to Annan and on to Dumfries. There, she halted, lifted her finger while with her eyes she searched further north and west. . .

"There," she breathed, her finger descending to point to a small village.

He looked, then looked up at her questioningly.

"That's Carsphairn village." Her words reached him on a thread of sound. "The road to the Vale heads west, less than a mile south of the village."

He nodded and drew the map closer. He studied the area she'd indicated, then checked the roads between Dumfries to that point. He glanced at Martha, then murmured, "Even though my trap is old and rickety, I should make it in a day."

She nodded. "Assuming the way is clear."

He flicked her a glance. "I believe it will be. But I'll need to get a good night's sleep."

She frowned, then turned her head away from Martha and mouthed, "Tonight?"

Certain no one could snore that deeply without being asleep, he risked murmuring, "No meeting. I'm working on our distraction. Be ready tomorrow—I'm not sure exactly when."

Gathering the map, he stood and refolded it. Sliding it into his pocket, he nodded politely, then turned and walked back to the inn.

Heather didn't immediately turn and watch him, but when she judged he would be most of the way back, she shifted and looked, and saw him striding along, nearing the stables.

When he disappeared into the inn, she stifled a sigh and faced forward once more. What was he up to? And why was there to be no secret meeting in the cloakroom to look forward to, and to reassure her, that night?

The following twenty-four hours were the longest Heather had ever endured. She slept fitfully, tossing and turning and wondering what Breckenridge was doing. The only reason he would have cancelled their nightly meeting was that he wasn't going to be in the inn. And if he wasn't, where the devil was he?

From the moment the new day dawned, she was tense, on pins. This was the day Fletcher expected the laird to arrive—the dangerous, mysterious, highland nobleman who had ordered her kidnapped and brought to Gretna Green. Both Fletcher and Cobbins had taken pains with their ablutions and attire. Even Martha had spruced herself up.

Heather felt thoroughly rumpled in comparison, in her dull round gown and clashing shawl, but her appearance didn't even feature on her list of concerns.

Breckenridge was playing least in sight. He hadn't been in the tap for breakfast, at least not while she and Martha had been there. Of course Fletcher had insisted they retire to the parlor and remain in seclusion there, so she had no idea if Breckenridge appeared later, but he didn't join the company for lunch, either. She didn't dare inquire directly, but to her relief Martha asked Cobbins where their friend was. Cobbins replied that Timms was preparing to leave, to drive on to Glasgow in easy stages.

The information settled her. The Glasgow road wasn't the one they would take. Laying a false trail was a sound, very Breckenridgelike idea.

The weather had turned bleak, the wind biting. When a group of sailors came into the tap, closely followed by three farmhands, Fletcher ordered her and Martha back to the parlor.

With ill-grace, she went.

An hour later, she was standing before the parlor window and staring across the inn's graveled forecourt, tempted to bite a nail although she'd broken the habit years ago, when three men came striding swiftly and purposefully down the lane.

They turned into the inn's forecourt and headed without pause for the front door.

Their uniforms stated they were from the local constabulary.

Their pugnacious expressions declared they were on the trail of some villain.

The first reached the door, opened it, and strode in. His companions followed on his heels.

Heather headed for the parlor door, risks and options colliding in her mind.

Martha looked up at her, frowned warningly.

Reaching the door, Heather signaled her to silence, then mouthed, "Police."

Martha dropped her knitting. She paled, then leapt up, grabbed the knitting, and shoved it into her cloth bag.

At the door, Heather carefully cracked it open a sliver. She'd already jettisoned the idea of flinging herself on the constables' mercy; Fletcher and his story, backed up by Cobbins and Martha, were simply too believable. But what the devil was going on?

Martha joined her at the door, locking large, strong fingers around one of Heather's wrists.

Heather didn't look at her, just breathed, "Sssh."

Through the narrow gap, she peeked into the inn's front hall. Alongside her, Martha crouched and peeked, too.

The man who'd led the charge into the inn was standing at the bottom of the stairs, talking rapidly, but quietly, with the innkeeper. The two clearly knew each other—hardly surprising in such a small village. The other two constables had taken up positions with their backs to the front door.

A crowd of patrons from the taproom, Fletcher and Cobbins among them, had left their pints and come to cluster in the archway separating the front hall from the tap.

The innkeeper nodded to the first policeman, then came hurrying across to his counter, a little to the side of the parlor door.

Heather couldn't see what he was doing, but from the sound of pages flipping, she could tell he was consulting his register.

The senior constable turned to scowl at the men crowding the tap's entrance. "You lot just sit yourselves back down. We want no bother from you."

Several brows were raised, but the men slowly turned and went back into the tap. After sending intense, searching glances toward the parlor, Fletcher and Cobbins retreated with the pack.

The constable by the stairs, the one who seemed to be in

charge, turned to the other two stationed before the door. "Keep an eye on them." With his head, he indicated the tap. "No one goes in or out."

The pair nodded briefly. "Aye, Sergeant."

The innkeeper left his counter and returned to the sergeant, still waiting at the foot of the stairs. The innkeeper said something; Heather couldn't hear what. But the sergeant turned and reached for the balustrade. "You'd best come with me."

With that, he headed up the stairs three steps at a time. The innkeeper hurried up in his wake.

After a moment, Heather whispered, "Do you have any idea what this is about?"

"No," Martha growled back. "But I don't like it."

They didn't have long to wait for the next act in the drama. Within minutes, the sound of heavy footsteps pounding down the stairs heralded the return of the sergeant. He reappeared at the bottom of the stairs with a long silver candlestick in each hand. Halting on the last step, he glanced at the innkeeper as he joined him. With his head, the sergeant urged the innkeeper on. "Go show them which ones."

The innkeeper nodded. The constables moved from the door, following him to the tap's entrance. Pausing under the archway, the innkeeper pointed. "Him, and him."

Pushing past the innkeeper, the constables moved into the tap.

Straining her ears, Heather heard one say, "If you'll come with us, sir, we have a question or two."

Someone replied, but she couldn't catch the words, or make out the voice. But. . .

"Won't take but a minute, sir. The rest of you just remain where you are."

She glanced at Martha. Whispered, "Were there any other guests staying in the inn last night?"

Eyes glued to the crack between the door and the jamb, Martha didn't reply.

Heather looked out again, just as her suspicion was proved correct. Fletcher and Cobbins, closely escorted by the two constables, walked reluctantly out of the tap.

The sergeant was still standing at the foot of the stairs, hefting the pair of candlesticks, one in each hand. Fletcher took note but merely raised his brows and met the sergeant's gaze. "What seems to be the problem?"

"These." The sergeant brandished the long candlesticks. "Disappeared from Sir Kenneth Baxter's house last night. Not a good place to pick to burgle, him being the local magistrate an' all."

Fletcher frowned. "So it would seem. But why are you talking to us? We know nothing of any burglary."

The sergeant made a scoffing sound. "Don't come the innocent with us, m'lad. Were you or were you not occupying the room at the head of the stairs, first one to the south— room number five?"

Fletcher's gaze remained level, but even from across the room, Heather could sense his sudden comprehension, see the equally instinctive tensing, the assessing of his chances. . . .

The sergeant and the constables saw the latter, too. Both constables' hands drifted to the grips of the truncheons hanging at their sides.

"Now, now," the sergeant reproved. "No sense in making this harder on yourselves than it has to be. You come along quietly, and—"

Fletcher held up a hand. "Just so we're clear, we had nothing to do with the theft of those candlesticks. Someone must have put them in our room—"

"That's what they all say."

"But our employer—"

"You just come along and you can tell your story to the magistrate—Sir Kenneth. Sure an' he'll be keen to hear it."

Before Fletcher could say more, the constables pulled his and Cobbins's hands back, manacled them, then turned them toward the front door. Just before he passed through it,

Fletcher sent a scorching look at the parlor door, then he was bundled outside.

Cobbins followed, led by the second constable. After pausing for a last word with the innkeeper, the sergeant, carrying the candlesticks, brought up the rear.

Heather eased the parlor door shut, then straightened and stared at the wooden panel.

Beside her, Martha jerked upright, turned to agitatedly look over the parlor, then pinned Heather with a narrow-eyed look. "How the devil did you manage it? You've been under our eyes all the time."

Heather blinked, met Martha's eyes. "I didn't." But she knew who had.

This had to be Breckenridge's diversion. He'd been out stealing candlesticks last night. And of course he'd stolen them from the magistrate—the one local guaranteed to be able to get instant police attention.

But what was she supposed to do now? Wait for Breckenridge to reappear? Or should she perhaps go to the police station and through them contact the magistrate . . . ? "No."

She could imagine the sensation when she explained she'd been kidnapped and held, through days of traveling, by the likes of Fletcher and Cobbins; despite Martha's presence, the scandal would be immense. Very likely of the sort she would never live down, Cynster or not.

So back to their plan of making a dash to the Vale and the safety of Richard and Catriona's household. Breckenridge had removed Fletcher and Cobbins. All she had to do was get free of Martha and she and Breckenridge could be on their way.

Refocusing on her erstwhile "maid," she discovered Martha clutching her bag of knitting to her ample middle, finishing a last visual survey of the room and inching toward the door.

Turning, Martha reached for the door latch. "I'm getting out of here."

Heather frowned.

Before she could respond, Martha eased the door open, looked out, then slipped out, leaving the door swinging.

Puzzled, Heather followed, pausing only to close the door after her.

The innkeeper had retreated to the tap; she could hear him regaling his remaining customers with the details of where they'd found the candlesticks—in the bottom of Fletcher's and Cobbins's bags in the wardrobe in their room.

Surprisingly silent despite her bulk, Martha tiptoed to the stairs and climbed quickly up.

Still mystified, Heather followed, all the way to the room they'd shared.

Martha dropped her knitting bag on her bed, then crossed to the wardrobe, hauled it open, and pulled out her capacious traveling satchel. Dumping it on the bed, she proceeded to toss Heather's clothes out of it. "You can have these back. No good to me, to be found with such fripperies."

Crossing to the other side of the bed, Heather reclaimed her evening gown, her reticule, and the second plain gown they'd given her, gathering them to her. The soft silk of the evening gown felt odd beneath her palms after days of rougher clothing.

Muttering imprecations, Martha dragged her own clothes from the wardrobe and crammed them haphazardly into the satchel. "Thank God I insisted they paid me my wages before we set out on this caper. Knew it sounded too easy to be true."

Shoving her knitting bag on top of the bundled clothes, then pulling the satchel shut, she paused to look at Heather, still standing, uncomprehendingly, on the other side of the bed. "Don't know about you—you can stay and meet this laird for all I care—but I'm leaving. Now."

"Where are you going?"

"I'm heading back across the border as fast as I can, for a start, then in Carlisle I'll get the mail coach to London—

tonight's if possible." Martha glanced at the door. "The sooner I get shot of this place, and out of Scotland altogether, the better. Before any of that lot downstairs decides to tell those flatfoots that we—you and I, missy—were here with Fletcher and Cobbins." Martha cinched her satchel closed. "They'll take us up as accomplices as fast as you can spit."

"Accomplices?" Heather froze.

"Aye—accomplices." Martha paused, eyes narrowed, then added in a growl, "And I'm thinking I wouldn't put it past Fletcher himself to tell the plods that, just to make sure he keeps us close, so he can still give you to this laird when he shows."

Hefting the satchel off the bed, Martha looked at Heather. "You didn't screech once, so I'll tell you this—if I were you, I'd get myself gone from here right quick." Martha glanced around the room one last time. "As for me, I'm off."

With that, she barreled toward the open door, paused to peek out around the jamb, then whisked out.

Heather listened to her footsteps fade . . . then she rushed to the door, closed it. Raced to the wardrobe and pulled out the satchel her captors had provided for her "luggage."

Tossing it on the bed, she rapidly gathered the few clothes she had, both her own and those her captors had provided, the brush and comb they'd given her. She shoved the few articles willy-nilly into the satchel, swiftly did up the buckles. "Where the hell is Breckenridge?"

Swinging the satchel to her shoulder, she swiped up her cloak, swung it around her shoulders, and whirled to face the door—just as it started to open.

Slowly.

Her heart was thudding. Frantically looking around for some weapon, she spotted the poker leaning against the side of the stone hearth. Carefully picking it up, she tiptoed to stand behind the door. Raised the poker high as the door swung wider.

Drew in a breath, steeled herself . . .

Recognized the dark head, the height, the profile.

Her pent-up breath escaped in a wheeze. Exasperation flooded her. "For God's sake—knock!"

Breckenridge swung to face her, took in the poker as she lowered it and set it down.

Took in her satchel and cloak.

He started to come around the door, started to close it.

With both hands, she pushed him back. Hissed, "We have to go! Now!"

In typical male fashion, he stopped, rooted to the spot. "Why?" He glanced around as if searching for something to explain her panic. "There's no rush." Looking back at her, he smiled, the epitome of self-satisfied male. "The magistrate wasn't amused. Fletcher and Cobbins will be tied up for at least a few days, possibly more. "

"Yes! And as their accomplice, so will I!"

"Accomplice?"

She saw the instant it struck him. The transformation from self-satisfied smug to fully alert warrior took no longer than a blink.

His face all sharp angles, not a soft curve in sight, hazel eyes hard, he glanced around the room. "Where's Martha?"

"Heading to London as fast as her legs will take her."

"Right." He met her eyes. "Just let me get my things—the map, my pistols."

Using both hands, she pushed him again; this time he consented to move. "Your room. If anyone downstairs decides to help the police by catching me, this is the first place they'll look."

He didn't reply, merely grasped her arm, hauled her out of the room, and shut the door. Releasing her, he steered her before him down the corridor, past the head of the stairs and into the other wing. Halting her before the last door before the narrow servants' stairs at the wing's end, he opened the door and urged her inside. Following on her heels, he quietly shut the door.

Heather stood to one side, out of his way, as he pulled two satchels from the wardrobe and swiftly, remarkably efficiently, packed clothes, then two pistols, powder, and shot, packed more clothes around them, tossed in a brush, stowed a pair of shoes in the second bag, then the rest of his clothes.

He was buckling the satchels' straps when he swore. Virulently.

She narrowed her eyes at his downbent dark head. "Don't you dare swear at me!"

He didn't look up, but she saw his lips tighten even more than they already were. "I wasn't swearing at you. I was swearing at the fact that we can't take the trap."

She blinked. "We can't?"

He glanced up at her. "You're right—they'll come after you, any time now. Fletcher will send them—it's the only way he can make sure you're held here, too. If we take the trap, we'll have to stick to the roads. When they find you gone, they'll search the inn—and within minutes they'll discover I've disappeared, too, along with my trap."

Her mind was racing again. "But they'll think you've gone to Glasgow. Cobbins thought that."

He shook his head. "I only told Cobbins and Fletcher that. I told the innkeeper I'd probably stay on for a few more nights." He swung his cloak around his shoulders, tied the ties loosely about his neck. "If the trap disappears, they'll guess you're with me and send riders out along all the roads. Even if they don't make the connection, they'll still send riders to all the nearby towns. And the horse . . . even if I stole one of the inn's stronger nags, riders would still catch us before Annan."

Grabbing up his satchels, swinging both over one shoulder, he beckoned her to him. Taking her arm, he led her to the door.

She put her hand on the panel to stop him from opening it. Looked up at him. "So we flee on foot?"

He looked down at her. "To begin with. We can hire a

135

carriage or a gig further on. We can look at the map later and see what our options are, but for now we need to leave— we'll go out across the fields toward Annan. We'll go as far as we can before dark, then take stock."

She absorbed the grim resolution in his face and nodded.

Removing her hand, she waited while he opened the door and checked that the corridor was safe, then she slipped past him and, obeying his guiding push, went quickly to the head of the servants' stairs. He moved past her and led the way down.

The stairs ended in a small hall between the kitchen and the back door. At that hour, with dinner being prepared, the kitchen was a hive of activity, with the ovens roaring and the cook screeching. They slipped out of the back door without anyone having any notion they'd been there.

Breckenridge closed the door behind them, then grasped her hand. He set off, striding quickly past the inn's stable. She hurried to keep up. Pausing behind the stable to help her over a stile into the field beyond, he murmured, "The fields are so flat, we'll need to keep the stable and barns between us and the inn for as long as we can."

Heather looked ahead. A line of trees marched along a slight rise a mile or so on.

From beside her, Breckenridge softly said, "If we can get that far without being seen, we stand a good chance of getting away."

They couldn't afford to be caught by the authorities. Even less could they risk being captured by Fletcher's laird.

When they reached the line of trees without any sign or sound of a hue and cry being raised behind them, Breckenridge felt only the very slightest soupçon of relief. The tension gripping him eased not at all. If he was taken up along with Heather, for aiding and abetting an accomplice to a crime who was fleeing from justice, then once the laird arrived in Gretna and was alerted by Fletcher, it was all too likely that said laird would be able to arrange for Heather to be released into his—the laird's—keeping. Then, while he—Breckenridge—remained locked in some cell, unable to do anything, the laird would disappear into the highlands with Heather as his recaptured ward.

If they were caught, nothing he could say, nothing she could say, would hold any power to alter that scenario.

That nightmare.

They trudged on across the fields. He glanced at Heather, took in her stoic expression. Despite the rigors of their flight, she'd uttered not one word of complaint.

Most ladies of the ton would be filling his ears with re-criminations and petty griping.

Then again, he'd always heard that Cynster ladies had spines of steel.

She was also, he judged, in significantly better physical condition than many of her contemporaries.

"Do you ride?" The question was out of his mouth before he'd thought.

She glanced at him, surprised by the comment coming out of nowhere, but then she nodded and looked ahead. "I love to ride. I don't get as much opportunity as I'd like what with being in London so much, but whenever I can manage it, I'll get on a horse." Her lips twitched and she glanced up at him. "Preferably one of Demon's."

He grinned. "His are the best."

"Do you have any?"

He nodded. "One definite benefit of being connected to the family."

"I love the exhilaration one gets when pounding along—I think that's what I enjoy the most."

He blinked. Decided hard riding wasn't the best choice of conversational topics. At least not for him. Especially not with her. "What about dancing?"

"I love to waltz. I even enjoy the older forms, the qua-drilles and cotillions. They might be less fashionable now, but there's a certain . . . reined power in them, don't you think?"

"Hmm." Where was an innocent topic when he needed one?

"Have you ever danced the gavotte?"

"Years ago." And he still remembered it. And of course the thought of dancing that particular measure with her, in full flight, instantly filled his mind.

Searching for distraction, he looked around.

"Get down." His hand on her back, he pressed her down into a low crouch. Hunkering down beside her, he looked into her startled face. "Riders on the road." They were walking parallel to the road to Annan, but a good two hundred yards to the south, using hedges and coppices to screen them from roadbound travelers.

After a moment, he grimaced. "Stay down."

Leaving his hand on her back to ensure she did, he swiveled and raised his head. Looked, then relaxed a trifle. "They didn't see us. They're riding steadily on."

She straightened her back. "Constables?"

Removing his hand, he nodded, looked again, then rose and gave her his hand. Gripping her fingers, he drew her to her feet.

She straightened, sighed, and looked down. "My evening slippers aren't holding up too well."

When he looked down, she slipped her fingers from his and lifted her hems enough for him to see the poor, bedraggled excuse for footwear she had protecting her small feet.

He bit back the curse that leapt to his lips. "Holes?"

"Not so much holes as they're not waterproof. They aren't designed for hiking through soggy fields."

He hadn't thought . . . and clearly neither had Fletcher, Cobbins, or Martha. He looked ahead. "We'll have to get you proper walking shoes. Perhaps in Annan."

She started walking again. "They're all right, at least for the moment."

Falling in beside her, he let the subject lie and put his mind to considering the more immediate details of their flight. He—they—had planned on driving to Richard and Catriona's estate, but now . . .

It was some time later—two miles or so later—when she spoke again. "It's a pity we can't slip back toward Gretna. I was hoping to hide somewhere close—close enough to get a glimpse of this mysterious laird when he arrives."

He grunted. "I'd flirted with the notion myself, but with the authorities as well as him looking for you, it's too dangerous." He glanced at her, then added, "I scouted around, looking for cover, but there wasn't anywhere we could have hidden and in safety watched the inn."

Heather met his eyes briefly, then nodded and marched on. She was starting to accept that he wasn't as arrogantly high-handed as she'd always thought—witness his scouting, trying to find a way to give her what she'd wanted even though he himself had never been that keen, never convinced that a glimpse would be worth the effort. He was probably right, yet he'd tried to find a way to accommodate her wishes.

Despite not getting what she'd wanted, the knowledge made her feel more content.

They walked into a sunset muted by churning clouds. Before the encroaching darkness deepened, Breckenridge paused to check the map.

"We should be nearly at Dornock." He looked ahead, squinted. "I can see roofs ahead—that must be the village."

"We can't just walk up and ask for shelter, can we?" She'd thought through the ramifications. "Those riders would have stopped and warned the villagers about us—about me, at least."

He grunted an assent. He surveyed the still largely flat fields, then touched her arm, pointed a little way further south. "There's a barn there, close enough to reach before the light fails. Let's see what it's like."

She didn't reply, merely started walking.

Tucked in one corner of a field, isolated and at least three fields from the nearest farmhouse, the barn proved sound and filled with hay. Much of it was loose, and the fragrance that surrounded them when they climbed to the loft was redolent with the memory of summer.

Breckenridge looked around. "We'll be warm enough up here, and safe enough." He glanced down at the ladder they'd climbed up. "The ladder isn't fixed—I'll pull it up for the night."

So she'd feel safe. Heather hid a grin; for a man whose expression she could still rarely read, he was becoming quite predictable in some ways.

Setting down her satchel, she slipped off her cloak, flicked it out, and spread it over a wide, deep pile of hay, then turned and sat, wriggling her hips to create a comfortable hollow. Reaching down, she eased off her poor slippers, studied them in the fading light. "I don't suppose we can risk a fire."

Looking up, she met Breckenridge's shadowed eyes.

After a moment, he shook his head. "No. Too risky."

But he'd thought of it. She nodded and set the slippers aside, used her cloak to rub her feet dry, then stretched out her toes, flexed her ankles, and reached beneath her skirts to massage her calves.

He cleared his throat. "We haven't any food, either."

She glanced up, faintly smiled. "I don't think going without food for one night is going to hurt either of us."

He held her gaze, after a moment said, "You're being very accommodating. I was expecting something rather closer to hysterics."

She snorted. "And what good would they do?" She raised a shoulder. "We're in this together, and doing the best we can. I don't expect you to perform miracles." Lying back on her makeshift pallet, she looked up at him. "And as long as you don't expect miracles from me, I daresay we'll manage well enough."

He stared at her, his expression, as usual, impenetrable. Of all the men she'd ever met, he kept his features under the most rigid control. Then he shrugged off the satchels he'd carried, set them near hers, and turned back toward the ladder. "I'm going to check around the building. I won't go far, and I won't be long."

Heather lay back, let her muscles relax, and tracked him by sound. He moved around within the barn, then went outside.

While she waited, she held onto a mental vision of him—imagined him walking around the structure, assessing it. Her brothers, her cousins, were protective men; she was accustomed to the foibles of the species. Breckenridge, however, although every bit as protective, if not more so, hid it better. She considered, then murmured, "No, that's not right." He didn't so much hide his proclivities as mute them, negotiate around them. Make them seem reasonable and sensible and justifiable.

His was a more subtle, but also more effective, approach.

If he'd been one of her brothers, or even one of her cousins, she'd have felt smothered by now—and she'd have been sniping and resisting his orders and restrictions for all she was worth, on principle if nothing else. But because he was reasonable and listened—or at least seemed to listen—to her wishes, then she could be reasonable, too.

Given her previous view of him, that she'd come to the point of regarding him as "reasonable" struck her as exquisitely ironic.

By the time he returned, darkness had fallen, but the moon was half full, shedding sufficient light to make out shapes even inside the barn. When he reached the top of the ladder, she slid her feet back into her slippers, stood, and shook out her skirts. "I need to go outside. I won't go far, and I won't be long."

He froze. She smiled sunnily at him, even if he probably couldn't see well enough to appreciate the effect. She'd given him back his own words. She'd trusted him, now he had to trust her.

With obvious reluctance, he shifted, allowing her to reach the head of the ladder. "It's dark."

"I'll be careful." She started down the ladder, then glanced up at him. "Just stay there."

Reaching the ground, she walked to the barn door, lit by light slanting down through a window high in one side wall. Pulling open the door, she glanced out, then slipped around the corner of the barn to attend to the call of nature.

She walked back inside five minutes later, only to find him waiting just inside the door. She narrowed her eyes at him, but he didn't meet her gaze, simply pulled the door closed, then lifted a heavy beam and angled it across the opening.

"If anyone tries to come in, they'll have to shift that— we'll hear them."

She humphed and walked toward the ladder, wondering if he'd thought of the beam before or after he'd followed her down to the ground.

He trailed close behind her, claimed her hand, and helped her onto the ladder. She climbed up, careful not to get her feet tangled in her skirts. Once she stepped free, he followed her up, then turned and, with surprising ease, hauled up the long ladder.

She settled back on her cloak and watched as, bathed in the faint moonlight, he maneuvered the ladder to lay it along the edge of the loft. Even though he was fully clothed, she still got an impression of the play of muscle necessary to achieve such a feat.

There was no denying Breckenridge was one of the ton's favorite rakes for good reason.

Smiling to herself, she relaxed on her makeshift bed.

He looked at her, then picked up his own cloak, shook it out, and spread it on the hay, not next to her but on the other side of their satchels. She inwardly humphed. While he sat, then lay back and settled, she sat up and pulled her satchel closer. Opening it, she hauled out the other plain gown and her evening gown. The silk, she hoped, would help to keep her warm.

Breckenridge, of course, had simply wrapped his cloak about himself. Given how warm he always seemed to be, he would probably be warm enough. She fussed, laying first the evening gown, then the plain gown over her, then she lay down and wrapped the skirts of her cloak around her.

She was, she told herself, warm enough. She wasn't likely to freeze.

Breckenridge spoke out of the thickening darkness; the moonlight was starting to fade. "We'll head for Annan in the morning—see if we can slip into the town, get some breakfast and shoes for you at least."

"Hmm. I suppose in a town rather than a village we'll have a better chance of escaping attention."

He didn't reply.

"Good night," he eventually murmured.

"Good night." Settling her head on one hand, she closed her eyes.

Silence fell.

Whether it was her hearing sharpening once she'd shut her eyes, or that the sounds only began some minutes after she and Breckenridge had become silent and still, rustlings started, at some distance initially, but as the minutes stretched, she could swear the furtive shifting of the hay was growing nearer, and nearer . . .

She was suddenly wide awake.

Suddenly in a greater panic than she'd been earlier in the day.

The only thought that occurred to her, the only possible way to secure relief, involved shockingly forward behavior.

To escape mice, she could be shockingly forward.

Rising, all but leaping to her feet, she grabbed up her

gowns-cum-covers, swiped up her cloak, and dashed past their mounded satchels to where Breckenridge had stretched out.

Through the dimness she could just make him out, stretched on his back, his arms crossed behind his head. He might have been silent, but he hadn't been asleep. She could feel his frown as he looked at her.

"What are you doing?"

"Moving closer to you." Dropping her gowns, she shook out her cloak and laid it next to his.

"Why?"

"Mice."

He let a heartbeat pass, then asked, carefully, "You're afraid of mice?"

She nodded. "Rodents. I don't discriminate." Swinging around, she sat on her cloak, then picked up her gowns and wriggled back and closer to him. "If I'm next to you, then either they'll give us both a wide berth, or if they decide to take a nibble, there's at least an even chance they'll nibble you first."

His chest shook. He was struggling not to laugh. But at least he was trying.

"Besides," she said, lying down and snuggling under her massed gowns, "I'm cold."

A moment ticked past, then he sighed.

He shifted in the hay beside her. She didn't know what he did, but suddenly she was sliding the last inches down a slope that hadn't been there before. She fetched up against him, against his side—hard, muscled, and wonderfully warm.

Her senses leapt greedily, pleasantly shocked, delightedly surprised; she caught her breath and slapped them down. Desperately; this was Breckenridge—this was definitely not the time.

His arm shifted and came around her, cradling her shoulders and gathering her against him.

"This doesn't mean anything." The whispered words drifted down to her.

Comfort, safety, warmth—it meant all those things.

"I know," she murmured back. Her senses weren't listening. Her body now lay alongside his. Her breast brushed his side; through various layers her thighs grazed his. Her heartbeat had deepened, sped up a little, too. Yet despite the sensual awareness, she could feel reassurance along with his warmth stealing through her, relaxing her tensed muscles bit by bit as, greatly daring, she settled her cheek on his chest.

This doesn't mean anything. She knew what he meant. This was just for now, for this strange moment out of their usual lives in which he and she were just two people finding ways to weather a difficult situation.

She quieted. Listened.

The sound of his heartbeat, steady and sure, blocked out any rustlings.

Thinking of the strange moment, of what made it so, she murmured, "We're fugitives, aren't we?"

"Yes."

"In a strange country, one not really our own, with no way to prove who we are."

"Yes."

"And a stranger, a very likely dangerous highlander, is pursuing us."

"Hmm."

She should feel frightened. She should be seriously worried. Instead, she closed her eyes, and with her cheek pillowed on Breckenridge's chest, his arm like warm steel around her, smoothly and serenely fell asleep.

Breckenridge held her against him, and through senses far more attuned than he wished, followed the incremental falling away of her tension . . . until she slept.

Softly, silently, in his arms, with the gentle huff of her breathing ruffling his senses, the seductive weight of her slender body stretched out against his the subtlest of tortures.

Why had he done it? She might have slept close to him, but she would never have pushed to sleep in his arms. That had been entirely his doing, and he hadn't even stopped to think.

What worried him most was that even if he had thought, had reasoned and debated, the result would have been the same.

When it came to her, whatever the situation, there never was any question, no doubt in his mind as to what he should do.

Her protection, her safety—caring for her. From the first instant he'd laid eyes on her four years ago, that had been his mind's fixation. Its decision. Nothing he'd done, nothing she'd done, had ever succeeded in altering that.

But as to the why of that, the reason behind it . . . even now he didn't, was quite certain and absolutely sure he didn't, need to consciously know.

Exhaling slowly, he let his senses expand, checking the barn for any intrusion, then settled to see out the rest of the night.

Chapter Eight

They set out for Annan a little after dawn. The day was cloudy, but the wind had softened. Given the state of her slippers, Heather was grateful it wasn't raining.

She'd woken to find herself wrapped in her gowns, her cloak, and Breckenridge's, too, but he'd been gone. He'd walked back into the barn as she'd reached the bottom of the ladder; by the time she'd gone out and come back in herself, he'd been climbing down the ladder with their satchels already packed and her cloak over his shoulder.

Side by side, they walked steadily westward. Skirting Dornock village—a few houses lining the road to Annan—to the south took them close to the shores of Solway Firth. The water was gray, but relatively calm. As the sun rose at their backs, the surface of the water took on a rosy hue.

They'd passed Dornock and could see the roofs of Annan ahead when Breckenridge stopped her with a hand on her arm. She glanced at him, saw him looking at the road a few hundred yards to the north. Following his gaze, she saw two riders—both constables, who had been heading west—slow to meet with a pair of their comrades riding in the opposite direction. The four milled, clearly exchanging news, then formed up two by two and headed toward Annan.

She and Breckenridge were traversing a wood, one with plenty of bushes between the trees; as long as they didn't move, they wouldn't be spotted. They held still and watched the four constables ride on. Heather looked ahead; judging by the roofs, Annan wasn't a large town.

As the constables reached the outlying cottages, she glanced down at her slippers. Considered, then asked, "How far to Dumfries?"

Breckenridge glanced at her. After a moment replied, "As the crow flies, which is more or less the route we're walking, about twelve miles."

She grimaced, raised her head. "We'd better get on, then." Suiting action to the words, she stepped out.

Breckenridge kept pace alongside her. She appreciated that he didn't make a fuss, or ask what she meant. She'd spoken first, intentionally absolving him of making any decision that would, as he would see it, adversely affect her well-being.

He held his tongue while they gave Annan a wide berth. For a while they walked along the firth's shores. When the road angled more northwest, enough to allow them back into the fields while maintaining their distance from it, he glanced at her more intently, studied her face. "We could stop at one of the smaller villages and see if we can get something to eat."

She almost smiled. His tone made it clear that he didn't want to risk it but felt he had to make the offer. "We could, but should we?" Halting in the lee of a hedge, beside a stile over which they'd need to climb, she met his hazel gaze. "It'll be much easier, and much safer, for us to slip into and then out of a large town like Dumfries. Any village we stop at . . . even if the people there don't try to capture and hold us, they'll certainly remember us and tell the next constable who rides past."

She wasn't telling him anything he didn't already know. Breckenridge held her gaze. "True, but at the same time, I'd rather you didn't faint. Me carrying you into Dumfries isn't going to make us less noticeable."

Her lips tightened. "I promise I won't faint. I can make it to Dumfries without food, and there's plenty of fresh water, at least."

They'd crossed numerous small streams; the area was riddled with them, and in this season most were in full spate. "If you're sure . . ." He waved her to the stile.

"I am." She reached up and grasped one of the rungs; the stile was a high one, the top higher than his head. She started to pull herself up, but her feet, still clad in her leather-soled dancing slippers, slid on the wet grass.

He caught her about the waist, steadied her.

"Damn!" She huffed, blowing errant strands of hair off her forehead. "You'll have to help me up."

Mentally gritting his teeth, he didn't let himself think, just slid his hands to her hips, gripped, and hoisted her up.

She stifled a gasp, seized the stile's highest bar, and quickly clambered up.

But then she stopped. On the top step of the stile, looking down the other side. After a moment, she said, "The ground's further down on this side than on that."

"Wait there." He climbed up, then swung around her, his long legs making the maneuver easy enough. He climbed down, dropped down to the ground on the other side, glanced quickly around, then turned to her and beckoned. "Come on."

She started climbing down. When she reached the last step, still too far from the ground for her to jump down, he gripped her hips again, lifted her clear, and set her down.

When he released her, she wobbled.

He caught her waist, steadied her. Glanced at her face. "All right?"

Her cheeks were a trifle pink, but whether from the exertion or something else he couldn't tell.

She nodded as he released her. "Yes, thank you." Raising her head, she faced forward, drew breath, then exhaled. "Come on."

Straightening his lips before she saw them twitching, he dutifully fell in beside her.

Halfway across the field, he said, "The reason I wondered

whether you would faint is because my sisters would have. When they were your age they used to starve themselves. If they didn't eat something of a morning, they'd be sure to fall limp before luncheon."

She met his eyes. "Your sisters are significantly older than you. Which makes them very much older than me." She faced forward again, nose elevating. "Fashions change."

"I know." He hesitated, then said, "I just wanted you to know that I didn't imagine you would faint because I think you're weak."

She looked almost as surprised by the explanation as he was. She recovered first, crisply nodded. "Duly noted."

And continued walking.

He kept pace, wondering at himself—wondering why he'd wanted to reassure her. He told himself it was because his sole aim that day was to keep her safe, and that would be much easier if she was speaking to him.

Despite their tonnish lives, both of them spent at least some time each year in the country; it showed as they strode along, both relatively long-legged, their pace an easy, swinging stride that ate the miles to Dumfries.

While they walked, he had plenty of time to dwell on the irony in the situation. A situation that now left him truly appreciative of the very aspects of her nature that had previously irritated him to a near-insufferable degree. Her inner strength of purpose, of will, her independence of thought, and the confidence that showed in her ability to think and act. Previously he'd found those qualities not so much challenging as abrasive.

He was thankful for them now. If she'd been a different sort of female, the sort he might previously have wished her to be, their situation now would have been infinitely worse.

Then again, if she'd been that other, meeker, milder sort of female, she'd have allowed him to haul her out of the inn at Knebworth and take her straight home.

He considered that, weighed it against the outcome of the path they'd taken instead . . . despite all, he couldn't find it in him to disapprove of her stance. Her insistence that she needed to learn all she could of the laird who had sent men to kidnap her or one of her family.

That sort of loyalty, of family protectiveness, was bred in the bone—in him and in her. He could hardly disapprove of something he himself considered sacrosanct.

He glanced at her. Wondered when she would realize what the outcome of this adventure of theirs would be. There was no alternative, none at all. Would she accept it? Or would she try to fight it?

Or would she, as he had, realize that there were far worse fates?

His lips kicked up briefly. Looking ahead, he saw another hedge, another stile.

This one was lower. When they reached it, he climbed over first, then took her hand to help her over.

Didn't release it when she joined him on the ground, instead sliding his fingers fully around hers before turning and walking on.

She shot him a glance, but then settled her fingers in his.

Hand in hand, they walked on to Dumfries.

Fletcher and Cobbins were sitting on rude bunks in a stone-walled cell at the rear of the Customs and Revenue Office in Gretna, slumped, resigned, and praying for deliverance, when the sound of a deep voice, cultured and even-toned, reached them.

Their heads rose. They straightened, straining to hear, to make out words, but the thick stone walls defeated them.

Cobbins met Fletcher's gaze. "It's him, isn't it?"

Slowly, still listening to the distant rumble, Fletcher nodded. "Yes. Thank God." After a moment, he added, "Let's hope he sees his way to getting us out of this."

On the words, a groaning grating told them the heavy door leading to the cells was being opened. As the sound died, they heard, "Thank you. This won't take long."

Someone mumbled something in reply, and the door groaned shut again.

Both Fletcher and Cobbins got to their feet. Both straightened their jackets, smoothed down their hair, rubbed their palms on their thighs.

Relaxed footsteps with a long, easy stride came down the flagged corridor. A second later, the man they knew as McKinsey appeared on the other side of the iron bars that formed the front of the cell.

He appeared even more powerful than they remembered him—as tall, broad-shouldered, as impressively strong, with a face hewn from granite, all harsh planes and sharp cheekbones, and pale, wintry, icy eyes. He was dressed for riding in boots and corduroy breeches, a well-tailored coat hugging his heavy shoulders.

After surveying them for a moment, he arched his winged black brows. "Well, gentlemen? Where's my package?"

Fletcher swallowed. "At the inn—the Nutberry Moss, like you told us."

McKinsey shook his head. "No, not so. I've already been there."

"She's gone?" Cobbins's shock was too genuine to mistake.

McKinsey noted it, then nodded. "She hasn't been seen since before your unfortunate arrest." He transferred his cold gaze to Fletcher. "Incidentally, how did that come about?"

"We don't know." Fletcher knew beyond doubt that their only hope lay in convincing McKinsey of their innocence. "We didn't steal the wretched candlesticks—why would we?" He snorted. "Let alone hide the blessed things in our room."

McKinsey considered him for a moment, then glanced at Cobbins. Then he nodded. "I believe you. I did a reasonably thorough check into your pasts before hiring you, and you've never before shown any inclination to rank stupidity."

"Exactly." Fletcher let his irritation—something close to offense at being taken for a simple thief—show. "Someone must have put the damned things there."

"Indeed," McKinsey said. "The question is who, and even more importantly, why."

Fletcher dared to meet his eyes. "The police?"

"No. I spoke with the innkeeper. The sergeant found the candlesticks where he claimed—in your bags in your room. And the innkeeper isn't aware of anyone else going upstairs that morning. His staff know nothing."

"What about Martha?" Cobbins looked at McKinsey. "The maid we hired, like you asked."

"Ah, yes—she, too, appears to have vanished."

"It wouldn't have been her got the candlesticks," Fletcher said. "Not her style either, and the idea of her finding the magistrate's house and creeping in of a night . . ." He made a scoffing sound. "That's nonsense."

Cobbins nodded. "She's not one for going out at the best of times."

McKinsey studied them, then murmured, "The choice of the magistrate as the victim of the burglary is, I suspect, revealing. Had it been anyone else, the constables would have been much less likely to leap into action as they did. In terms of getting you two out of the way—I am, of course, assuming that that was the purpose of the candlesticks, to remove you both so that the package you were holding for me could be spirited away—the ploy was carefully and very cleverly thought out. So . . . who knew about the girl and was clever enough to devise and effect such a scheme?"

A moment passed, then Cobbins looked at Fletcher. "Timms?"

McKinsey's brows rose. "Who is Timms?"

Fletcher was frowning. "An unemployed solicitor's clerk. Said he was on his way to Glasgow and stopped at the inn—he came in a few hours after us, I think."

"And he stayed?"

Fletcher nodded. "Seems he had a wound—war wound possibly—that was playing up."

"He said because of driving so far in his rattly old pony trap," Cobbins said. "And that was true enough. His trap was ancient."

"So he arrived after you, and was still at the inn when you were arrested?" McKinsey asked.

"Not sure if he was still there." Fletcher exchanged a glance with Cobbins. "He said he was getting ready to leave and drive on to Glasgow in easy stages. He'd waited around long enough."

"What does this man look like?"

"Not as tall as you," Fletcher said. "Not as big. A bit slighter all around. Brown eyes."

"Hazel," Cobbins corrected. "And dark hair—very dark brown. Dressed like a clerk, dark clothes, ordinary stuff. Always appeared a bit scruffy—like he needed a new razor and had lost his hairbrush."

Fletcher nodded agreement.

"How did he speak?" McKinsey asked.

Fletcher shrugged. "Well spoken enough, like you'd expect a London solicitor's clerk to speak." He frowned, and looked at McKinsey. "No real accent, now I think on it. A bit like . . ."

McKinsey smiled chillingly. "A bit like me?" After a moment, he murmured, softly, to himself, "I sincerely hope not." More loudly he asked, "Did Timms get to know the girl?"

Fletcher pulled a face, shook his head. "Not that I saw. He nodded to her—knew she was with us—but he swallowed our story and kept his distance." He glanced at Cobbins.

"Saw him stop beside her and speak with her . . ." Cobbins screwed up his face in thought. "Day before yesterday, it'd be—when she and Martha went for a short walk. We kept watch—one of us—from the inn. Timms was out walking. He stopped beside the girl and sat down—not close—to

154

look at his map. But Martha was right there, next to them, the whole time."

"What about at night?"

"Martha's good at what she does," Fletcher said. "She always took all their clothes, hers and the girl's, and slept on them, so if the girl tried to escape, she'd have to do so all but naked. And they always shared a room."

"Hmm." After a moment, McKinsey nodded. "All right. Here's what we'll do. I'll speak to the magistrate and explain that you'd been south to collect a package for me, that you had it at the inn, but then someone—we have no idea who—stole his candlesticks, put them in your room, and alerted the constables. Once you were taken up, my package disappeared." His wintry eyes met Fletcher's. "I'm confident the magistrate will understand—especially as he has his candlesticks back, and no real evidence to say you two actually took them and it didn't instead happen as I'll claim. Indeed, my missing package can be taken as proof of your innocence of the theft."

Fletcher and Cobbins both nodded. Neither ventured any comment.

McKinsey smiled coldly. "Indeed. In return for my assistance in gaining your release, gentlemen, and for the payment I'll leave waiting for you at the inn—not, sadly, the payment you would have received had you handed over my package as arranged, but enough to satisfy you in the circumstances—in return for both those things, you will oblige me by leaving Gretna and heading back over the border, and forgetting all you ever knew about this episode. Forgetfulness would definitely be in your best interests. I don't care which town you make for, but I do ask that you remain out of Scotland for . . . shall we say the next year?"

There was enough refined menace in McKinsey's eyes to have both Fletcher and Cobbins nodding. Fletcher cleared his throat. "Seems fair."

"Indeed—it is. Eminently fair."

"But what about the package—the girl?"

McKinsey's icy gaze fixed on Fletcher. A heartbeat ticked past, then McKinsey softly said, "I will hunt down my package. I don't believe I will require any help."

Fletcher swallowed, nodded. "Right. Of course."

McKinsey held his gaze for an instant more, then turned away. "I bid you farewell, gentlemen. I'll arrange for your freedom, but it won't happen immediately. Sit quiet, say nothing, and you'll be free by this evening."

Fletcher and Cobbins listened to his footsteps retreat, heard the door to the cells groan open, then shut again.

When silence returned, Fletcher glanced at Cobbins. "That's one scary bugger."

Cobbins nodded and sank back on the bunk. "Don't know about you, but I'm glad we won't be meeting him again."

The man who Fletcher and Cobbins knew as McKinsey was very glad he'd decided to use an alias.

After speaking with the magistrate, who, while he might not be able to place him, had recognized his true station well enough to readily acquiesce to his request that his hirelings be released without charge, McKinsey returned to "reward" the constables, then recruit them in searching for his missing package, and arrange for Fletcher and Cobbins to be held until evening before being released.

By then he would be on his way, whichever way that was.

Mounted on his favorite chestnut gelding, he rode back up the highway to Gretna Green, and the Nutberry Moss Inn. The constables, vocal cords loosened by the largesse he'd distributed, had volunteered that the older woman they'd assumed to be one of Fletcher and Cobbins's accomplices had fled back over the border into England the previous evening; they hadn't bothered giving further chase. Of the girl, however, they'd had no sign.

That the girl must have fled, either alone or, more likely and very possibly worse, in the company of some bounder passing himself off as a solicitor's clerk, preyed on his mind. That definitely wasn't how his plan was supposed to have played out.

But he'd long ago learned the need to flow with fate, to take whatever clouts she sent him and survive. Manage and make the best of things had long been his creed.

In this case, that meant learning where the girl had gone, then following her and rescuing her. Getting his plan back on track and making restitution in whatever way he could, to her at least. Her family would be something else again, but that was too far in the future for him to worry about now.

First, find the girl. Second, get rid of the bounder.

Drawing rein in the Nutberry Moss forecourt, he smiled easily at the young lad who came running to take his horse. He dismounted and handed over the reins. "I'll be maybe an hour, no more. Just walk him a little, then rest him."

Eyes round with awe, the lad tugged his forelock, and reverently led Hercules away. The big gelding had come by the name through having to carry the weight of him on his back.

He walked into the inn. Fletcher and Cobbins would have been surprised to witness the persona he deployed with the innkeeper. He didn't need to frighten the man, so he didn't.

"Timms?" The innkeeper consulted his register. "Aye, m' lord. He came in later on the day your men arrived."

"And when did he leave?"

The innkeeper scratched his ear. "Can't rightly say that he has left, m'lord. His bags and clothes are gone, the girls tell me—all his personal things—but his writing desk is still there, and his trap and his horse are still in the stable. He didn't say anything to me about moving on just yet—said his wound was still playing up. He's paid up for another two nights."

"I see." He thought, then said, "Fletcher and Cobbins will be released later today—they'll be back to claim their luggage." He withdrew a sealed packet from his inside pocket. "I told them I'd leave this for them—if you could make sure

157

they receive it?" The innkeeper nodded and took the packet, stowing it under the counter. "In the meantime, however, if I could see their rooms—the two Fletcher hired, and if I could just look into Timms's room. No harm if there's nothing personal in there."

"Indeed not, m'lord. The room the women used was number one, at the end of the corridor to the left. Fletcher and Cobbins were in room five, that's just by the top of the stairs, and Timms was in room eight—end of the corridor to the right."

He smiled. "Thank you. I'll just have a look around—I won't trouble you further."

"No trouble at all, m'lord. Just call if you want anything."

He climbed the stairs and checked the women's room first. There was nothing left, no belongings of any kind, not even hairpins on the dressing table. Presumably the girl had at least had time to pack, then.

Moving to Fletcher and Cobbins's room, he noted their bags had been left in the wardrobe. Passing on to Timms's room, he stuck his head in, saw, as he'd been told, that the wardrobe, gaping open, was empty. Other than an ancient traveling writing desk on the side table by the bed, there was no sign of any belongings anywhere.

Crossing to the writing desk, he raised the lid. A few sheets of yellowing parchment, an assortment of old nibs and pens, and a small bottle of ink nestled inside. None of the sheets bore any helpful name or address, or, indeed, any mark at all. There was nothing to suggest any of the implements had been used in years; even the piece of blotting paper was blank. Releasing the lid, he raked the room one last time, then walked out.

Stepping into the corridor, he pulled the door shut—and looked consideringly at the narrow servants' stair in the shadows at the corridor's end. When he'd called at the inn earlier, the innkeeper had related the sequence of events that had culminated in Fletcher and Cobbins's arrests. The two women had remained in the parlor, as far as anyone had known. Only much later, when one of the serving girls had thought to look in, surprised that the women hadn't rung for afternoon tea, had their absence been discovered.

The parlor door had been open when he'd come in. Assuming the two women had been inside when the constables had arrived, they would have heard, quite possibly seen, all that had transpired. Martha, certainly, had seen the implications. That explained her rapid and effective flight. And, of course, Martha had left the girl to fend for herself. But if Timms was behind the scheme of the candlesticks, then where had he been? Neither the innkeeper nor his staff had sighted him after breakfast that day.

Looking back down the corridor all the way to the women's room, he felt sure Timms had been there, in his room, playing least in sight while the constables had removed Fletcher and Cobbins. Then . . . he looked again at the stair. If it led to where he thought it did . . .

He went silently down it.

As he'd suspected, the stair debouched into a tiny hall between the kitchen and the inn's back door. He wasn't easily overlooked, yet even he managed to slip past the open doorway of the kitchen and slide out of the back door without being seen.

"So that's how Timms got in and out without being seen by the innkeeper or anyone else."

Stepping off the single step outside the back door, he looked across the inn's stable yard, which was at the side of the inn, on the west, rather than at the rear. If Timms had taken the girl and come out this way . . . why hadn't he taken his trap and driven off?

He walked across the yard and into the stable. The young lad, the stableman, and two helpers were all gathered about a stall admiring Hercules. The lad saw him and jumped to attention. "Do you want him, then, m'lord?"

He smiled. "No, not just yet." He let his smile flow on to

159

the stableman. "I wanted to take a look at Mr. Timms's trap."

The stableman was happy to oblige.

While answering eager questions about Hercules' pedigree, he examined the trap; it was indeed as rickety as Cobbins had made out. As for the nag that went with it . . . if Timms and the girl had taken to the road in the trap, they would have been caught by the constables, who, he'd been told, had ridden out along all the roads in an attempt to capture Fletcher and Cobbins's accomplices.

He'd told Fletcher and Cobbins that he would attend to the matter of the girl himself, but he'd seen no reason not to make use of the constables. He'd used the same story he'd given Fletcher to explain the girl's captivity, and had enlisted the aid of the police in keeping watch on the roads and taking the girl up if they happened to find her.

Thus far, all reports from the riders who had, he'd been assured, been sent out along all the major roads leading out of Gretna Green had been negative. No one had sighted the girl, and the constables had a fair description.

He was learning to respect Timms's intelligence.

Thanking the stableman, saying he'd be back for Hercules in a few minutes, he walked out of the stable and paused, looking back at the inn.

Then he turned and surveyed the land around about. Flat fields. With his height, he could even see a glimmer of light off the firth a mile or so south.

If Timms had been clever enough to have foreseen the danger in using the trap, then he would also have realized that if they'd walked away across the fields in almost any direction they would have been easily spotted from the inn, if not from the ground floor, then certainly from the upper floor.

In any direction but one.

Turning back, he viewed the stable, with its high roof above the hayloft. It effectively blocked the view of the fields directly behind it.

He walked around the stable, to the short stretch of grass at the rear.

To the stile that gave access into the field beyond.

He was a highlander born and bred; he could track most things over rocky ground.

Tracking a man and a woman over soft, damp earth was insultingly easy.

But the boot print he found by the stile bothered him. He stared at it for a time before he realized why. Then he stamped his own boot print close by and compared the two.

And felt grimness as well as puzzlement steal through him.

Timms—whoever he was, and he was increasingly certain the man was no unemployed solicitor's clerk—was wearing extremely well-made riding boots.

The girl, in contrast, was still shod in dancing slippers.

Straightening, he looked across the field. They'd made for the trees cresting a rise, just over a mile away. Once past those . . . given they'd avoided all the police patrols, they must have kept to the fields.

Easy enough for him to track, given he now had a direction. And with the firth to the south, with just a narrow strip of land between the road and the shore, he could make good time along the road, and just periodically check to confirm their direction.

Finding them wouldn't be hard.

Lips setting, he turned and strode back to the stable. Nearing the door, he called for his horse.

Chapter Nine

Breckenridge, with Heather beside him, walked into Dumfries in the early afternoon.

The first thing he saw as, still walking comfortably hand in hand they headed toward the main street of shops, was two constables loitering on the corner of one of the main intersections.

Avoiding them wasn't difficult, but the sight reminded him just how careful they needed to be. Reemerging from an alley between two shops, they joined the crowds thronging the main thoroughfare.

"Just as well we waited until Dumfries." Heather drew her cloak closer. "Annan wouldn't have been crowded enough to risk being on the main street."

Breckenridge grunted.

She glanced up at him. "Are there others close?"

He could see over the heads of the bustling hordes. "I can't see any along the street, but I suspect there'll be more at the big intersection up ahead." He glanced down at her. "We'll be safe enough if we stay among the crowds. If we see any uniforms getting close, we'll nip down a side street." Dumfries was thankfully well supplied with those. He raised his head, scanned again.

"Speaking of which." Using his hold on her hand, he drew her out of the crowd and down a narrow cobbled alley to where a small sign swinging above a door proclaimed the place within to be the Old Wall Tavern. Halting before the door, he met her gaze. "We need food first, then some shoes for you."

She peered through the thick glass in the window beside the door. "This looks all right."

He opened the door and, remembering that they weren't gentry for the moment, walked in, towing her behind him. He chose a table around a corner, out of sight of anyone looking in.

The serving girl came bustling up. "You can 'ave your choice of the last of lunchtime's shepherd's pie, or there's venison pie for dinner that's just come out of the oven."

They both opted for the venison pie. Breckenridge ordered ale for himself and watered ale for Heather. When the serving girl left them, he murmured, "No tea, much less wine in places like this."

Heather shrugged; her lips curved as she looked around. "Truth be told, I'm rather curious. I've never had watered ale before."

He grunted again, saw her shoot him a look that suggested his communication skills needed polishing. He pretended not to notice. He couldn't have told her what he felt about her comment, much less what he felt at that moment—had felt increasingly over the last hours.

Her feet hurt. Not that she was limping, but especially once they'd hit the cobbles and stone paving of the town, she'd been placing her feet carefully. Of course she'd said nothing, had complained not at all, but that only made him feel even more . . . whatever it was he felt. And no matter what she'd said, she had to be feeling faint from lack of nourishment. Females couldn't go without food for as long as men, especially females who had no fat to speak of stored about their person.

He told himself the concern he felt over her not eating— over not being able to feed her—was simply residual terror that she would fall at his feet in a faint . . . but he knew very well it wasn't that. Or not simply that. He'd actually felt torn

163

over which of her ills to attend to first—her feet or her stomach. Feeding her had won out purely because he'd spotted the little tavern and it had looked safe.

Safety—hers—remained his principal concern.

The venison pie proved surprisingly tasty.

Breckenridge's conversational abilities—Heather knew he had them—remained in abeyance, absent, but she'd seen behavior like his before, in her brothers and her cousins, when they were absorbed with protecting females they, for whatever reason, considered in their care. Why grunts should so predominate she had no idea, but if anything she found his inability to engage his customary glib tongue amusing.

Admittedly, she was grateful, too. Grateful for his protection, which was something she'd never thought to be.

When they'd cleaned their plates and drained their ales— she'd found her watered ale unexpectedly refreshing—he left coins on the table, then escorted her outside. Immediately they stepped out of the door, he reclaimed her hand, as if by some right. She settled her fingers within the reassuring clasp of his and decided not to dwell on it.

They rejoined the crowds in the High Street, ambling along, searching for the cobbler's shop the serving girl had told them of. Breckenridge walked close beside her, by his sheer bulk protecting her from the bustling shoppers. If he'd done such a thing in Bond Street, she would have been incensed. Here, far from home, she found his nearness—even his hovering when she paused outside the cobbler's shop to study the wares displayed in the window—comforting, reassuring, simply soothing.

She knew all too well that in men like him, protectiveness had a bad habit of converting to snarling possessiveness, but in the circumstances, she would accept the risk.

"Those boots might do." She pointed to a pair of half boots, heavier than any she owned, but they were the only pair that looked anywhere near small enough for her feet. "Let's go in."

She opened the door and, to the tinkle of a bell, walked into the shop. Breckenridge glanced around outside before following her in; he had to duck to pass through the doorway.

At the rear of the small shop, the cobbler, a small, wiry man with a pair of pince-nez perched on his nose, looked up from the shoe he was mending.

Heather smiled. "I need a pair of walking boots." She gestured to the window. "I wonder if I might try on that pair?"

The cobbler looked pleased. He came out from behind his counter. Wiping his hands on a rag, he nodded to Breckenridge, then eased past them to reach into the window. "Good eye, you have." He turned with the boots in his hand. "These are a fine pair. Did all the work myself, so I know."

"It's the size that concerns me." Heather turned to look for somewhere to sit.

"Have a seat on the bench there, mistress." The cobbler pointed to a narrow bench along part of the side wall. "And we'll see if these will do for you."

Heather sat and slipped off her evening slippers, quickly pushing them back behind her stockinged feet and her skirts the better to hide them. If the cobbler saw . . . she doubted many ladies came walking into his shop in all-but-destroyed London ballroom slippers.

Breckenridge saw. Realized. He reached out and lifted the walking boots from the cobbler's hands. "I'll help her."

Going down on one knee, letting his back and shoulders shield Heather's legs and feet from the cobbler, he set one boot down, took the other in one hand, and with his free hand reached for her foot.

Found it—closed his hand around a slender arch encased in the sheerest of silk stockings.

She jumped at the contact.

A part of him did, too.

A blush rising to her cheeks, she somewhat breathlessly said, "Don't forget I'm ticklish."

He glanced at her, met her gaze, and knew she was lying.

165

She wasn't ticklish, but she was sensitive, especially when he was touching, cradling, all but stroking her as-close-to-naked-as-made-no-difference foot.

One part of him cursed; the rest was fascinated.

Looking down, he steeled himself and slipped the boot he held onto her foot, braced the sole as she pushed her foot in and settled her toes. He glanced at her face. "All right?"

Holding his gaze, she moistened her lips, then nodded. "Yes. Let's try the other."

They managed getting her other foot shod with rather less sensual drama. He got her to stand and hold her hems up a trifle so he could lace the boots. Then, swiping up her discarded slippers, surreptitiously crushing them in one hand, he rose and stepped back.

She walked the three paces across the small shop.

While the cobbler was distracted, Breckenridge shoved the slippers into one of his satchels. Heather turned, saw, paused until he reclosed the satchel, then walked back.

He met her gaze. "How are they?"

She nodded. "They'll do."

The cobbler, initially put out at having his role in fitting a young lady usurped, rediscovered his smile.

While Breckenridge negotiated the price, then paid, Heather walked back and forth, ostensibly to break the boots in as best she could, in reality to try to calm the surging tide of sensual awareness that had, at Breckenridge's touch, all but swamped her.

Even now, she could feel the seductive warmth of his large, hard palm, the reined strength that had sent shards of thrilling sensation lancing through her.

Ridiculous in a way, but who would have thought her foot could be so sensitive? So sensitive in such a very improper way?

She was still dwelling on the revelation when he escorted her from the shop, back into the midafternoon bustle.

As they started along again, merging with the shoppers, he lowered his head and grumbled, "Didn't Martha have the sense to provide you with thicker hose?"

She nodded. "But they were so coarse I couldn't bear to wear them—they scratched."

Breckenridge fleetingly closed his eyes. The image her words conjured—of the finest, most delicate silken skin lining sleek, feminine inner thighs—wasn't one he needed to dwell on.

Opening his eyes, he looked ahead, then nudged her toward another alley. "There's two constables wandering slowly this way. We'll have to go around."

The street they came out on was lined with market stalls selling all manner of fresh produce. They exchanged a glance, then he stood watch while she selected and bargained for apples, some dried fruits, a loaf of seed bread, and a large bag of nuts. He saw a stall selling water skins and added one to their haul. Satchels bulging, they continued on, keeping a wary eye out for ambling constabulary.

They eventually found themselves on Buccleuch Street. "We should get off the pavements." He nodded toward the window of a coffeehouse opposite. "Let's go in there and check the map, and work out our best way forward."

Crossing the street, they entered the coffeehouse, which proved to be quite large and helpfully ill lit. Heather led the way to a table in the shadows along one wall and toward the rear.

A girl came bustling up. He ordered coffee, and after some discussion, Heather ordered a pot of tea and two large plates of scones.

He arched a brow as the girl departed. "Still hungry?"

Heather shrugged. "I'm sure their jam and scones will be lovely—country-made usually are." She suddenly looked conscious, then fixed her eyes on his. "We have enough money, don't we? I mean, don't you?"

He nearly laughed at her look, then waved. "Plenty. I got more when I stopped in Carlisle. Money isn't on our list of concerns."

"Good." She propped her chin in one palm and met his eyes across the table. "We have concerns enough as it is."

He nodded. "How are the boots?"

"Quite good. He was right, the cobbler. They are well made."

"All right. So . . ." He pulled the map from his coat pocket, unfolded, then refolded it so the section they needed was exposed. He set it against the wall between them, so they could both see it. "We're here." He pointed to Dumfries. "And Carsphairn—the village—is there. How to get from here to there is what we need to decide."

The girl returned with his coffee, Heather's tea, and two plates piled high with buttery scones. For ten minutes, they were silent, but after polishing off his second scone loaded with blackberry jam and cream, he picked up his coffee mug, sipped, and returned his attention to the map. "Nice scones."

"Hmm."

The sound made his lips twitch. It was one of the things he was learning to like about her; she appreciated the small pleasures.

How she would react to larger, more intense pleasures . . .

He blinked, and forced himself to refocus on the map. "Let's list all our options first. We could hire a gig and drive—the most obvious way to get from here to there."

Heather poked a bit of jam-laden scone past her lips. "Or we could hire horses and ride—and if we did that, we could go cross-country, not by the major roads. We could take this route." With one fingertip she traced a minor road—more like a country lane—that went across and over the hills.

He considered it. "That route looks shorter, but it'll almost certainly take longer because of the climbing and switching back and forth through the passes. Against that, it will almost certainly be free of patrolling constables, and at this time of year, there's little likelihood of the passes being blocked—the way should be clear."

Heather took a long, revivifying sip of her tea, then sighed and set down the cup. "But we can't risk hiring a gig or any carriage, not even horses, can we?"

Breckenridge met her eyes, then grimaced. "I've been toying with the notion, but I can't see how to do it without leaving some trace. The constabulary isn't foolish—they'll have alerted all the stables. And we have to assume we have the mysterious laird on our heels, too. He must have arrived in Gretna by now. We can't afford to assume we're free of him, and he'll certainly check every possible place we might try to hire from."

Heather nodded briskly. "If we can't hire horses, then we'll have to walk."

Breckenridge hesitated, his eyes on hers, then quietly asked, "Are you up for that?"

Not, she noted, could she manage that; he really was remarkably attuned to women.

Suppressing a smile, she nodded. "I walk quite a lot when at home. These hills may be higher than the Quantocks, but they're not horribly mountainous, either. I'll manage."

He looked at her, then said, "If you can, then I'd prefer to play safe—to do everything we possibly can to avoid both the constables and the laird if he's searching. How long it takes us to get to the Vale is less important than that we reach there safely."

She nodded again. "I agree. For us, the less-traveled way, the least likely way, is the best option."

He reached for the map. "The country lanes, then." He consulted the map, then said, "We need to head out on the main road to Glasgow. The road we want gives off that a mile or two out of town."

She looked past him, out through the front window of the coffee shop. "The light's starting to wane. We should go."

They drained their mugs. Crumbs were all that was left of the scones.

The girl came to take their payment.

"Which is the road to Glasgow?" Breckenridge asked.

The girl pointed right. "Go straight along the street, across the bridge over the river, then turn right. You can't miss it."

Breckenridge thanked her and left a small tip—the sort an unemployed solicitor's clerk might leave.

The girl bobbed and, smiling, showed them out.

Stepping into the street, Breckenridge saw two constables walking the pavement, but by fate's blessing they had their backs to them and were walking away from them, away from the bridge over the river. "Come on." He'd already taken Heather's hand. He glanced at her head, at the shawl she had slung about her shoulders. "Can you wind the shawl about your hair? It'll make you a trifle less recognizable."

She drew her hand from his and complied.

Then she reached for his hand again, just as he reached for hers.

Together, hand in hand, side by side, they walked steadily, resisting a very real urge to hurry, along the street, across the bridge, and out of Dumfries.

The highlander calling himself McKinsey rode into Dumfries an hour later. The first thing he noted as he walked Hercules along, heading toward High Street, was a number of constables either watching the main road or patrolling the pavements on foot.

The constables were searching for a girl. He, however, was searching for a couple.

He'd found their tracks in the fields immediately southeast of the town, had seen where they'd veered to join the road leading into the town proper. He debated sharing his insight with the constables but decided against it. The constables here most likely wouldn't know that it was he who had insti-gated their search, which would necessitate detailed explanations, but more importantly, should he find the girl and the bounder she was with, he wanted to be free to deal with the man in his own way—silently and anonymously.

Turning off the main street into the yard of the Globe Inn, he left Hercules safe in the stable and headed on foot into the warren of streets that formed the center of the town.

He was Scottish; he could ask questions and, by and large, people would happily answer. All he needed to do was allow a touch of his native brogue to slide into his voice.

He'd found the barn where the fugitive pair had spent the night. He'd tracked them steadily on; somewhat to his surprise they hadn't stopped at any village, not even in Annan, to eat. From what he'd understood of how they'd left the inn at Gretna Green, they shouldn't have had any food with them. Which meant that by now, they should be dizzy with hunger.

Eating would be at the top of their list of things to do in Dumfries. As it was market day, the town would have been crowded throughout the day; they would have had excellent cover. More than enough to avoid the notice of the constables patrolling the streets.

From their tracks, he estimated that the pair had entered the town at least three, possibly four hours ahead of him. Starting at the lower end of High Street, he stopped at every eatery and asked after his brother and his lass, explaining that he'd missed them and was trying to catch them up; from what he'd learned of Timms, the relationship would pass well enough.

He struck gold early at the Old Wall Tavern just off High Street. The serving girl couldn't tell him anything about the pair's eventual direction, but she sent him to the cobbler a little further north along the main street. There, he learned of their purchase. Remembering the girl's slippers, he wasn't surprised, but he couldn't decide whether the purchase of walking boots specifically implied anything.

The cobbler, when applied to, shrugged. "Only pair I

had in her size, so it could have just been that that made her choose them." A second later, the old man grinned. "Mind you, you should warn your brother—he's been living in Lunnon too long. Charged 'im the full Lunnon price, I did, and he didn't turn a hair. Just pulled out the coins and handed them over. Not short of the ready, is he?"

He tipped his head, smiling as if in amused agreement. "No." Pushing away from the counter, he walked to the door. "I'll be sure to remind him. He's been away too long."

Stepping out of the shop, he closed the door—and let his easy expression fall away. Plenty of money, and neither the serving girl nor the cobbler, both of whom had seen both him and Timms up close, had batted a lash at the notion that they were brothers.

Timms, the bounder, the supposed unemployed solicitor's clerk, was taking on new dimensions.

Lips setting even more grimly, he turned and continued up the street. The cobbler had had no insight into which road the pair had been making for, but he'd noticed that they'd headed north from his door.

More than an hour later, after he'd exhausted every possible place they might have stopped at, or been spotted from, all along High Street and then west out along the road to Edinburgh, he stalked back toward the center of the town. Could they have decided they were safe enough to stop in Dumfries for the night?

Given the number of constables about, given how careful the pair had thus far been, he seriously doubted it.

Halting at the top of High Street, he looked west into the setting sun, down the length of Buccleuch Street to the bridge over the Nith. And remembered Fletcher saying that Timms had been on his way to Glasgow. Of course Fletcher had also believed Timms was an unemployed solicitor's clerk, but . . . what if, whoever Timms was, he really had been heading for Glasgow before becoming distracted by the Cynster chit?

Stifling a sigh, he started down Buccleuch Street, stopping at every shop, asking after his errant sibling and his lass.

The girl in the coffeehouse remembered them.

He could barely believe his luck. Not only had she in passing overheard them agreeing to go on by foot, but later they'd asked her for directions to the Glasgow Road.

Thanking the girl with his most charming smile as well as a couple of coins, he sat down and ordered coffee and a large slice of ginger cake.

While he drank and ate, he weighed his options. It was already dusk; night would soon close in. Setting out now . . . he would run the risk of missing his quarry, passing them all unknowing in the dark. If the pair followed their previous night's pattern, they would find some barn or perhaps a farmer's cottage in which to spend the night, then be out on the road again early in the morning.

He knew the Glasgow Road. Knew the long, open stretches that lay between Dumfries and Thornhill. Mounted on Hercules, catching up with the pair tomorrow, arranging to come up with them on one of those long, lonely stretches, would be simple, easy, and certain. He'd have plenty of opportunity to watch them from a distance, to gauge what was between them, and then decide what to do.

And then do it.

Meanwhile . . . better that he and Hercules spend a comfortable night, then set out refreshed in the morning.

Decision made, cake consumed, and coffee drained, he rose, dropped payment and a sizeable tip on the table, then headed back to the Globe Inn.

Chapter Ten

The light had faded from the western sky, leaving a sunset of swirling purples and blues, when Heather and Breckenridge walked into the tiny hamlet of Gribton.

They'd turned off the main road to Glasgow about two miles north of the bridge in Dumfries, onto the lane they'd chosen to follow across and over the hills. A stone circle sitting in a field bordering the lane had caught their interest, but they hadn't dallied. Breckenridge's map was reasonably detailed; they'd felt confident enough of finding their way, but had wanted to put as much distance as possible between themselves and Dumfries before seeking shelter for the night.

The lane would take them through a series of passes between various peaks. With luck, they would reach the main pass tomorrow, and might even reach the Vale, but for tonight they had to find some resting place.

Which had led them to Gribton. As they'd walked further inland, the landscape had changed from flat near the firth to rolling pastures, with denser hedgerows and taller trees. They'd spotted the roofs of Gribton as the sun had started to dip beneath the horizon. Rather than risk continuing on to the next village along the country lane, they'd turned off it down a track that had led to the five cottages clustered around a country crossroads.

Breckenridge halted in the middle of the track, in the middle of the cottages. "Which one?"

Her hand still in his, Heather surveyed their choices. "Let's try the middle one." Neat, whitewashed, with a sound slate roof, the cottage nestled between two trees just off the track. It appeared the most prosperous of the five abodes.

With her beside him, Breckenridge halted on the stoop and knocked on the green painted door.

The woman who opened it wore a harassed expression, instantly explained by the bevy of children who came racing up to crowd behind her. Ineffectually pushing them back, she looked at Breckenridge, then at Heather. "Yes?"

Breckenridge nodded politely. "We were wondering, ma'am, if you could put us up for the night. We're on our way up into the hills. We'd be happy to pay for a room if you have one."

The woman looked torn, but then glanced at the brood clustering behind her and sighed. "I can't. But"—looking back at them, she waved further down the track—"if you ask at the last cottage, the old couple who lives there, the Cartwrights, could most likely put you up. Their son and his wife moved up to Glasgow a couple of months back, so they've the room and could use the coin, too."

Breckenridge smiled; Heather did, too. "Thank you."

With nods all around, they retreated, leaving the woman to shoo the children back and shut the door.

Returning to the track, they headed for the last roof they could see, that of a cottage sunk within a small plot of garden. Before they reached its boundary, Breckenridge halted.

When Heather stopped, too, he drew her to face him. "We can't expect to get more than one room, and to get that room, they'll need to believe that we're man and wife."

Even if he could get another room at one of the other cottages, there was no way he could leave her alone in a separate building, not with the mysterious laird possibly following them.

Somewhat to his relief, she merely shrugged. "So we'll let

them believe we're married, and if they ask outright, we lie."

Releasing her, he tugged the signet ring off his little finger, then reached for her hand. "And you wear this"—he slid the ring onto the third finger of her left hand—"so with any luck they won't even think to ask."

She held up the hand as if admiring the ring, then swung the seal around so only the band showed and nodded. "All right."

It wasn't quite the way he'd imagined putting a ring on her finger, but . . .

Retaking her hand, he led her on to the gate in the low hedge before the cottage, and through it to the front door.

This time an old man, long and lanky once, but stooped now, answered his knock. When Breckenridge inquired about a room, the old man turned and called, "Emma?"

The old woman who bustled to the door was as short and round as the old man was tall and thin. When she heard of their request, she smiled sweetly. "Yes, of course. Come you in."

The old man stood back and waved them inside. Breckenridge ushered Heather in, then followed, stepping into a neat parlor.

"This way." The old woman beckoned. "I'm Mrs. Cartwright, and that"—she waved back at the old man—"is Mr. Cartwright, of course."

Heather was grateful Breckenridge had thought of giving her his ring. It felt warm and strangely heavy on her finger. They followed Mrs. Cartwright through the tiny kitchen to a door in the rear wall.

Opening the door, Mrs. Cartwright set it swinging and stepped back to let them past her. "We added this room on when our son married. I'll just get a candle so you can see to set down your bags."

Heather stepped into the small, spare room. There was only one window, in the end wall, but it was heavily curtained. Most of the floor space was claimed by the bed, one wide enough for two, pushed into the far corner. A tiny cabinet stood in the nearer corner, leaving only a narrow walk space at the foot of the bed and along one side.

"Here." Mrs. Cartwright returned, shielding a candle flame.

Heather took the candlestick. "Thank you." She moved to set it on the corner cabinet.

Breckenridge, who'd halted at the foot of the bed, shrugged off the two satchels he carried and set them down, then removed his cloak.

Setting down her satchel beside the cabinet, Heather unwound her shawl, then slipped off her cloak. She turned as Mrs. Cartwright said, "You'll find the sheets aired, and there's two blankets on. I always keep the room ready in case our son and his wife come for a visit."

"Thank you—I'm sure we'll be very comfortable." Much more comfortable than in a hayloft. Heather smiled. "We've been traveling for a few days. We're grateful you could put us up."

"Oh, nonsense. We're glad to be able to. Now." Mrs. Cartwright fixed her surprisingly bright blue eyes on Breckenridge. "Have you eaten? Mr. Cartwright and I have already had our tea, but there's some soup and bread, if you'd like it?"

"Thank you," Breckenridge said. "That would be very welcome. We had lunch in Dumfries, but that was a while ago."

"Oh, I know how you lads eat, never fear." Mrs. Cartwright patted Breckenridge's arm, then bustled out. "I'll just set the soup pot back on the fire."

Heather pressed her lips tight, holding back a laugh as she bent to blow out the candle. Breckenridge looked faintly stunned at being called a "lad." But he followed Mrs. Cartwright back into the kitchen, stepping in to relieve her of the heavy soup pot and lift it onto the hook over the kitchen fire.

Without being asked, he crouched and tended the blaze.

Mrs. Cartwright smiled down at him approvingly, then looked at Heather. "Come along, dear, and I'll show you the necessaries."

The "necessaries" proved to be a small bathing chamber-cum-washhouse giving off a tiny back porch, and an outhouse beyond. The main chamber contained a pump, which Mrs. Cartwright said came off the outside well.

"Plenty of water, bracing cold though it may be." Mrs. Cartwright pulled a clean towel from a shelf. "I'll just leave this towel here for you, dear." Setting the towel on the washstand, she glanced around. "My son built this for us when he and his wife were living here."

"You must miss them," Heather said.

Mrs. Cartwright sighed. "Aye, we do, but you can't keep young people from living their lives, now, can you? Wouldn't be right."

She led the way back into the kitchen. Heather followed her in, then excused herself to return and make use of the "necessaries." After washing her face and hands, she felt considerably more presentable. A tiny mirror hanging above the basin allowed her to neaten her thoroughly disarranged coiffure. If her London maid could see her, she'd faint.

Feeling considerably more the thing, she rejoined Breckenridge and Mr. and Mrs. Cartwright in the kitchen. Breckenridge and Mr. Cartwright had settled to discussing the land around about and local farming.

Mrs. Cartwright ladled out two steaming bowls of soup and set half a loaf of bread and two pats of butter on the table, then directed Breckenridge and Heather to "eat up."

They sat and did, while Mr. Cartwright produced a pipe and quietly puffed, and Mrs. Cartwright filled their ears with a catalogue of little things—like the harvest she hoped to get this year from her prize damsons, and speculation that their son and his wife would return for a few days at Easter.

It was a curiously soothing half hour, a reminder that, despite their flight and the potential threat posed by the mysterious laird, life still went on in myriad calm and quiet ways.

By the time she mopped out her soup bowl with a piece of bread, Heather felt a lot more inwardly settled and satisfied than the soup alone could account for.

This was the country. The Cartwrights, like all country folk, retired early. They bade Breckenridge and Heather a good night, and left them seated about the kitchen table, a single lighted candle between them.

Heather studied the flickering flame, then sighed. "We should get to bed, but I'm going to seize the chance to have a proper wash first."

Breckenridge pushed the candlestick toward her. "Go ahead."

Heather rose, and with the candle retreated first to their little room to fetch her cloak and shawl, then out to the bathing chamber. There she set her teeth, stripped to the skin, washed, dried herself, then, teeth close to chattering, hurriedly re-donned her chemise, wound the shawl about her torso, then enveloped herself in her cloak. Slipping her feet, now clean, back into her new walking boots, swiping up her gown, she rushed back into the kitchen and straight through into their little room, saying as she passed, "I've left the candle in there for you. There's another one in here. I'll light it in a moment."

Breckenridge watched her streak past. Any impulse to laugh was slain by the thought that she almost certainly wasn't wearing much beneath her cloak.

Which wasn't going to make the night any easier for him, trying to find sleep while in the same room as temptation incarnate.

Why *she* now figured as temptation incarnate to his lustful mind wasn't a question he wished to dwell on.

Rising, he retreated to the bathing chamber and made use of the facilities, taking his time in the hope—almost certainly vain—that she would fall asleep before he returned to the room. He examined his beard, now grown in and thickening, and made a mental note to hunt out his shaving kit in the morning. And washing and combing out his rumpled hair wouldn't be a bad idea either.

Eventually acknowledging that there was a limit to how long he could put off the inevitable, he picked up the candle and headed back to the kitchen. He checked that the fire was nicely banked, then pushed open the door to their room . . . to see Heather snuggled down in the bed, closer to the wall, leaving more than half the bed vacant.

She was lying on her side, the covers outlining the quint-essentially feminine curves of her hip and shoulder. Her hair was down. She'd brushed it; gleaming strands of gold laced the ivory pillows.

She'd left the candle burning on the cabinet beside the bed. Shifting her head, she looked at him as he paused in the doorway.

Her expectation couldn't have been clearer.

Moving slowly, thinking furiously, he stepped into the room and shut the door. He hadn't got much sleep in the barn the previous night; if at all possible, he'd like to sleep tonight. Blowing out his candle, he crossed to place it with the other still burning on the cabinet. Keeping his eyes from Heather's, he moved back to the end of the bed, sat, and pulled off his boots. Setting them by the door, he straightened, glanced around at the available floor, then bent to pick up his cloak.

"What are you doing?"

Without looking her way, he flicked out his cloak, let it fall. "I'll sleep on the floor."

From the corner of his eye, he saw her jerk upright. Fleetingly—instinctively—he closed his eyes, then peeked sideways through his lashes. She'd clasped the covers over her breasts as she'd sat up—thank Heaven; beneath the sheet, all she appeared to have on was her flimsy chemise.

The candlelight flashed off the gold band on her finger. His ring. The sight momentarily transfixed him. He shook off the effect, told himself he might as well get used to it; that band and all it proclaimed would be real soon enough.

Predictably, she frowned at him. "Don't be ridiculous!" The words were a forceful whisper. She hesitated, then said, "I know a bed is—stupidly in my view and very likely yours, too—considered to be a somewhat different proposition than a pile of hay in a barn. But I'm no princess, and you're no lowly knight. We're in this together, and there's no reason we can't share this bed."

Oh, yes there is. He was tempted to tell her why, graphically, but stating such facts aloud might not help.

Stating, for instance, that he no longer trusted himself to keep a proper distance—not after last night, not after the events of the day. A thousand little things had abraded his control; he didn't need it stretched further, put under more strain.

And on top of his own compulsive desires, there were hers to manage as well. She was attracted to him; most women, most ladies, were. And young unmarried ladies—like her— were the worst; as a rule, they glorified him, more or less casting him as some sexual god. That was simply a fact— one he'd grappled with all his adult life—and as he knew to his cost, in a deeper sense that type of adulation meant nothing at all.

In this, he trusted her even less than he trusted himself.

And while not being able to trust himself to keep her at arm's length—even though she was virginal, totally inexperienced, enthusiastic rather than accomplished, in uncounted ways the antithesis of the sophisticated ladies whose beds he occasionally deigned to grace—was of itself distinctly odd, that was another issue he didn't want to dwell on.

Not now. Certainly not here.

Slowly turning his head, he met her gaze, his own steady, his expression impassive. "I'll sleep on the floor because we don't need any further complications in our relationship at present."

When he was serious, as he was now, most people had the sense to give way.

Her lips thinned. Her eyes narrowed on his. "I realize,"

she stated, her tone sharper, but still at a whisper, "that you want to be bullheadedly protective, honorable, and all the rest. But in case you haven't noticed, the temperature is already falling, and will assuredly fall even more dramatically before dawn, and as there's no fire I'll freeze, and be too busy shivering to sleep, so if you really wanted to be protective and honorable you'd lie down here"—she jabbed a finger at the bed beside her—"and keep me warm."

She held up the finger. "Furthermore, if you look down, you'll see that the space between the bed and the wall is significantly narrower than your shoulders—which is why you're standing at an angle right now. If you try to sleep there . . . what if you turn over and knock yourself out on the bottom of the bed? Who's going to protect me from that damned laird if you're unconscious?"

Hands rising to his hips, he narrowed his eyes back at her. That she was attempting to manipulate him shouldn't be a surprise. Regardless . . . his ring continued to flash in the light, taunting him. "I—"

Up shot her hand; the ring flashed again. "I haven't finished yet."

Heather held his hard gaze, driven by she knew not what to win this argument. The notion that he would rather sleep on the cold floor than in the comfort of the bed beside her offended her, infuriated her, at some level she didn't truly understand. If they were partners, equals, together facing all this, then they should share the bed; that was all there was to it.

And she knew what particular scruple was, beneath all his excuses, keeping him from complying.

"You don't need to imagine that by sharing a bed with me you'll compromise me—or rather that that fact will affect my future life in any degree."

He blinked; in his usually unreadable face she detected a moment's confusion.

"Yes," she went on, "I'm perfectly well aware that after a

journey such as this my prospects of ever marrying will effectively be nil. But they already were."

Because the one man she might possibly have married had never seen her as a marriageable female. He stood before her now, and almost certainly still saw her as a too-young young lady. Witness this argument.

He stood before her refusing even to share a bed, even in these circumstances, arguing as only he would, deeming it an unwise "complication," no less.

Regardless of anything, they never would, never could, marry now. The only reason he would now offer for her hand was because he felt forced to it by honor, by circumstance— a reason for marriage she would never accept. A reason her mother, her sisters, her aunts, all her female acquaintance would understand that she could never accept.

To have a man forced to marry her would be anathema.

To have *Breckenridge* forced to marry her . . . was unthinkable.

"I know society as well as you do." She continued more calmly, but no less decisively, "I'm twenty-five. In a few months, I'll be declared formally on the shelf, and that will be that. I've already decided what to do with the rest of my life—this journey and its outcome won't materially affect my plans."

He was frowning. After a moment, he asked, "These plans of yours—what are they?"

As if he didn't believe she truly had any.

She smiled, tight-lipped. "I like children, and I know Catriona has many under her wing, quite aside from her own. I'd already thought to visit the Vale this summer and stay for a time, learning more about what Catriona and her staff do, then go home to Somerset and explore what I might do there. So, you see, I have it all worked out—this journey merely moves my plans forward a few months. Whatever social repercussions flow from my kidnapping and this subsequent flight with you won't affect me in the least—in large part I won't even be aware of them, of what the ton might think and say."

Holding his gaze, yet as usual totally unable to read his expression, she decided that, in this instance, total honesty would serve her best. "And just to make matters crystal clear, while I comprehend that society might well deem a marriage between us the only acceptable outcome, I will not be a party to any socially dictated marriage. I would never marry a man who only sought to marry me to preserve his, and possibly my, honor." She paused, still holding, or more accurately now trapped by his hard hazel gaze, by eyes that seemed to bore into her with an intensity she couldn't quite comprehend.

She drew in a tight breath, fractionally tilted her chin. "So I trust that's now clear. And that now you understand that no part of this journey, including you sleeping beside me in this bed, is going to change my future in any way, you will simply shut up"—she let her eyes blaze, let her chin firm—"and damn well lie down!"

To cap her performance—her clear challenge—she glared, jerked up the covers, slid down in the bed, turned on her other side, away from him, and slumped down in the bed.

Leaving Breckenridge staring at one belligerently hunched shoulder.

And struggling with a riot of emotions.

He felt . . . insulted. Infuriated. He wanted to shake her.

To shake some sense into her stubbornly dismissive mind.

In all her wonderful plans, her careful planning, she'd forgotten one thing.

She'd forgotten him.

Fighting a nearly overpowering urge to stomp about the room, to rake his hands through his hair, clutch at the locks, then continue arguing with her—raging at her if need be—he clenched his jaw and glared . . . while beneath the churning feelings that part of him that had more in common with a warrior-general than any civilized,

184

sophisticated, bound-by-convention gentleman swiftly re-assessed.

He'd thought—clearly wrongly—that she hadn't seen the social implications of her kidnapping and his involvement in her rescue. Instead . . . the element she hadn't seen was that he might hold a different view from hers.

Hands locked on his hips, he stalked silently to the side of the bed. Staring down at her, he revisited his thoughts and requestioned his conclusions, his adamantly held belief that he and she *had to* marry. That that was the only way he could countenance this adventure ending.

His belief, his certainty, his absolute, unshakable conviction hadn't altered, hadn't shifted, hadn't been undermined by her arguments in the least. So . . . lips setting grimly, hands still on his hips, he narrowed his eyes on her. It appeared he had a significantly greater challenge before him than he'd foreseen.

The simple truth—one she refused to acknowledge—was that in the wake of this adventure, he being him and she being her left *him* with no alternative but to marry her. Not simply because society would otherwise howl and fig-uratively, if not literally, call for his head, nor because he needed a wife and she was in many ways the ideal candidate, but because, over and above every other consideration, on that plane on which he'd long ago vowed never to venture again but with her found himself walking on anyway, mar-rying her was now . . . mandatory.

To him their marriage was now a foregone conclusion.

And the warrior within him refused to give that up.

He looked down at her, at the sheen of the candlelight ca-ressing the silken smoothness of her shoulder, at the golden glimmer of her wheat-blond hair. The only reason he had, to this point, fought to keep the sexual barriers between them up and functioning was because he'd foreseen that if he gave in to the increasingly sharp prodding of his instincts and seduced her, using as his excuse the fact that society would dictate they had to marry anyway, she would later view him as having taken advantage of her. Of him using the situation to unfairly tie her to him, of him capitalizing on her relative social naivety to ensure they married, that all played out as he wanted regardless of what she thought or felt.

He'd thought that seducing her would leave her resenting him, resenting him for strengthening his claim on her. It was one thing for her to view society as forcing them to marry, quite another for her to view him as actively forcing marriage on her, too.

Given he'd assumed that she hadn't seen the social implications, that reasoning had been sound.

But she had seen, had considered, and had instead set her mind on not marrying at all, not him or any other man.

That changed things. Fundamentally altered the landscape.

Staring down at her, he assessed the new terrain.

If once they reached the Vale, she held to her present stance and refused to marry him, refused to bow to the dictates of society . . . seducing her now wouldn't necessarily give him any useable lever with which to change the outcome.

He knew the Cynsters, all of them, knew that if she put her delicate foot down and refused to marry him, established intimacy notwithstanding, while all the men would be on his side, the women—potentially all of them—might very well side with her. And the Cynster women were a formidable force. If push came to shove, he suspected that they would prevail; when it came to all things family within the Cynster clan, they were the ultimate authority.

So seducing her wouldn't strengthen his hand, not in that way, but . . . in seducing her, he had one more ace up his sleeve. He wasn't widely acknowledged as the ton's foremost rake for no reason.

And she was attracted to him. He had little doubt that attraction arose from the usual fascination most young ladies felt for a man of his lauded experience, but it gave him a place to start.

And looking at the entire scenario objectively, what had he to lose? As matters stood, the only way he could win her hand was to convince her to bestow it on him of her own accord.

He reviewed his options one last time, but nothing varied, nothing changed. No other option reared its head.

Accepting, embracing his new purpose, he considered the space beside her, then shrugged off his coat, unknotted his kerchief, undid the laces at his throat and wrists. He glanced at her, knew she was listening for all she was worth. Stooping, he stripped off his hose, undid the closures at his breeches' knees, then blew out the candle, stripped off his breeches.

Clad only in his shirt, reaching over the bed's head, he drew back the curtains covering the window in the rear wall, allowing faint moonlight to flood the small room, then he lifted the blankets. As he'd assumed, she was lying under the soft sheet. He slid into the bed on top of the sheet, leaving that as a last barrier between them.

Not that it would hold back the inevitable.

Laying his head on the pillow, he let himself relax as far as he was able.

Looking up at the ceiling, he waited for nature to take her course.

For fate to raise her head and have at them both.

Heather didn't know whether to grin triumphantly or just feel vindicated when she felt the bed dip at her back. Sliding her hand over the edge of the mattress, she clutched to hold herself in place as he settled . . . then realized she'd have to keep clutching if she didn't want to roll back into him.

Regardless, all but immediately she felt the temperature rise.

Telling herself she could now go to sleep, she closed her eyes.

Waited for her senses to subside.

To calm.

They didn't. Her lungs remained tight, her breathing too restricted for her to possibly succumb to slumber.

Her skin prickled, acutely aware. Her mind refused to let go of the information that he'd undressed before lying down.

She'd seen naked men before—her younger cousins and their friends swimming when they hadn't known she and her sisters had been near.

Instinct warned that what she'd seen then would be significantly different to what lay stretched out in the bed behind her.

It didn't matter. He wasn't for her.

Determinedly closing her eyes, she lay still and *willed* herself to sleep.

Dreams came even though she remained awake. Haunting, tempting thoughts of what it might be like. With him. To lie with him, to touch and be touched. . . .

As her life now stood, she was never going to lie with any other man. She wasn't going to marry, was never going to need the virginity she still possessed, was never going to gift it to any man . . . so what use was it now to her?

Was she really going to let the opportunity to be made love to by the ton's foremost rake slip through her fingers?

Especially when the alternative was to remain a bitter old virgin to the end of her days?

Especially when she knew that he was as attracted to her as she was to him, attracted in a purely sexual way. They'd never really liked each other, so what else could it be but sheer lust?

And she didn't think him so arrogant and insensitive, so distant, hard, and ungiving now, not after the last days.

The notion of sharing a brief, passionate liaison with him before commencing the rest of her lonely life held serious appeal.

Of course, she'd have to make the first move, and knowing him, he'd make her spell out her wishes, possibly even make her beg. . . .

She inwardly sniffed. She wasn't that innocent, or at least not that naïve. If he lusted after her . . . perhaps she might make him beg?

That idea held significant appeal.

But how?

It didn't take many minutes to decide that that was one of those questions that the longer one thought about it, the less easy finding an answer became.

So . . . first step. She released her grip on the mattress.

She turned over and even without trying found herself rolling into him.

He was lying on his back; her hand came to rest on his chest. He was still wearing his shirt and was lying on top of the sheet, not under it, as she was.

He'd been staring upward. Slowly he turned his head, and through the moonlight that poured through the window above them met her gaze. Then he arched one faintly supercilious brow.

She cleared her throat. "I . . ."

When she couldn't find suitable words, that damned brow arched tauntingly higher.

She glared into his eyes.

Then she pushed up, slapped one palm to his bearded cheek, bent her head, and pressed her lips to his.

There was nothing tentative about her kiss—it was full of fiery purpose and determination.

Even less uncertain was the response that surged through him, then raged into her.

Passion.

Unleashed, searing. Relentless.

For one dizzying moment it ripped her from the world, cindered her senses and left her reeling . . .

Then he reined it in. Ruthlessly, with an ironclad will he drew the heat and the tempestuous fury back in. Until he held both in the palm of his hand.

But he didn't break the kiss.

Instead, with that same ironclad, utterly unopposable will, he took control of the exchange. Until he was kissing her with slow, drugging intensity. Long, unhurried kisses that supped and tasted, that kept the heat within her simmering. Kisses laced with promise, with a leashed hunger that spoke of desire, and passion, and intimacy, and tantalized her. Mesmerized her. Made her want.

Made her ache with that wanting.

Then he surged up, rolled, and she was on her back.

Her lips parted on a gasp as she sensed him so close, sensed the heated hardness of his muscled chest a mere inch from her breasts.

Breckenridge took advantage to sink deeper into the kiss, to send his tongue gliding past her luscious lips into the honeyed sweetness beyond. He found her tongue and stroked, inwardly smiled as he set himself to tempt and taunt her into playing, into learning to engage with him in the more intimate exchange, one he knew she'd never shared with any other man.

She'd never taken a lover, but she was going to take him.

And he was going to take her, slowly, elaborately, and very thoroughly.

His hips lay alongside hers, separated by the tangled sheet. Propped on one elbow, he held his chest above hers, hands locked about her wrists, pressing them into the pillow on either side of her head as he slowly, thoroughly, ravaged her mouth, claimed every silken inch.

She was panting and heated when he at last raised his head.

He waited for her lids to rise, from a distance of mere inches looked into her stormy eyes. "Do you know what you're doing?"

She stared into his eyes, then the tip of her tongue slid over her lower lip and her gaze lowered to his mouth. "Do you?"

His laugh should have been supremely confident, but to his ears it was a trifle ragged. "I've been down this path before."

Her eyes returned to his, open challenge darkening the blue. "Not with me."

That was undeniable. He'd never seduced a woman with any serious intent before. He'd never had to exert himself as he intended to exert himself that night. "Which brings me to my next question."

"I didn't know interrogation would form such a large part of your play."

"And I didn't know you would want to play at all"—he caught and held her gaze—"and I still don't."

She didn't look away. "I would have thought I'd made my wishes plain."

"Tell me in words."

Her eyes flared. She drew in a deep breath, stopped—cut it off—when her breasts brushed his chest. She hesitated, but then didn't draw back, instead left the crests of the pert mounds teasingly touching, shifting the linen of his shirt against his skin.

It took considerable effort not to react.

"I want you to make love to me." She uttered the words clearly, deliberately. Her eyes remained challengingly locked with his. "I want you to be my lover." And as if that wasn't inducement enough, she added, "My one and only lover."

Beyond his control, his lips curved, not with humor, with intent. He would be her one and only lover; that was his aim, his goal. But he intended to claim the position forever, not just for a night. "If I oblige"—looking down at her, he sensed the will behind the delicate curve of her jaw—"we'll do it my way. No demands, no directions. You follow my lead."

She shrugged a bare shoulder. "You're the expert."

"Exactly. So you agree?"

She studied his eyes, clearly sensing there was some motive behind his request that she didn't understand. She would soon enough.

Drawing in a tight breath, she nodded. "All right. Your way."

He smiled even more intently, then lifted over her, and slowly lowered his body to hers. The sheet formed a barrier from waist to feet; his shirt as well as her flimsy chemise screened her breasts from his chest.

She stopped breathing, stiffened slightly, but the widening of her eyes, their glazing as her distracted senses slid away to explore, and the sudden leaping of her pulse beneath his fingertips assured him she wasn't about to change her mind and resist.

Releasing her wrists, his weight still partially on his elbows, he slid both hands into the silk of her hair, framed her face, then held it, tipped it to him, and kissed her.

Deeply, more intently, than before. Arousingly, with just a hint of urgency. Using every ounce of sensual guile he'd ever learned, he probed, caressed—there, and there—stroking the spots where she was most sensitive, the places within the succulent heaven of her mouth that most powerfully evoked her nascent passions.

They rose to his call. Slowly, steadily he drew them up, to him, until he could send them, all elemental want and smoldering heat, sliding through her to sink beneath her skin. And melt her.

He didn't rush, saw every reason not to. He took his time, until she was shifting, instinctively searching, her body rising, surging evocatively under his. His weight kept her pinned, held safely immobile so she couldn't exert any undue influence.

Only then did he break from her lips and send his own questing. Over the delicate, so feminine line of her jaw, down the long, arching line of her throat.

Heather caught her breath when he licked the pulse point at the base of her throat, then placed a scorching, open-mouthed kiss over the spot, then suckled lightly. Teasingly.

He seemed to know exactly where to kiss, where to touch. How to touch.

She'd expected—hoped for—nothing less.

His hands slid from her hair, from her face as he shifted lower in the bed. His retreat freed her forearms, her hands. Lids still lowered, seeking by touch, she brushed his cheek, his jaw, then ran her fingers back into the dark bounty of his hair, gripped lightly as his lips traced a path from her collarbone across to the ribbon strap of her chemise.

At least he hadn't suggested she'd been swept away by his kiss, that because of it she didn't know what she'd asked for.

She had been swept away, into a sea of pulsing passion unlike any passion she'd ever dreamed existed. Just that short exposure had been enough—to addict her, to make her yearn. After that . . . stating that she wanted him as her lover hadn't been so hard. She would have given him whatever words he'd wanted for another taste of that drugging delight.

Forcing open her suddenly heavy lids, she peeked down, watched as, having paid homage to the curve of her shoulder, he caught the ribbon tie with his teeth, tugged until the tiny bow unraveled.

Then with his cheek, his jaw, he eased the fine material down.

His beard brushed her skin, just the lightest abrasion.

She gasped, felt her spine arch, pressing her upper breast to his lips. Her lids fell as she felt those wicked lips curve against her skin, then shuddered as they artfully traced, tantalizing her with their touch. With caresses that caught and held her senses, then led them on a slow exploration.

Of her own body. She'd never known her skin could be so sensitive, that her nerves could spike with such sharp sensation. Had never known that the mere brush of his lips over her bare nipple could make it tighten to such a degree that she felt real pain.

Pain he drowned beneath sensation as he laved, then drew the damp bud into his hot mouth. Suckled slowly, gently, then increasingly powerfully.

She arched on a strangled gasp.

He released her tortured flesh instantly—and she immediately wanted him back.

Hands gripping his skull, she tensed her muscles to direct him, but his bearded chin brushed across her chest to her other breast. . . .

Sensing her hesitation, knowing its cause, with a mental smile Breckenridge settled to repeat the long-drawn process of educating her senses as to how much she could feel, how much fascinating sensation he could press on her solely with his lips, his tongue, his mouth, caressing and sampling her sumptuous breasts.

He hadn't realized they would be quite so distracting, so absorbing. He'd expected to have to force himself to go slowly, but instead . . . uncovering her, discovering her, was proving to be a delight all its own, unexpectedly compelling.

Her breasts weren't large so much as perfectly formed. Her skin was more satin than silk, fine and smooth and thoroughly caress-worthy. Her pert nipples, now ruched into tight buds, were exquisite.

He was an expert; he knew. Knew the scale of feminine allure to the last degree.

She rated very highly.

To his senses she topped the scale.

Not what he'd expected, not at all, but a revelation powerful enough to completely focus every male instinct he possessed.

On her.

Even as he drew the fine silk of her chemise further down, exposing more of her delicate skin to his lips and tongue, even as he slid lower in the bed, beneath the covers, to continue her education and his, he was conscious of the slowly escalating thud of desire in his veins.

Not demanding yet, nowhere near commanding yet, but it was there, assuredly there.

He wanted her, and he always had. As his fingers tangled

in her rucked chemise and he drew the silk down below her waist, uncovering her navel, he could admit that, embrace that. It didn't matter now that he had her in his arms, all but naked.

He drew back, pushing up in the bed to look, to examine. Shifting to settle alongside her, the covers held back by his shoulders, letting the moonlight fall in a pearlescent wash over her smooth skin, highlighting her curves, casting mysterious shadows, he set his other hand on her breast, carefully cradled the flesh, then shaped it, stroked, caressed.

Learned by a different sort of touch.

Felt her gaze on his face as he possessed her flesh by gentle degrees. Then he closed his hand and kneaded. Knew when her lids fell; heard her breath catch.

She stirred, but he kept her there, his to savor in the moonlight.

His to examine until he'd had his fill, until he'd filled her senses with his knowing.

Lips were more intimate than hands; touch, caresses, usually came first, but with her he'd instinctively known that starting with touch would have been too mundane, that it wouldn't have surprised her senses sufficiently to capture them.

Not as he'd wanted them caught.

Caught so that he held them, wholly his to command. His to lead, as he'd told her.

He bent his head and kissed her, took her lips again in a long foray into pleasure while his hand firmed on her breast, then he found the pebbled nipple and rolled it, then squeezed.

Drank her shocked gasp, sensed the moan she fought to hold back.

And was content.

She was no longer in danger of taking a chill. When he finally lifted his head, released her breast and slid down in the bed once more, her lips were swollen, her skin rosy, her breathing harried, edging toward a pant, yet still she watched him from beneath her long lashes, waiting for his next lesson.

Lips and tongue first; touch could come later.

He held to that principle, licked and laved his way over her tensed midriff, down past her waist to nibble unexpectedly at the edge of her navel, surprising her into a choked laugh.

He looked down at her quivering belly. At his fingers, long and tanned, spread over the ultrafine skin. "Ticklish?"

It took her a telling moment to find breath. To reclaim her tongue. "No . . . your beard."

"Ah, yes." Tactile abrasion, a useful addition to his sensual armory.

He looked down to where the near diaphanous folds of her chemise inadequately screened the soft brown curls at the apex of her thighs.

Sensed the expectation that sank talons of anticipation into her flesh, let it grip her, then calmly turned his attention elsewhere, to her long legs.

Reaching down, he found one foot, traced the arch, then slowly trailed the pads of his fingers up and around, over her calf, circling her knee, then traced, barely touching, up the sensitive inner face of her thigh, stopping a bare inch from those mesmerizing curls and the infinitely softer flesh they concealed.

She'd stopped breathing again, sucked in a desperate breath then held it as he repeated the long, lingering caress from the sole of her other foot to the top of her inner thigh. This time he let his fingertips continue upward, blazing what he knew she would feel as a line of fire up her hip, over her waist to circle her breast, then rising as he surged higher in the bed to frame her face, and kiss her.

With a great deal more passion than he'd allowed to show earlier. A hint of the potent passion she'd originally unleashed with that first bold kiss.

As he had with all the women he'd ever bedded, he kept

a sure hand on the reins, sank into her mouth and claimed, then fed her desire, and fire, and flames.

Waited until she was burning, until she arched into him, desperate and wanting.

Then he realized her hands had gone to his waist, slipped beneath the shirt to rise, skating over the sides of his chest.

Her touch distracted him.

Enough for her to pull back from the kiss and gasp, "Off—off! I want to touch you."

So much for no demands. He hesitated, but she was determined, bunching the fabric and struggling to haul it up.

He growled, then drew back; rolling to her side, he seized the bunched hem and, half sitting, hauled the shirt off over his head.

He hissed as her hands, small, scorching, demanding, found his chest.

Even as he wrestled to free his arms from the sleeves, she greedily spread her palms and caressed. A quick glance showed him her face, delicate features limned in silver moonlight—and then he couldn't look away.

Could only prop there, brace his senses, and let her have her way.

She met his eyes only briefly, but sensing his acquiescence, her lips lightly curving she embarked on an exploration, touching, tracing, learning each and every line of muscle, circling his flat nipples, then pushing her hands wide over the heavy muscles defining his upper chest, then sliding her palms higher to stroke the firm muscles and heavy bones of his shoulders.

He watched her face. She was enthralled—there was no other word for it. And while more women than he could count had looked on him with even greater lasciviousness, her appreciation was infinitely sweeter.

Ultimately she used her weight to push him fully onto his back. He told himself he allowed it because he was burning with a sensual curiosity he'd never before experienced—wondering what a virgin might think to do next. Luckily the rucked sheet still separated their lower bodies; if it hadn't, he doubted she would have been so successful in keeping her concentration so clearly fixed on returning the pleasure he'd given her . . .

Her intent was novel enough to capture him.

To have him let her come over him and take his mouth—to have him lie back and let her kiss him as she would, as deeply as she dared, as tauntingly, as challengingly.

Even while his senses purred and gorged themselves on her promise, on the unstated acknowledgment of the surrender her kiss declared would soon be his to claim, while he held her steady above him and let her kiss him with fiery abandon, some part of his mind was noting, registering, storing away the observation that few women he could recall had ever been as bold as she, as insistent.

Most had lain back and let him love them; few had exerted themselves to freely love him back. And to take delight in that loving; as she drew back from the kiss, her sensuously sultry expression declared she was definitely delighting.

Admittedly she was a virgin, but he doubted all virgins were this giving.

In mimicry of his loving of her, she skated her lips over his jaw, then down his throat to its base. From there she licked and laved her way to the flat disc of one nipple, licked, lapped, sucked—then nipped. The strange little pain shot fire to his groin; as she switched to his other nipple, he raised a hand to cup her head.

Before he could stop her she nipped again, and he jerked, pulled taut by the lancing sensation. The short exhalation of her near breathless laugh, redolent of pleasure and delight, turned him harder than iron.

He hauled her head up to his, kissed her with enough heat and fire to wrench the reins once more from her grasp. With the hand cupping her head, he held her to the kiss; his other

198

hand he sent skating down the svelte planes of her naked back, slipping under the barely there chemise, down to the curve of her derriere.

Caressing the sweet globes, then kneading evocatively, he waited until she was panting, gasping, close to demanding, then he stripped the crushed chemise down, baring her hips, her bottom, then her sleek thighs, baring her to his touch if not his gaze.

He tipped and rolled her over as he stripped the flimsy garment down her calves, then slipped it from her feet. Left it lying somewhere amid the rumpled sheets. All with the kiss unbroken.

Then he gathered her to him, let her breasts, peaked and aching, brush against the hair on his chest, then drew her closer yet, crushed her to him, feeling the soft mounds flatten against his harder flesh as he increasingly evocatively plundered her mouth.

As her hand rose, uncertain now, to touch, then gently stroke his cheek.

That touch nearly undid him, filled with a simple, innocent longing, one the experienced rake within him recognized and thirsted for.

Hungered for.

But he had his plans, his necessary goals.

He pushed her down into the bed, ignored the increasingly urgent impulse to simply strip the sheet from between them and sink his throbbing member into the slick, scalding softness between her thighs. Instead, he abruptly broke the kiss, slid back and down in the bed, with hard hands gripped her thighs and spread them wide, ducked his head as he wedged his shoulders between, and set his lips first to her curls, then at her strangled gasp, one filled with shocked realization, traced lower. Put out his tongue and lapped delicately.

Heather felt her heart pound, thought she might die. Sensation sharp as shards streaked down every nerve; heat shot along every vein. She couldn't breathe, but no longer seemed to need to; her hands blindly clenched in the sheets in a vain effort to anchor her whirling senses. She could barely believe that he would do such a thing . . . yet some part of her was eager to feel it, know it, experience whatever he would show her.

She'd initiated this new journey; contrary to her expectations, from the moment she'd kissed him, finally pressed her lips to his, she hadn't felt the slightest qualm. The slightest fear, nor any real modesty; on every level this—him and her together like this, naked and heated in a bed, his hard hands and hot mouth roaming her body, claiming her, his body hers to delight in and pleasure—seemed utterly right.

Grappling with the unstoppable cascade of sensations he artfully, expertly, sent crashing through her, she shook her head, gasped, tried to reach him, but could only clench her fingers in his hair and hang on. The tip of his tongue swirled about the sensitive bud tucked beneath her curls, and her world quaked; she tensed, tried to pull away, but he shifted before she could, set one heavy arm across her waist and held her immobile while he ever more blatantly tasted her, licked and traced until she was mindless, until she felt flames licking over every inch of her skin, set alight and racing by the abrasion of his beard against her inner thighs, intensified by the echoing rasp of his wicked tongue over flesh that grew only more sensitive with every deliberate stroke.

The flames flared, roared, and sank into her flesh, claimed that, too, cindering every inhibition along the way, until she was waiting for his next touch, panting and so damningly eager for the next sliding lap of his tongue, wanting and needy and hungry for something—for one last critical touch . . .

He kept her there, on the cusp of some cataclysmic revelation, sipping and tasting, even as the heated tension within her built, even as it coalesced into a solid knot at her core. Until she was writhing beneath his arm, all but fighting him, but for what she didn't know . . .

Breckenridge pushed her as hard as he dared, as far as he judged she could bear. In the instant that instinct told him the time had come, he felt a sharp surge of elation. He pushed her thighs wider, pressed nearer, and slid his tongue past her entrance into the heated channel beyond—

She shattered; he only just remembered to reach up and muffle her keening cry.

Her body bowed, caught in the throes of ecstasy for the very first time.

He licked, lapped, then licked one last time, savored her tart ambrosia on his tongue for one last, lingering moment, then he pushed first one finger, then worked a second as well, into her still rippling sheath, pumped his hand, his fist pressed against her swollen flesh as he rose over her, as he settled his hips where his shoulders had been.

Lowering his head, removing his hand from her mouth, he replaced it with his lips. With a kiss so unadulteratedly passionate that she gasped, then, small hands clinging, grasping wildly, she rose to him again.

Desperate and hungry, eager and yearning, frantically reaching for him.

He drew back from the heated exchange. Worked his fingers in her sheath, stretching her, readying her.

His own head was spinning. He rested his jaw against her hair, registered her sobbing breaths. "Sssh, sweetheart. Soon."

She gasped, "*Now!*"

And reached for him, found him hard and throbbing, filled her palm with the heavy head. Small fingers reached and stroked, traced the flaring rim.

He cursed, seized her hand and drew it up. Pressed deeper between her thighs and, drawing his fingers from her scalding sheath, guided his erection into her snug entrance.

Pressed in. Just an inch.

Felt her catch her breath. Start to tense.

Swallowing a curse, with his free hand he seized her nape

and hauled her to him, back into a kiss that was ravenous beyond belief.

Felt his reins fray as he pushed her deeper into the bed, trapping her beneath him; holding her to the flagrantly passionate, near-violent exchange, he gripped her hip, anchored her, pushed deeper, then, caught in a haze of erotically charged, passionate need, driven by wracked urgency, he withdrew, thrust powerfully through her maidenhead, and sank heavily home.

Pressed deeper still, forced her to take every last inch.

And felt his reins snap. Felt control fall away as she cried into his mouth, froze for barely a heartbeat, then clamped, tight as a glove, all along his length.

Need, desire, and passion beat at him with fiery wings, tore at him with talons tipped with raging hunger.

He wanted to go slowly, wanted to show her every small facet of the glory, but she moved beneath him, undulating, urging, and any hope of regaining control vaporized.

Primal need roared; he withdrew and thrust again, hard, heavily, taking and claiming.

Gone was any glimmer of sophistication. Gone was any mask; there was no way to hide. Not from this.

Not from the passion, the need, and the want that rose through him and answered her primitive call.

Not from this elemental claiming.

And she was with him, writhing beneath him, hips lifting to take all he would give her.

Heather was caught in the passionate fury, ensorcelled, enslaved, by the driving urgency. Captured, trapped, by the shattering intimacy.

By the sheer feel of him, hot, hard, and heavy at her core, with each powerful thrust filling her, completing her, with each relentlessly deep penetration claiming her, her senses, her body, her heart.

That driving rhythm was all she knew, the compulsive beat

her all, her everything. In that moment, nothing mattered beyond having him, holding him, knowing him like this.

Being with him—his—like this.

Locked in their kiss, she could no longer breathe, breathed through him. Didn't care. Breathless, dizzy, with pleasure and passion spiraling ever higher, she clung and rode with him, delighted, desperate, needing, wanting . . .

Desire dampened their skins; slick and heated, they shifted and slid. Fingers gripped, tightened. Held on. Held together.

Breckenridge was blind. Lost. For the first time in his life, fully victim to the spell. Then beneath him she rose, peaked again, sobbed again, and softly keened his name. Her nails raked and scored his back, her sheath contracted, rippling powerfully along his length, drawing him on, urging him on, milking and stroking . . . desperately breaking from the kiss, head lifting, tipping back, teeth gritted he fought to stifle his roar as his climax surged over and through him, as it shattered him, wracked him, razed him.

And left him drowning beneath a wave of completion so intense he couldn't breathe.

He collapsed half on top of her, too wrung out to move, his lungs working like bellows, his heart thundering, pounding.

Gradually, it slowed. Sensation, muted awareness returned, enough to register the gentle stroking of her hand, the soothing touch calming, strangely claiming.

He wanted to find his sophisticated armor and put it back on—before he faced her, before she saw . . .

Before he could move, she did; turning her head to his, pushing back the damp hair from the side of his face, she touched her lips to his jaw, then, her lips curving sleepily, touched those swollen lips to the corner of his.

"Thank you." The words were a sigh, the softest of feminine exhalations. "That was . . . thrilling. And . . . so very fine."

He nearly humphed. Fine? The intensity had damned near killed him, and she labelled the moment "fine?"

She fell back, fully relaxed on her back in the bed.

After a moment, he turned his head and looked at her. Studied the madonnalike expression that had claimed her face, the bliss that infused her features.

He filled his lungs, then managed to summon sufficient strength to disengage and lift from her. Slumping on his back alongside her, he stared up at the ceiling, but there were no hints or clues written there.

For the first time in his extensive career, he didn't feel, even now, in control. He felt . . . exposed. Uncertain. Not his usual polished, urbane, somewhat boredly smug self.

Yet he was the one who was supposedly used to this, accustomed to all the nuances. Who knew all the appropriate moves to make, and when to make them.

She . . . he glanced at her again, at her face.

Hesitated, then gave into impulse and reached for her. Drawing her to him, he pulled the covers over them, then settled her against him, cradled within his arm, her head pillowed on his chest.

She made a humming sound, then her limbs eased against him.

He dipped his head, placed a kiss on her forehead. "Sleep."

He felt her lips curve, but she didn't reply.

Instead she slid her hand up, curled her fingers against the side of his throat, and relaxed into his arms.

Inexplicably satisfied now as well as sated, he closed his eyes. And found slumber waiting, dreamless and deep.

Chapter Eleven

The following morning, Heather woke to find Breckenridge already up and gone from the bed, and the tiny room. Blinking awake, she yawned, stretched . . . felt the pull of muscles unaccustomed to the, for her, novel activities of the night.

Those activities . . . had surpassed her wildest dreams, her most exotic fantasies.

A smile unfurled across her face; warmth still flowed through her, unexpected yet welcome.

Then she remembered, lifted the sheet, and looked . . . "Thank heaven." She had bled a little, but her crumpled chemise had been trapped beneath her and had caught the few drops.

Relieved, she climbed out of the cocoon of the covers, hurriedly dressed, sans chemise. Peeking out of the door, she saw only Mrs. Cartwright making pikelets on the griddle; her back was to Heather, and the sizzling masked most sounds. Peering around the jamb, Heather saw the doors to the back porch and the bathing chamber beyond standing ajar. She slipped out of the bedroom, whisked out and into the bathing chamber, shut and latched the door, then she relaxed, grinned, and set about her ablutions.

Her mood remained sunny through breakfast, taken with the Cartwrights and Breckenridge, who'd appeared from outside when Mrs. Cartwright had called. Apparently he'd been chopping wood to help the old couple. With the extra coins he insisted they take on top of payment for room and board, Heather felt they were leaving the old couple happier and better off for their stay.

They left the cottage with the sun climbing higher into the morning sky, walking out of Gribton hand in hand, their satchels on their shoulders. When they regained the lane, their route to Dunscore and Kirkland beyond, Breckenridge, whose face had remained unreadable throughout the morning, halted and pulled out his fob watch.

He consulted it, grunted, then tucked it back in his pocket. "Just nine o'clock." Looking ahead, he grasped her hand more firmly and started walking. "I had another look at the map. We might reach the Vale, or at least be close enough to it by nightfall to risk going on without halting, but, more likely, the way will become more mountainous the further we go, which will slow us considerably." He glanced at her. "We'll probably have to find somewhere to spend one more night."

Still smiling, she blithely nodded. "There'll be somewhere—a hamlet or a farmhouse. Just like last night." *Just* like last night.

His only reply was another grunt.

Her smile deepened. They walked on in companionable silence as the sun slowly rose and beamed down upon them. It was a glorious spring day, with birds singing and bees buzzing in the undergrowth bordering the lane. The sky gradually lightened to a cerulean blue. Everything seemed fresh, dew-sparkling, filled with intrinsic promise. She drank it all in, felt her heart swell and overflow with a similar brightness.

She felt like skipping or dancing along, but in deference to the grunter beside her, kept striding evenly by his side. He'd long ago mastered the need to adjust his pace to hers. They progressed toward the hills rising ahead of them at a steady rate.

It was impossible, of course, to keep her mind from revisiting the events of the night. The feelings, the physical sensations. The intimacy, that indefinable heart-to-heart, body-to-body connection, the power of the moment, the bliss-filled aftermath.

Thanks to him, her eyes had been well and truly opened. She couldn't believe she'd been willingly avoiding, and therefore missing the benefits of, the activity for all these years.

Then again, she seriously doubted any other man would have lived, or could now live, up to her expectations, not those she'd previously had, and even less those she now possessed.

The truth was, if she'd known how it would be, she would have waylaid Breckenridge years ago.

The notion made her smile, yet brought her thoughts circling back to them, to the inevitable. Despite the indescribable pleasure, she knew to her bones that her path hadn't changed. She would never accept a socially coerced husband, no matter how incredible a lover he was. The events of the night might have further shaded her evolving view of him, and she could but hope that he'd revised his view of her, yet in terms of their separate future paths nothing had truly changed.

What had perhaps altered was their immediate future. Their next days.

She glanced at him. Quite aside from her losing her virginity, something between them had subtly shifted. Perhaps it was a change that always happened when a man and a woman were intimate. She couldn't tell, but she did feel both closer to Breckenridge and a lot more easy in his company. On many levels.

What exactly that might lead to . . . she considered the prospects as they marched on.

From the corner of his eye, Breckenridge watched her. Took in her serene, yet pensive, expression. He would give a great deal to know what she was thinking. Experienced as he was with women, he'd long ago learned not to try to predict how their minds might work; they inevitably surprised him, and he was sure she'd be no different in that respect.

She might even be worse, God help him.

Worse because he actually wanted—possibly needed—to know what she thought.

To his mind, seducing her had shored up his right to, once they reached the end of this journey, claim her hand. Even if she hadn't yet realized it, being intimate had tipped the scales between them. Irreversibly.

It had changed other things, too. Just the thought was enough to stir one of those other things.

Fighting not to grip her hand tighter, he willed the possessiveness that after the night had only grown more powerful to subside. To lie quiet and not unnecessarily attract her attention.

She was a Cynster female; if she got a clear view of how he now regarded her, she would guess his plan and cease cooperating. Keeping his true feelings for her—feelings and emotions he found unsettlingly intense—concealed, at least from her, was therefore essential.

He walked along, steady and sure, a part of his awareness constantly scanning their surroundings, watching for any danger, while inside he grappled with the changes the night had wrought.

In opening the door and stepping over the threshold into intimacy, he hadn't expected anything he hadn't encountered a thousand times before. Instead . . . all he could remember, all that was blazoned on his mind, was the shocking intensity, the unsettling vibrancy, of the moment. And the wave of emotions that had crashed through him in its wake.

Powerful emotions connected to sexual congress were an entirely novel experience for him.

Unsettling enough, but the not-so-subtle vulnerability that now ran beneath all else made him . . . nervous. That was the only word that adequately described what he now felt.

Regardless, last night had set his path in stone; she was the lady he would have as his wife . . . and if joining with her was an experience beyond anything he'd experienced with any of his previous many lovers, that might well be because in his mind he'd already decided she was his.

She was special; she was to be his wife. Understandable if he now saw her as more precious to him, and that the need to wed her now possessed a very sharp, very definite edge. Having her as his bride was now, to him, an absolute imperative; after last night, there was no other possible way forward.

They came to a section where the lane had been almost washed away by a gushing streamlet. Logs had been placed to one side of the lane to help those on foot cross the quagmire. He stepped up first, balancing, then holding Heather's hand more tightly, sidestepped along. Holding up her skirts with her other hand, she shuffled after him. He seized the moment while she was concentrating on her feet to search her face, her expression.

Stepping off the logs onto firm ground once more, he steadied her, then assisted her off and onto the thick, damp grass. Looked again at her face, briefly met her eyes.

Then he turned, and, her hand still comfortably locked in one of his, they set out walking once more.

He couldn't guess what, exactly, she was thinking, but that little smile that flirted about her lips, the still pleasured, pleasant, encouraging light he'd glimpsed when her eyes had met his . . . all suggested that she wouldn't be averse to a repeat of their previous night's engagement.

Given he was committed to having her as his wife, and as he seriously doubted she'd yet changed her mind about the future direction of her life, then patently he had more ground to make up, more work to do on that front. Clearly it behooved him to do everything possible, to use every opportunity that came his way, to both change her stubborn mind and to tie her to him as securely as he could with passion, pleasure, and desire.

The prospect was intriguing, challenging, and, given their past history, held considerable appeal.

Considering his possible options, he walked steadily on.

In the fullness of the morning, the man calling himself McKinsey rode out of Dumfries and headed north up the Glasgow Road.

He was confident of finding the Cynster chit and her escort; within a few hours at most, he should have them in his sights. Once he did . . .

He'd spent a good few hours of the night considering the best way to proceed. Given that he was increasingly sure that the man with her was no solicitor's clerk, nor had ever been one, he'd decided that observation first would be the wisest course.

The road contained many long, open stretches; once he located them, watching them from a distance while they remained unaware of him would be easy enough.

Once he'd studied how they interacted and gained some notion of the nature of their connection, he would know what to do. It might be possible to use what had happened to his advantage; the situation might yet advance his cause, or be rejigged, redefined, to do so.

His mind awhirl with possibilities, he rode steadily on, the sun warming his back, the regular tattoo of Hercules' hooves filling his ears. His expression, however, remained set, his lips a straight, uncompromising line.

No matter what transpired, regardless of all else, regardless of his and his people's needs, courtesy of the disruption of his plan, his principal imperative now had to be saving Heather Cynster.

He had to make sure she was unharmed, that her future— whether with him or another—was certain, assured, and held the degree of comfort she would otherwise have had, had he not been forced to kidnap her.

A twist indeed; that certainly hadn't been his original aim. But as matters now stood, his conscience wouldn't allow him to follow any other course.

Swallowing a frustrated sigh, he rode steadily on.

* * *

Heather and Breckenridge were nearing Kirkland when, with the sun shining high overhead, they stopped by the banks of a stream to eat some of the provisions they'd bought the day before in Dumfries.

Sitting on an outcrop of sun-warmed stones above the burbling water, they ate and looked back at the rolling hills through which the lane had slowly ascended. Even though they'd been climbing for some time, the folds of green blocked their view to the south. From all they could see, they might have been the only people in the world. Yet all around them nature bustled, rich and vibrant. Hedgerows were budding and the bare branches of trees were softening in the first flush of leaf.

Heather reached into one of the satchels and pulled out an apple. Recalled the old woman she'd bought it from, in the market at Dumfries. Now, Dumfries seemed far away, much further in her past than a mere twenty-four hours. Between then and now . . . it was as if plunging into intimacy with Breckenridge had divided her life into a "then" and a "now."

She glanced at him and couldn't help grinning. He was wolfing down some bread and a piece of hard cheese, his gaze scanning the fields below them. With his beard darkening his cheeks and concealing the austere, arrogant, distinctly aristocratic lines of his face, he appeared rumpled and disreputable, and oddly more human, his godlike handsomeness dimmed, veiled.

It was still there, of course. Every time she met his eyes, she saw him as he truly was. As she'd seen him last night, with the moonlight gilding every powerful line of his naked torso. His current incarnation as just another man was merely a temporary aberration. Once they were back in civilization, he would shave off the beard, revert to his usual clothes, and once again become Breckenridge, the ton's foremost and favorite rake.

Until then, however, he was as he was . . . and what he was, was, to her mind, hers. She was the only one who would ever see him like this, in this moment. Only she would ever know how he'd behaved toward her during this journey. Quite aside from introducing her to the pleasures of the flesh, he'd behaved so very differently toward her than when in London.

Facing forward, she lifted her face to the sun, felt it combine with a wisp of breeze to caress her cheeks. She closed her eyes. Drank in the small pleasures.

She would always remember this moment, the gentle zephyr of warm wind washing past her. The London rake in clerk's disguise sitting beside her.

Her lips curved. Her mind ranged irresistibly on.

She'd already made up her mind about tonight. They would definitely have to stop at some cottage or find shelter in a barn. Either way, she was determined to reexperience the pleasures she'd enjoyed last night, and if possible press him to extend her horizons.

Once they regained civilization, their liaison would end, if not immediately, then very soon afterward. She didn't have any firm idea how long it might last—how long she could stretch it out, how long she might hold his interest, widely acknowledged as peripatetic when it came to his lovers—so it was plainly in her best interests to ensure she gained as much out of the short time she would have with him.

During the short time in which he was hers.

She sat in the sun, with him beside her, and gave herself up to imagining.

Breckenridge glanced at her, took in the delight that showed in her face, then looked back down the lane—and reluctantly concluded that even if they appeared to be all alone in the landscape, they weren't. In another place, another time, in a safer situation he would have been tempted to use the moment, seize it to further his new agenda, but her safety trumped his compulsion to do all that he could to tie her to him.

Besides . . . he hadn't yet grown reconciled to the fact that, in doing all he could to tie her to him last night, while he might have succeeded in that, he'd simultaneously bound himself even more irrevocably to her, moreover in ways he didn't yet fully understand.

Ways he didn't yet want to understand.

He glanced at her again; his eyes were drawn to the ripe curves of her lips . . .

Dragging his gaze from her, he shifted, then grabbed the satchels, closed them, and got to his feet.

She looked up at him, brows rising, that odd little— sirenlike—smile still on her lips.

It suddenly occurred to him that he had no idea how much she'd seen, how much she'd guessed.

Hardening his heart along with his expression, he held out a hand. "We should get on. We've some way to walk yet if we're to be sure of reaching the Vale tomorrow."

She tilted her head, regarded him for an instant, then nodded and set her hand in his, let him pull her to her feet. "Thank you."

He waited while she brushed down her skirts and shook them out, then handed her the satchel she'd been carrying. "We should join a larger road up around the next bend. Kirkland should be a little further west."

She merely nodded, reached out, and slipped her hand into his.

He grasped it lightly, settled her fingers within his clasp as he led her from the stream, back into the lane.

Hand in hand again, with her striding easily— transparently contentedly—by his side, they walked on toward Kirkland.

The man masquerading as McKinsey was in a far more deadly mood as, inwardly cursing, he rode south, heading back to Dumfries along the Glasgow Road.

If all had played out as he'd originally planned, he would have been, at that moment, back in the highlands, almost home, with Heather Cynster in tow, and his estate and all those on it would soon be safe once more. Instead . . .

Grim-faced, he was forced to halt every traveler heading

213

north and ask after the pair, forced to stop at every cottage, barn, tavern, every possible resting place, had to sidetrack and check for any sight of them down every lane giving off the road.

He'd reached Thornhill without finding them—which had meant they'd either halted somewhere and unknowingly he'd overtaken them, or they'd turned off the road and headed elsewhere.

Where, he had no idea.

It had been no part of his plan to call attention to himself by approaching dozens of people along the road and asking questions, but he had no option. At least the stretch of road south of Thornhill didn't have that many lanes giving off it, and most had a cottage or farm close by the corner. At that time of day, with the sun shining brightly, everyone was out in their fields; easy enough to inquire whether they'd seen his brother and his lass.

Remounting after questioning another crofter and once again getting a shake of the head, he settled in the saddle, picked up Hercules' reins, eased the big gelding into a canter, and wondered if the Cynster chit was worth the effort.

If she hadn't escaped with some unknown bounder . . .

Inwardly sighing resignedly, he rode on. No matter what arguments he wove, there was simply no way he could let the silly chit run off into the wilds and come to harm, given the blame for her being in the wilds at all and not safely in the bosom of her family in London lay entirely at his feet. His fault. Her potentially perilous circumstance was undeniably and solely an unintended outcome of his tortuous plan.

It was up to him to set things right.

Jaw firming, he tapped his boot heels to Hercules' side and shifted into a gallop.

Chapter Twelve

I n the late afternoon, with Heather beside him, Breckenridge walked into a tiny hamlet that, according to his
map, gloried in the name of Craigdarroch. In unspoken
accord, without a word or even a glance exchanged, he
and Heather halted and considered the three cottages clustered just ahead of them on the slight upslope above the lane.

"I don't suppose there's a larger village around the next
bend?" With her head, Heather indicated the next curve in
the lane, the next outcrop of hill that hid their way onward.

"Not according to the map. It doesn't show a larger set-
tlement for quite some way, so we can't risk going on." He
glanced at the western sky. "The sun might still be shining,
but it won't be for long."

They'd reached Kirkland a little after midday and had
continued on along a larger lane that ran over the hills joining Thornhill and New Galloway. That lane had been better
surfaced, but it had still tacked and turned, climbed and descended, albeit never steeply. Nevertheless, the going had
been slow—there was no chance they could reach the Vale
that day. They'd passed through the village of Moniaive
an hour or so ago, and following the route they'd selected,
they'd turned off onto the much narrower, pitted lane-cum-
track that had brought them to Craigdarroch.

He hoped their taking a less obvious route out of the hills
would throw any pursuer off their trail.

At his side Heather stirred. "Let's try the last cottage. It
looks to have an extra room added at the rear."

He looked, then nodded. Grasping her hand more firmly, he walked with her to the red-painted door of the white-washed cottage at the end of the short row. They halted on the stoop. He adjusted the satchels on his shoulder, then raised his hand and rapped.

A moment passed, then a woman opened the door. She looked surprised to see them. Alarm briefly flared in her eyes as she looked at him; she quickly moved the door closer to closed before asking through the narrower gap, "What is it?"

Before he could respond, Heather stepped forward; slipping her left hand from his grasp, she gripped his sleeve, pressed . . . in warning? "We were just wondering, mistress, if you have a room we might hire for the night. We're on our way to visit my family, but the going was harder than we'd thought, so we need a bed for the night."

Breckenridge saw the woman's eyes drop to Heather's hand on his sleeve—the hand on which his signet ring still gleamed—and held his tongue.

The woman looked at Heather in her rumpled gown, her hair escaping from the bun she'd fashioned that morning, her normally alabaster skin faintly pinkened by the sun, then considerably more carefully looked at him. She looked him down, then up, then she returned her gaze to Heather. "He's your man?"

"Yes. He's mine."

"He" managed not to glance inquiringly at Heather. Her answer had been instant, assured and absolute; from the corner of his eye, he watched her chin tilt upward a fraction, as if challenging the woman to comment unfavorably on him.

He couldn't remember the last time he'd been viewed by any woman in a less-than-favorable light, but he wasn't slow. Clearly the woman distrusted large and physically strong men. Ducking his head, doing his best to lower his shoulders and seem less intimidating, he shifted his feet and murmured, "I'd be happy to cut wood for you, mistress. Did that for the couple we stayed with last night, back down by Gribton. In addition to the coin, of course."

The woman glanced again at Heather, then she nodded and stepped back. Holding the door wider, she waved them in. "I'm Mrs. Croft. I'm a widow, so I have to be careful, you see. But I won't deny the coin—and the wood—will come in handy."

Heather glanced around the cottage's tiny sitting room. An open door in the middle of the rear wall led into a lean-to kitchen, a deal table at its center. A door in the wall to the right of the front door no doubt gave onto the cottage's main bedroom. The hearth and chimney were built into the rear wall, to the right of the kitchen door. Further to the right, a narrow stairway led upward, turning to disappear behind the chimney.

After shutting the stout front door and slipping a heavy iron latch into place, Mrs. Croft waved to the staircase. "The spare room's up there. Take a look, set down your things. The washroom's out the back through the kitchen." She hesitated, her gaze skating over Breckenridge to fix on Heather's face. Then she nodded as if she'd made some decision. "You've come at the right time—I was just starting in on filling the pot. If you fancy, I can do you a decent dinner and a good breakfast, too, as well as the room."

"Thank you." Heather smiled in honest relief. "That would be most welcome." Remembering what they'd paid the Cartwrights, she suggested the same sum.

Mrs. Croft all but beamed. "That'll do nicely—if you're sure you can spare it."

Breckenridge, head bowed because he was standing beneath one of the low ceiling beams, rumbled, "Seems fair. And I can start filling your woodbox before the light goes, if you like."

A small fire was already burning in the hearth.

Mrs. Croft glanced at the wooden crate beside the fireplace. It was half full of logs. Without meeting Breckenridge's eyes, she waved. "Oh, you can leave that til morning. You've been walking all day by the sounds of it, if you've come up from Gribton, and the light's already fading."

And then they would leave her with a full woodbox.

Breckenridge ducked his head even lower. "The morning, then."

Heather had to press her lips together to hide her smile. He looked so . . . not him, trying to make himself appear innocuous. "We'll just go up then."

Mrs. Croft nodded. "I've a bell—I'll ring when the plates are on the table."

Heather started up the stairs. At the turn she glanced back and saw Breckenridge, about to follow, angle his shoulders sideways just so he could fit. She'd never considered the difficulties associated with being so tall and broad-shouldered; continuing up the short flight, she stepped onto a tiny landing before a simple door.

Opening the door, she walked into a small, but fastidiously neat, room. Windows at the rear looked across the rising meadow behind the cottage. The room had been built over the kitchen, spanning the space between the cottage's original roof and the raised bank behind; the room's floor was the kitchen's ceiling.

A wood-framed bed occupied the center of the room, with its head against the wall below the windows and its foot toward the blank wall of the chimney flue. There was space enough for a small chest of drawers against the far wall and a washstand against the wall beside the door.

Heather crossed the room and set her satchel down by the chest. She turned to see Breckenridge, having closed the door, pause with his hand on the chimney.

Seeing her looking, he said, "With the fire downstairs, we'll be warm enough up here."

Slipping the satchels off his shoulder, he walked to the corner beside the washstand. As he straightened from setting the bags down, a knock sounded on the door.

Mrs. Croft's voice reached through the panel. "I've brought a pitcher of warm water—thought you might like to use the basin in there."

Waving Breckenridge back, Heather hurried to the door. Opening it, she smiled at their landlady. "Thank you. That was kind."

Handing the pitcher over, Mrs. Croft wiped her hands on her blue-striped apron and immediately turned away. "Aye, well, you're welcome."

Heather watched her descend the stair, then held the heavy pitcher out for Breckenridge to take. He relieved her of it and set it on the washstand.

Closing the door, Heather murmured, "I wonder what happened to her."

Breckenridge cast her a glance, then tipped still steaming water into the waiting basin. "Her husband probably beat her."

The way he said it, his tone, made her think he recognized something in the way Mrs. Croft reacted to him. *That's why you've been trying to appear harmless.* She thought the words but didn't say them, instead accepting his waved invitation to make use of the warm water.

After rinsing the dust of the lanes from her face, then patting it dry with the thin towel hanging from the side of the washstand, she left him availing himself of the rest of the water and went to inspect the bed.

Drawing down the coverlet, she examined the sheets, then pulled the coverlet back up and sat on the mattress, bouncing to test it. "The linens are fresh, and the bed"—slipping off her walking boots, she lay back and stretched out full length, her head on the pillow—"quite comfortable."

Turning from setting the towel back on its rack, Breckenridge regarded her.

Closing her eyes, she let her muscles go lax on a surprisingly contented sigh. Now she was off her feet, lying supine in relative comfort, with dinner arranged and nothing more to do . . . she could think of what else might be, what else she might accomplish if she put her mind to it.

Breckenridge drank in her expression, saw the smile flirting about her lips—and found himself drawn irresistibly to the bed. His legs came up against the opposite edge of the mattress; he was tempted, so tempted, to reach out and run the backs of his fingers down one delicate cheek. . . .

Unwise. He knew where even the most innocent touch would lead, and she'd been walking all day. Better to let her catch her breath before instigating the next stage of his plan.

His plan to ensure she married him.

That when the time came, she wouldn't argue but instead would happily agree.

He might have his work cut out for him, but it was, after all, work at which he excelled. There was no need for him to be a cad and press his case immediately; he had time.

Reluctantly turning away, he sat on the edge of the bed and, reaching out, hauled one of his satchels closer. Pulling out the map, he unfolded it.

As he studied their route onward, beneath his feet he could hear the occasional clang of a pot, the clunk of a stove door. He concentrated on the map, estimating the distance they still had to traverse, gauging the likely terrain, adding up the hours. Despite his focus, some part of him registered the cadence of Heather's breathing; he knew she wasn't asleep. "We're more or less in the middle of the passes up here—we haven't much more climbing to do. An hour or two, and then all the rest is downhill. If the Vale is where you say it is, we should definitely reach it tomorrow, but it'll probably be midafternoon before we get there."

"Hmm."

He heard the consideration underlying her response, decided he didn't need to torture himself with imagining what she might be thinking.

Staring at the map, he heard another rattle and clang from downstairs. Thought of Mrs. Croft, and the flash of alarm that had shown in her eyes. He'd seen it before, knew what it usually meant. And whenever he came across such responses . . . he was always left wondering how, let alone why, any man would hit a woman. Just the thought of hitting a woman—any woman—literally sickened him. He knew his own strength, had fought with men his own size often enough to know just how powerful, how damaging an uncontrolled blow from him might be—to a man. To a woman?

The entire notion of beating a woman—the why of it, the how of it—was simply beyond his comprehension.

Not that he hadn't met women who'd qualified as unmitigated bitches—the one who had taught him the true value of love sprang to mind—but no matter how much they might have deserved retribution in full measure, he'd always been of the mind to leave that to fate.

In his experience, fate usually caught up with most wrong-doers, and often in exquisite ways no human agency could match.

Despite his wishes, his thoughts circled back to the woman on the bed at his back. Her and her kind—no matter that he knew the worst of them, all the bored matrons who scratched and clawed at each other, then plastered on a false smile and tried to lure him to their beds—they were women of his class, and the protectiveness he felt toward them was inbred and innate. He could no more turn against them than he could cut out his own skeleton, his attitude to them was that deeply ingrained.

As for Heather . . . even as his mind focused more definitely on her, he felt something in him rise. Something steely, forged, and ungiving.

He would never raise his hand to her, but he'd kill any who did.

That was a conundrum about himself—about him and other men like him, like the Cynsters and their ilk—for which he'd never found any rational explanation. They would never, could never, be violent toward their women but would unhesitatingly respond with unparalleled violence were any to threaten said women.

He was perfectly aware—had been for years—that that propensity lay within him. Only now, however, with Heather, had it—it wasn't an emotion, was it? . . . no, better to call it an ingrained attitude—achieved its full and somewhat unsettling potential.

Unfortunately, knowing that how he felt was normal enough for men like him didn't make dealing with the associated impulses any easier.

The bed behind him dipped. He assumed she was turning over and settling for a nap, but then the mattress immediately behind him dipped deeply, and she was there, pressing close, her front to his back, her breasts soft mounds against the hard planes on either side of his spine as she settled on her spread knees and sent her hands sliding around him.

Without thought, one of his hands left the map to trap her questing hands against his chest. "What are you doing?"

He raised his head, then tipped it slightly as she nuzzled beneath one ear.

"I'm trying to seduce you into putting the hour we have before Mrs. Croft rings her dinner bell to good use." The warm waft of her breath was followed by the gentle caress of her lips. Then she drew back and murmured in his ear, "Is it working?"

Heather didn't think he'd answer, at least not in words. She was operating on a combination of instinct and impulse, and had no idea if he would be willing to play. If tonight was to be their last free of all social restraint, then to her mind she needed to make the most of it. She had no idea if after they reached the Vale he would consent to continue a liaison, and even so, any affair between them would necessarily end when he returned to London, which he presumably would once she was safe under Richard and Catriona's roof.

He'd gone still. Not exactly frozen, but—

Before she could blink she was flat on her back on the bed,

staring up at him as he hung over her, his arms braced, his palms sunk in the mattress on either side of her, caging her. His eyes, hard hazel bright with greens and gold, held hers. "Exactly what were you thinking of?"

Clearly her seducing had worked. "I was wondering . . ." Looking into his eyes, she wondered if she dared say the words aloud. Decided she did. "You must have had many encounters with ladies at ton balls and parties—encounters where time was limited and the risk of discovery and exposure very real." He and she would never share such encounters; if she wanted to know, she would have to ask now. Reaching up, greatly daring, she stroked a fingertip down one lean cheek to the corner of his lips. "So here we are with an hour on our hands—a stew will take at least that long, I think—but with Mrs. Croft downstairs, we can't afford to make much noise. . . ."

When he didn't respond but simply watched her, waiting, she boldly arched a brow. "So what would you do?"

He considered; she saw calculation briefly gleam in his eyes. "First point to consider: we—me and any lady in such a situation—would necessarily keep our clothes on."

Why the notion sent excitement lancing through her she had no clue; she was sure she'd prefer to be naked with him, especially in the soft, late afternoon light. She summoned a pout. "I can't see that that applies here. We'll have plenty of time to get dressed again before Mrs. Croft rings her bell."

His expression was readable when he wished it; he appeared faintly patronizing. "I thought you were interested in an authentic experience—and there's no need at all for it to be that fast."

Another frisson of excitement skated down her spine. She tilted her head. "Well, if you insist. So . . . ?"

"So we most likely wouldn't have a bed, either—and even if we did find a convenient bedroom, we couldn't take advantage of the bed, not like this."

She frowned. "I suppose not. So what—"

He rolled away from her, off the bed, capturing one of her hands and tugging her up after him. She scrambled from the bed, and he drew her up beside him. "Let's start from the beginning—the door."

Breckenridge towed her to the door, then swung around. Putting his back to the panels, he pulled her into his arms—framed her face, tipped it up, and slanted his lips over hers.

And kissed her voraciously.

He pressed her lips wide and claimed, no by-your-leave, no hesitation.

And she met him, eager and brazen, encouragingly wanton in her uninhibited response.

No scented ton lady had ever been so direct. So honest.

He took her mouth as he wished and she gave, joyously surrendered, then joined him in a heated duel of tongues.

It wasn't hard to summon the appropriate hunger, the scintillating edge of desperation that should infuse such moments, feeding the titillating sense of illicitness.

It was the forbidden, the illicit, that most fascinated and ensnared.

He knew theory and practise so well, yet with her in his arms it seemed different, new. The well-trod path seemed fresh, exciting, enthralling, where usually faint boredom prevailed.

He didn't feel bored when she pushed his jacket wide and spread her small hands over his chest, then clutched, gripping the linen as if she would rip it from him.

On a mental curse, clinging to the kiss, he surveyed their options, immediately realized there was only one. The bed was the only useable furniture, but how best to use it? How best to further his own ends while capitalizing on her curiosity?

With an inner shrug, he let his rakish instincts free, let them provide the answer.

Releasing her face, but refusing to release her from the kiss, he reached down and swept her up in his arms.

He strode to the bed, turned, and sat upon it, cradling her in his lap.

She wriggled to face him, clapped her hands to his cheeks and wildly kissed him back.

Supporting her with one arm, after a giddy moment during which the contest could have gone either way, he reseized control of the heated kiss, then sent his free hand questing.

Up to her throat, to tip her face to precisely the right angle for continuing a kiss that was rapidly becoming all consuming.

Once she was fully engaged with the incendiary mating of their mouths, he let his hand slide, down to her breast.

And fractured her concentration.

He palmed the firm mound, then gripped lightly, squeezed . . . when she gasped through the kiss, he settled to knead, to know, to possess.

If it had been up to him, he would have forgotten about dinner and instead bared her breasts and feasted. But she'd set the stage, and he was willing and able, and more than experienced enough, to perform as required.

So he kneaded her breasts until both were swollen, full and heavy and aching, filling her bodice until the material drew tight and she restlessly shifted, seeking relief.

For which there would be none, not yet.

Releasing her breast, he sent his hand skating lower, fingers pressing, tensing on the taut curve of her belly, then sliding lower still to, through her skirts, press artfully between her thighs.

Heather caught her breath. She couldn't breathe but through the kiss, relied on its heat, its simmering passion, to anchor her whirling senses. His fingertips pressed again, harder, deeper, stroked evocatively, and she lifted her hips to his hand, wanting, shamelessly demanding. Her gown and her chemise shielded her flesh from his touch, but nothing could mute the sensation of his hard fingers outlining what lay beneath, tracing and knowing . . . the damned man knew too much.

On a breathless gasp, she tried to pull back from the kiss, but he wouldn't let her. He held her trapped within the scorching exchange, the evocative plundering she'd invited and now couldn't pry any part of her senses from. But she needed to—

His fingers left her. Before she could react—before she could protest—her skirts rucked slightly as he reached beneath. His fingers and palm cruised her calf, and she sighed.

Waited.

He gave her all she wished for—the fire, the heat, the oh-so-knowledgeable play. Until she was aching and empty and wanted him there . . . then one long finger slid deep inside her, and she shattered.

Felt her senses implode into a million shards of bright, brilliant glory.

As they realigned, she felt his hand working between her thighs, two large fingers stroking deep, keeping her fires smoldering, then she realized he'd finally released her lips and lifted his head. In extremis, her hands had slid into his dark hair, her fingers mindlessly tangling in the locks. Forcing open lids weighted with passion, she looked at his face—and saw that he was looking elsewhere.

Saw that he'd rucked her skirts to her waist, and his attention was fixed on his hand as it flexed between her widespread thighs. . . . She shuddered and closed her eyes.

"Do you want what comes next?"

The words reached her on a low rumble, their tone matter-of-fact, but his voice gravelly . . . She now recognized the deeper cadences of desire.

"Yes." Her answer wasn't in question. Opening her eyes, she captured his. "I want the entire performance. I want you inside me—I want to feel you there, filling me. Taking me."

It was his turn to shudder and briefly close his eyes. Breckenridge dragged in a breath, through the pounding of his pulse in his ears heard her demand, "So how?"

Drawing his fingers from her sheath, his hand from between her thighs, flicking her skirts down, he stood with her in his arms. Met her eyes as he turned to the bed. "Like this."

He tumbled her facedown onto the covers, then caught her hips and drew them up and toward him. "On your knees."

She obligingly settled upright on her knees. Sitting on her ankles, she glanced over her shoulder. Frowned. "How—"

He caught her face, kissed her, held her steady for one long-drawn engagement, then released her and pressed her shoulders down, stepping between her ankles as he did.

"Oh," she said, and leaned forward on her hands.

"Indeed." He flicked up her skirts, one hand cruising the dew-damped curves of her luscious derriere as with the other he released the buttons at his waist.

His erection sprang free, turgid and heavy. Sliding his fingers once more between her thighs, stroking the swollen, scaldingly slick folds, he parted her, then eased the broad head of his erection to her entrance, then slid slowly, heavily, home.

All the way to paradise.

The sound that fell from her was a shivery, thankfully breathless, moan.

"No sound," he reminded her. Grasping her hips, he eased slowly out, then took his sweet time easing all the way back in. As he'd told her, there was no need to make this quick.

So he drew the moments out, made every touch, every sliding glide last, strung every second out until the tension drew tight as a wire, until it stretched taut enough to cut.

He listened to every sound he wrung from her, savored each, accepted that at the end he would have to reach around her and muffle her scream . . . he was determined that she would scream.

Preferably his name.

With every slow penetration, every achingly slow impression as her sheath stretched and accepted him, then clamped so tight, delicate and powerful at the same time, he felt

227

something in him rise. With every artful, expert possession, although who was possessing whom was moot, he sensed that novel something grow and swell, a new part of him, a new facet of him that hadn't been there before.

That new element, whatever it was, delighted in the pleasure, not just the pleasure he gave and her freely communicated appreciation, but even more the pleasure he received with every caress of her sumptuous body.

She knew it was him. For her, in this, there was only him, and that was certainly different. That somehow added another, unique and addictive, dimension to their joining—to this act he'd performed so many times before but had never before felt so invested in.

As she rode his slowly accelerating thrusts, she turned her head enough for him to glimpse her profile—her eyes closed, an expression of sensual bliss in place, a smile of exquisite delight curving her lips . . . the sight made his breath catch.

And then they were moving faster, harder, striving as together they raced for the peak.

Heat rose. Need swelled and grew.

The arousing sounds of their mating enveloped them— the slap of skin against skin, their ragged, desperate breaths, the muted sobs that fell from her lips.

Passion caught them.

Held them in an invincible grip and ruthlessly, relentlessly, drove them on.

Until they were clinging to sanity, desperate, greedy, beyond needy, so close to the sensual abyss yet still not there. . . .

Pressing deep, her bare bottom riding evocatively against his groin, he bent over her, reached around, slid one palm over her parted lips, filled the other with one swollen breast, found her ruched nipple, gripped and thrust harder, deeper, more forcefully as he squeezed.

She cried out and came apart, pressing back against him

as he continued to fill her, deeper and still deeper. Her sheath contracted, clutched, and drew him irrevocably on—he let go and followed her into the blinding ecstasy, glorying in the moment, in the sheer heat and fury, the mind-melting, bone-dissolving cataclysm of sensation that slammed into him, into them, that set her keening as they crested the final peak.

They fractured.

And fell.

Into a void of indescribable bliss.

He collapsed upon her, managed to slide to the side enough so he didn't crush her.

They were both struggling for breath, helpless and weak, limbs like jelly, nerves unraveled.

Eventually he gathered enough strength to disengage, then he rolled onto his back the better to fill his chest.

After a moment, she rolled, too, so that she lay on her back alongside him.

He glanced at her just as she drew in a breath and blew it out in a huff.

"That was . . . *amazing.*"

He grinned and refocused on the ceiling. Intention accomplished, goal achieved.

Tomorrow they would reach the Vale, and Richard and Catriona's roof. As a guest thereunder, he couldn't in all conscience visit Heather's bed, so whatever inducements to matrimony he wished to impress on her had to be proffered now.

And if later she was keen to play further, he was—would be—more than willing.

In his educated experience, they together—she and he—were significantly more than amazing.

They nodded off and woke to a handbell ringing downstairs. Rolling out of each other's arms and off the bed, they quickly washed, straightened their clothes, then headed down the narrow stair to find Mrs. Croft setting down plates on the deal table in the kitchen.

The aromatic stew piqued Heather's appetite. Complimenting Mrs. Croft, she took the chair the widow waved her to—the one between Mrs. Croft's and the stool at the end of the table to which Breckenridge was directed. Mrs. Croft cast him a glance as he sat, then she said a brief grace, and they settled to eat. For several moments, the only sound was the scrape of spoons on the metal plates.

Heather noted that Breckenridge, as he had before, slumped, slouched, and attempted to draw in on himself. He kept his eyes on his plate, and other than a brief word in appreciation of the stew, said nothing at all.

Which admittedly seemed to settle Mrs. Croft. She applied herself to her plate with similarly silent zeal.

Her own appetite appeased, Heather searched for a topic of conversation. Through the open doorway, her eye fell on a pile of mending in a basket in the sitting room, set beside what was clearly Mrs. Croft's armchair. "Do you take in mending, then?"

Mrs. Croft glanced at her. "Aye. There's quite a few gentry houses hereabouts. Used to be a sempstress at one before I married Croft, so I make my way with it now."

"If you like, once we've washed the plates, I could help you." It was the one practical thing she could do—she was an excellent needlewoman.

Mrs. Croft blinked, but then slowly nodded. "If you've a mind to, I wouldn't say no." With her head, she indicated the pile in the basket. "I need to get that done as soon as maybe."

Which was how Heather came to spend a strangely comfortable evening sitting beside the fire sewing up hems and repairing ripped seams. Breckenridge did wonders for Mrs. Croft's opinion of him by offering to wash the plates and pot so she and Heather could get on with the mending.

Later, he stood, ducking his head in the doorway, and asked the widow to point him to the axe and woodpile. "I'll be up early and get that woodbox filled for you before we leave."

By then Mrs. Croft had largely lost her wariness of him. She readily rose and showed him where everything was, then returned to her chair alongside Heather's.

Breckenridge followed the widow back into the sitting room. He stood in the shadows and watched for a time—watched Heather's face as she set tiny stitches in some dandy's shirt. She looked surprisingly domesticated.

Hiding a smile, he shifted, attracting both women's attention. He bobbed his head. "I'll go up, then. Good night."

He included Mrs. Croft as well as Heather with his nod.

Reaching the stairs, he climbed, smiling again at the tableau he'd left before the fire. He was still smiling when he entered their room.

Heather felt peculiarly settled as she sewed. Whether it was the satisfaction of doing something active and helpful with her own admittedly small hands, or the knowledge that, once she finished and went upstairs, Breckenridge would be waiting for her in the comfy bed, she wasn't sure, but she felt happier than she could logically explain.

Another half hour of dogged industry and between them she and Mrs. Croft emptied the basket.

"Well!" Mrs. Croft looked at the neatly folded linens, as if stunned they'd accomplished that much. "I have to say, mistress, that you're quick with that needle. I truly do thank you . . ."

When the widow's voice trailed away, Heather looked at her inquiringly.

Mrs. Croft met her eyes, then tentatively offered, "Your man—he's a good man, isn't he?"

"A very good man." There was no hesitation in her answer.

"Aye, well, I had a good man, too—Croft was a simple woodsman, but he had the best of hearts." Mrs. Croft's lips pinched. "The one afore that, though—he was a blackguard. All smiles and honey and handsomeness, but he had a black heart. So I know the bad, but I know the good when I see it, too. Your man—he might be handsome as sin, but his heart's true. If you're wise, you'll hang on to him and not let him go."

Heather smiled but couldn't bring herself to lie. She had every intention of parting from Breckenridge with the same matter-of-fact attitude with which he would undoubtedly view the end of their liaison. "Thank you," she murmured. "I'd best go up to him."

Mrs. Croft nodded. "I'll see you in the morning."

Heather took the single candle the widow held out to her, then carefully shielded the flame as she climbed the stairs.

The door at the top had been left ajar. She nudged it open and went in. In the wavering light of the candle, she saw Breckenridge stretched out beneath the covers.

He wasn't asleep. He turned his head to watch her as she eased the door shut, then carried the candle to the chest of drawers. Setting it down, she glanced at him. "Mrs. Croft is now convinced you have a good heart."

He smiled and looked up at the ceiling.

She quickly stripped, debated whether or not to leave her chemise on, then hauled it off over her head, pinched out the candle, and rushed to dive under the covers Breckenridge helpfully raised for her.

She burrowed closer, and discovered, as she'd assumed—and hoped—that he was naked, too. All but plastering herself to his side, she sighed as his heat reached out and enveloped her. Being skin to skin with him was soothing on the one hand, pure temptation on the other. She felt rather than heard his deep chuckle, then he raised his arm, slid it about her shoulders, and drew her nearer yet. Pillowing her cheek on his upper chest, she sank against his strength, relaxed into his embrace.

Heaven. She was quite sure this, in its smallest-of-pleasures way, qualified.

Breckenridge's jaw shifted against her hair, then he

pressed a kiss to her forehead. "Sleep. We've another long day ahead of us."

She considered the command for all of a minute, considered the subtle tension infusing his every muscle, a tension that had been there since she'd walked into the room, then shifted her head and through the moon-etched dimness looked into his face. "I'm not that sleepy. I'd rather explore more."

She remained distantly amazed that she found it so easy to make such immodest demands, yet with him she felt assured, confident in a connection that made such directness acceptable, that made the usual veiled references to passion irrelevant, if not absurd.

Studying his shadowed eyes, she didn't doubt that he would be happy to oblige.

The faint moonlight lit her face. Breckenridge read her expectation in her eyes, the queenly assumption that he would fall in with her suggestion—followed by the shift of her attention inward as she formulated what she would ask him for this time—

Raising one hand, cupping her head, he raised his and kissed her.

His turn, this time, but he was wise enough not to give her any chance to debate the point.

He kissed her deeply, slowly reclaiming the slick sweetness of her mouth, heavily stroking her tongue with his, luring her deeper into an exchange that progressed to the rhythm of their heartbeats.

Steady.

Sure.

An exchange that escalated slowly, keeping time with that elemental beat that built on the rising tide of desire. He fought to hold back the sharp edge of need, of greedy hunger, and give her pleasure undiluted, uninhibited, unrestricted, unrestrained.

She wanted to know, so he showed her.

He led her into a landscape of sensual lushness created by touch, by tactile sensation, by long-drawn intimate exploration capped by sexual revelation. He guided her on through valleys of pleasure colored by rainbows of glitteringly sharp delight, onto plateaus where untempered passion ran so luxuriously and deliciously deep that it swamped their senses and left hers reeling.

His senses were too well drilled to reel, yet even he found his breath catching, found himself momentarily caught in the wonder. By the wonder.

A glorious, shimmering, glimmering wonder heightened by every erotic caress, every illicit, longed-for, yearned-for touch.

When he rolled and rose, tipping her beneath him, cradling her bottom and settling her under him, her thighs pressed wide by his, it was all he could do to deny the impulse to let his reins fall and simply gorge . . . but he had his plans, his own agenda, and even as he clung to both and, looming over her, his head bowed as he continued to fill her mouth, kept the tempo rigidly reined, he knew to his soul that this was the way.

That new entity within him that she called forth glowed like a beacon, a guiding light that led him, that invested every sweep of his hands, every possessive touch, with emotional meaning.

An emotional element he'd never before played with, worked with, bent to his will. It seemed to flow through him, coloring and heightening, lacing the tantalizing with the riveting to call forth and hold her fascination. To hold her.

They were both learning tonight. He as well as she.

The long-experienced lover that was so much a part of him, a cynical, world-weary part, saw and acknowledged that novel element, regarded it with unalloyed suspicion, but the rest of him didn't care. The rest of him, the better part of him, the part of him that was the man behind the reputation, was too immersed in savoring the sharper delight, the heightened pleasure, the brighter, scintillating glory of their passion.

His mouth locked with hers, he flexed his spine and entered her, long, slow, and easy.

She closed around him, scalding and slick, taking him in, hips tipping in wordless entreaty, accepting and ready, wanting and needing.

Giving, surrendering.

Claiming.

What followed was nirvana, pleasure beyond pleasure.

Heather followed blindly where he led. She was no longer herself but a creature of passion, infused with it, awash with it, buoyed by it as she rose to his call and embraced him, took him in and rode with him, clung and shared the indescribable delight . . . with him.

They moved together, joined in passion, wrapped in heated desire, linked by a seductive ribbon of emotion stronger than forged steel.

If she'd been able she would have examined that binding, that elemental linkage, more closely, but her senses weren't hers and her mind was suborned by the cataclysmic pleasure of his loving.

His mouth remained locked on hers, drinking in her inarticulate moans. He'd taken his weight on his elbows, his shoulders and heavily muscled upper arms caging her beneath him. His chest, the raspy hairs that adorned it, abraded her tightly furled nipples with every powerful, surging thrust. His hips were wedged between hers, pinning her to the bed, her body surrendered, his to fill, his erection, heavy, rigid, hot silk over steel, buried deep inside her; with every repetitive, rhythmic motion, he withdrew only so far, then pushed solidly, forcefully, powerfully back, filling her more deeply, and ever more deeply.

Relentlessly rocking her to ecstasy.

Breathing was beyond her. Nothing mattered but the sensual communion. The meeting of the physical and the sensual in which she and he were so deeply engrossed.

Never had Breckenridge experienced such absorption, such depth of sensual abandon. Normally he always had a part of his awareness monitoring his surroundings, on watch, keeping guard . . . not tonight.

Not with her.

He was as ensnared as he knew her to be.

They moved together in an intimate harmony he'd never before known, never before experienced, never dreamed could be.

Beneath the covers, they danced in the darkness, bodies joined in hot, slick, breathless desperation as passion escalated in a rising crescendo.

Long, voracious, rapacious kisses built their hunger until it was raging.

Explicit caresses, intimate and uninhibited, drove desire higher still, until passion became a whip.

Until possession reared and seized. Gripped and held.

And hurled them to the peak.

Desperate and yearning, striving and wanting, they shuddered and clung, his body plunging one last time into hers.

Glory erupted. Scintillating and brilliant, it flashed down every nerve. Pleasure indescribable surged through every vein.

And they shattered.

Fractured.

Lost touch with the physical plane.

Lost themselves in the void . . . then ecstasy swept in and claimed them.

Renewed and remade them.

Leaving them floating, slowly sinking back to earth, to a reality that had altered, changed.

Head bowed, he hung over her, their kiss finally broken, their bodies slowing, then halting, muscles quivering.

In that instant he knew, had a moment of blinding clarity.

Through the sound of his sawing breaths, her softer pants, he heard the inner truth. Knew it.

He'd intended her to be caught—to be captured by the sensual delight so she would yearn for it, want more of it, so that when he offered for her hand, when he offered the prospect of constant indulgence, she would agree.

He'd intended to fashion a net from the silken ropes of passion, one with which he might hold her.

He'd intended to trap her.

He hadn't intended to become ensnared, too.

Yet he was.

Even as the knowledge resonated in his brain, satiation slammed into him, rolled inexorably over him, heavier, denser, and laced with contentment, with that simple peace he'd never known.

Resistance wasn't possible.

With a muted groan, he summoned the strength to lift from her, disengaging only to slump half over her, still wrapped in her arms.

His place.

Where he should be.

Closing his eyes, he surrendered.

The moon was riding the sky when McKinsey walked Hercules into Kirkland.

He'd picked up the trail of his fugitive pair at New Bridge. They'd turned off the Glasgow Road there, and for some godforsaken reason had headed this way. Luckily, given how late it had been by the time he'd found their trail, the lane they'd chosen had had few turnoffs and had been bordered by numerous small crofts and farms all along the way. He'd been able to verify the pair's progress without having had to waste too much time.

He'd pushed hard—they were on foot, and even with his delay they couldn't have been that far ahead of him—but the failing daylight had forced him to slow.

Now it was all but pitch, too dark to risk riding on.

He paused to look along the narrow road, saw the lights burning in what appeared to be an inn in the middle of the short row of cottages. Stifling a sigh, he trudged on.

He'd get a room at the inn and start afresh at first light. He'd have to cast around and make sure they'd come this way—that they'd passed through Kirkland and headed on. After losing them this morning, he wasn't going to make any assumptions about where they might be heading.

But he wished he knew why.

Heather Cynster's reputation was, he judged, irretrievably ruined by now. Once he confirmed that, his mother would have got her wish, and he and his would be safe once more, but that wasn't as he would have had it.

The best-laid plans . . . too often went awry.

Especially when women were involved.

He truly hadn't wished the silly chit any harm, but . . . regardless of what had occurred between her and the man who was traveling with her, his intentions remained unchanged. He would follow, catch them up, and make sure she was protected—either by that opportunistic bastard, or by himself.

Whichever way she preferred it.

Drawing near the inn, he raised his head, drew in a tired breath, and made a mental vow. Tomorrow, one way or another, he would make atonement for his recent sins. He'd find the fleeing pair, and then he'd learn what fate had planned for Heather Cynster—and what fate, fickle female, had planned for him.

Chapter Thirteen

hey bade farewell to Mrs. Croft soon after the sun had sailed into the blue sky. Heather had woken in the ghostly light of predawn to find the bed beside her empty. Almost immediately she'd heard the distinctive *thunk* of a log being split outside.

By the time she'd risen, washed, and dressed, made the bed and packed their satchels, then finally gone downstairs, Mrs. Croft had been busy in the kitchen, tending pans on her stove, and Breckenridge had been perched on the kitchen stool, sipping from a steaming mug of coffee.

With a cheery good morning, Heather had slipped into the second kitchen chair and had promptly been regaled with a catalogue of Breckenridge's virtues, from which she'd gathered he'd cut enough wood to last Mrs. Croft into the next week.

They'd parted from the widow on excellent terms. Heather had approved of the sizeable tip Breckenridge had left on the washstand upstairs.

They set out from Craigdarroch, striding easily into a morning that looked set to be fine, although mist still clung about the nearby peaks and shrouded their way up ahead.

Breckenridge had taken her hand again; she'd refrained from pointing out that the lane was relatively even and she was unlikely to trip.

Truth be told, she wasn't sure why he insisted, albeit wordlessly, on holding on to her, but she wasn't about to eschew the contact. Even as they strode along, it was pleasant to feel the connection, the implied closeness.

A hundred yards further on, it occurred to her that his hold on her hand might be read as possessive, as indicating some degree of possession . . . she was immediately distracted by her response to the thought, to the possibility—which, in her experience, with a man of his ilk was quite high—that his action, whether unthinking or deliberate, was a sign that he saw her, in that typical, inherently male way, as *his*.

Some part of her wasn't at all bothered by the notion of him seeing her as *his*.

Given her aversion to possessively protective, ergo arrogantly high-handed males—such as her brothers and cousins—that lack of antagonism struck her as strange.

Strange, but somehow comfortable.

Their hearty breakfast of porridge and honey stood them in good stead as they marched steadily on. As Breckenridge had predicted, the lane rose for several miles, wending around the flanks of hills and through a large stretch of forest. But then they climbed a rise and, halting on the crest, saw the land and the lane gently fall away into a green valley. Beyond, in the distance, another line of hills marched in a hazy purple line across the horizon.

Heather pointed. "Those are the hills at the back of the Vale." Lowering her arm, she searched the far side of the valley, then pointed again. "And that's about where the Vale itself lies, but we can't see the manor from here."

Breckenridge nodded. While Heather looked ahead, trying to pick out familiar landmarks, he glanced back along their trail—and froze.

From where they stood, he couldn't see much of the lane they'd walked that morning, but by a fluke of the landscape he could see all the way back to just outside Moniaive.

To the horseman riding confidently along, following their trail.

To be accurate, the man was riding along on the same narrow lane they'd followed, but they were well out in the country and as yet had seen no one else traveling the lane. . . .

Turning, Breckenridge retook Heather's hand. "Come on. Let's get going."

She threw him a curious look but consented to stride along again.

If he could see the man, then if the man glanced up, he might see them. Best, Breckenridge thought, that they headed for the Vale as rapidly as they could. With Heather beside him, he could only go so fast, but he set a good pace and she obligingly kept up.

While shooting speculative glances his way.

Finally she asked, "What is it?" Her eyes narrowed on his face. "What did you see?"

He briefly met her eyes, considered not answering, or even lying . . . instead replied, "A man on a horse. A good-looking horse."

Her eyes widened. "You think he's the laird?"

She immediately craned her head to look back.

He tugged her forward. "He's well back—just out of Moniaive, I think. And I can't tell if the rider might be our villain. It's easier to see that the horse is of good quality, but the man is dark-haired and looks to be large."

"And he's wealthy enough to own a good horse."

He nodded, striding on at an increased pace, one she could only just manage. "But we've passed the entrance of quite a few drives, quite a few large estates. Mrs. Croft mentioned there were several about. The man could just be a local riding home. Regardless, I'd rather not meet him on such a desolate stretch."

A little way along, she predictably said, "What if we—"

"No. We are not setting a trap, or finding some place to

watch as he rides by, on the off-chance he's our villain." He glanced at her warningly. "We need to concentrate on getting you safely to the Vale." And he wasn't about to let any potential villain get between them and that goal.

He was carrying one of the pistols he'd bought in his coat pocket. It was primed and ready, but if he drew it and leveled it at their pursuer . . . there were far too many variables in that scenario. What if the horseman had a gun, too, or worse, a shotgun?

If it had just been him, he would have been tempted to do exactly as she wanted, but with her by his side he couldn't afford to attempt any action that had an even long-odds risk of leaving her without protection. He couldn't risk tangling with the man on horseback in case the rider *was* their villain and he—Breckenridge—lost the encounter.

It went against the grain to run, but . . .

He glanced at her. "Tell me if I'm going too fast for you. We'll walk on without stopping. We can eat while we walk."

She held his gaze for a moment, then, somewhat to his surprise—he'd expected some protest, at the very least a tart comment—she nodded and looked ahead. "All right."

After a moment, Heather added, "I can keep up this pace for a while longer."

He nodded and they strode on, his hand clasping hers more firmly than before.

She'd been tempted to press her point, but then she'd looked into his eyes, felt his tensed grasp . . . understood. He needed to keep her safe. Yet instead of trying to shield her from the reality of the potential threat at their heels, instead of lying or spinning her some tale about why they needed to hurry on, as her brothers assuredly would have, he'd treated her like a sensible adult and shared the truth and his deductions with her.

For that alone she felt compelled to do what she could to make things easier by acceding to his wishes.

She hadn't thought of it before, but clearly being intimate

with her had rescripted his view of her; he certainly wasn't treating her like a schoolgirl anymore.

She wasn't about to complain about that—indeed, accepted female wisdom, the kind passed on by Lady Osbaldestone and Heather's aunt Helena, Dowager Duchess of St. Ives, held that the correct response when a male of Breckenridge's class improved his behavior was to reward him.

Five steps on, she abruptly halted. He immediately swung to face her, agate storm clouds in his eyes. She stepped into him, framed his face with her hands, tugged him down as she stretched up and kissed him.

Despite their situation, she sensed the leap of his response, like a hungry hound, one he quickly released and drew back.

Inwardly smiling, she broke the kiss; opening her eyes, she lowered her hands.

He frowned down at her. "What was that for?"

She let her smile show. "Just a thank-you." Retaking his hand, she started on down the lane.

In two steps he was by her side again. He stared at her face—she felt his gaze—but then he humphed and looked forward.

Resettling his hand once more around hers, he strode on.

Inwardly delighted, still smiling, she set herself to keeping pace.

They reached the first landslide a mile or so on. From the crest of the rise, the lane had descended more steeply than on the way up, its surface increasingly gouged and eroded by the runoff from the thaw and the spring rains.

"Careful." Halting Heather, Breckenridge eyed the loose shingle, a load of scree that had come loose from further up the hillside to slide over the lane, burying it. He'd crossed scree before while walking in the Peak District; he knew what to do. "Follow as closely as you can in my footsteps."

Still holding Heather's hand, he picked his way across.

Despite a small slip or two, they reached the other side without serious incident.

Blowing out a breath, Heather looked back over the unstable patch. "That'll slow a horse, won't it?"

He nodded. "He'll have to be extremely careful, but it's not so deep a horse won't be able to negotiate it. The horse just won't want to, so it depends on how good the rider is, and how well the horse knows him."

"If the horse trusts him." Settling her hand in his, Heather waved ahead. "Onward."

The second landslide was a half a mile further on, another stretch of scree, rather more extensive than the last.

Breckenridge felt a lot more confident once they were across it. "If he's still following, that will definitely slow him down."

They set off again. The sun rose ever higher as they swung along. If anything, the surface of the lane deteriorated even further, until it was unlikely the rider would be able to ride, not if he valued his horse.

About them, spring seemed determined to take hold, to wrest the land from winter's drab grip. Swallows and larks swooped high above; a cuckoo called from deep in the woods that formed a solid green barrier ahead.

The lane led straight on between the trees. Bushes grew thick, increasingly tall as they descended from the more desolate heights. Breckenridge glanced back several times, but the lay of the land, the twists in the lane, hid any pursuer from his sight.

They reached an intersection. A wider lane ran to both left and right. They paused and looked both ways. The tree- and bush-lined lane looked identical in both directions.

"Right, I think," Heather said. "If I remember correctly, there'll be a small loch on the other side of the lane just a little way along."

Hauling out his map, Breckenridge consulted it, then nodded. "Right."

They'd kept up a good pace, and the lane, unrideable in some places, would have slowed the rider if he was still on their trail. Nevertheless, Breckenridge felt his instincts stir as they turned onto the wider, and much better surfaced, lane.

The loch Heather remembered was soon visible through the trees on their left. Long and thin, it followed the lane, or rather the lane followed its shore, steadily heading northwest.

He had to quash the urge to keep looking behind. He would hear a rider approaching from a good distance away; he'd have enough warning to take cover, and with the bushes lining the lane now so plentiful and thick, they'd be able to find a decent hiding place.

Although he had no idea if the rider was still following, and hadn't instead turned off along the way, his instincts kept flickering. He'd never felt so on edge, so . . . protectively aware. And while the wiser part of him understood that his acute reaction was due to the fact that it was Heather walking beside him, that it was she—the lady he'd all but formally claimed as his bride—who was at risk, most of his conscious mind didn't want to dwell on any concomitant implications.

He just wanted her safe in the Vale.

Heather walked steadily beside Breckenridge, at the fastest pace she could manage. She wondered if he thought she was oblivious of the tension gripping him, that all but hummed through him. His face, unreadable though it remained, had taken on a graven cast, the lines of the austere planes more harsh and honed.

He was totally and completely focused on the danger that potentially followed in their wake.

She, meanwhile, felt none of the fear she certainly would have felt had she been fleeing alone. She wasn't unaware of the danger, yet with Breckenridge beside her, her mind remained clear. If danger did indeed catch up with them, she would need her wits about her—not least to ensure they both got free and he didn't do anything recklessly and possibly unnecessarily brave.

That he might—that, if the situation to his mind called for it, he would—she had not the slightest doubt.

The irony wasn't lost on her. As they marched on through a golden afternoon, she remembered perfectly clearly what had taken her to Lady Herford's salon on that fateful night over a week ago.

She'd been looking for a hero.

And she'd found one.

He definitely wasn't the hero she'd imagined finding, but he was a hero nonetheless.

Not that he was *her* hero, the one she'd been seeking. He was hers only temporarily, not hers for life. Once she was safe in the Vale, they would part, and the connection they now had would come to an end.

Regardless, in the current circumstances, she would appreciate the hero she had.

The long, narrow loch eventually ended. They walked on in silence. The lane emerged from the trees to cross an open stretch, then a wood closed in on the lane from the left. The lane was leveling out. Just ahead, a roof appeared through the trees, then another roof became visible on the other side of the lane.

"That must be Knockgray." She picked up her pace, conscious of an impulse to rush ahead. "Once we reach it, the entrance to the Vale is close."

Breckenridge glanced back, looked hard as they once more passed into shadow. No sound reached him, no telltale drum of hooves, yet his instincts prickled, ruffling and rising in warning.

He could see nothing among the trees back beyond the open stretch. Facing forward, he strode on, senses alert. Just a little way further and she would be safe.

They strode rapidly into the tiny village. A farm worker

and a woman in a cottage garden turned their heads and watched their progress, then went back to their toil.

"This way." Heather pointed left, then led him into a straight, narrow lane that cut directly down an incline. At the bottom of the incline, the lane met a well-paved road.

"There!" Heather pointed.

Lifting his gaze beyond the road, Breckenridge saw what at first glance appeared to be the entrance to another lane directly opposite the one they were in, but once they'd descended the first few yards, he saw that the lane was in fact a drive, the entrance flanked by shoulder-high stone cairns, with drystone walls stretching to either side.

The further they descended, leaving Knockgray behind them, the more obvious it became that the lane opposite was the entrance to a significant private estate; the stone walls stretched unbroken to either side, and the land enclosed looked prosperous and well tended, far more so than any farm they'd yet passed.

"This is the road to Ayr," Heather almost gaily announced as they reached the intersection. "Carsphairn, the village, is that way"—she pointed to their right—"and Ayr is far beyond it. To the left lies New Galloway."

Breckenridge nodded, mentally orienting their position on the map. Keeping his hold on her hand, he led her across the road. "How far is the house?" A sense of impending danger still rode him.

"The manor—Casphairn Manor—is about two miles on." She glanced at him as, pausing in the entrance to the driveway, he glanced back up the lane.

The lane was so straight that he could see all the way to the top, to where it met the lane through Knockgray.

Heather squeezed his hand. "You don't need to be so worried—we're here now."

He met her eyes. "Two miles is still two miles."

She grinned and started walking. "True, but I can't imagine, Catriona being who and what she is, that anyone would dare follow us into the Vale—not if they meant to do us harm."

That gave him pause, and another question. "Catriona—exactly who and what is she?"

Heather's lips were distinctly curved. "She's the Lady—the Lady of the Vale. She's . . . well, I suppose those who don't understand would call her a witch." She briefly met his eyes. "A very powerful witch."

"What about those who do understand—what do they say of her?"

"That she's the Lady, and she keeps the Vale and all its inhabitants safe and prosperous."

"We're not inhabitants."

"I'm family and you're protecting me—believe me, that puts us under her wing."

He pulled a face and didn't argue, but he'd be damned if he dropped his guard because of a witch who might or might not be sitting two miles ahead. And who might, or might not, be watching, let alone be of a mind to assist.

They walked straight on, due west, for a quarter of a mile, then the lane, more a well-graded carriageway, curved around a low hill to the south. Once around the bend, they would be out of sight of anyone pursuing.

Heather strode toward the bend, her gaze fixed eagerly ahead.

Releasing her hand, he halted and turned, letting her walk on while, yielding to instinct, he searched the route they'd followed, scanning their trail all the way back up the lane to the intersection in Knockgray—

And the rider, dark-haired and well-built, sitting his chestnut at the very top of the lane, his gaze trained on them.

Breckenridge didn't need a closer look to know—beyond question—that the man had indeed followed them; he was the same rider he'd seen before. And now . . . the rider's stance, his focus, positively screamed his interest.

He was almost certainly the mysterious laird behind Heather's kidnapping.

He fit the bill. Not just in physical parameters but in every other way as well. There was a menace in his stillness, some intangible, primitive quality Breckenridge recognized even across the distance separating them and interpreted without the slightest difficulty.

The man was a warrior—warrior-born, like him. A worthy foe, one no sane man would discount.

Breckenridge stood, watched. Hands rising to his hips, he waited.

But the rider didn't move, neither forward nor back.

A standoff. Breckenridge finally accepted that.

The man, the laird, whoever he was, wasn't inclined to venture onto Vale lands.

And while Breckenridge was certain the man was their enemy, he couldn't—wouldn't—leave Heather and give chase. Even if he'd had a horse handy, he wasn't about to leave Heather, even if she was less than two miles from safety.

By the time they reached the manor, even if he and Richard rode out as soon as they could, the rider would be long gone.

For a full minute, he stared at the rider, returning look for look, then, hands falling from his hips, he turned and stalked on, following Heather deeper into the Vale.

The man who wasn't McKinsey sat his horse at the top of the steep slope and looked down and across the road at the couple retreating around the bend. He watched them disappear around it, saw the man who had stood and stared back at him, warriorlike and challenging, put out a hand to steady the woman. In the last instant before they passed out of his sight, the man's hand slid down to engulf the woman's.

Heather Cynster. He didn't know her, but now he'd laid eyes on her he was faintly relieved that fate had intervened and sent someone else—some other warrior—to rescue her. She looked like she'd be a handful; her confidence even under such circumstances, the proud set of her head, the fluidity of her stride, suggested intelligence, courage, and an independent will.

A termagant would have made his life difficult. Even more difficult than it already was.

It was perfectly possible he'd had a lucky escape, that he should thank the man—the gentleman-warrior—for taking her off his hands.

Now he'd seen the man, it was clear he no longer had to worry about the Cynster chit's future, let alone her safety. That had been his principal concern, the reason he'd felt compelled to follow them, but it was transparently obvious that the gentleman who had walked protectively, a touch possessively, by her side had taken both her future and her safety into his hands.

Timms, the unemployed solicitor's clerk, who was no more a clerk than he himself was.

Although the distance between them had been too great to have any hope of identifying the man—or to run the risk of the man identifying him—like recognized like. It wasn't simply the set of the man's shoulders but how he held them, not just the long length of his rider's legs but how he moved.

The man—Heather Cynster's protector—was of his own class, a nobleman. He would take his oath on that.

And the man's name was definitely not Timms.

He was tempted to leave, to turn and ride home and consider his obligation to Heather Cynster at an end, but one question remained: Why had they walked up that particular lane?

The lane appeared to strike west toward the next range of hills, the Rhinns of Kells, that ran along the other side of the valley. But those hills were more rugged than those the pair had already crossed; the way through them would be far from easy. Surely they weren't intending to make their way over the range?

His uncertainty communicated to Hercules, who shifted forward several steps and tossed his head. Calming the great beast, he looked down again, then stared at the cairns and drystone walls he could now see flanking the entrance to the lane, suggesting it was actually the carriage drive leading to some country house.

There was no sign on the stonework—a carved stone plaque or anything similar—to give a clue as to which house it might be. Although he knew the general geography of the region, he didn't know whose estate it was . . . but he had an inkling.

Regathering Hercules' reins, he turned the big gelding and trotted on along the lane through Knockgray. A few inquiries at the nearest tavern should give him the details he required to set his mind completely at ease.

The lane joined the Ayr road just south of the village of Carsphairn. A small country tavern in the middle of the village appeared perfect for his needs. Dismounting, he left Hercules tethered in the inn yard and went in.

Slouching on the bar, he ordered a pint of ale. A few comments on the weather, and a speculation about the upcoming harvest, delivered with a strong hint of his native brogue, and he was accepted and free to say, "Passed the entrance to an estate just a little ways back." With a tip of his head, he indicated the road south. "Didn't say whose it might be, but the land looked lush."

An old codger seated on a stool along the bar nodded. "Och, aye—that'd be the Vale."

"Vale?"

The old man exchanged a glance with the barkeep, then shrugged. "Vale o' Casphairn, it be. Owned by the Lady, and her husband, Mr. Cynster."

"Good man, Mr. Cynster." The barkeep polished a glass. "Comes in here now and then."

He nodded easily and let the subject drop, asking instead about the state of the road to Ayr. Not that he intended to go that way, but they didn't need to know that.

He remained at the bar, slowly sipping his ale, feeling relief, now complete, slide through him. He'd studied the Cynsters enough to have stumbled across the information that Richard Cynster had married some lowland witch, who, it seemed, owned the Vale of Casphairn.

Little wonder why Heather Cynster and her protector had headed down the Vale's drive.

And that meant they were now safe. Back in the bosom of the Cynster clan.

Setting down his empty mug, he saluted the old man and the barkeep, and left the tavern. Despite the total failure of his plan, he felt oddly lighthearted; although the outcome wasn't what he'd planned, what he'd wanted, much less what he needed, he felt irrationally pleased that—thanks to fate—he'd avoided disaster. A disaster he wouldn't have been able to easily live with, that would have darkened the rest of his days.

Outside, he greeted Hercules, then mounted. The gelding sensed his lighter mood and pranced, anticipating a run. Grinning, he patted Hercules' powerful neck, then turned the horse out into the road, dropped the reins, and let him fly.

Clinging, crouched low, hands sunk in the streaming mane, the air whistling past his face, he felt the powerful bunch and release of the horse's muscles beneath him, and for that moment simply savored the thrill.

The freedom.

Illusory though it was, he'd take what he could of it, what surcease he could find.

Home.

On one level, the most visceral level, the thought made his soul sing.

On another, more immediate plane, it brought unwelcome reminders of what waited for him there—of the chaos and catastrophe it was his lot to avert.

His role to make right.

However he could, however he might.

Whatever he had to do, he would. He had no other choice. But that was for tomorrow. For today, he was free.

Afternoon was waning into evening, the sun dipping behind the western hills, leaving shadows lengthening and the air cooling, when Heather and Breckenridge walked up the last rise and into the wide forecourt before Casphairn Manor.

The manor was a large, many-gabled stone building with three storeys under the slate roof and three turrets reaching to the sky. Built of dark gray stone, the house was irregular in shape yet seemed somehow balanced, settled on a slight rise with a small river coursing past. Gardens, currently bursting with life, filled the gentle slope between the house and the river. Breckenridge had glimpsed a jumble of outbuildings behind the house, with all the trappings of a busy, productive farm.

They weren't even halfway across the forecourt when the massive double front doors flew open and three children raced out.

"Heather!"

"Mama, Papa—Heather's *here*!"

Breckenridge suppressed a wince; after the silence of the wide valley, the serenity and peace, the high-pitched screech was an aural assault. But then he glanced at Heather, saw the quality of the smile that split her face as she stepped forward and opened her arms wide, and decided he would have to forgive the hooligans. Anything that gave her that much joy . . .

The two eldest children slammed into her; he put his hand to her back to steady her, though she hardly seemed to notice as she fiercely hugged the pair.

"Lucilla!" Heather placed a kiss on one shining coppery-red head, then hugged the black-haired boy and released him. "Marcus."

She transferred her attention to the youngest of the three, bending as the girl reached her so the child could fling her arms about her neck. "And Annabelle." After exchanging another near-violent hug and kiss, Heather straightened and looked toward the door, just as her cousin Richard came striding out. "Is your mother at home?" she asked the children, her gaze on Richard.

"Yes, but she was in the nursery with Calvin and Carter," Lucilla reported, "so she'll still be rushing down the stairs."

Breckenridge fixed his gaze on the tall, black-haired gentleman striding across the gravel. He knew Richard, thank God, and Richard knew him. This was going to be awkward enough as it was.

Richard's cornflower-blue eyes rapidly assessed Heather, then he swooped and swept her up into a tight hug. "We've all been worried, you ninnyhammer. About time you showed up somewhere."

"Believe me," Heather said, returning the hug, "we came as fast as we could."

Easing his hold on her, Richard held her at arm's length, then, apparently reassured as to her health, he released her and turned his narrowing gaze on Breckenridge. After an instant's hesitation, Richard nodded curtly and held out his hand. "Breckenridge."

"Richard." Breckenridge clasped the proffered hand, shook it. "I assume you've heard—"

"Heather! About time!" Relief, albeit collected and calm, rang in the words.

Glancing at the house, Breckenridge saw a vividly beautiful lady walking smoothly their way, skirts and shawl gently streaming behind her in the light breeze. Hair the color of bright copper-red lit by the sun was gathered in a knot on the top of her head, strands wreathing loose to frame a face with delicate features and a surprisingly firm chin. Richard's witchy wife was a little taller than average, slender and curvaceous rather than svelte. Breckenridge had met Catriona only once before, at Caro's wedding. Now, as then, she effortlessly exuded an aura of calm, of confidence and serene assurance.

Reaching Heather, Catriona enveloped the younger woman in a warm embrace, kissing her cheek.

Beaming, Heather returned the hug and kiss. "We had to come here—I knew you wouldn't mind."

"Mind? Of course not! We're simply thankful you've arrived safe and sound." Catriona's eyes, vibrant green flecked with gold, shifted to Breckenridge. She looked at him for a moment—truly looked as few others ever did, deeply enough to make him wonder what the devil she was seeing—then her radiant smile lit her face and she extended her hand. "Breckenridge. If Richard hasn't already said so, we're indebted to you for rescuing Heather and conducting her to us in safety."

There was a certain satisfaction in Catriona's voice. Ignoring it, Breckenridge took her fingers and—for the first time in too many days—called up his usual persona and bowed over the delicate digits. "Catriona. A pleasure, although I might wish it was in different circumstances."

Her lips quirked. "Indeed, I imagine you might. However"—turning, she held out her arms and waved, effortlessly gathering her brood, Heather and Breckenridge, and her husband, and directing them all back toward the house—"you're here now, so let's get you inside before the light fails and the wind blows cold."

Falling in beside Richard at the rear of the small company, with the children dancing ahead and shooting questions one on top of the other at Heather, Breckenridge seized the opportunity to say, "We had to walk from Gretna, which is one reason it's taken us so long to reach here."

Richard briefly met his eyes, his own gaze hard. "I'll be interested in hearing the full tale."

They reached the door and followed the others in—into a welcome of a sort Breckenridge had never before weathered. People came from everywhere. A motherly woman swept up, all concern and warmth—the housekeeper, a Mrs. Broom. After greeting Heather, she literally patted his cheek in delight, thanking him effusively for his gallant rescue.

A much older man, wizened and worn, hobbling along with a cane, directed a young footman to close the door, then beamed as Heather, turning and seeing him, smiled, seized his gnarled hand, and pressed it.

"McArdle—it's good to see you again. Are you keeping well?"

"As well as can be expected, miss. So kind of you to ask."

The swirl of greetings and people passing into and through the hall continued, a warm, engaging, welcoming tide that gradually shifted them on. Richard paused to speak with a dour, rather hatchet-faced man called Henderson about sending word south to the rest of the family. Catriona meanwhile was issuing orders to McArdle and Mrs. Broom regarding rooms. Amid the rising cacophony, Cook, a jovial rotund woman who was a testament to her trade, assured Breckenridge that she'd have just what he and Heather would like ready for dinner, and suggested they might want scones in the interim.

He gave silent thanks when Catriona, overhearing, agreed.

A tall, queenly woman with gray-streaked dark hair came down a curving stair shepherding two black-haired little boys. Without the slightest hesitation, the instant their chubby feet found the floor, the toddlers made a beeline, first to Heather, who picked each up and bussed their cheeks soundly, then the pair swept past their mother, tugging briefly at Catriona's skirts before, launching themselves at their older siblings, they noisily insisted on their right to join in whatever game was developing.

Suddenly realizing that the older woman who had accompanied the black-haired demons downstairs had halted on the last stair, her steady gaze fixed on him, Breckenridge turned his head and met her eyes.

Like Catriona, she studied him for a moment, then she

smiled—with a touch of the same smug self-satisfaction Catriona had displayed.

"That's Algaria," Richard informed him, reappearing by his side.

"Is she a witch, too?"

Richard nodded. "She was Catriona's mentor. Now she watches over the children, and when she thinks Catriona's not looking, mentors Lucilla."

Breckenridge switched his gaze to the copper-haired young girl. "She's . . . ?"

"The next Lady of the Vale, apparently—that's how it works." Richard eyed his offspring, loosely gathered around his wife, with poorly concealed pride. "According to Algaria, the reason we had twins was so that Catriona would have a girl to be the next Lady, and I would have a boy to train to be the next Guardian of the Lady, which is apparently my role. Mind you, given Lucilla is a Cynster through and through, as is Marcus, I don't know how well she's going to take to having her brother as her guard."

Reminded of the willfulness of Cynster females, Breckenridge glanced at Richard. "Before you send off that note, I should tell you our tale."

"Indeed." Organizing complete, Catriona had turned in time to hear his words. "But let's adjourn to . . ." She met her husband's eyes. "The library, I think."

Richard nodded. Catriona dismissed the children, sending them upstairs with Algaria, with the promise of scones, clotted cream, and jam to sweeten the banishment. Together with Heather, Catriona, and Richard, Breckenridge repaired to a comfortable room at one side of the manor. The ladies claimed the sofa, facing the fireplace in which a cheery fire crackled. Sinking into a large armchair angled beside the hearth, Breckenridge took in the masculine decor. The library was, presumably, Richard's domain.

As Richard sat in the other armchair, a maid bustled in,

ferrying a large tray with the promised sustenance. Catriona poured as Heather and Breckenridge fell on the fare—scones, clotted cream, and, if he wasn't mistaken, damson jam, plus sandwiches stuffed with ham.

From the corner of his eye, he saw Catriona shake her head at Richard, plainly signaling him to hold off his inquisition until Breckenridge and Heather had at least taken the edge from their appetites.

Silence reigned for several minutes, then Heather set down her plate, picked up her cup and saucer, and sat back with a contented sigh. "We haven't really had that much to eat, not since we left Gretna Green."

Catriona blinked and fixed her gaze on Heather. "Gretna Green?"

Heather nodded. "That's where the kidnappers took me. But I should start at the beginning."

She promptly did.

After a moment's consideration, Breckenridge sat back and let her tell their tale in her own way, in her own words, from the moment she walked into Lady Herford's salon.

For which Heather was sincerely grateful. She knew her cousins—knew Richard—too well not to recognize what was behind his unusually stiff reception, not so much of her but of Breckenridge. She was determined that no whisper of blame should attach to him; she was all too conscious of just how understanding and supportive he had been, even to the extent of reigning in the overprotective impulses that beat in him just as much as in her cousins.

She felt beholden to him, immensely grateful for his steady, unwavering support. She seriously doubted many other men would have done as he had—accepted and bowed to her wish to learn what she could of the truth of the kidnappings in order to better protect her sisters and cousins.

Instead of arguing, he'd done what he'd been able to do to keep her safe, which in turn had allowed her to continue with her role as kidnapee with confidence, in the sure knowledge that if anything had threatened her, he'd stood in the shadows, close, ready, willing, and able to haul her to safety.

Everything he'd done, all the rules he'd broken, he'd broken for her, and she would not hear of him being held to blame.

To his continued credit, he interrupted only to add those details she hadn't known, such as how he'd come to locate her at the inn at Knebworth. Her refusal to escape with him that night made Richard frown, but her reason for doing so forced him to bite his tongue.

Between them, she and Breckenridge told the story of her kidnapping and his subsequent pursuit in concise but accurate detail.

Breckenridge was impressed by how clear and open Heather was; one glance at Catriona's face, then Richard's, reassured him that they, too, had realized that, for all the attendant drama, Heather had sailed through the ordeal with no real damage—no lasting fear. Not just from her words but also from her tone and irritated expression as she recounted their failure to find any real clue to the identity of the mysterious laird, it was clear she was more exercised by the need to learn what lay behind the kidnapping than anything else.

Of course, she'd skated, very neatly, over the small matter of their intimacy. She'd remembered to return his signet ring as they'd approached the manor, so not even that detail remained to raise awkward speculation. Nevertheless, Breckenridge felt, sensed, Richard's suspicious glance, but he pretended not to so he wouldn't have to meet it. He fully intended to speak with Richard as soon as he could and make a clean breast of the situation, but not with the ladies present.

Not with Heather present, and until Breckenridge was sure which way Catriona would lean, he wasn't inclined to include her in his confidence, either.

Regardless, he knew that Richard's initial stance—the battle-ready tension that had thrummed through his large frame when he'd met them in the forecourt—had faded, steadily receding as Heather recounted all that he, Breckenridge, had done in order to protect her.

Heather didn't see the half of it, but Richard did. The occasional, increasingly understanding glances Richard threw him bore witness to that.

Reaching the end of her recital, Heather concluded, "And so we walked down and into the Vale."

Breckenridge stirred, finally met Richard's eyes. "The horseman—he followed us to the edge of the Vale."

"What?" Heather stared at him. "I didn't see him."

"He halted at the top of the lane down from the last village—Knockgray?" When Richard nodded curtly, Breckenridge went on, "I glanced back before walking around the bend—the one where you lose sight of the lane down. He was there, calmly sitting a huge horse—a prime piece of horseflesh. I waited, but he didn't make any move to follow. Eventually, I rejoined Heather and we came on. Clearly he didn't follow."

Catriona's eyes grew distant, but then she shook her head and refocused. "He didn't set foot on Vale land—I would know."

Breckenridge hesitated, then said, "That suggests he knew the place."

Richard grimaced. "Not necessarily. People often feel an aversion to entering the Vale if they intend to do harm."

Heather, still absorbing the fact that Breckenridge hadn't mentioned the horseman, felt grateful for Catriona's power. If the horseman had decided to run them down . . . but then Breckenridge had had a pistol in his pocket, so most likely he would have been safe.

Richard smoothly rose. "I'd best send a courier south, posthaste."

Heather looked up. "Can I send a note, too? To Mama and Papa?"

"That," Richard said, "would no doubt be best." He waved

her to the desk that sat at the far end of the room, before the velvet curtains drawn against the evening gloom.

While Richard and Heather sat at the desk and composed their respective notes—Heather's to her parents, Richard's to Devil, his half brother and head of the family—Breckenridge sat by the fire and asked Catriona about the Vale. He was curious, and she was happy to indulge him, educating his ignorance, as he suspected she saw it. He didn't mind; he felt strangely comfortable, more relaxed than he'd expected to be.

More relieved.

The irony in that occurred to him when, the letters dispatched with a rider, Catriona swept Heather off upstairs to find clothes and luxuriate in a bath, leaving him at last alone with Richard; given the necessity of leg-shackling himself to Heather, his relief was surely misplaced.

Before he had a chance to assemble his wits enough to find the right words to broach the subject, Richard, returning to stand before the fire after closing the door on the women, then detouring to pour them each a glass of much-need whisky, looked down at him as he handed him a glass, caught his gaze, and stated, "I appreciate and accept that you had to do everything you've done. I know Heather well enough to realize that she left you with no real choice. That said, given the circumstances, given who you are and who she is, what now?"

Breckenridge appreciated Richard's directness. Holding Richard's gaze, he succinctly stated, "I'd rather assumed a wedding was in order."

Richard studied his face, then blew out a breath. "You'll agree to marry her?"

He would *fight* to marry her, but he saw no need to admit that. "It seems to me that our principal goal in this has to be to protect her reputation. The way I see it, given she's to be my bride, that's of paramount importance—without her reputation intact, she won't be able to fulfill the social position that should be her due."

Richard nodded. "You'll get no argument from any Cynster on that."

"Just so." Breckenridge paused to sip the whisky; it was a seriously fine malt, too good to gulp. "The reality as far as the ton is concerned is this: I have to marry and reasonably soon, and Heather is already twenty-five. After this Season, if she doesn't marry, she'll be considered to be on the shelf. The tale I suggest we tell is that, as we already knew each other, some kind soul—Lady Osbaldestone springs to mind—suggested that we would suit, or rather that both our situations could be resolved with one ceremony. Consequently, in lieu of Heather and her parents visiting Baraclough, it was agreed that we should meet privately here, under your and Catriona's eyes, to decide if we could agree on a wedding."

"Why aren't Martin, or at least Celia, here, too?'

"Because Celia has two other daughters to chaperon through the balls and parties, and her sudden disappearance from the social round, together with Heather, would have occasioned considerable speculation, which both families were keen, given the true circumstances, to avoid."

Richard considered. Head tipping, he said, "From what we've heard, the family's managed thus far to keep Heather's disappearance a secret. Celia and the ladies have put about some tale that Heather's taken ill and might have something catching, so none of her friends and their mothers are falling over themselves to call."

Breckenridge inclined his head. "That will work. When our truth becomes known, they'll no doubt dub the tale romantic."

Richard snorted. He sipped, then glanced at Breckenridge. "Two quibbles. First, it's a commonly held axiom that Cynsters marry for love."

Breckenridge shrugged. "It simply didn't happen in this case, and with Heather having reached the age of twenty-five without tripping over her one true love, she decided a viscountess's coronet, with a countess's tiara to come, was preferable to remaining a spinster."

Richard nodded. "Fair enough. The other quibble is why meet here, rather than at Baraclough?"

Breckenridge smiled cynically. "That's easy. Because Baraclough's a short drive from London, and anyone might have dropped by to see m'father while we were there. The Vale, on the other hand, is a very long way from the curious ton."

Richard grinned. "Ah—I see." After a moment of thought, he nodded. "That just might work."

"What might work?"

They both glanced up to see Catriona closing the door behind her.

She came forward, brows arching in query.

Richard explained, not the need for a wedding—that, Breckenridge realized, Richard and Catriona had already discussed—but that he, Breckenridge, was willing to marry Heather, and the story they would tell to cloak her absence from London, thus protecting her reputation from the censorious ton.

At the end of Richard's exposition, Catriona remained silent for a heartbeat, then looked at Breckenridge. "Have you discussed this with Heather?"

He felt his lips thin, disguised the reaction by raising his glass. "No. Not yet."

"Well." Her brows rose. "I suggest you do. However, in the meantime, you had better repair to the room Henderson's prepared for you, and restore yourself to your customary sartorial state." Her eyes scanned both pairs of shoulders before her. "Richard can lend you some clothes." She rose.

Breckenridge perforce rose, too. As he set down his glass, Catriona continued, "It'll be dinnertime soon. All else can wait until later."

She somehow succeeded in shooing both him and Richard from the room. In the hall, she instructed Richard to find

Breckenridge some clothes and dispatched her husband up one turret stair, then she handed Breckenridge into the care of Henderson, to be led up another winding stone stairway to his room and an awaiting bath.

Hands on her hips, Catriona stood at the bottom of the spiral stairs and watched Breckenridge ascend. When he passed beyond her sight, she continued to stare, then she slowly smiled, shook her head, and with that faintly patronizing smile still flirting about her lips, swanned off to attend to her other duties.

Returning from Breckenridge's room, having escorted thereto and introduced Worboys, his terribly correct gentleman's gentleman, who naturally had insisted that only he could adequately clothe a gentleman of Breckenridge's caliber and had therefore usurped the task of selecting and carrying a selection of garments drawn from Richard's wardrobe to Breckenridge, Richard reentered the large chamber he shared with his witchy wife to discover her already gowned for dinner. Seated before her dressing table, she was brushing out her long hair.

Firelight danced along the gilded red strands.

Dragging his eyes from a sight he still found mesmerizing, he closed the door, shook off the distraction, and remembered what he'd meant to ask. Catching her eyes in the mirror, he let a frown color his. "What was all that about?"

He didn't need to elaborate—she knew what he meant. Her "all else" that was to wait until later. He wasn't at all sure what tack she was taking, but he was perfectly clear on where he stood.

At least, he thought he was.

She refocused on the lock of hair through which she was drawing her brush. "Did you notice how eager Heather was, how intent she was, on ensuring you, I, and, by extension, the family, understood that Breckenridge was in no way to blame for the length of time she's been away?"

Halting behind her, watching her face in the mirror, Richard slid his hands into his pockets and shrugged. "Understandable enough. She's never been one for lying, or even gilding the truth, so she'd feel horrendously guilty if we rained fury on Breckenridge's head for an outcome that was, in fact, her fault."

"It was in no way her fault." Catriona's tone didn't materially change, but he heard the censure nonetheless. "Any fault in this lies at the feet of the kidnappers, and more, on the head of this mysterious laird."

Richard tipped his head. "All perfectly true, but that's not how society will see it."

"Perhaps not, but we've strayed from the point." Setting down her brush, she raised her hands and swept back her hair, preparatory to winding it into her usual neat knot that never remained neat for long. "What I found most interesting in the tale of their adventure was firstly Heather's efforts to make it clear that the outcome was entirely due to her decisions, not Breckenridge's, *and* that he, patently, had not just accepted those decisions of hers, accepted her right to make them, but had then supported her, selflessly and largely, it seems, without complaint. *That*, I find most interesting, don't you?"

Richard frowned, considering. After a moment he replied, "I really can't see what else he could have done. This is Heather, after all. Much as none of us like it, she's a Cynster to her toes, and with a threat against her sisters and possibly Henrietta and Mary, too, in the wind, she would have been like a terrier with a bone—impossible to detach and lead away."

Catriona held his gaze for a moment, smiling fondly in a way that told him he'd missed some utterly obvious point, then she softly said, "Tell me—what is Breckenridge?"

Not who, he noted, but what.

He knew what she meant, could follow her argument, but . . . he pulled a face. "We can't tell what really went on—

how much argument there actually was—but I still believe that, no matter what he did, Breckenridge wouldn't have been able to turn Heather from her path."

It was Catriona's turn to lightly shrug. "Perhaps not. I suspect we'll never know, and I'm not sure it's relevant, not anymore."

She started to slip pins into her topknot.

Richard studied her face. She wasn't wearing her "Lady" mask, the serene assurance she could project even in the face of disaster, yet she was happy, genuinely pleased with the situation.

Frowning, uncertain over just what she in fact saw, what she was expecting—what it was in all this that she saw and he didn't—he ventured, "You do realize, don't you, that they'll have to marry?"

Her smile widened. "You do realize, don't you, why the Lady steered them here?"

Richard straightened. "The Lady?" His witchy wife did not invoke her deity without good cause, and he'd learned to be wary when she did. "She's involved in this?"

"Well, of course. Where else would she send a pair of lovers who need to sort themselves out?" Hair anchored to her satisfaction, Catriona swiveled on her dressing stool and leaned back to look up at him. "You of all people ought to know that the Vale is a place for lovers who fail to see the obvious to realize what is meant to be."

Richard hesitated, but had to ask, "They're meant to be?"

Catriona shook her head at him. "You really need to pay more attention. Even I knew they were meant to be, and I've only seen them together twice before." She spread her hands. "And now here they are, and all is plain."

"It is?"

"Of course! So our role is to encourage them to remain here until they see it, too." Rising, she undid the wrapper she'd worn over her alabaster shoulders, largely bared by the wide neckline of her dinner gown. "I doubt it'll take too long—Heather's never been blind, and I rather doubt Breckenridge is either. Indeed, his reputation would suggest that when it comes to women, he sees more than most."

That won't save him. Richard kept the words to himself.

Laying the wrapper aside, Catriona shook out and resettled her gown, then swung around and presented him with her back. "Lace me up—and then you'd better change, too. The gong will ring at any moment, and we should be in the drawing room when they arrive—I want to see their faces."

Having no real quibble with that plan, Richard put aside his confusion along with his misgivings, set his long fingers to her laces, and complied.

He didn't truly care if the Lady was involved, just as long as Heather and Breckenridge fronted the altar. Ensuring that happened was his duty to the family, but how it came about . . . no one would care.

Tying off Catriona's laces, then turning to doff his clothes and don the garments Worboys had left out for him, the words he'd uttered to Breckenridge replayed in his mind. He didn't think of himself as prescient, yet it seemed his words had been a warning.

Cynsters married for love.

If he was interpreting the Lady's interest in Heather and Breckenridge correctly, and he was fairly certain he was, then it seemed he'd have the honor and the unmitigated delight of welcoming Breckenridge—Breckenridge of all men, the ton's foremost and favorite rake—to their club.

Grinning to himself, he shrugged on his evening coat, settled the sleeves, then followed Catriona to the door.

Chapter Fourteen

Hours later, arms crossed behind his head, Breckenridge stretched full length beneath crisp linen sheets, luxuriating in once again being in a bed that could properly accommodate his length. Relaxing with a sigh, he waited for Morpheus to make an appearance.

His mind drifted back over the recent dinner, taken with the rest of the household in a great hall that seemed to have changed little over the centuries, with the family and guests gathered about the high table, raised on a dais at one end, and the rest of the household, chattering and cheerful, spread about tables on the floor of the hall.

Revisiting the scene, he found himself smiling, remembering the warmth, the affection, the sharing of life that had flowed so effortlessly around and about the high table, about the hall in general, effervescent streams of ephemeral connection glimmering with laughter and smiles. Even he, an unknown entity, had felt included, bathed in the glow.

His own family, the Brunswick household, interacted in a manner that he recognized as similar, but here in the Vale, the joy and the simple pleasure of family were more easily perceived, more openly expressed.

It had been an interesting evening.

In more ways than one.

His mind ranging further, he sifted through the myriad conversations, examining the undercurrents, both over the dinner table and in the two hours they'd later spent in the drawing room. While he wasn't surprised by Richard's standing down, as it were, what he now sensed from his host was . . . something more akin to sympathy.

Which seemed strange. Richard feeling sorry for him because he was being forced to trade his rakish freedoms for marriage to a Cynster female simply wouldn't wash. All male Cynsters viewed their female cousins as akin to princesses of the house; Richard and the others would see any man who married one of the girls, no matter the circumstances, as being honored, rather than being an object of pity.

Richard eyeing him with sympathy made him uneasy.

Contributing to that underlying unease was Catriona's confident, embracing acceptance. She knew that he and Heather would have to marry, yet he'd detected no disapproval of such a socially dictated union.

Catriona had been Richard's wife, and thus within the Cynster fold, for more than nine years; it was difficult to believe that she hadn't yet been infected with the "Cynsters only marry for love" creed.

Especially given her connection to her mysterious "Lady."

What had rung more true was Catriona's veiled warning that, once Heather was reminded of the social reality, of what society would expect and demand, she might jib.

Just the thought . . . he felt his muscles tensing, tried to relax them again.

Tried to push the disturbing notion away, tried to bury it, but the prospect of having to let her go rose like a specter—and hardened his resistance. He didn't want to let her go—couldn't imagine how he could live with such an outcome. How he could meet her and pretend nothing had changed. He could prevaricate with the best of them, but that would be beyond him. The idea of him retreating to his previous distance—of allowing her to once again view him as an uncle—was laughable.

He shook himself, then resettled in the bed. In the interests of finding sleep that night, he focused on the positive—of what would come once they married. They'd use Brunswick House when in London, but other than the obligatory times when they would be looked for in the capital, he rather thought they'd spend their days at Baraclough. His father would like that, and so would he.

The truth was he'd like a chance to build a home—not just the house but the family to inhabit it—along the lines of what Richard had here. Richard was patently at peace, and if this life suited Richard, it would suit him. Would satisfy and fulfill him.

He hadn't thought of it before, but that was what he wanted. What he wanted to achieve—the road he wished to follow for the rest of his life.

The only hurdle, it seemed, was getting Heather to accept that she had to marry him in the absence of any protestations of love. Luckily, in that he would for once have society, and the grandes dames in general, on his side.

Lips curving, he closed his eyes, composed his mind—and tried to find slumber.

It should have been easy; the bed was more than comfortable, and with the stone walls so thick, no sounds disturbed him.

He tossed. And turned.

Sat up, thumped the pillow, lay down again.

In the end he lay on his back and stared up at the ceiling. He was tempted to get up, find his fob-watch, and see how long he'd been lying there, but while it felt like hours and hours, by the distance the moonbeams had traveled across the room, it hadn't been more than one.

He knew of one activity guaranteed to lead to sleep, but the convoluted tenets of gentlemanly honor forbade him to seek Heather's bed, not while under Richard's roof.

Besides, he didn't even know where her room—

The click of the door latch had him turning his head. Had every muscle in his body snapping taut.

Heather eased the door open as silently as she could, relieved when the hinges remained blessedly silent. She'd guessed which room, which turret, Breckenridge would be in, but she'd had no idea if she was correct.

She'd had to wait until the entire household had retired, wait until her eyes had been well adjusted to the darkness that prevailed in the manor's corridors, but at no point had she imagined simply passing the night in her room, in her bed, alone.

Tonight, or if she was lucky tomorrow night, would be her last chance to sleep in his arms. She saw no reason to pass up the opportunity. Once he made up his mind to leave . . . she was determined she wouldn't cling but would behave with the sophisticated savoir faire he was no doubt accustomed to in his lovers.

They were lovers, nothing more. Circumstances had brought them together, and circumstances would soon part them. She'd known how it would be when she'd seduced him; she wasn't foolish enough to believe that he'd fallen in love with her in the space of two days.

Through the hours of two richly physical nights.

The door was finally open enough for her to step into the room and peer through the moon-washed dimness at the bed. . . .

He was there.

Her heart leapt. Literally leapt in her chest, which seemed quite silly of it, but she definitely felt it.

He lay on his back, bathed in soft, silvery light. The sheets rustled as he came up on one elbow to look at her . . . the sheet slid down, exposing his chest.

Her mouth went dry. Her lungs slowed.

Then she remembered what she was about—she'd have time for staring later. Whirling, she shut the door as silently as she could, then turned and padded over to the bed.

He watched her draw near, as she halted by the side of the bed asked, "What are you doing here?"

She met his eyes, in answer tugged loose the tie of her robe, then shrugged the garment from her shoulders, let it fall, the silk sliding down her naked body to the floor. "You're not going to argue, are you?"

His gaze had fallen to her breasts. After an instant's hesitation, he murmured, "No. Of course not," even as, his eyes still locked on her, he raised the covers.

She slid under them, scooted closer as he let them fall.

Caught her breath at the delicious sensation of skin meeting skin. His was so much hotter, his body so much harder.

So potently male.

He reached for her, drew her to him, beside him, half under him as he bent his head and she tipped up her face and their lips met.

Curious . . . even though his lips met hers, moved over hers until they parted and his tongue slid within, heavily stroking with his customary expertise, she sensed he was holding back, was somehow aloof . . . he was thinking.

But then he refocused, intent as well as assured as he pressed closer, closed one hand, knowing and sure, about her breast, and took possession of her senses.

And the dance was different again, a delicious, delightful waltz of the senses as their bodies met, pressed together and parted, as his hands played over her flesh, and his mouth drifted, paying homage before demanding his due.

She rose beneath him, restless and seeking, yet his control never faltered; with faultless execution and experienced command, he orchestrated a consummate performance that, exactly as she wished, educated her senses, opening doors on a different sensual plane, leading her further, leading her on—

Into passion that stole her breath.

Into need so powerful she ached.

Into heat that flowed effortlessly beneath her skin and burned.

Into desire so sharp she felt cut free from the world, cocooned in his arms, in the soft billows of the bed, surrounded by him and the beauty he wrought.

Held, willingly snared, by the pleasure he lavished upon her.

The pleasure built, threatening to sweep her away, but she had her own agenda. She fought, held back the tide, managed to snatch breath enough to gasp, "No. My turn."

It took several long minutes of heated wrestling to convince him that she was in earnest, that she wouldn't let him sway her, but, eventually, on a muted groan he consented to roll onto his back, and let her have at him.

Let her caress and have her fill of him.

Let her drench her senses, drown them in him.

She might never have another chance at this, and of all men, she wanted to learn this with him.

To learn what pleasured him, which caresses built his tension in the same way his built hers. Which slow strokes most teased his senses, which pulse points were most sensitive to the pressure of her lips, to the rasp of her tongue, to the soft suction of her mouth.

She learned quickly, learned well. In those heated moments, his body was hers, surrendered to her wishes, to her will. Hers to explore, to know, to delight in.

She drank her fill.

Breckenridge struggled to hold on to any semblance of control. His fingers locked in the silk of her hair, he endured the exquisitely erotic possession, one he rarely allowed.

That he'd allowed her of all women, innocent as she was, to pander to his fantasies in such a way defied all logic. She was one of the few who had ever challenged his control, ever threatened to strip his civilized veneer from the primitive male beneath.

Chest tight, every muscle tensed to rock, he lay back and, jaw clenched, hung on . . .

Until, predictably, she went one step too far. The instant he felt her delicate fingers drift to his scrotum alarms sounded in his head—rising to a screech when she torturously slowly drew the hot haven of her mouth from his aching erection, then angled her head—

Before her mouth, her kiss-swollen lips, could make contact he surged up, flipped her over, and had her flat on her back beneath him again, pressing her heavily into the soft mattress as he angled his lips over hers. And took over.

Took charge, took control.

He wasn't interested in giving it back.

Once he was certain her wits were reeling, once her hands lost their questing intent and lay passive against his chest, he drew back and slid down the bed, grasped her thighs, lifted them wide, and set his mouth to her softness.

Turn and turn about.

She'd given him this chance; he fully intended to use the engagement to bolster his hold on her.

He focused all his considerable expertise on taking her where she hadn't yet been, and was rewarded with a soft, breathless, mindless scream as she climaxed.

For the first time. He wasn't of a mind to skimp on the night, yet continued to be aware of the primitive male within—the being she called forth, drew forth so effortlessly that primal needs beat just beneath his skin.

When she crested again, driven by his fingers buried deep within her sheath, he could hold back primitive impulse no longer. He positioned himself, and sank into her.

Gloried in the way she accepted him, not just so deeply into her body, but into her arms. They reached up and around, grasping all of him she could as she rose beneath him, her breath all but sobbing as she wordlessly urged him on, tipping back her head to offer him her mouth . . . he hauled in a breath and dived in.

Took, claimed.

Not just her mouth but all of her.

He pushed her, cajoled, demanded, wrung, and seized every last gasp of her passion.

Every last sob, every last evocative moan—he wanted it all.

And she gave.

Without reservation, with no inhibition.

He knew the difference, valued the gift.

Treasured it.

Closed his eyes, held it to his heart as she shattered beneath him, and this time he let go and allowed himself to follow her into oblivion.

Where satiation ruled and bliss rolled in on a long slow wave, and pulled them under.

Wrapped in each other's arms, they slumped in the bed, and surrendered to bliss-filled dreams.

He woke sometime later, summoned enough strength to disengage and lift from her. She turned with a murmured protest, snuggling back into his arms, settling against him, her softness a blessing, her nearness a comfort.

Slumping beside her, half beneath her as she seemed to prefer, he let sleep drag him back under . . . but just before it did he realized what had previously kept him awake.

Clarity often came in moments like that, on the edge of consciousness.

He hadn't been able to fall asleep because she hadn't been in his arms.

Obvious.

Lips gently curving, relaxed to his toes, reassured to his soul, he let consciousness slip away, and slept.

Heather woke to pleasure, to sensation so sweet her toes curled.

To whispers of seduction.

Unable to resist, unwilling to draw back, she let him sweep her away.

Let him take her, have her, slide deep into her body and fill her. Complete her.

From behind, he slid deep, and thrilled her.

Then he rocked her to paradise.

And followed, muffling his hoarse shout in the hollow of her throat.

Hand sunk in his hair, her body arching in his hands, she held him deep inside and gloried.

As the golden tide slowly washed through them, then receded, pulled back and left them racked, she listened to her heart thud, felt the echo of his heartbeat at her core, and clung.

To the closeness.

To the intimacy.

To the indescribably joyous sense of being one.

Slowly their muscles relaxed, their wits returned to them.

She had no regrets that she'd become his lover.

Her only regret was that their time would soon end, and she would lose this—this chance to forge such an incredible connection, one that transcended the physical and edged into the spiritual.

Eyes closed, she felt him draw back, disengage. Felt the connection break, fade.

He slumped, heavy and hot at her back.

For long moments silence reigned while their heartbeats slowed and their breathing evened, and they drifted back to the here and now, to the glow of predawn lightening the sky beyond the windows, to the distant sound of larks heralding the dawn.

His arm lay heavy across her waist, the long fingers of one hand gently cradling her breast.

She felt him stir, then he settled again.

Then he spoke, his voice deep, still edged with passion's rasp. "We need to face facts."

She tried to frown, but her muscles were still too lax. Reluctantly she started marshaling her wits. "What facts?"

"We need to get married."

She jerked away from him enough to turn and stare. "What?" She couldn't have heard aright.

But he was wearing his impassive mask, and his gaze, all

gold and green, remained steady. "There's no other way—
we need to get married, and that's all there is to it."

"What?"

She pulled away, pushing away from him, her expression
one of shock, if not horror; Breckenridge fought the urge to
grab her and haul her back. To hold her. He forced himself to
lie still, kept his voice calm, his tone uninflected. "You can't
possibly be that naïve—you know our world. Given we've
been away, together and alone, for so long, then a wedding is
the prescribed outcome."

Her eyes had flown wide with—he would swear—sheer
and utter surprise. Now they darkened, the soft blue-gray
clouding, roiling with emotion.

"No." Her chin firmed. She scrambled out of the bed,
grabbed her robe, and started shrugging into it. "This is
what comes of letting Richard talk to you alone."

He started to sit up.

Robe gaping, she pointed an imperious finger at him.
"No—don't try to deny it. He spoke to you, and told you you
had to offer, but—"

"He didn't." Despite his best intentions he was speaking
through clenched teeth. "Yes, he asked what I thought, and
I told him I would marry you, and that's the sum total of the
words we exchanged on the subject."

Cinching the robe's tie, she narrowed her eyes at
him. "Richard might not have dictated, but he's good at
intimidating—all of them are."

"No one had to intimidate me—"

"What you and he have failed to understand is that I do
not wish to marry you—not you or anyone else! *Yes,* I seduced you, but that didn't mean I expected you to offer for
my hand, and I most assuredly never meant for us to marry!"

Why not? He bit his tongue, refused to utter the too-re-
vealing words. Drawing his knees up beneath the sheet, he
leaned forward, loosely clasping his hands around his calves
. . . wondered if he could lunge and grab her . . .

She took a large step back. Dragged in a breath. Never

took her eyes from his. She drew herself up, appearing almost regal. She inclined her head a fraction. "I appreciate that given the circumstances, you believe you're honor-bound—"

"Honor has nothing to do with it."

"—that you feel obliged to offer the protection of your name to shield me from scandal, but as I informed you earlier, I've turned my back on the notion of marriage and have my life, my future, already organized, and as that doesn't involve returning to live in London, much less among the ton, then any scandal is irrelevant, so any obligation you might feel is misplaced."

"Your family won't think so."

Her chin tipped up. "Perhaps, but they're not me. Regardless, while I thank you for your kind offer, I must decline."

With that, she whirled away.

"Damn it, come back here!"

"Why? So you can attempt to browbeat me into accepting your offer? I thank you, but no."

"We need to discuss this like sensible adults."

"There's nothing to discuss. I am not going to marry anyone, but I am especially not going to marry a man forced to the altar by notions of honor and obligation."

"Damn it! No one's forcing me—"

Reaching the door, she swung around and pointed at him. "You don't want to marry me—you know you don't. Admit it."

He hesitated.

"Aha—see?" Her eyes glittered. "You don't want to marry me, I don't want to marry you, and there's no reason why we should, so we won't, and that's that."

Hauling open the door, she rushed out and shut the thick panel behind her.

He stared at the door. "I do want to marry you."

The words were too quiet to carry beyond the room.

After a long moment, in which she didn't return, in which

278

he wondered why he was hoping she would, he exhaled, then ran his hands over his face.

"Now what?"

Unsurprisingly, no answer came.

Increasingly grim, he tossed back the covers and rose, one thought resonating in his brain.

She might have her future organized, but what about him?

If she had her way, the future he'd imagined the previous night, the pleasant future that had started to take shape in his mind, would remain nothing more than a fantasy, a golden vision of what might have been. . . .

Jaw setting, he hauled on his clothes.

She wasn't getting away from him that easily.

Chapter Fifteen

He found her at the high table in the hall, breaking her fast with porridge drizzled with honey. Although there were others nearby, groups of men at two of the lower tables chatting and exchanging predictions for the day, there was no one else at the table on the dais.

Drawing out the chair beside her, he sat.

A little maid appeared and bobbed at his elbow, then asked if he'd like some porridge. He managed a smile and agreed. The maid flitted off; the instant she was out of earshot, he said, "There's no point running. We have to sort this out."

Heather slanted him a glance filled with . . . irritation?

Before he could be sure, she shifted her gaze back to her bowl. "By which you mean we need to organize a wedding?"

"There is no other choice."

Her lips tightened, but the maid returned at that moment with a steaming bowl of porridge.

He thanked the girl, helped himself to honey from the glass jar on the table, then slowly stirred the golden nectar into the thick oatmeal. "The situation is simple—I am, in case you've forgotten, commonly held to be the foremost rake in the ton. I didn't come by that reputation by playing cards at White's." He kept his voice low, but his accents were clipped; he couldn't find his usual, suavely persuasive tone. "Given that—who I am—then any gently bred unmarried lady with whom I even nominally spend one night alone will be deemed ruined, and marriage is the only acceptable way to mitigate that outcome—and before you start arguing, whether I in any way was at fault in bringing about that night alone is of not the smallest consequence, any more than the question of whether anything of an improper nature actually transpired is."

He felt his jaw tighten, scooped up a mouthful of the sweetened porridge. Before raising it, he cast a swift glance sideways; her gaze was still lowered, but she was listening. "Add to that that you are who you are—one of the Cynster princesses—and there is no question but that a wedding between us is mandatory."

She glanced sharply at him. "According to society."

He didn't deign to reply; she knew the reality.

The porridge was surprisingly good, nutty-flavored, smooth, and creamy. Looking down, he scooped up another mouthful. Savored, swallowed, then went on in the same low, tight tone, "As there is no chance of avoiding matrimony, I see no benefit in trying to fight the tide. There's no reason we can't wed. I'm already under sisterly edict to find myself a wife, and you're unattached"—he realized he knew that for fact; if she'd harbored any feelings for any other gentleman she would never have allowed him to seduce her—"and our families move in the same circle to the point that a match between us would be considered an excellent one on all counts. Given all that, there's no impediment whatever, no hurdle, no difficulty, standing between us and the altar."

"Except for one fact." Heather set down her spoon, her appetite gone. She met his hazel eyes. "I care nothing for society's approbation, not over this."

She didn't have to fabricate the tension in her voice, the underlying determination fueled and given an edge by growing anger. "Understand this—I am adamantly opposed to marrying"—*you*. Despite her best efforts, the lie stuck in her throat. She dragged in a breath, substituted, "Under such circumstances. I have no ambition to marry, not you, not any man, just because society says I should!"

281

It wasn't just her voice that was unsteady; her head was reeling; she felt faintly dizzy.

When he'd first stated, so baldly, that they would have to wed, she'd been so shaken it had taken all her concentration to rush out of his room before she'd given herself away.

Because the instant he'd raised the prospect of them marrying . . .

Anger had her by the throat and was threatening to strangle her. Welling fury at herself as much as with him. How the devil had she allowed matters to reach such a pass? Had some unforgivably witless part of her been secretly hoping and praying he would, after a few nights of passion, suddenly discover he was in the throes of love with her?

Drawing a tight breath, she held his gaze. "I am not interested in marriage to a man who doesn't want to marry me."

His lips tightened; his expression darkened ominously.

She tipped up her chin. "As I intend to remain in the country and henceforth eschew society, I see no reason to pander to its dictates. This is my life we're discussing, and I'll live it as I please."

He was listening, his attention locked on her—it was one of the things she loved about him, the way he focused so intently on her to the exclusion of the world . . . *no!*

She blinked, shoved aside the distraction. She had to cling to her anger—anger at him for, even if unknowingly, suddenly dangling a prospect she'd never imagined before her, offering her everything that, to her utter shock, she now realized she wanted with every fiber of her being.

Except there was a nasty, slimy worm spoiling the rosy apple. He'd offered her everything her stupid heart had apparently all along desired, except for the one, vital, crucial element necessary to make it work.

She wanted him as her husband—had she always? She had a lowering suspicion her previous prickly attitude to him had been a symptom of unrequited regard—but no matter that her giddy heart had leapt at his bald statement, no matter how rosily some foolish, hitherto unknown part of her wanted to paint their prospective future, no matter how much she yearned to walk into that future with him by her side, just as they'd walked over the mountains to the Vale, she wouldn't—*couldn't*—marry him like this, without so much as a whiff of love.

Hardening her heart, and her determination, she placed an elbow on the table and, eyes locked with his, leaned closer the better to emphasize her point. "Consider this. What sort of lady would I be if I willingly married a man coerced into it? How do you imagine that would make *me* feel?"

He frowned. "I didn't say . . ." He shifted, faintly grimaced. "You don't need to be willing in the sense of turning cartwheels—you just need to accept it's what has to be, as I have."

"No."

"We don't have a choice."

"Yes, we do!" She glared at him.

Brows rising, expression mildly supercilious, he stared steadily back.

She exhaled through her teeth and faced forward. "You're not thinking clearly."

Damn him! She'd assumed that despite their intimacy, he would continue to see her as far too young for him and, when she offered him an honorable way out, that he'd be hedonistic enough to admit they wouldn't suit and grasp the chance to return to and continue his self-centered rakehell's life.

Turning back, she met his eyes, tried again. "You don't want to marry me—I don't want to marry you. And there's no reason we need to wed because I intend to devote my life to taking care of homeless children, and I don't need a husband, much less a socially sanctioned, spotless reputation for that."

She couldn't marry him. Especially not him.

If she did, he'd break her heart—nothing was more certain, more written in stone. He would break her heart because he didn't love her back.

She pressed her lips tight; inside she felt like screaming. The only way out of this miserable mess was to say *No*, and stick to it, no matter what he said. Say no, and insist. "I'm not going to change my mind. Eventually you'll realize that, and go back to London, and all the scented ladies awaiting you there."

His eyes narrowed fractionally; she'd hit a nerve.

"That's where you belong." She tipped her head southward. "In London, prowling the ballrooms and the boudoirs. Being leg-shackled to me won't be in your best interests. If it's honor that's keeping you arguing, then I hereby absolve you of all obligation." She hauled in a breath, held it, then let it out with, "I'm not that desperate to marry that I'll allow anyone to hold a gun to your head and force a marriage upon us both."

She pushed to her feet, looked down into his eyes. "It's not right for us to marry. Accept that . . ." She waited as, pushing back his chair, he slowly, gracefully, rose, too. Looking up, keeping her eyes on his, she continued, "Accept that there's no reason for you to remain here—you can leave whenever it suits you. Regardless of all and anything else, I am not going to hold you back from your life, nor am I going to turn aside from mine, just because society thinks we should."

With a curt nod, she went to swing away.

Breckenridge reached for her arm, halted her. Immediately had to fight to gentle his hold.

As he met her widening eyes, he continued to battle, as he had throughout their exchange, to subdue his inner self, the primitive male who knew she was his, irrevocably his, and had no reservations about making that plain. Keeping all sign of his inner snarling fury from his face, from his hands and eyes, demanded every ounce of self-control he had; he didn't have brain enough left to counter her arguments.

284

Not without risking his leash slipping and letting her see far too much.

He couldn't afford to forget she was a Cynster, and therefore very far from slow-witted. One slip . . . and she might glimpse enough to start wondering.

To start scheming.

Yet he couldn't let her go.

"If we marry . . . there's no reason you can't follow your . . . vocation. With my wealth behind you, you'll be able to be much more effective in—"

"No."

His lips thinned. "If you married me, you'd be much more successful."

"Perhaps." She lifted her chin, met his gaze directly. "But not even for that will I marry you."

Despite his control, he felt his face harden. "Why not?"

She studied his eyes. A long moment passed, then she quietly said, "If you don't know the answer, then that's proof we shouldn't wed."

His inner male roared. "What is this?" He couldn't keep the growl from his voice. "Some secret test?"

Her eyes flashed at his tone; with a swift jerk she pulled her arm free. Inclined her head in clear and haughty warning. "I'm going to spend the morning with Catriona. I'll see you at luncheon."

She turned and walked out of the hall.

He kept his feet planted and watched her go. Frustration welled. Secret test, indeed. The test, it seemed—the challenge before him—was to weave a net of social compulsions and seduction, then use it to capture her, tie her up, and drag her to the altar . . . his primitive self liked the thought.

Savored it.

He would, he swore, do it—tie her up with passion and duty if need be, and marry her, stubbornness, willfulness, and all.

And—the true challenge—he would do it all without discussing or alluding in any way to what he truly felt for her.

To the feelings he had no intention of owning to, of ever letting out into the light of day.

Even for a rake—perhaps especially for a rake—some acts were simply too dangerous to contemplate.

Heather followed the stone stairs down to the dungeon below the manor. Whether it had ever functioned as a dungeon, she didn't know, but it was now Catriona's workroom. As she'd expected, she found her cousin-by-marriage there, busily compounding one of her remedies.

Bunches of herbs dangled from the massive blackened beams that crossed the ceiling, sending aromatic scents wafting in the warm air currents rising from the fireplace in which a small fire crackled and hissed. The chamber was large, lit by small windows high in the walls, and also by lamps burning fine oil. Algaria sometimes worked alongside Catriona but these days was more often to be found in the nursery, atoning for past sins by watching over Richard and Catriona's children, especially Lucilla, the next Lady of the Vale.

Meanwhile, the present Lady of the Vale was standing at one end of the large central table busily grinding something in a mortar. She glanced up as Heather halted at the other end of the table, and smiled. "I thought you'd be by."

Pulling up a tall stool, Heather plopped down on it. "Breckenridge is pressuring me to marry him."

Catriona quirked one fine brow. "What did you expect? You and he have been traveling alone together for . . . how long? Eleven days?"

Heather thought back. "No—we weren't traveling together until we escaped from the others, so it's only been three days." She grimaced. "Not that that matters."

"Three days, three nights." Catriona shrugged, glanced again at Heather's face. "You had to have known Breckenridge would do the honorable thing."

Heather saw no reason to equivocate. "I have absolutely no intention of marrying him."

"Hmm . . . he is a rather daunting proposition." Catriona paused to examine the contents of her mortar, then wielded the pestle again. "But if he's too much for you to take on, then while I would be the last to claim a complete understanding of the ton and all its ways, given yours and Breckenridge's respective backgrounds, I gather an acceptable alternative would be for you to marry some other gentleman, perhaps some second son nearer your own age, more gentle-tempered and meek, some mild-mannered and suitable suitor who was willing to overlook your abduction and its outcome— meaning the time you've spent alone with the ton's foremost rake—someone agreeable to marrying you, presumably for your position and wealth, thus resurrecting your reputation." Catriona frowned. "Mind you, I've never quite grasped just how and why a marriage can repair an otherwise irretrievably damaged reputation."

Heather barely heard Catriona's last comment; she was too immersed in horror at the vision Catriona's earlier words had evoked. "It's not . . ." She blinked, strengthened her voice. "While I have no wish to marry Breckenridge, the notion of marrying some milksop who was willing to overlook . . ." She focused on Catriona. "That's an even worse prospect."

"Ah. I thought perhaps you might have had some gentleman in mind."

"No! It's not that." Heather dragged in a breath. "The truth is . . . I've decided that marriage is not for me."

Ceasing her pounding, Catriona looked up. "Oh?"

Heather nodded. "We—Eliza and I, and Angelica, too, but she's three years younger, so not yet nearing her last gasp, but Eliza and I especially have been searching . . . well, for the right gentleman."

Catriona's lips curved. She glanced down. "Searching for your hero?"

"Yes! Exactly. We know what we want—what sort of man he has to be. But . . ." Unbidden, the image of Breckenridge filled her mind—not as she'd so often seen him, the epitome of polished sophistication prowling the ton, but as he'd been while he'd held her hand and they'd walked through the hills. What had she been searching for? What manner of man?

A man who loved her.

Breckenridge didn't qualify, not in that respect.

Pushing his image from her mind, determination firming, she refocused on Catriona. "It's clear I'm not going to find the gentleman for me, not now this has happened, so I've decided that as fate has effectively decreed that I won't find love, then instead I want to devote my life to helping children who are homeless and alone—who don't have what we, the three of us and our whole family, were born with. So I wondered if I could stay here and learn from you. I know you oversee the care of a small army of such children. I thought that I might stay up here for a time, until summer comes and any scandal over my abduction has blown over. By then I'll have learned so much from you and your helpers, I'll be able to go home to Somerset and see about setting up a similar system there."

"Hmm." Frowning, Catriona reached into a hessian bag of herbs, drew out a handful, and added the leaves to the mortar. Picking up the pestle, she looked at Heather, paused, studying her, then looked down and started grinding again. "That's a laudable ambition, and not one I would discourage. However, you have to remember that for me, looking after stray children is but one activity that's part of a greater whole. I'm the Lady of the Vale, and that's my vocation— the position and the job I was destined to fill. Looking after my strays is a part of that." She paused and met Heather's eyes. "But it's only one part of my larger life."

Heather frowned. "I'm not sure I follow."

Catriona worked at her herbs. "What I'm saying is that before you create such secondary aspects of your life, you need to focus on the core, the central plank . . . I suppose what I'm saying is that first, you need to define and secure your destiny."

"But can't my destiny be to look after stray children?"

Catriona raised her head and looked at Heather. A look from vivid green eyes that searched and somehow saw beneath skin and flesh to the essence that lay beneath.

Heather held still, unflinchingly met that incisive green gaze.

After a moment, Catriona visually drew back. "That isn't what I see, what I sense, for you."

When Heather looked her question, Catriona's lips curved, faintly rueful. "Your destiny is intertwined with that of some man's."

"You can see him?"

"Not in terms of flesh and blood, face and features—I see his . . . aura, if you like. His inner being."

"And my destiny's tied to his?"

"According to the Lady, your destiny lies in dealing with a man . . . if not Breckenridge, then someone like him, of his ilk." Catriona's lips quirked. "A man like your cousins—the Lady knows, I can recognize their like well enough."

"So . . . I'm destined to find my hero after all?"

"Indeed. All you have to do is . . ." Catriona frowned. "The word I'm being pushed to say is 'see' him—perhaps that means recognize him."

Heather thought about that. Catriona's prophecies didn't come often, but they had a startling propensity for coming true. "Perhaps . . . after I learn about looking after children from you and go back to Somerset—" She broke off; Catriona was shaking her head. "No?"

"To the Lady, your plan to learn about looking after stray children is a diversion . . . at least at present." Catriona tipped her head, as if listening to something far distant. "She views it as you trying to avoid the life you're meant to live."

After a moment, Catriona refocused on Heather, studied

her face, then wryly said, "I suspect you won't want to hear this, but all my instincts are suggesting you should look more closely at Breckenridge."

"He doesn't love me. He only wants to marry me because he feels honor-bound to do so."

"Are you sure?"

Heather frowned. "All I can go by is what he says . . ."

"Has he told you he *doesn't* love you?"

"No, but . . ."

"But he's said nothing to lead you to believe he does?" When Heather nodded, Catriona smiled. "That, I have to tell you, means nothing. Whoever your hero is, he is definitely like your cousins, and dragging an admission of love from men like them is never easy. They positively hate exposing their finer feelings, even admitting they have such things, not if they can help it. . . ." Catriona paused, looking struck.

"What is it?"

Lips curving, Catriona met her eyes. "It just occurred to me that the current situation between you and Breckenridge . . . if he was in love with you, given what I've just said about men of his type, don't you think he would seek to exploit the situation so that he could marry you without ever having to declare his heart?"

Heather didn't even have to think to know the answer. "He's as devious and as manipulative as they come." She grimaced. "So I truly will have to consider him more closely."

Catriona nodded. "And in doing so you might want to remember that the love of such a man—as I and your brothers' wives and all your cousins' wives will freely testify—is very much worth fighting for."

Heather humphed. "If only I had some confidence that if I scratched that oh-so-polished exterior, I might find my hero . . ."

"Love rarely comes with guarantees of any kind. And with a man like him, you'll have to be prepared to risk your heart to have any chance of him exposing his." Catriona paused, then added, "One observation that might stand you in good stead. Breckenridge is truly a hedonist to his toes. The counter-side to that, however, means that if he actively pursues a goal, you can be sure that goal is something he truly wants. Otherwise he wouldn't bestir himself."

Given what Heather knew of him, that rang very true.

She sat and considered. Catriona went back to working her herbs.

Minutes ticked by as Heather thought over all Catriona had shared, and she felt something within her settle, accept. So . . . her search wasn't over yet. And she wasn't finished with Breckenridge yet.

Looking up, she met Catriona's understanding, knowing gaze.

"Lots to think about?"

Heather nodded. "Yes—and thank you for . . . reading me. I know you don't do that for everyone."

Catriona's lips kicked up. "I was told to."

"Ah." Heather slipped off the stool. Being around Catriona when she was being the "Lady" could be a trifle disconcerting. "I think I'll go up and see the children—"

"Wait." Catriona checked her mortar, then set it aside. "Finally that's done." A faintly puzzled light in her green eyes, she looked at Heather. Then she shook her head. "For some reason, I'm supposed to give you this." Reaching into her apron pocket, she drew out a chain, fine gold links interspersed with small, round, purple beads with a pink stone pendant, a crystal of half a finger's length.

Walking around the table, Catriona raised the chain; reaching Heather, she slipped it over Heather's head.

Catching the hexagonally cut crystal, Heather studied it. "There's something written on it—etched into the sides."

"The language is so old not even Algaria knows what it is."

Heather glanced up. "It's old?"

Catriona nodded. "My mother's, and hers before that. I used to wear it before I married Richard." Reaching inside the neckline of her gown, she drew out the pendant depending from the chain she wore—a similar, delicate gold chain, but interspersed with pink beads and the pendant was purple. "But then Richard gave me this one—his mother's—which is older still." She pointed to the purple crystal. "This is amethyst, which invokes intelligence." Dropping the pendant back between her breasts, she pointed to the pink pendant on the chain around Heather's neck. "That's rose quartz, which resonates with love."

Chin down, examining the necklace, Heather fingered the small purple beads. "And these are amethyst, too?"

"Yes. The construction you have signifies a melding of love and intelligence, with love the principal force. It's an appropriate charm for a young lady seeking to look into her hero's heart."

"Thank you, but it must be valuable." Heather looked up. "Are you sure—"

"Yes." Catriona smiled. "Courtesy of the Lady, I know my passing it to you is right. You're supposed to wear it until you've found and secured your hero, then pass it to Eliza, then Angelica." Catriona paused, then her brows rose. "And apparently it then goes to Henrietta, and finally Mary, before coming back here to Lucilla." She opened her eyes wide. "It seems the Lady has quite a few destinies already in mind."

Heather tucked the pendant inside her bodice. "I have to admit that knowing I have the Lady on my side is reassuring."

Catriona smiled. "I knew I was to hand it to you—that's why I brought it with me this morning. But I didn't know the rest, about the others. I suspect being told that Lucilla will indeed eventually find her hero was my reward for doing what I was supposed to for you."

Heather fingered the necklace. "It must be a wrench, giving up something of your grandmother's."

"Yes, and no." Catriona picked up her mortar and carried it to a bench. "I've learned over the years not to question—to just believe and obey."

Smiling back, Heather turned to leave. "I'm going to the nursery—do you have any message?"

"Just tell the twins to stop fighting over their knucklebones. Oh." Catriona looked up. "One other thing—remember that a man who declares his heart too easily will leave you wondering whether he truly meant it—and the converse is even more true."

Brows arching, Heather thought, then nodded. With a wave, she started up the stairs.

In midmorning, Breckenridge rode past the spot in the manor's drive where, the afternoon before, he'd stood and watched the man he was sure was behind Heather's kidnapping looking down at them.

"He sat his horse at the top of the lane"—he pointed to the lane leading down from Knockgray—"and just watched us." After a moment, he added, "I didn't get any sense that he was interested in coming closer." He glanced at Richard, mounted on a raking black beside him. "Is there something Catriona does to repel invaders?"

Richard snorted. "I don't ask, but I suspect those intending harm would, these days, find it strangely difficult to cross our borders. It wasn't always so, but she's grown progressively stronger with the years."

When they reached the Ayr road, Richard nodded up the lane. "Let's see if we can pick up his trail."

They rode quickly up the lane, slowing as they reached the top of the steep rise. Leaning from his saddle, Richard studied the ground, then smiled. "Nice big horse, with nice, extra-large hooves." He wheeled his mount, trotting on along the lane past the cottages of the village. "This way." When they reached the end of the tiny village, and the trail led on, Richard grinned and straightened. "Excellent. This lane rejoins the road near Carsphairn. With any luck the locals will have seen him."

Breckenridge brought the bay he was riding up alongside.

"If he's anywhere near as large as he looked, it shouldn't be too hard to know if they'd seen the right man."

"How big was he?"

Breckenridge glanced at Richard, measuring his height against the height of his horse. "If his horse was larger than yours—and that might well be the case; it looked massive—then he's at least a few inches taller than you, and broader by a considerable amount, at least in the shoulders and chest."

"A big beggar, but as you say, that should make him easier to track. What color hair?"

"At a distance, black."

They each glanced at the other's head. Breckenridge's hair was a sable brown, while Richard's was true black. But picking the difference at any distance . . . Richard grimaced. "Dark hair, then."

It didn't take them long to reach the spot where the lane joined the Ayr road. Just before the junction, a neat cottage bordered the lane. An old man sitting on the porch in a rocking chair held up his hand in greeting.

"Fine day, Mr. Cynster."

"Indeed it is, Cribbs." Reining in his prancing black, Richard asked, "Tell me, did you see a large man on a large horse go past yesterday afternoon?"

"About four o'clock," Breckenridge added.

But Cribbs was already nodding. "Couldna' missed him, big as he was. Lordling or laird, by the look of him. Nice chestnut gelding he had under him. Must have been strong as an ox, the horse, to carry his weight."

"That sounds like the man we're after—did you see which way he went?"

"On toward the village." Cribbs nodded north, toward Carsphairn.

"Thank you." Both Richard and Breckenridge saluted and trotted on.

Once on the better-surfaced road, they let their horses

stretch their legs, on and up around the next bend. When they reached the parish church, Richard reined in. "There's only one watering hole—Greystones."

Breckenridge followed Richard to a neat, low, whitewashed building a little way along the road. Richard rode down a narrow alley alongside, and they dismounted in the gravel yard behind the tavern. Leaving their horses tethered to a post, Richard led the way through an open rear door. Both he and Breckenridge had to duck beneath the low lintel. Straightening once inside, Breckenridge found himself in a cozy tavern bar.

With walls half paneled in dark wood, and dark wood tables and chairs, and a long bar running along one side, all lit by the fire in a stone hearth and the sunlight pouring through twin windows facing the road, the long, narrow room was comfortably warm and full of good cheer.

"Mr. Cynster, sir! And what can I get ye?" The barman's gaze tracked past Richard to Breckenridge. The man nodded in smiling greeting. "And your friend, too."

"Two ales, Henry—and your ear." Grinning, Richard fronted the bar, leaning on the raised counter.

Breckenridge ranged alongside, his gaze scanning the other occupants. Four old codgers with nothing better to do than sit indoors, sip ale, and watch the road—just what he and Richard were looking for.

The barman set down two pint pots filled to the brim with frothing ale. Breckenridge turned to accept his with a murmured thanks. He sipped, then cast Richard a glance Richard had been waiting for. Breckenridge grinned and wordlessly toasted Richard. "Your secret?"

The ale was ambrosia.

Richard shrugged, swallowed. "I've just never seen the need to mention it at the manor, at least in female hearing."

The barman returned from carrying the fresh pints Richard had sent to the four older men, all of whom called their thanks and toasted Richard before gratefully drinking.

Henry, the barman, pulled out a cloth and industriously wiped the counter. "So what can I help you with, sir?"

"A large man on a big chestnut gelding rode past yesterday afternoon." Richard turned to include the four older men. "Did any of you get a good look?"

"Better'n that," Henry said. "Came in here, he did. Stopped for a pint."

"Aye," one of the older men said, "and asked after the manor. Wanted to know what lay down the drive."

Henry nodded. "That's right. Good looking gentl'man, he was."

"Taller than me," Breckenridge said, "and broader, too?"

Henry and the others gauged Breckenridge, who was a touch taller than Richard.

"Aye, that'd be right," one of the older crew opined. "Handsome, he was, too, but not as handsome as you."

Breckenridge good-naturedly lifted his pint at the resulting laughter.

"So was he lowland or highland?" Richard asked.

"Highland, definitely, or me mother's an Englishwoman," one of the regulars called.

The others all nodded.

"Never seen him 'round here before," Henry said, "and he did say he was just passing through."

"Rode on away to the north," the old man closest to the window offered. "And that horse of his was something to see. Massive in the chest, and strong, I'd warrant."

"Close to, what did he look like?" Richard asked Henry.

"Black hair—black like yours. Eyes . . ." Henry paused, then shivered. "To tell the truth, if he hadna been such a personable chap, those eyes woulda given me the willies."

Breckenridge lowered his pot. "How so?"

"Pale they were—put me in mind of the ice that forms on yon burn in winter. Cold and pale, but with something flowing underneath."

A moment of silence gave due note to Henry's poetic turn.

"What about his features?" Richard asked.

Henry grimaced, looked to the others. "Pretty much what you'd expect from a laird, I'd say."

"Aye—clean-cut, well-shaven. His clothes were quality, too. And his boots."

No matter how they angled their questions, they learned nothing more.

After draining a second pint each, Breckenridge joined Richard in bidding the five men in the tavern farewell, then walked back out into the rear yard.

Both he and Richard halted in the yard, looking up at the sloping field behind the tavern while they pulled on their riding gloves.

"Not much to go on, beyond confirming he's a laird—they wouldn't have got that wrong."

"And his eyes," Breckenridge said. "Of everything we've learned about him, his eyes are the one thing that's most distinctive. That, combined with his size, combined with his being a laird . . . it might not be enough for us to identify him, but it should be enough to recognize him if he comes after Heather again, or goes after one of the other girls."

"True." Richard caught his horse's reins and swung up to the saddle.

Breckenridge mounted more slowly, juggling possibilities in his mind. Settling in his saddle, he met Richard's eyes. "There's an outside possibility that the man who stopped here was simply what he claimed—a highland laird passing by on his way north. He might have simply been curious about us walking ahead of him."

"But you don't believe that." Richard held his skittish black in.

"No." Breckenridge turned his bay into the alley back to the road. "Because I can't deny the similarities between the descriptions Heather and I independently wrung from Fletcher and Cobbins, and what we just heard."

He rode out and back onto the road. Richard ranged alongside and they cantered south, back toward the Vale.

"So how are the wedding plans progressing?" Richard asked, once they were out of the village.

"They aren't." Breckenridge heard his clipped tones, heard the irritation beneath. Didn't care if Richard did, too. "She's taken some nitwit notion into her head that I don't need to marry her, that she's going to go off and manage an orphanage in the country, or some such thing, so her social ruination doesn't matter."

"Ah." Richard nodded sagely. "She's playing stubborn."

"*Playing?*" Breckenridge shot him an irate look. "She's the definition of the word. I've already tried talking her around. Twice."

"I hate to break it to you, old son, but it won't be your honeyed words that change her mind."

Breckenridge snorted. "I've tried that, too—so far all that's gained me is . . ." *An even deeper sense of being irrevocably linked to her.*

Richard glanced at him curiously. "What?"

Breckenridge pulled a face, growled, "Damned if I know."

Richard grinned. "Well, whatever it takes, just console yourself with the thought that the end result will be worth it."

Breckenridge cast Richard a sharp glance, saw the open contentment in his face. Felt compelled to ask, "So what did you have to do?"

Richard's smile deepened. "The same thing we've all had to do—prostrate ourselves at their dainty feet, swear undying love, and mean it."

Easy for you. He didn't say the words, because even as they formed in his head, he knew they were unlikely to be true. Richard was very like him, even down to the true nature of his birth. Richard had been the scandal that had been no scandal; Helena, Richard's father's duchess, had claimed him as her own shortly after his birth and his natural mother's death in childbed—and no one with a brain in their head argued with Helena.

Breckenridge was a bastard, too, but it had been his father

who had opened his arms to him and claimed him, also from birth.

Both he and Richard had grown to manhood in the midst of the ton, with all the wealth and privileges pertaining to those who belonged to the upper circles of the nobility. Yet he suspected that Richard, just like him, had always carried a question buried in the deepest recesses of his brain. A question that had to do with rightful place.

In Richard's case, he'd had to find one, and he'd patently succeeded here in the Vale. It couldn't have been easy; even though he'd spent less than a day on the estate, Breckenridge had sensed that it was Catriona who stood at the heart of the place, yet Richard had carved his own place, and had clearly earned it, by her side.

For himself . . . Breckenridge's question was slightly different. He had a place waiting for him—his father's shoes. When his father died, he would become the Earl of Brunswick. Even though he already performed many of the duties, did much of the day-to-day work managing the estate, he still wondered if he would measure up when the time came.

For some reason, he knew that if he had Heather by his side, he would.

That if she were there, blithely expecting him to be all he could be, then he would be everything he needed to be, and, possibly, more.

Cantering beside Richard, Breckenridge turned into the Vale drive and rode steadily toward the manor; in the peace and the quiet, broken only by the tattoo of their horses' hooves, he tried to analyze why he was so convinced he needed her, and only her, to succeed in his future life . . . in the end, decided he had no clue.

But perhaps Richard was right.

Breckenridge had more at stake than Heather knew, than he could ever let her know, but perhaps making some concessions, revealing enough to engage her curiosity and, ultimately, her interest, would serve.

That, and taking a more aggressive, more commanding line in the liaison she apparently imagined he was going to allow to end.

Breckenridge next met Heather at the luncheon table. The seat beside her was empty; he claimed it, but Richard and Catriona's older children—their first set of twins, Lucilla and Marcus—had joined the company about the high table and had selected the chairs opposite.

He quickly realized that the eight-year-old twins were determined to do what they saw as their social duty and keep the conversational ball rolling.

The topics they chose ranged from gentlemen's hair styles—comparing Richard's with his—to comments about the source of the lamb roast, identified by name, and Algaria's dandelion wine, to speculation over whether they would have cause to visit London soon.

The pair cheerily discussed the latter at length, all with wide-eyed, innocent curiosity, which fooled him and Heather not at all.

He and she exchanged a glance, then both set themselves to divert attention to any other topic but the one that, transparently, was uppermost in every mind.

A brief glance over the hall confirmed that virtually everyone was living in eager expectation of hearing an engagement announced at any moment. Although the observation only fueled his frustration, the underlying irritation over not yet having secured her agreement to a wedding, in the circumstances, he kept his lips shut.

He did consider using nonverbal means to pursue his objective, but aside from them being too closely watched, he couldn't, he realized, predict how Heather would react. With any other lady with whom he was engaged in a liaison, he wouldn't have hesitated, but not with her, not least because his goal wasn't simply to continue said liaison.

He'd never before wooed a woman. For one of his expertise, the realization that wooing wasn't as easy as seducing was unsettling.

When the platters were empty and all were satisfyingly replete—and Algaria summoned the terrible twins to their afternoon lessons and shooed them before her from the hall—he reached out and, under the table, tugged Heather's sleeve. Leaned nearer as she turned to him, captured her gaze and murmured, "We need to talk."

She studied his eyes for a moment, then nodded. "All right."

He eased back, considered. "Do you know somewhere we can talk without being interrupted or overheard—and preferably not seen?"

She grimaced. "Not being visible from the house isn't easy, but if we go into the herb garden we'll be far enough away. No one will be able to eavesdrop or easily approach, or to see our faces."

He nodded, rose, and drew back her chair.

She led the way out of the emptying hall; ignoring the questioning glance Richard sent him, as well as Catriona's serene regard, he strolled in her wake.

The herb garden was, perhaps predictably, large; it filled the wide swath of downward-sloping land that separated the manor's walls from the banks of the small river. In the irregularly shaped beds, some specimens had only recently shaken free of winter's hold and were tentatively unfurling green buds, while other plants were bursting forth with new foliage in bountiful profusion. At the bottom of the slope the river rushed along in full spate, gurgling over rocks, splashing against boulders embedded in the banks. The sound was happy, cheery, strangely soothing.

Hands in his pockets, he followed at Heather's heels further, lower, into the thickly, richly, informally planted garden. Birdsong became drowned by the drone of bees flitting through the lavenders and the many and various other blooms he couldn't name. The sun was high, its beaming warmth washing over the plants; the tapestry of scents that rose to wreathe around them was enough to make him giddy.

Heather led him toward the river, to a small indentation in the lower side of one bed, a curve carved into the rising bank and walled with stone. Within the curve, more blocks had been laid to create a bench. Walking to one end, with a swish of her skirts, she sat. He halted. When, looking up, she arched a brow at him, he inwardly shrugged and sat alongside her.

The sun shone, a gentle benediction, upon them; the warmed rock surrounding them cocooned them, the fine mist thrown up by the rushing river an occasional refreshing caress.

"Good choice." Leaning back, he rested his shoulders against the wall's upper edge and fixed his gaze on her face. Her profile was all he could see. "We need to settle this—and no, don't tell me it's already settled, because it's not." He paused, making a determined effort to if not eradicate the terse accents from his voice, then at least mute them.

Eyes closed, she tipped up her face in sensual appreciation of the sunshine. "You'll see it my way soon enough—just give yourself time."

Not gritting his teeth took effort. "I won't change my mind, and contrary to your assumption, we don't have unlimited time. For all we know, your parents might already be on their way—we need to have an agreed position before they arrive."

At the mention of her parents, Heather turned to stare at him. Then she frowned. "I wrote and told them that I'm perfectly well, and that there's no need for them to come all this way."

"That may not convince them, but regardless, we need to discuss, sensibly, rationally, the prospect of a marriage between us. You may have formed an attachment to an imagined future without a wedding ring, but realistically, in our world, that isn't an option, not for you."

So Catriona had informed her. The weight of the rose

quartz pendant against her skin reminded her of what else Catriona had said; she wasn't therefore averse to further discussing the subject of a potential union. She faced forward. "Very well—why don't you make your case?" And perhaps if she listened and closely observed, she might get some hint of what, beneath the words, behind his so often impassive mask, was really going on inside him. "Your case beyond the obvious social imperatives, that is."

"Difficult given my case is based on the obvious social imperatives."

"Nevertheless, you might at least *try* to find a broader foundation."

From the corner of her eye, she saw him look up as if imploring divine aid—or perhaps more prosaically asking *why me?*—and had to hide a smile.

Eventually he lowered his head and leveled his hazel gaze at her. "All right—let's try for a broader perspective. You're a Cynster, well bred, well connected, well dowered, and more than passably attractive."

She inclined her head. "Thank you, kind sir."

"Don't thank me yet. You're also opinionated, willful to a fault, argumentative, and at times irrationally stubborn. Be that as it may, for some reason I don't comprehend, we managed to rub along reasonably well through the last week or so, when we had a common goal. I take that as an indication that, were we to marry and jointly take on the common goal of managing my father's estate, the estate that will in time be ours, we would again find ourselves on common ground, enough at least to make a marriage work."

He'd surprised her.

Leaning back, she looked at him. He'd angled his shoulders into the curve of the wall, stretching one arm along the upper edge, long legs stretched out so that his boots brushed her hems. At ease, relaxed and debonair, he appeared the epitome of the sophisticated London rake, which, of course, he was.

He was also an enigma.

At some point during their hike through the mountains, she'd realized that no matter what he allowed her to see, there was something different, something even more attractive, beneath his polished veneer.

"You'd share the responsibilities of running the estate?" She hadn't expected him to speak of such matters.

"If you wished to involve yourself with it." He studied her face. "There are, for instance, the usual number of children to be rescued in and around the estate as you'd find anywhere else in the country."

She humphed. "So I would remain at Baraclough, overseeing the household, while you swan about in the capital?"

Glancing down, he brushed a leaf from his breeches. "Contrary to popular belief, I don't spend all that many weeks in the capital these days—I'm mostly at Baraclough."

"Hmm. All right." She nodded. "That's something for me to consider. So what else can you tempt me with?"

Breckenridge hid a wry smile; he'd guessed that, in common with her female Cynster mentors, she'd be drawn to the prospect of managing a large household and the estate's people. Organizing ran in the blood. "I believe I mentioned that I'm under sisterly edict to marry. Unsurprisingly, a large and pertinent motive behind my sisters' prodding is the desirability of me begetting an heir, or more, thus securing the succession. Perish the thought the estate might ever revert to the Crown, so you could view your role as my future countess as in part holding the ton line against King George and his cronies."

She narrowed her eyes on his. "That's the most inventive way I've ever heard of saying you want children."

His lips curved, then he let the expression fade. "I do—but do you?"

She looked forward. "Yes, of course." After a moment she added, "I can't imagine not wanting children, truth be told."

"Well, then, we're in agreement on that."

"Don't get carried away—you haven't yet convinced me we should wed."

He hesitated, then said, "Perhaps it's time to examine your reasons for refusing." He fixed his gaze on her face, once again in profile. "You're not hesitant because of my . . . for want of a better phrase 'irregular paternity,' are you?"

He'd thought he was asking not because he imagined she would hold that against him—he didn't—but because it was an exccllent gambit to elicit her sympathy . . . yet as the words left his lips he realized that, somewhere deep inside, that question of belonging, of being seen as him and still accepted in his role, lingered.

To be banished by the look she turned on him—a frown that conveyed mystification along with incipient offense.

"Don't be daft!" Her frown deepened. "That hadn't even entered my head. Why would it? It's not as if you're not as well-born as I, and you are Brunswick's heir, after all." Waving back at the manor, she faced forward. "And just think of Richard."

Heather paused, honestly stunned that he'd even imagined . . . but perhaps that wasn't it. Wasn't the real reason he'd brought up what had to be, for him, a sensitive subject. Eyes fixed unseeing on the river, feeling her way, she went on, "You're you—you're too old, too experienced, too worldly to be judged by any other criteria than who and what you *are*." She glanced briefly his way, encountered his customary unreadable façade. "On how you behave."

Gazing again at the river, she tipped her head his way. "And much as it pains me to acknowledge it, you've been nothing but protective and honorable—indeed, throughout our adventure you were close to a pattern-card of the gentlemanly virtues."

"Close to?"

"You argued too much and you're far too stubborn."

"You can talk."

"Precisely—I can." She glanced at him again, this time met

his gaze. "You might be an expert in seducing women, but if there's one thing *I* am an expert in it's arrogantly aristocratic gentlemen and how they behave—I've been surrounded by the cream of the species since birth—and you are readily recognizable as one of their number."

With a nod to emphasize her conclusion, she looked back at the river again.

She wasn't too surprised when he didn't immediately speak, didn't rush to push any further point.

It didn't last, of course.

"All right—so it's not my birth, and clearly you don't feel overly challenged by me or my station. You don't feel out of your depth dealing with me."

When she made a scoffing sound and flung a dismissive glance his way, he caught it, held it.

"So what, then"—his voice deepened, softened, the suave tones sliding over her skin—"will it take to convince you that you should—indeed, ought to—marry me?"

He let her look into his eyes, for once didn't keep his mask between them.

Let her see he was in earnest, sincere in wanting to know.

She drew in a long breath, then looked back at the river and let out a long, slow sigh. Wondered why she was bothering. If he truly didn't know . . .

Perhaps she should tell him.

"Very well. As you're so determined to hear them, these are my reasons." She'd never voiced them before, not all of them, yet if Catriona was right and he might be her hero . . . it behooved her to try to find the words. "I long ago decided that the one element I would never agree to marry without was true . . . affection." Recalling Catriona's views, she substituted the less specific, less, for men, frightening word. "An affection strong enough to last the years, powerful enough to guide and inform, deep and broad enough to be the foundation of a shared life. I want passion and laughter, interest and inclusion, a partnership at least on a practical level, and something even deeper on the personal.

"I want . . . to be wanted, to feel necessary and needed, to know I fill a role that only I can fill." She paused, then forced herself to go on. "But even more than that, I want that depth of affection to be offered to me, Heather Cynster, not because I *am* Heather Cynster, well-connected heiress and"—she flicked a glance his way—"considered by some to be more than passably attractive, but because I'm *me*." She tapped her chest, felt the pendant beneath her bodice. "I want to be wanted, needed—and married—because of who I am, not what I am."

Suddenly seeing the parallel, she caught his gaze. "In light of your query regarding your birth, you should understand how I feel—how important to me it is to be valued for myself, and to know it."

Breckenridge held her gaze—and wondered how he'd managed to let her maneuver him into such a position. Into the narrow gap in a cleft stick. Because he did understand—more than that, he felt the resonance of her words reach deep, to the man he truly was. Felt his true nature react, respond, effortlessly drawn forth by a compulsion to satisfy her need.

To blurt out words he had no intention of saying, to lay before her the assurance, the capitulation, she was searching for—a vow that she would forever and always be the focus, the fulcrum of his life . . . the admission hovered on his suddenly reckless tongue.

He'd had no idea his probing might precipitate such a link, that her answers might deepen his susceptibility even more. He'd been looking for a way to avoid stirring his emotions. Instead . . .

She wanted him to tell her he loved her.

But that meant he'd have to hear the words himself.

Words he'd sworn never again to utter. He'd sworn to never again open himself, his heart, to that much pain. . . .

He knew the pain, still carried the scars.

Never ever again.

Their gazes remained locked. He could almost feel her willing him to open his mouth and speak. . . .

Time suspended, lengthened, and he started to suspect she knew, had seen, at the very least suspected what he himself was pretending to be blind to.

The prospect shook him, helped him keep his lips firmly shut.

When he didn't speak—when she accepted he wasn't going to—her lids lowered, then she drew fractionally back, tipping up her chin as she turned to face the river. "Regardless of any arguments you or others might proffer, I will not marry without that particular affection."

A declaration, a ringing challenge.

He stirred, muscles tensing, then forced himself to relax again. "This 'affection.' "

The terse words were on his lips before he'd thought, placed there by that elemental male who considered her already his. Who heard her intransigence as a clarion call to action, who interpreted her challenge as an affront.

But aggressive insistence wouldn't trump her stubbornness. Wouldn't prevail.

He had other weapons at his disposal, ones he'd honed over decades in the ton.

"Yes?" Brows arched, she glanced at him.

"Perhaps . . ." Resuming his rake's persona, investing every movement with languid grace, he shifted forward, closer. Held her gaze. "You could teach me what it is you need." He let his gaze drift from her eyes to her lips. "I've always been considered a fast learner, and if I'm willing to learn, to devote myself to the study of what you truly want . . ."

Her lips parted slightly. He raised his gaze once more to her eyes, to the stormy blue. Read her interest, knew he had her undivided attention.

Inwardly smiled. "If I swear I'll do all I can to meet your requirements, shouldn't you accept the . . . challenge, if you like, to take me as I am and reshape me to your need?"

Holding her gaze, resisting the urge to lower his to her tempting lips, he raised a hand, touched the backs of his fingers to her cheek in a tantalizingly light caress. "You could, if you wished, take on the challenge of taming the ton's foremost rake, of making me your devoted slave . . . but you'd have to work at it, make the effort and take the time to educate me—arrogantly oblivious male that I am—all of which will be much easier, facilitated as it were, by us marrying. After all, nothing worthwhile is ever attained easily or quickly. If I'm willing to give you free rein to mold me to your liking, shouldn't you be willing to engage?"

She was thinking, considering; he could see it in her eyes. She was following his arguments, her mind following the path he wanted it to take.

Shifting his fingers to lightly frame her chin, he held her face steady as if for a kiss.

"And just think," he murmured, his eyes still locked with hers, his lips curving in a practised smile, "of the cachet you'll be able to claim as the lady who captured me."

Her focus sharpened. She looked into his eyes, studied them.

Then she rolled her eyes and lifted her chin from his fingers. "You're really very good, but that's not going to work."

He stared at her. He'd had her; she'd been with him, following, coming around. . . .

Facing the river, as if she could hear him she shook her head. "There were an awful lot of ifs and buts in that, and none of them changed anything." She glanced at him, her eyes narrowing, her gaze sharpening. "You didn't expect to charm me into marrying you, did you?"

Yes, I did.

Lips pressed tight, he slumped back against the wall, looked up at the sky. Few women were immune to his persuasive charm, but, of course, she had to be one. Inwardly swearing, he rapidly canvassed his options.

Dropped all pretense and sat up. "Listen—we cannot go on as we are with absolutely nothing decided."

"On the contrary, there's nothing to decide. You made an offer motivated by honor, and I refused."

"That's not the end of it."

"Yes, it is—and if all you have to say is simply a restatement of what you've already said, then I believe we have nothing more to discuss." Nose in the air, Heather tensed to rise.

Breckenridge's hand clamped heavily on her arm. "No, you don't—just sit still and listen."

His growl, the possessive grip, spurred her temper. She whipped around and glared at him. "Why? So you can browbeat me into agreeing?" She shook off his hand and surged to her feet.

He stood, too, quickly facing her, blocking her way. "Heather—"

"No!" Temper in the ascendant, she poked a finger at his chest. "It's *your* turn to listen—and listen well. If you don't feel the degree of affection for me that I require in my prospective husband, then I will not marry you—and I am not about to agree to a wedding on speculation!"

His face decidedly grim, his expression for once some indication of his temper, he glared at her. "Damn it! There's only so much I can give—that I can offer you."

"You can give whatever you want—if you truly wanted to!"

He shifted closer, looming nearer, his eyes agate hard boring into hers. "We need to get married. That's an inescapable fact. We have to come to some arrangement so our wedding can proceed—which means you have to grow up, set aside any rosy, starry-eyed notions, and deal with the realities of our world. You need to reassess, you need to be reasonable, then you need to tell me what I can give you that will enable you to agree to become my wife."

She held his gaze. And felt fury burn.

Because she was starting to suspect that Catriona might

be right, that behind his smooth, polished façade, Breckenridge might actually feel for her everything she wanted him to feel.

More, that he might know he did, but—witness his charming words, his roundabout arguments—for some impenetrable male reason he was unwilling to declare that truth, not in any way, shape, or form.

So he was going to be difficult. But if there was any chance at all that he, arrogant, infuriating, and irritating though he was, was her fated hero, that he and this was her chance to seize a future as glowing as any she'd ever dreamed, then there was likewise no chance that she would—that she could—give up and walk away.

The love of such a man is worth fighting for.

Catriona's words rang in her head.

Rising up on her toes, eyes locked with his, she simply said, "Give me one *good* reason why I should."

His temper was as close to the surface as hers. She all but saw the hot words leap to his tongue—but he pressed his lips even tighter together, holding the impulsive, sure to be revealing response back. . . .

Eventually, his tone rigidly controlled, he replied, "We need to get married because that is the only acceptable outcome."

She held his gaze, felt his will, implacable and utterly compelling, beat about her.

Felt her own stubbornness well. Harden.

Felt her temper surge, hot and scalding.

She opened her mouth to give him a piece of her mind— fury clogged her throat.

"*Arrrgh!*" She flung up her hands, swung on her heel, and stormed off through the gardens.

Breckenridge watched her go. Heard the gravel crunch beneath her feet, read the fury in every stride, the anger investing every line of her svelte form.

The words he'd uttered, and those he hadn't, echoed in his

head. *We need to get married because that is the only acceptable outcome . . . to me.*

If he'd been honest enough, brave enough, to give voice to the last two words . . . would she have let him get away with just that?

He inwardly scoffed. A fool's hope. When it came to that particular "affection," she, like her like-minded sisters, would insist on her full due. If he gave her any definite hint that he felt anything of that nature for her, she wouldn't rest until she had him on his knees swearing undying devotion. And offering her his heart on a platter.

Something he could never do.

The one thing he would never trust any woman enough to do again.

Heather reached the manor's side door and disappeared inside.

He thought, consulting the morass of ill-used feelings churning inside, then, jaw setting, stalked off along a different path—the one that led to the stables.

Standing a few feet back from the window in the turret room below the bedchamber she and Richard shared, Catriona, arms crossed, watched Breckenridge stride toward the stables. "Well, that looks promising."

"Indeed." Beside her, Algaria nodded. "I wasn't sure before, but now . . ."

"I wasn't sure either." Catriona turned to the room. "Not that she was the right one for him, or that he was the one for her, but after that performance, there can be no doubt."

She used the chamber as a sitting room, and Algaria often brought Lucilla and Marcus there for their less formal lessons. The elder twins were seated cross-legged on the floor, sorting various leaves, learning the plants their mother and the Vale folk used for various ills, both in themselves and their animals.

"Be that as it may"—Algaria turned to watch the twins—"I sensed from the first that he's . . . very contained."

Catriona nodded. "That's why I was most unsure about him—he appears so outwardly open, so charmingly at ease, yet inside there are walls. Thick, impenetrable walls."

Algaria nodded. "If he's ever to have her, he'll need to take those walls down himself."

"Or at least open a door and let her in." After a moment, Catriona went on, "All we can do is have faith—and watch to see what happens next."

Chapter Sixteen

Ten hours later, Heather lay in the four-poster bed in the room she usually occupied at the manor. Fingering the chain about her neck, she stared up at the canopy above.

Most of the manor's occupants would by now be snoring. If she intended to join Breckenridge, then it would be safe to go to his room now.

Cloaked in comfortable darkness, she didn't move, just lay staring unseeing upward.

Thinking, reviewing. Planning.

Scheming.

She had, at his request, declared her position—told him what she wanted from any man she would agree to call husband. She'd made the effort, plumbed her deepest feelings and bared her dreams . . . and what had been his response?

Silence. Then he'd tried charming her.

When that hadn't worked, he'd reverted to heavy-handed, domineering arguments.

She'd given him the opportunity to bare his deepest feelings—even a hint would have sufficed—but instead he'd held firm and told her nothing.

Admitted nothing.

For the rest of the day, through the long evening, he'd held to a rigidly correct distance. If it hadn't been for the heat in his gaze she might have thought he'd decided to return to treating her as he had over the past years in London, that as far as he was concerned the interlude between London and the Vale had never occurred . . . but those dark, smoldering glances had given the lie to that.

He'd admitted nothing yet remained unswervingly fixed on marrying her.

All of which left her in a complete quandary.

Did his refusal to admit he felt any strong "affection" for her mean that he did but was—in typical male fashion—doing his very best to hide it?

Or instead had he refused to give her any hope because he truly didn't feel any real affection for her, only lust, something he presumably would know all about, and recognizing that, he was too honorable to pretend to feel the "affection" she required in order to falsely gain her agreement to marry him?

She could hardly fault him if the latter were the case.

And if it was, she wouldn't be marrying him.

Which very definitely meant she shouldn't get up, slip through the corridors, and make her way to his bed.

She might actively want more experiences to build her store of memories against the lonely years ahead, but . . . going to him would prolong his belief that if he persevered, he would eventually wear her down—wear her out—and she would agree to marry him without the vow of "affection" she sought.

In that, he wouldn't succeed, but there was, unfortunately, another pertinent consideration.

What if she fell pregnant?

There'd be no avoiding the altar then. Even more so given he needed an heir.

Introducing a child into their equation was the only twist capable of forcing her to put aside her requirement for "affection" and marry him regardless.

That was something he might guess.

Something he, given his continuing determination to wed her, might seek to use if she continued to refuse him, and then she'd never know which of his potential reasons—true "affection" or mere honor linked with lust—was his real motivation.

So . . . no further indulging.

At least not unless she had better proof that he truly did love her.

She wasn't afraid of using the word, yet simply thinking it evoked a wellspring of yearning, a hollow need that encompassed her heart, and had grown deeper and broader over recent days.

An emptiness she prayed would one day be filled, by a partner, a lover, a husband who loved her.

She sighed, then sat up, thumped her pillow and slumped down on her side, her cheek pillowed on soft linen.

Not the same as being pillowed on his chest.

Nowhere near as soothing.

But it was safer this way.

Besides . . . it was entirely possible that abstinence would make the heart grow fonder.

Whether it might make his heart any easier to read was another matter altogether.

She wasn't coming.

Hands beneath his head, Breckenridge lay on his back, stared up at the ceiling, and felt the realization sink to his marrow. He wasn't sure whether to feel relieved or aggrieved.

In the end, aggrieved won out.

How was he supposed to convince the damn woman to marry him if she avoided him? Especially if she avoided him here, at night, in the arena in which his persuasive powers were strongest?

Perhaps he should go to her?

He debated the option for a full five minutes but reluctantly conceded that if she didn't come to him, then he couldn't go to her. Such an act would smack of a need he was trying hard to hide; the suggestion that he would rather not be parted from her for even one night was simply too revealing.

Besides, if she didn't want to sleep in his arms . . .

The thought shook him but effectively refocused him on the question of why she hadn't come slipping through his door.

All conceit aside, he knew she'd enjoyed their interludes every bit as much as he had, and even if she wished to hold to her stance of not marrying him, why would she deny herself a pleasure that, if she prevailed, she wouldn't have available for many days more?

Why put an early end to their liaison?

To punish him for not admitting to "deep affection"?

Or to prod him into admitting the same?

Or both?

The more he thought of it, the more he was convinced the answer lay somewhere along those lines.

Lips twisting wrily, he turned on his side, pulled the covers over his shoulder, and closed his eyes.

What was sauce for the gander in that regard was also sauce for the goose.

Breakfast the next morning was the usual noisy, warmly inclusive Saturday morning meal Heather recalled from previous visits to the Vale.

Sadly, the effervescent buzz of conversation, punctuated by the clink of cutlery and the chiming of crockery, only made her temples throb more definitely.

She hadn't slept well. And she knew at whose feet to lay the blame.

Breckenridge sat alongside Richard toward the other end of the table; between sipping tea and nibbling toast, she cast dark glances his way—glances he chose to ignore.

Rising temper did nothing to ease her burgeoning headache.

Finally the meal, shared with the entire household, was at an end.

Seated at the middle of the high table, Catriona rose and

looked at Heather. "I need someone to take a basket to one of the farms—some items to help a new mother. Her babe's only two months old. Can you take it?"

A nice long walk in the fresh spring air was exactly what she needed. She nodded and pushed back her chair. "If you'll tell me the way, I'll be happy to."

Catriona glanced at Lucilla and Marcus, seated to Heather's right. "Why don't you two act as guides?"

"Yes, please!" Marcus shot up from his chair.

Catriona smiled. "It's the Mitchells' farm."

"We know the way," Lucilla assured her. Looking at Heather, Lucilla added, "We won't let you get lost."

Heather felt her lips curving for the first time that morning. "Thank you. I'll put my faith in you." She arched a brow at Catriona.

"Megan Mitchell, and the babe's Callum. He's a healthy boy, but if you sense anything amiss"—Catriona included Lucilla with her eyes—"be sure you tell me when you get back."

"Yes, Mama." Coming around the table, Lucilla took Heather's hand, then peeked down. "Good—you have your boots on. So we can go and collect the basket straightaway. Cook will have it ready."

"Yes, all right." Allowing herself to be towed around and off the dais, Heather exchanged a laughing glance with Catriona, then surrendered and let the twins drag her on—all the while pretending not to notice the increasingly black frown on Breckenridge's face.

The instant Heather disappeared through the archway leading to the kitchen, Breckenridge cut across Richard's dissertation about the local crops to ask, "How far is the Mitchell farm?"

His expression mild, Richard replied, "About a mile and a half, maybe a bit more, further into the Vale."

In the act of swanning past, Catriona paused. "You don't need to worry. They'll be perfectly safe. The way's all on Vale lands, after all—I would know if anything threatened."

With that, she passed on.

Richard cast him an understanding glance. "I take it you'll be busy this morning?"

Breckenridge grunted and left it at that. Richard didn't need more of a reply.

After a few seconds' consideration, Breckenridge rose, nodded a farewell to Richard, who smiled, but wisely said nothing, then Breckenridge left the hall and headed for the manor's front door.

He circled around through the herb garden; he was standing concealed in the shadows cast by one of the irregular corners of the manor when Marcus ran out of the back door, followed by a skipping Lucilla. Heather brought up the rear, a basket on her arm.

The basket didn't appear to be that heavy. Breckenridge reluctantly rejected using its weight and his offer to carry it as his excuse for joining the expedition. Given the situation between him and Heather, he knew well enough that this was the wrong time to push her—to press his company on her—but equally he wasn't able to simply stand by and watch her walk out effectively unescorted.

She might be perfectly safe, but his inner male wasn't about to risk it.

Once the threesome were far enough ahead, he set out in their wake, walking slowly, hands in his pockets, and making good use of any available cover.

Heather reached the Mitchells' farmhouse after half an hour of pleasant rambling along the winding river, then up a sloping path through a stand of trees to the small, south-facing plateau on which the farmhouse sat.

The sun bathed the front of the whitewashed building, glinting off the windows flanking the green-painted door. One of the windows was open a crack; as Heather approached, she could hear the baby fretting.

She paused before the door, hesitated, but then raised her hand and rapped.

A pale face appeared briefly in the window, saw her, saw Lucilla and Marcus running up from where they'd dallied among the trees, and abruptly disappeared.

Half a minute later, the door opened to reveal a harried-looking young woman smoothing down her skirts. "Yes?"

Heather smiled. "Megan Mitchell?"

The woman bobbed. "Aye, miss."

"I've brought you some things from the manor." Heather indicated the basket on her arm. Megan Mitchell was, she judged, younger than she.

The young mother's gaze fell to the basket. "From the Lady?"

"Yes. She thought you might find these things useful." Heather saw the relief in Megan's face as she spied the loaf of bread in the basket. "Might I come in?" Heather glanced back at Lucilla and Marcus, now playing a boisterous game of tag on the swath of grass before the farmhouse. "And if the baby—Callum, isn't it?—is crochety, perhaps we'd best leave those two outside." Turning back to Megan, Heather let her smile turn understanding. "Meanwhile, perhaps I can help you—at least hold Callum while you get some chores done."

Megan all but sagged with relief. "Thank you, miss, that would be most kind. But I wouldn't want to impose—"

"You won't be. I'm happy to help." Stepping over the threshold as Megan stepped back, Heather took in the almost painfully neat space, kitchen and sitting room rolled into one. Despite the austerity, there were small touches of warmth here and there, most to do with the baby, grumbling and grouching and waving his tiny fists in the bassinet set in the sunshine before one window.

"Here." She handed over the basket. "You take care of that, and I'll make Callum's acquaintance."

Megan took the basket and set it down on the table. Heather felt her watchful gaze as she went to the bassinet, leaned over to coo, then play with Callum's batting fists.

The baby's eyes were wide, just coming into a definite

blue. A tuft of fluffy brownish hair decorated his pink crown; with his button nose, round face, and pink cheeks, he looked very like a doll come to life.

"I've helped my sisters-in-law, cousins, and my cousins' wives with their babies." Heather spoke without looking at Megan, as, acquaintance made, she carefully lifted Callum into her arms. "Between them, they've had quite a few, and I can assure you most were far more fractious than this sweet boy."

Callum looked into her face as if fascinated by the different cadence of her voice.

Megan watched, but then, reassured by Heather's confident handling of little Callum, relaxed and gave her attention to the basket. She unpacked it, briskly setting the various items about the kitchen. "Please do thank the Lady—and I 'spect Cook—for the loaf. Helps if I don't have to bake."

"I will." Heather rocked Callum in her arms. He'd settled like a lamb, still staring up at her, possibly at the curls that fell from the knot on the top of her head.

Some minutes later, "Hmm . . . miss, do you know what this's for?"

Heather turned to see Megan holding up a bottle of what looked to be medicine. Still gently rocking and jiggling Callum, Heather walked over. The bottle contained a pale syrup. "Can you open it for me?"

When Megan obliged, Heather touched a finger to the rim of the bottle, then tasted. "Ah, yes. Dill essence in syrup." She smiled. "Catriona—the Lady—is looking ahead. It's for when the colic sets in." Realizing from Megan's mystified expression that she didn't know of the joys awaiting her, Heather explained.

Megan looked at the bottle with new respect. "She's a wonder, the Lady. Do please give her my most humble thanks."

Heather inclined her head, then wandered back to the shaft of sunlight. Looking down at Callum, still wide awake, but utterly quiet, she said, "He seems quite settled."

321

"Aye—he likes to move a little, just as you're doing." Megan set the empty basket down by the door. Then hesitated.

Without looking up, Heather murmured, "If you'd like to attend to any chores, I'm happy to keep him amused."

"If you're sure . . . ?"

Heather smiled. "Yes. Will we be out of your way here?"

"Oh, aye. It's the washing I need to finish, and if I can get the pot on, that will be a blessing."

Swaying slightly, Heather stood in the sunshine before the window, rocked Callum in her arms . . . and thought of how she might feel if the baby were her own.

Of course, if she followed that thought to its logical conclusion, the baby would have dark hair and hazel eyes. She couldn't imagine having any other man's child, which, she suspected, said quite a lot. Breckenridge had mentioned wanting children, and she'd immediately seen herself rocking his son. She'd wanted that dream, but it was only a part of the wider whole.

Of all they—he and she—might have, if only . . .

If only he loved her enough to tell her so.

During the night, in between her fitful bouts of sleep, she'd revisited her decision, as one did in the dead of night when one tried to find a way through a shifting maze, questioning at every turn. She'd wondered if, perhaps, she could manage without him declaring he loved her.

Pointless to pretend she didn't care for him, that she wasn't, indeed, in love with him. If she hadn't been, she would never have been wasting so many hours thinking and obsessing about him and his inscrutable ways.

So could she agree to marrying him without knowing, without being certain, that he loved her in return?

No matter how she'd twisted and turned, the answer had remained the same.

Because she loved him, she couldn't risk marrying him without the assurance.

Because without that assurance, she would live in constant fear, never feeling safe in her love, never certain that he wouldn't break her heart by turning to other ladies.

She was neither blind nor witless. She knew his reputation had been wellearned.

But other rakes had changed; she knew of several who had become pattern-cards of virtue after they had wed.

But they'd all been in love; head over heels, undeniably in love.

Only love was a guarantee that he would be hers for ever more.

And she was who she was; she needed ever more.

So no, she needed to hear his love declared . . . or at least communicated in some unequivocal way. Even if he never said the words, as long as she knew.

Words were only words, after all, easy to say, easy to forget.

Actions spoke louder. . . .

Were there any actions, any undeniable clues that he did indeed love her despite his refusal to say the fateful words?

Was there any chance she might convince herself of his love without him having to make a declaration?

No immediate answers sprang to mind, but if she did find such a clue, convinced herself it was real and true, even if he never admitted to loving her, wasn't love—securing love and building a life together based on that emotion—worth the risk? Worth almost any risk?

Catriona had warned that in order to secure Breckenridge's heart, Heather might well have to risk hers. Was this what Catriona had meant?

When all the rest was stripped away, was she willing to risk her heart to secure the future she yearned for?

What if she risked all and didn't win? Didn't gain the reciprocal love, the husband, and the life she wanted?

Risk, indeed.

"There, now." Megan came forward. "I'm all done for the morning, and m' bonny bairn is sound asleep." Smiling softly, she reached for the baby.

Heather relinquished the warm bundle, watched Megan's face, so full of maternal love as she gazed down at her sleeping son. "I'll leave you now."

Megan looked up at the whisper, smiled. "Thank you, miss. You've made my day much easier—needed a helping hand I did, and there you came along."

Heather's smile deepened. "Thank the Lady."

With a salute, she picked up the basket and stepped through the still open door.

The sunshine beamed down. Halting on the stoop, she closed her eyes, listened to the song of the birds, the buzz of insects, the piping voices of Lucilla and Marcus now playing in the shade of a tree by the edge of the meadow.

A moment of peace in an otherwise thought-filled, thought-provoking day.

Opening her eyes on a sigh, she stepped out, heading back along the path toward the trees. "Come along, you two. It's time to go back."

Lucilla waved. Marcus whooped, then led the way down the path, gamboling like a lamb, Lucilla, on his heels, calling out encouragement.

Heather laughed. Feeling much lighter, she lengthened her stride, empty basket swinging from one hand.

She'd reentered the dappled dimness beneath the trees when a flitting shadow at the edge of her vision had her turning her head sharply. Enough to catch a glimpse. Enough of a glimpse to guess.

Smothering an oath, she stepped off the path, tramped through the low underbrush to a large tree five yards off the path.

Rounding the wide bole, she halted and glared. "What the *devil* are you doing here?"

Breckenridge opened his eyes. Eyes he'd closed in momentary exasperation. "What do you think I'm doing here?" When in doubt, turn the question back. Inspiration struck. "I'm doing what I've been doing since I left Lady Herford's salon—protecting you."

She narrowed her eyes at him, anger and aggravation in every line of her face. "Has it ever occurred to you that if, in her ladyship's salon, you'd done the sensible thing and pretended not to notice me, rather than decided to 'protect' me by hauling me out and sending me home, then none of this would have happened?"

Guilt washed over him, but it was a more fundamental fear that seized him by the throat and kept him silent. He stared impassively down at her as the seconds ticked by, then finally asked, his voice flat and uninflected, "Would you really rather *none* of this had hap—"

"Forget I said that." She brusquely waved a hand as if erasing her comment. "That's not the point. The point is that there is no danger here—there's no need for you to be following me. I don't need a guard in the Vale." She waved at the surrounding hills. "I'm at no risk here!"

"You might be." Her aggravation abraded his. "For all you know Fletcher and Cobbins might have followed us here and just be waiting for the right moment to seize you again."

"What?" She blinked. Her face paled; she looked toward the track. "Lucilla and Marcus. They've run ahead—"

"No—I take it back." Disgusted that he couldn't even let himself scare her, he hissed out a breath through clenched teeth. "There isn't any imminent threat."

She frowned at him. "How can you be sure? You just said—"

"I know what I said." Gripping her elbow, he urged her back toward the path. "But Richard sent riders—trackers—around the boundaries, and they found no evidence anyone had crossed, and all the Vale people have been alerted, but no one's seen any stranger lurking." They reached the path and he released her. Scanning their surroundings, he grimaced. "And much as I don't want to dwell on whatever witchy powers Catriona wields, she says there's currently no threat on Vale lands, and as everyone else seems to think she would know . . ." He shrugged.

He matched his stride to hers as she started back along the

path. Thrusting his hands in his pockets, eyes on the path, he felt forced to concede, "It's unlikely you're in any danger here, but having got you this far safely, there's no reason to take unnecessary risks."

He felt her sharp, still annoyed gaze on the side of his face. Made no move to meet it. Instead steeled himself for her next attack.

When he refused to meet her gaze, Heather humphed, looked ahead, and tried to sort out her feelings. Tried to decide what she felt.

The trees ended and the path dipped down to the river's edge. Ahead, the twins had paused to toss stones into a pool; they looked back, saw Breckenridge and her, waved, then ran on.

Striding freely along the more level path as it followed the burbling river, she couldn't help but remember her earlier enjoyment in walking the other way alone. Couldn't help but note and wonder why she felt the same enjoyment, yet a somehow deeper, more complete sense of contentment now, just because Breckenridge was walking by her side.

He wasn't even holding her hand, yet the connection was still there, ephemeral perhaps, yet undeniable.

Even though she was annoyed with him.

She might jib at him surreptitiously "guarding her," yet she couldn't deny that the sense of being guarded, of being watched over, had grown on her. At least when it was him doing the watching. And she'd be lying if she said she didn't appreciate his attention in having thought to check on the kidnappers, on whether they might pose any continuing threat.

Having him walking beside her, a large, undeniably physically capable, protective male, made her feel safe. Safe in a way that reached soul-deep.

In a way that she would lose, would no longer have, and most likely would never know again, once he returned to London.

The thought sent a spike of loss lancing through her.

"You might as well start practising not following me about—you'll be leaving for London soon, after all." Turning her head, she met the unreadable hazel of his eyes as he glanced at her. Tipped up her chin as the long, lonely hours of the previous night replayed in her mind. "There's nothing to keep you here, not now. So when will you be leaving?"

He held her gaze, his expression like granite, as impassive as ever.

Breckenridge didn't misinterpret her challenge, didn't miss the flash of stubborn pride in her eyes. But they both had a surfeit of that particular emotion. "You'll know when I know." He kept his tone even, his gaze level—meeting her challenge with his own. "Of that, you can be absolutely sure."

Her chin rose another notch as, with a faint arching of her brows, she looked ahead.

Facing forward, too, he concentrated on walking on unaffectedly, unthreateningly, by her side, subduing—denying—the compulsion to halt, haul her into his arms, and make clear in unequivocal fashion that he had no intention of ever letting her go, of ever permitting her to escape him. His inner male didn't appreciate that she'd even entertained the thought, much less given it voice.

But his civilized self was too experienced to give into such reckless impulse. She'd backed away from implying that she wished their liasion had never been . . . he needed to tread warily, to give her time to come around. This was not the moment to pressure her.

Not yet.

As they walked back to the manor, the morning bright about them, he turned his mind to planning the next stage in a conquest unlike any other, one from which he could no longer walk away.

A conquest he couldn't afford to lose.

* * *

After lunch, Breckenridge joined Richard in his library. They'd discovered they shared a passion for fly-fishing; tying lures was an occupation whose attraction never waned.

On one side of the library, they sat at either end of a narrow table reserved for the task. Tiny boxes containing hooks, beads, and feathers of every conceivable sort were spread over the tabletop, along with various coils of line and an assortment of implements.

Richard was using a viselike stand to hold the lure on which he was working. Breckenridge preferred to use a simple clamp.

Silence reigned, companionable and soothing, while they each concentrated on their creations. The long case clock in the corner ticked on.

Eventually Breckenridge tied off the lure he'd constructed, snipped the end of the line, then carefully released the lure from the clamp and set the lure aside.

Setting down the clamp, he leaned back in his chair, stretched.

Noting that Richard, too, had reached the final, less exacting stages of construction, Breckenridge hesitated, then leaned forward again. Selecting a hook, he started the process of assembling the various feathers and beads for another lure.

Eyes on his task, murmured, "One question I feel compelled to ask: Before they agreed to marry, did all the Cynster females behave as irrationally as Heather is?"

He glanced briefly up, but Richard didn't look up from the lure he was tying off as he unperturbably replied, "Prickly at the best of times, then 'have-at-you' the instant you set a foot, nay, a toe, wrong?"

"Exactly."

"Then yes." Richard straightened, tipping his head as he examined his lure. "It seems to be a family failing, even when they're not Cynster-born."

Breckenridge humphed.

He was carefully placing the fresh hook into his clamp

when Richard continued, "There seems to be this prevailing wisdom, not just over marrying for love, but what that actually equates to. They seem to all have it firmly in their heads that without some cast-iron assurance, preferably in the form of an open declaration from us, then no matter the reality of any love, that love won't be solid and strong."

Unwinding the vise to release his completed lure, Richard grimaced. "It's almost as if they think that unless we state our feelings out aloud, we won't know what they—our feelings— are." He snorted. "As if we somehow might not notice that our lives have suddenly shifted to revolve solely about them and their well-being."

Breckenridge grunted in masculine agreement.

"Sadly," Richard said, selecting another hook, "it appears futile to expect them to go against the familial grain."

Silence lengthened once more as they both became absorbed—Richard in making his next lure, Breckenridge letting his fingers go through the motions while his mind weighed Richard's words against his own reading of his and Heather's situation.

That she required, and was indeed angling for, a clear declaration of his feelings rang all too true. A bare second's thought confirmed his continuing antipathy to giving her any such declaration. Quite aside from the vulnerability he would feel over acknowledging that she was so emotionally critical to him, to his future, to his happiness—a vulnerability shared with Richard, and all the rest, all the other men like him who'd been fated to fall in love, something akin to inviting a permanent itch between his shoulder blades, or more accurately, an exposed feeling over his heart—all of which was bad enough, there was the not-so-small matter of his experience with love, with ever having been foolish enough to utter that word.

The thought of doing so again . . .

His entire being—his sophisticated self as well as his inner male—balked.

Obdurate, unyielding, immutable.

Yet he needed to win her agreement to their wedding.

While his fingers shaped and twisted, placed, balanced, and bound, he juggled the issues. There had to be some way forward.

He had to find some way of meeting her need that didn't involve him making any syrupy declaration of undying love. He wasn't expecting her to make any such reciprocal declaration; he might prefer her to love him back, prefer that she returned what he felt for her with equal fervor, but he wasn't prepared to consciously hope that that would actually be the case.

Other than gaining her agreement to wed him, he wouldn't make any further demands of her. He had no further caveats; as she wanted children, that subject didn't need to be specified.

Which left him still facing the central critical issue: How to declare that he loved her in exactly the way she wanted to be loved . . . his throat constricted just at the thought.

All his vaunted charm and glib persuasiveness weren't going to be of any help; a verbal declaration simply wasn't an option. If he was unwise enough to try . . . an aborted attempt might only serve to infuriate her, to convince her that he wasn't in earnest, that he would never measure up, and had no intention of ever measuring up, to her requirements.

No way forward there . . .

His fingers stilled. He stared unseeing at the half-made lure as the clock ticked steadily on, and the one possible way forward, the one real option available to him, blossomed and took shape in his brain.

Chapter Seventeen

nce the manor had settled for the night and there were no more candles bobbing along the corridors, when silence had fallen and enough time had elapsed for the last stragglers to have found their beds, Breckenridge opened the door of his room and stepped out into the darkness of the turret stairs.

Closing the door, he waited for his eyes to adjust to the darkness. Luckily the manor's narrow, stone-walled stairwells and corridors were largely free of furniture he might bump into, with only the occasional wall hangings to act as landmarks. Otherwise the corridors all looked much the same, especially in the dark.

Hoping he wouldn't get lost, as soon as he could make out the stairs, he descended to the floor below, the first floor above the hall, and started along the gallery that Worboys, Richard's valet, who had been tending his few clothes, had helpfully told him led to Heather's bedchamber.

When he'd baldly asked which room she occupied, Worboys had answered readily, confirming his suspicion that the entire household was eager to play matchmaker. As in this instance their goal—to see him and Heather wed—was the same as his, he'd accepted Worboys's aid with nothing more than an inner wince.

He needed to forge a way forward with Heather, to gain her agreement to their wedding. To accomplish that, he had to convince her of the depth of his feelings, and as he couldn't utter the requisite words, that left only one possible means of communication.

Luckily, it was a means at which he excelled. Although he hadn't previously used those means in such a way, he felt reasonably confident his experience and expertise would prove sufficient to convey what she required.

On top of that, he saw no reason to spend another night alone. From what Richard had shared, from all he himself had seen, given what he understood his problem to be, keeping his distance was unlikely to aid his cause.

The mouth of the corridor down which Heather's room lay loomed ahead. He rounded the corner—

She barreled into him.

He caught her. He knew it was her, instantly recognized the alluring warmth and feminine softness of the body plastered to his.

His senses leapt. She was wearing her silk robe again, and nothing else. His hands tightened on her upper arms, long fingers encircling, holding.

"Oof!" She blew strands of tumbled hair from her face, then looked up.

"Your room." His inner male salivating, he tried to turn her.

"No." Hands against his chest, she resisted. "Your room. You have a bigger bed."

A pertinent consideration. He nodded, released her, and stepped back, taking her hand in his. Anticipation escalating with every step, he led her back through the corridors to the landing before his door.

Lifting the latch, he sent the door swinging wide, held it open, and waved her in.

He followed.

He would give her no time to talk, to question and expect answers. To argue. Words were of no use to him; better to avoid any verbal exchange.

Ahead, she slowed.

He turned and shut the door.

Turned back—

And she was there.

She stepped close. Eyes locking with his, her hands sliding up his chest, over his shoulders to twine about his neck, she stretched sinuously up, silk susurrating against his coat. Lids lowering, she drew his head down to press her lips to his.

And kiss him.

Kiss him in a manner patently intended to circumvent all discussion, all questions.

Kiss him in a way that made his head spin, that made him—*him*—giddy.

Giddy with a need she pledged herself to fulfill. To sate, to satisfy.

With her lips a firm pressure tempting his, her mouth a luscious offering, she wordlessly promised to engage, indulge, and gratify whatever desires he wished.

His temptress incarnate. A siren like no other.

Her lips parted beneath his; with her mouth, succulent and sweet, offered as a delight, with her tongue a fiery brand inciting—nay, demanding—his response, she flagrantly invited him to state his need. His wish, his want.

She pressed closer, the firm mounds of her breasts impinging against his lower chest, her hips meeting his upper thighs, her taut belly cradling his rampant erection, the long, slender lengths of her thighs sliding against his in an evocative promise of sweet passion and tempting heat, and pleasure without reservation.

One hand rising to palm her head, to frame her jaw, he was kissing her back before he'd thought—but his response required no thought, no logical consideration.

If she was offering, he would take.

Gladly.

His other arm banding her waist, he drew her flush against him, sensed the hitch in her breathing, the momentary tensing, then she melted, and gave. Yielded.

Even as he slid the reins from her grasp, as he took charge of the kiss, took control of the exchange and settled to plunder the delights of her mouth—slowly, savoring, claiming as his due—even as he instinctively, intuitively assessed, and planned the tempo of the interlude, the rhythm and the cadences of the dance to come, he wondered at her agenda.

Clearly she had one.

Equally clearly, hers didn't involve words, either.

Regardless, with their mouths fused and heat and desire stirring, welling, rising, and swirling through them, with her hands sliding from his nape, one upward to tangle evocatively in his hair, the other cruising over his shoulder, then sliding down his chest to slip beneath his coat and fragment his focus, with her body the ultimate distraction in his arms, he had no space left in his head to pause and think. To question, even mentally, what she was about.

No doubt he would learn later. For now . . .

She'd given him the perfect lead, the perfect opening to demonstrate and display all he wanted to and needed to reveal, so she would see and know, and so understand, all the things he couldn't say.

All he felt for her.

All that filled his heart.

He couldn't have wished for a better opportunity, a more helpful setting of their stage.

Now all he had to do was capitalize on the moment.

Heather knew he was planning. Even as he'd reacted to her blatant invitation and then pressed for control of the kiss, even as she'd relinquished the reins and let him take charge, she'd known he had some end of his own in mind.

He hadn't been surprised when she'd run into him in the corridor; he'd been on his way to her room.

He'd been intent on instigating another interlude . . . letting herself flow into his kiss, setting herself to follow wherever he led, she was curious to see what he would do, where he would lead her, and even more curious as to why.

That, after all, was precisely why she'd left her room and headed for his. She'd tried encouraging him verbally; she'd tried abstinence. Neither tack had yielded the desired result. So she'd decided to try one last, infinitely more risky, throw of the dice.

He angled his head and deepened the kiss, his lips commanding, his tongue demanding. She let herself respond openly, without guile or reservation. Sent her tongue to tangle with his, to stroke, to invite, to incite. To ignite the passion and set flame to the desire that smoldered between them. She kissed him back with fervor, let her need infuse her lips, her mouth, her body as she pressed against him. Into him.

As she wordlessly asked, and made it perfectly clear she would if necessary plead, or even beg.

She hid nothing. Nothing of her reaction as he sank deeper into her mouth, as he evocatively plundered and heat and sensation rolled through her. Sinking her fingers into his hair, she gripped his scalp as his tongue caressed, then heavily, provocatively probed, and desire slid, hot and heavy like syrup, through her veins. To ultimately pool, a mass of heated yearning, low in her belly.

A familiar, slow-building ache.

She stirred against him. Splayed one palm on his chest, over his heart. Rolled her hips against him in blatant entreaty.

Wordlessly encouraged. Flagrantly incited.

Deliberately provoked.

With her lips, her tongue, her body, and her hands, she strove to make her want, her hunger, and her need blatant, to write it in large capitals on their sensual slate . . . in the resulting moment of vulnerability, fleeting though it was, she sensed why he might hesitate to be so emotionally naked.

Yet she couldn't afford not to try—not to put her need on display, not to expose it fully. Catriona had told her she might have to risk her heart in order to secure his. She wanted him—wanted a future with him—enough to take that risk.

In her heart she prayed that he wouldn't fail her, that he wouldn't turn aside from her desperately yearning need. That he would acknowledge it, not ignore it.

That he would meet it, match it, and not simply use it.

She was wagering her heart that what had grown between them was not just about physical satiation but meant more, not only to her but to him as well.

She was wagering that if she took the plunge and exposed her heart first, he would respond, that he would follow her lead and take the risk, too—a lesser risk if she had risked first, if he already knew that she loved him.

She was wagering that if she showed him her love, unequivocally and without reserve, then he would reciprocate and show her . . . enough at least for her to know that he felt a similar connection, that underneath his reservations he loved her in the same way.

How to make her point . . . at some stage she would have to convince him to cede the reins to her.

But not yet.

Not when he was lavishing heat and pure pleasure on her mouth, and slowly steering her to the bed.

The back of her legs hit the mattress. His hands shifted to her waist, gripped, steadying her, even as he surged deeper into her mouth, rapacious and hungry.

Greedy for her.

Expectation, a sharp spike of sensual anticipation, flashed through her. In its wake flames rolled in, desire and need escalating, sapping her resolution, cindering her will . . .

In sudden desperation, she pulled back, broke the kiss. "No."

His was a seduction of mind as well as body. If she let him sweep her away, let her mind become ensnared in the passion and delight, she would never have the wit, let alone the will, to take the lead and do what she'd come there to do. She stared through the dimness, holding his gaze.

Then, with deliberation, she licked her kiss-swollen lips. Felt as much as saw his gaze lock on them. "Me, first." The words hung between them, sultry yet definite. "My turn to dictate."

He was an expert in this sphere and, at least with her, he'd never acted other than deliberately. Control was something he exercised so effortlessly, so completely on the physical, sexual plane . . . she doubted he realized that that very control and how he deployed it might reveal, might reflect, what he felt.

She was entirely willing for him to lead their dance and reveal whatever he might, but not until she'd made her statement, her wordless declaration. Sliding her hand from his hair, retrieving the other from beneath his coat, she gripped the lapels, leaned in and, instead of kissing him, ran her lips in a feather-light caress along his jaw, distracting him as she pushed the coat off his shoulders.

Leaning back, into his hard hands—they'd moved to rest at the back of her waist, hard, heavy, heating her flesh through the single layer of flimsy silk—she stripped the coat down, tugging and pushing until he obliged and drew first one arm, then the other, free of the sleeves.

Feeling his heavy-lidded gaze on her face, she extended one arm and let the coat fall where it may.

"Just as long as I get my turn, too."

Reaching for his cravat, she glanced up, briefly met his gaze. Glimpsed the banked passion in his eyes. "We can share, but I lead first."

Switching her attention to her fingers, she swiftly undid the simple knot he favored.

He didn't immediately answer but eventually said as she drew the strip of linen free, "If you insist."

"I do." Her determination had returned in full force. Sending the cravat to join his coat, she fell on his waistcoat.

Looked up as she freed the last button. "To do what I want, I have to be in charge."

"You do?" When she nodded, then tugged, he obliged by shrugging off the waistcoat. "And what do you intend to do?"

"I'm not going to tell you." Stepping closer, she looked into his eyes, her fingers swiftly undoing the buttons closing the front of his shirt. "I'm going to show you." She looked down.

"Are you." Not a question; a skeptical statement.

She didn't respond; leaving his shirt hanging open, she caught one of his hands, flicked the button at his cuff free, then did the same with his other hand, other cuff.

"In this arena, you're going to show the foremost rake in the ton . . . what, exactly?"

She looked up, met his gaze, held it as, between them, she flicked the button securing the flap on his trousers free. "I'm going to show you something no other lady ever has." Without taking her gaze from his eyes, she slid her hand past the gaping flap, reached in and found him, stroked, then boldly took his rigid member into her palm. "I'm going to do to you what no other lady ever has."

She was going to make love to him.

It had occurred to her that there was a reason the act was described that way. A reason she could use. An exchange she could exploit to communicate what she needed to convey, then encourage him to use the same language to reply.

Brazen and bold the ploy might be, but if it worked . . . she was more than willing to try.

He'd sucked in a tight breath. She sensed rather than saw his muscles tense, turn steely hard as she let her fingers trace, trail . . . then she closed her hand.

His lids fell; hands again splayed on her back, his fingertips pressed harder.

Gripping him firmly in her fist, she shifted closer still; the silk of her robe brushing his bare chest, she stretched up and set her lips to the sensitive spot beneath his jaw, below his ear, then traced a path down to where his pulse thudded at the base of his strong throat. Her fingers tightened about him, and she heard a soft hiss. She placed a long, lingering kiss over his pulse point, then laved lightly with her tongue, sensing the heat of him through his skin, tasting the wildness, the hungry desire, that prowled beneath.

Savored the strength of him, borne in his touch as his arms closcd, and his hands, large and so male, spread over her back and held her.

Held, but didn't urge, didn't guide; hc waited, his breath shallower than usual, to see what she would do.

Inwardly smiling, she set herself to fulfill her self-appointed task. Slowly, on a long, caressing stroke, she drew her hand from the hot rod of his erection; she needed both hands to properly worship the width of his chest, the wide muscles that spanned it, the flat discs of his nipples curtained by wiry dark hair, to properly appreciate the heavy, solid bones of his shoulders, the warm resilience of the heavier muscles that framed his upper back.

Spreading the halves of his shirt wide, she pushed the linen off his shoulders, then paid due homage to all she'd uncovered with her lips, her tongue, her teeth, with the hot wetness of her mouth.

All the while shifting, sensuously sliding, her silk-encased form against his rock-hard frame.

She sensed his fascination, his indulgence, felt him shift as, drawing his hands from her he reached behind his back and stripped the shirt free, let the garment fall.

His hands returned to cradle her back, shifting over the silk of her robe.

She nipped lightly at one nipple. Heard his breath hitch, felt the spike of reaction that flashed through his muscles.

Felt the heat spread beneath his skin.

"What are you doing?"

She looked up, met his gaze, darker now, passion smoldering behind the bright hazel. "I'm doing as I wish, what I want—what I need to do."

Heat was steadily rising, in him, in her, between them; she should have felt the night's chill but instead felt only the building glow of desire, the slow burn of encroaching passion.

Raising one hand to his cheek, she drew his lips to hers, kissed him again, openly demanding, taking his mouth rather than giving hers . . . surprised that he allowed it, she was enthralled enough to ask for yet more. To take more.

When she drew back and their lips parted, they were both breathing quickly, and the heat had flared to a nascent conflagration.

Eyes on his, sensing, all but seeing the steely control he was exerting, their breaths mingling, she murmured, "You're being very good."

His reply was a dark rumble. "For now."

She took note of the implied warning and gave him no chance to retake the reins; pushing back against his hold, she slid her hands, palms to his warm, deliciously heated skin, down from his upper chest, over the rock-hard ridges of his abdomen, down and wide to either side of his waist, then skimmed her hands lower, down his lean hips, catching his trousers, sliding them down.

Her hands reached his upper thighs, and the garment slid of its own accord down his long legs to pool about his feet.

She followed it down, sliding from his hold and sinking to a sideways crouch. Saw the powerful muscles in his flanks, his upper thighs, lock. Ignoring the sudden grip of his hand on her shoulder, she drew down one stocking, with a nudge of her arm got him to lift his foot so she could free it of stocking, shoe, and trouser leg. After repeating the actions with his other foot, she pushed shoes, stockings, and trousers back and away across the floor, then, swiveling to him, her hands sliding up the back of his bare calves, gripping the wide muscle for balance, she looked up—all the way up to his eyes.

Legs braced, fingers trailing her shoulders, his spectacular body naked, the powerful contours limned by faint moonlight, he looked down at her; in that moment he appeared more beautiful, more powerful, than any god.

Before he could move, she ran her palms upward, over the backs of his knees, then further still, tracing the backs of his thighs up, up to the curve of his buttocks.

Through the dimness she saw his jaw clench. Felt his fingers shift, his hands start to reach for her.

Smoothly shifting to her knees, she drew her gaze down his body, down to where his erection jutted proudly, just below her face. Drew her hands in, closed both about the hot, heavy length.

Heard the rush of his indrawn breath, heard its tightness. Sensed the sudden leap of tension in his body, the steeling of muscles already taut.

She could all but taste his flaring expectation; bending her head, touching her lips to the exquisitely soft, broad head of his erection, she gave herself over to meeting it.

To fulfilling every desire he might have, to, with her mouth, her lips, her tongue, her teeth, lavish pleasure upon pleasure on him.

She took him deep into her mouth, lightly sucked, then used her tongue to slowly stroke. Felt his entire body lock, felt his hands drift, sightless it seemed, until they found her head. Until his fingers could tangle in her hair, and grip.

Hold on.

As she pleasured him.

As she devoted every iota of will she possessed to impressing on him her intent. Her message. Her wordless declaration.

She knew they were in his room, by the foot of his bed, but her senses drew in and she lost touch with the world as she set herself to this—to loving him.

To this sensual demonstration that she did.

Breckenridge stifled a groan, a moan of sheer pleasure,

when she took him deeper yet, drawing him further into the hot haven of her mouth, then using her wicked tongue to torture him with delight.

With sensual pleasures he'd rarely known, rarely allowed any other woman to give him. Why he'd never understood; her mouth on him there was nothing less than paradise—a slice of heaven in the mortal world.

Head high the better to breathe, to haul breath into lungs that had seized, he glanced down through his lashes and watched her—and felt something inside him shift. Expand, then grow stronger. More definite.

Take larger, sharper, more indisputable shape.

Through his hands on her skull, his fingers locked in the silky strands of her hair, he felt her deliberation, her unswerving will.

In the suction of her mouth, in the strong, rasping, strokes of her tongue, read her driving purpose.

This was not a bid to try something new.

This was no exploration but deliberate worship.

This was passion leashed and channeled. Wielded with intent. An intent to . . .

She drew him deeper yet, until the muscles of her throat caressed the sensitive head of his erection. All thought fractured, irreversibly fragmented as she suckled hard, then stroked with her tongue.

As her fingers stroked his scrotum, then one hand closed about his balls and she played . . .

He hauled in a tortured breath, ground out, "Enough." The word was rough, gravelly, barely decipherable, his customary sangfroid, his usual detachment, long gone.

She responded with a tortuously slow, deliciously rasping, stroke of her tongue.

His control quaked; his balls started to tighten.

Barely stifling a curse, he slid a thumb between her luscious lips, eased his throbbing member from the wet suction of her mouth, drew free. Grasped her shoulders and pulled her up—into his arms, up onto her toes, into an embrace that was just this side of desperate.

Into a kiss that burned and scorched and tasted of passion run wild . . .

He was out of control, or so close to it as made no odds. For an instant, blatantly, flagrantly feeding from her yielded mouth, feeling her small hands spread on his chest, he teetered on the cusp of simply giving in—for the first time in more than fifteen years letting his inner self free, letting the primal male have his way and simply gorge.

Simply take her, own her, possess her, with no thought to shields or guile or protection.

No thought of concealment, of deploying any veil or screen.

He couldn't. Too dangerous.

Even in this extremity, his mind still grasped the need for self-protection.

Sunk in her mouth, his arms wrapped about her, crushing her silk-encased body to his, he fought—and found strength in the subtle perfume that was her, that rose from her flushed skin and wreathed through his brain, and somehow anchored him.

Found even more strength in the touch of her palm against his cheek. In the way she responded—fully, openly, with her own flaring desires and heightened passions—to the rapacious demands of the kiss.

She was a steady flame, a beacon, guiding him back to sanity. To his customary control.

To the ways and means he'd intended to employ.

To his purpose.

Heather kissed him back and waited to see what direction he would take. When he'd wrenched control back, so driven and absolute, she'd hoped he would drop his shields and let her see. . . . But then he'd steadied.

For one fleeting instant she'd considered challenging him, but she knew she didn't have that power. Accepted instead that at that point she had to yield the reins fully, that if he needed them, needed her this way, then she had to meet that need.

A need that was hot, molten, passion in the night.

That he communicated effortlessly in the heavy stroke of his hand over her breast, knowing and possessive.

Openly so. If he had any message for her in what followed, possession was his theme.

His clearly communicated motive.

His fingers found the rose quartz pendant, for fleeting seconds toyed, but then his attention refocused.

His lips remained on hers, his kiss devastating and demanding. Commanding as his hands roved her body, as through the silk he sculpted, weighed, and assessed, then he stripped the silk away, let it fall to the floor, and set his palms, fingers, mouth, lips, and tongue to her naked skin, to her aching flesh, and branded.

If desire was a flame, he burned her.

If passion was a whip, he scourged her.

If need was a tempest, he called it down and sent it raging through her.

Until on his knees before her, he closed his big hands on the backs of her thighs, parted them and, largely supporting her, set his mouth to her softness.

And feasted.

Hands sunk in his hair, she could only cry out. Eyes closed, she could barely cope with the sensations—heightened and deepened and ever more powerful—that he sent streaking through her.

His tongue stroked, and her world rocked.

He'd tasted her there before, but that had been in a bed, in a tangle of sheets, not exposed like this, naked in the moonlight.

That she was his for the taking had never been so clear. So blatant.

So inescapable.

Even as, eyes closed, head tipped back, she clung and sobbed as he razed her senses, some tiny part of her mind recognized and approved.

Encouraged her to give herself over to this, to letting him have his way . . . because that was a part of loving him, too. Simply letting him be him.

Accepting him as he was, without any reservation at all.

The power of passion was his to command, the currency of desire his weapon. With his tongue he pressed her further; with laving strokes and quick rasps he raced her up the ragged peak, then he thrust in just enough to send her soaring.

To have her nerves unraveling and sensation splintering.

A small scream escaped her—and then he was there, on his feet, his arms about her, his hot, hair-roughened skin against hers, the steel of his body wrapping around hers as he held her, embraced her, kissed her—and she tasted her nectar on his tongue.

Supped it from his mouth as he fed her, as he slid one hand between her thighs and repetitively speared her.

And the climax rolled on and on. . . .

When it finally started to fade, he swept her up in his arms and carried her around the bed. Kneeling on the mattress, he laid her upon the silk coverlet, then followed her down, stretching out alongside her, one hand splaying, openly possessive, on her belly as he leaned over her.

And proceeded to lead her to paradise again.

By a longer route this time, one where progress was steady but slow, where each stage extended and stretched . . . until every last iota of pleasure had been wrung from it; only then did they move on.

Slower the way might be, but it was infinitely more— richer, more intense, every second, every heartbeat, more vested with feeling.

He caressed her, and she returned the pleasure. Their bodies met, naked and yearning, their bare limbs tangling, intertwining. Flushed, desire-dewed skin slid across skin, brushed, pressed, and nerves sparked. Sensation spread in slow, heated waves, rose and ebbed only to rise higher and slowly sweep them on.

Their hands roved each other's bodies, pleasure their only intent—to give, to receive, to share.

To watch the other writhe, gasp, and then sigh.

To do the same, give the same, in reply.

Together they progressed through passion's landscape. First he led, then she. Never before had they been together quite like this, sharing like this, no battle for supremacy but a true joining, the switching back and forth effortless, smooth as a thought, as an unvoiced desire.

Their gazes touched, locked, often held. Their heated breaths mingled, were shared when their lips met, or washed over each other's skin.

Sensation expanded, heightened, became acute. Every touch carried heat, carried meaning.

Every caress meant more, weighted with feeling. With emotions unstated, yet so very real.

She took it all in; dazzled by the vibrancy, she drank in the wonder, savored the delight, saw in his face, behind his austere features, saw in the brilliant gold and greens of his eyes, a similar appreciation of their bounty.

This was them—the truth of them.

Breckenridge knew it, felt it to his soul, felt that truth echo there, resonate, sink deep, and belong. Owned.

He let himself do it—set true control to one side and let himself follow the path, and without reserve let himself respond to her as his inner male wished, the savage edge of his passion held at bay by the deeper and needier want that was this.

Being able to share *this*.

With her.

His woman. His lady. His one and only true lover.

He'd never followed this path before, yet even now sensed

the danger. But if this was the route he needed to travel to bind her to him, he would take the road and accept the risk without hesitation.

They needed no words, which was just as well, because he had none. None that could do justice to *this*.

To the closeness, the true intimacy.

When he pressed her thighs apart, intending to settle between, she murmured and resisted—hand on his shoulder she urged him back. Moving to the slow tempo—the magic that had him in its grip—he obliged and rolled onto his back.

Allowing her to come over him. To straddle him and, naked in the moonlight, take him in. And ride him.

A slow dance; she rose upon him, then slid back down, using every muscle to caress.

To pleasure.

With the strange necklace about her throat, the pendant nestled between her bare breasts, she looked like a pagan goddess. Hands firming about her hips, he held, but didn't guide. Let her set the pace.

Mesmerized by the sight.

Trapped by her heavy-lidded gaze as she moved upon him and . . . cherished him.

He felt her intent, sensed it in her focus, her unswerving devotion to his pleasure.

The knowledge ripped through him, triggering an avalanche of emotions, feelings, impulses, a welter of powerful reactions that surged and tumbled through him.

Teeth gritted, he tried to hold them back, to give her her time.

As if sensing it, she shook her head wildly, golden hair flying about her shoulders. "Come with me. Now."

At her husky demand, the dam within ruptured. His hands gripping tighter, holding her hips, he surged beneath her, thrusting up as she sank down.

In short order she was sobbing, her hands locked on his

wrists, her head tipped back as she rode the heavy, pounding beat he set.

His own breathing ragged, he half sat, propped on one arm, and set his mouth to her breast.

Suckled hard, fiercely, and drove her on.

Thrust even deeper, and she screamed and came apart.

Need clawed within him, mindless and desperate, yet he wanted more—the final culmination.

The ultimate benediction that, for the first time in his life, was within his grasp.

He tipped her over, rolled with her, pressed her thighs wider, and with one powerful stroke, resheathed himself in her scalding heat.

And pressed her on.

And she was with him.

Fearless, she clung, and with him plunged back into the raging furnace of their need.

Into the passion and the greedy flames, into the roaring conflagration, straight into the vortex of that breathless, mindless, tearing need.

No gentle giving, but a raging, reckless striving, a desperate reaching for some perfect accord.

Together they reached for it.

And flew. Through passion's fire, through desire's flames, beyond the pinnacle of their joint need.

Their senses imploded, reality fractured, and ecstasy streamed in.

She screamed. He groaned.

Glory blossomed, swelled, and took them, filled them, wracked them, then wrought them anew.

And they let it. Merged beyond the physical, they held tight, bodies slick, skins afire, lungs laboring. Gazes locked, breaths mingling, they clung, and let the moment speak.

No simple homage but a true reverence, a beyond-the-self prostration before some greater god, something that went far beyond them.

A surrender like no other to the something that linked them, that joined them.

That had from the first tapped them each on the shoulder, pointed at the other, and said: *That* one.

That power flared in them, through them, erupted, and engulfed them.

Held them and fused them.

They became it and it was them.

It shone in their hearts, overwhelmed their senses, illuminated their souls.

The moment stretched, waned, faded.

Oblivion beckoned, and they closed their eyes, felt that precious moment pass . . . let it go.

Let themselves fall into soothing darkness, to where satiation buoyed them on a golden sea, and the familiar world was a heartbeat away.

The night closed around them and wrapped them in her arms.

Exhausted, they slept.

The chill of deepening night washing over him eventually drew Breckenridge back to the world. He resurfaced reluctantly. Easing from Heather, from the warm clasp of her body, the haven of her arms, he drew back, lifted from her, then slumped beside her. Only to recall that they lay on top of the covers.

Gathering his strength, he rolled off the bed, loosened the covers, eased them from beneath her, dragged them down, then climbed beside her and drew the sheets and coverlet up, flicking them over them both.

She murmured and turned to him, snuggled her way into his arms, then sank back into slumber.

Through the dimness he studied her face but could read nothing in her relaxed features.

He didn't want to think of what had passed between them, the depth, the connection . . . the revelation. They'd gone far beyond the mundane, the usual, the customary; they'd touched, breached, some other plane.

Something he was certain she couldn't have failed to see, to recognize; they'd been there together, very much hand in hand.

Which meant that all should now be well, that she would have no further quibbles over accepting his suit.

Closing his eyes, he felt his lips curve. He slid into a dreamless sleep.

Chapter Eighteen

"Heather!" Stepping out under the archway from the great hall, Breckenridge started after Heather as she walked down a corridor leading deeper into the manor. At his hail, she halted, turned, and smiled.

Something inside him clenched at the sight. He couldn't remember ever feeling this nervous, this on edge.

He forced an easy smile and continued toward her. Aside from them, the corridor was deserted; that wouldn't last.

They hadn't had a chance to speak that morning; they'd exchanged not one word about the night. He'd woken in good time but had lain there like a dope and just watched her sleep. By the time she'd stirred, stretched like a cat, opened her eyes, and smiled—very much as she was smiling now, with that glow that warmed him filling her eyes—it had been too late for anything; she'd had to rush to get back to her room before everyone and the twins had been about.

Breakfast about the high table with everyone in attendance had been no place to broach the subject of matrimony, regardless of how confident he was that she would, now, accept him. After last night, how could she not?

She'd been so passionate, and had matched him so well, had been the female reflection of all he was as a male, her actions, her need, mirroring all he'd felt, that he'd dropped every last shield and simply been.

A terrifying freedom. One he'd grasped with all he had in him, but now, in the aftermath, in the cool morning light, the sense of vulnerability, of having said too much even though he'd uttered not one word, haunted him.

Rode like a specter at the edge of his vision and threatened him.

At least she couldn't have missed his revelation. His truth.

Lips still curved, he halted before her, looked down into her soft blue-gray eyes.

Heather met his gaze and felt her heart literally swell. This was the moment; expectation cinched tight.

She'd spent every minute since she'd left his room trying to imagine what he might say. She no longer needed any declaration, just a word, a touch—any allusion to what they'd shared last night. One word, even a look, would do, would serve to acknowledge their new reality. Then they could move forward, into their new life.

Fighting to keep her anticipation reined, not to jig with impatience, or clutch at the pendant between her breasts, when he didn't speak, she prompted, "I have to join Algaria in the herb garden—I told her I would yesterday, and she truly does need my help."

Something shifted—behind his eyes, a subtle shift in his usual difficult-to-read expression. Gaze lowering, he inclined his head, the movement redolent with his habitual grace. "Yes, of course. I won't keep you." He hesitated, then diffidently, almost offhandedly, said, "I was just wondering about our return to the capital. We'll need to announce our betrothal and face down the inevitable brouhaha."

He paused.

Still waiting for her word, she didn't respond.

Drawing breath, he met her eyes, went on, "I should draft a notice for the *Gazette*—I should probably send that ahead of us, to set the scene, as it were. We should also send letters to our families—they'll need to be prepared."

He fell silent, waited.

Heather knew her expression had frozen—to hide the

eruption of anger that was searing through her. She felt like screaming.

What did she have to do to get him to admit he loved her?

He *did*; after last night, she was sure he did. . . .

She inwardly rocked, felt as if the ground beneath her feet literally shifted even though she stood on solid stone.

He was an acknowledged expert . . . could last night have been a sham, a pretence, something he'd concocted to satisfy her? Knowing what she wanted to see in him, had he simply given her that, even though it hadn't been true?

Had last night simply been another conquest to him, albeit with a different goal?

She'd made her declaration first—her wordless confession of her love for him. Had he then pulled the wool over her eyes?

Hurt, deeper than any she'd ever felt, sliced through her.

She blinked, looked into his eyes—desperation rising, searched but couldn't see.

Anything.

Any glimmer of the love she'd expected to find shining there.

That didn't mean the damned man didn't feel it—he always kept his emotions so contained . . . but the purpose of last night had been to reassure him, to encourage and allow him to give her just *one word,* one hint, however oblique, that he loved her.

If he didn't . . . she'd already gone over that argument. She couldn't go forward without any acknowledgment.

He'd grown uncharacteristically restive. Now he shifted. "Think about it and let me know later." He half turned to walk away.

"No—wait." As he turned back, jaw firming, she tipped up her chin. "You're laboring under a misapprehension. I haven't yet accepted any proposal—indeed, none has been made—certainly not in any form of words I find acceptable."

His face, his eyes, hardened. She drew breath, held his gaze, and strove to make his options crystal clear. "You know what I want. Until you give me the assurance I need, I won't be agreeing to any wedding, especially not with you."

She didn't wait to hear what he thought of that. Swinging around, she stalked off, down the corridor to the side door.

Rooted to the spot, Breckenridge watched her go. Watched, and felt his chest slowly constrict. Tighten until he couldn't breathe.

Last night he'd done what she'd wanted and exposed his heart—and that still wasn't enough for her?

Especially not with you. He felt like he'd been kicked in the gut; he'd heard those words before.

Of course, last time—fifteen years ago—Helen Maitland had laughed as she'd uttered them.

Swallowing a vicious curse, his face like stone, he turned and walked away.

Just as he had fifteen years before.

He'd left Helen Maitland without a backward glance.

Heather Cynster was a different matter.

A different female.

A different proposition altogether.

He'd ridden out with Richard, hoping the fresh air and exercise would wipe the turmoil from his brain, but no luck. Breckenridge strode out of the manor's stables and headed across the cobbled rear yard, then remembered and detoured toward the herb garden.

Halting in the shade of the manor's walls, he scanned the sloping garden. He spotted Heather immediately, cutting swags of some herb with a pair of shears. Surveying the rest of the garden more closely, he thanked his stars; Algaria wasn't there.

He started down the winding path. Heather was facing the other way; she hadn't seen him yet.

Regardless of her intransigence, he wasn't about to walk

354

away. And much as he might like to dismiss her insistence on some "assurance" as feminine pigheadedness, that would get him nowhere.

You know what I want.

So she'd stated, yet that was the point that had him stumped.

She must know that a declaration of love from him—the foremost rake in the ton—simply wasn't in the cards. Even discounting his experience with La Maitland, which admittedly Heather knew nothing of, his all-but-constant dalliances with the married ladies of the ton—something she did know about—had left him with a very definite notion regarding the value of love.

Namely that one should place no faith in it at all.

To him the word love had no real meaning.

Or if it did, it wasn't anything good, fine, and desirable.

No lady of the ton would believe a verbal promise of undying love from a gentleman of his reputation.

Besides, she'd been there, with him, every gasp of the way last night. She was intelligent and observant; she couldn't possibly have missed the essential truth he'd revealed, so she had to be clear on that much, at least. She had to know the depths of his feelings for her, had to comprehend the true nature of his commitment. He'd exposed his heart in no uncertain fashion; she had to have seen and understood.

She'd done her own share of exposing and revealing, too. If he'd noticed, observed, and interpreted what she'd done, how she'd behaved, as a reflection of the truth of how she felt about him, then there was no chance whatever that she'd been blind and hadn't seen his reciprocation for the wordless declaration it had been. Women were far more attuned to such nuances, and actions definitely spoke louder than words in that arena.

That issue, that side of things, was done with. Taken care of.

So what else did he have to reassure her of?

Especially not with you.

He assumed that was an allusion to his reputation, but in

what way, from what perspective, in reference to what, he had no clue.

Ladies like Heather Cynster should come with translation cards.

He had to get her to agree to their wedding, ergo he had to find some way of reassuring her in whatever way she deemed necessary.

Which meant he first had to ferret out what she wanted to hear.

She heard his footsteps as he neared, glanced his way, then turned, long sprigs of feathery growth in one hand, sharp shears in the other.

He halted two paces away.

She met his gaze, arched her brows.

He hesitated, then shifted to sit on the low stone wall edging the raised bed from which she was snipping.

Heather turned back to the wormwood she was harvesting. "I presume you didn't come here just to sit in the sunshine."

"No, but the prospect does have a certain allure."

Her lips started to twitch; she straightened them. "Don't try to charm me—it won't work."

He sighed, a touch histrionically.

She clipped another frond. She wasn't going to make this any easier for him—

"Earlier, last time we talked out here, we touched on most of the usual elements that are factors in a decision to wed."

His voice was smooth, the tones relaxed, as if he discussed such matters every day.

"Station, wealth, estate, children. The role I play now, and the one I'll eventually inherit as Brunswick's heir, and the role you would play by my side. In addition to that, of course, there'll be the accompanying social round commensurate with being my viscountess. During those times we reside in London, there'll be plenty of opportunity for you to socially shine. Assuming you wish to."

She glanced at him, let her puzzlement show. "Why do you imagine that's important to me?"

He didn't frown, but she detected a certain darkness in his eyes. "I thought that might be something you'd want to do."

She sent him an exasperated look and turned back to her clipping.

After a brief pause, he went on, "You'll have to redecorate the house—houses, come to think of it. The London house as well as Baraclough. My mother died over a decade ago, and Constance and Cordelia have had their own establishments for even longer—both places are in dire need of a woman's touch. You'll have free rein—"

She made an exasperated, frustrated sound and whirled on him. "Why are you telling me this?"

His frown materialized—blackly. "I'm trying to tell you whatever it is you want to hear." When she glared at him, he capped that with a distinctly terse, "Am I getting close?"

"No!"

He stood; she swung to face him. His jaw looked like iron; a tic flickered beneath one eye as he loomed intimidatingly and glowered down at her. "What the devil is it you want me to say?" He flung out his arms. "For God's sake! Tell me and I'll say it."

That was what she was afraid of.

Her temper rising, provoked by his, she pressed her lips tight, kept her eyes locked with his, and tried to ignore the yawning emptiness inside.

He was telling her all the things she didn't need to hear, and nothing of the one thing she did. She was increasingly afraid she'd made a tactical error the previous night; clearly he'd interpreted her wordless declaration correctly—and now that he knew she loved him, he thought everything was settled. . . .

It would have been if he hadn't been what he was—such an expert that, on reflection, on deeper thought, there was no earthly way she could be sure that his side of their night's exchange hadn't been anything other than, as he'd just stated, him giving her—telling her—what he'd thought she'd wanted to hear.

Now he thought she would marry him with no more said.

Holding his gaze wasn't easy, not when, with him this close, every sense she possessed was reminding her of what had passed between them in the night.

"If you don't know—"

"I don't."

"—then"—she glared belligerently up at him—"telling you won't fix it."

His eyes narrowed to agate shards. "If you refuse to tell me what you want, how can I give it to you?"

"It's not what I want, it's what I need."

"Which is?"

His heart, the fool. She needed his heart.

They were all but nose to nose. Clenching her jaw, she forced herself to say, "I told you that in order to marry I required true . . . affection." She had to grit her teeth to get the lesser word out, but there was no point badgering him to say he loved her—he just might oblige, but all that would do now was assure her he didn't mean it.

That he was only saying it because he'd decided that them marrying was absolutely imperative for both their reputations . . . would he have behaved as he had last night, then demand this morning that she name the wedding day if that was his goal? She didn't need to think to know the answer was yes.

That he might, if pressed hard enough, even utter the word love, just to get her to agree to marry him.

The more she pushed, the less likely this would work out well. But she had to try. "And I wanted that depth of affection offered to me freely—*not* because of my standing, because of who I am, my name, and *not* because my reputation needs saving—but because I'm *me*."

He was blocking the sun, so she couldn't be sure, but she thought he'd paled. Dragging in a breath, she concluded, "*That's* what I want, and if—"

"That's what I thought last night was all about."

His flat tone halted her mid-rant.

She searched his eyes, could read nothing beyond an implacable determination.

"I thought"—he continued in the same cold, impossibly even tone—"that last night was all about your *true* affections. I thought it was about exchanging opinions—if not vows—on that score. I thought last night was about us examining our *affections* and thereby taking a step closer to the altar."

Oh, God. Wildly she searched his eyes, trying to convince herself she wasn't looking at the confirmation of her worst fears.

He'd known; he'd recognized what she'd been doing and had with cold deliberation—the same deliberate planning with which she'd approached the exchange—given her what she'd wanted. He hadn't been swept away by passion, hadn't been moved by her wordless declaration—he'd been as deliberate as she in using the act to communicate what he'd known she'd wanted to hear . . . he'd come looking for her intending to do just that.

She'd received the response she'd schemed to get, but now she had no reason to believe he'd meant it, rather than that he'd seized the opportunity she'd engineered as the surest route to his desired goal.

The hollowness inside intensified.

His hazel eyes bored into hers; his voice dropped to a lower register. "Are you telling me last night *wasn't* an indication of your true affections?"

She glanced aside. Forced her shoulders to lift in a small shrug, then elevated her nose. "Last night . . . was just another night. Wasn't it?" She glanced fleetingly at him, saw nothing but an increasing stoniness in his features, looked away and hurriedly went on, "It was, I grant you, somewhat more intense, but . . ."

Why the devil had she let herself expose her heart so? It *hurt*. Just thinking that he'd deliberately intended to engage with her, to persuade her like that even though he didn't—clearly didn't—love her slashed like a blade through her heart.

Dragging in a breath, raising her head higher, she baldly lied, "I wasn't aware it was anything all that special. It wasn't on my part."

Silence greeted her pronouncement.

She couldn't look at him, didn't dare. If she did, he would see the emotions roiling inside her.

"I . . . see." There was a tone in his voice that she'd never heard before.

She wanted to look at him but didn't. The too-exposed, too screamingly vulnerable part of her couldn't.

She sensed him draw in a huge, deep breath.

Then he more crisply, almost normally, said, "If you'll excuse me, I've just remembered something I need to do."

Before she even glanced his way, Breckenridge turned and started walking back along the path, heading toward the rear of the manor, back the way he'd come.

He kept his head high, his shoulders straight.

He'd suffered rejection before.

He couldn't remember it hurting like this.

Last night hadn't been anything special on her part. What he'd seen as exposing his heart—and his soul, come to think of it—had meant nothing to her.

Suppressing the urge to swear and kick something took effort.

Just as well—the effort distracted him.

He knew better than to get on an unfamiliar horse in such a temper. In such turmoil. He kept walking. Out past the stables, out along a track between two fences.

Picking up his pace, he strode fast and furiously. Only

when he was out of sight of the manor's turrets did he halt. Hands on his hips, breathing hard, he hung his head.

Closed his eyes.

He'd thought . . . tipping back his head, he blinked up at the blue, blue sky.

He'd thought she loved him.

But no.

For some reason, the foremost rake in the ton was impossible to love.

Perhaps because he *was* the foremost rake in the ton . . . but that had been a reaction to not being loved by Helen Maitland. He'd thought to show her what she'd declined by becoming the noble lover all the ladies like her begged to grace their beds . . .

And he'd somehow made himself unlovable in the process.

He didn't know how he'd done it; if he knew, he'd try to change.

But no. Too late. He was what he'd become, and no matter what he thought had occurred in the dark passionate watches of the night, Heather Cynster wasn't about to give her heart to him.

Back in the herb garden Heather stood where he'd left her, her gaze fixed on the spot where he'd passed out of her sight.

He'd gone.

Simply turned on his heel and left . . . because he'd realized his tack hadn't been working and so had abandoned it and gone off to think of some other way to pressure her?

Probably.

She'd thought back over the words they'd exchanged, but her conclusion remained the same. Last night he'd deliberately set out to use the very same route she'd thought to use to demonstrate her love for him, but his intent had been merely to tell her what he'd realized she wanted to know. While she was truly in love with him, he wasn't truly in love with her.

He wanted to marry her because he'd made up his mind that that was the correct thing to do, and he'd decided it would suit him well enough.

After what she'd just learned, he would need to think again.

As for her . . . she would have to accept that there was no future for her with him.

That there was fated to be no *them*.

He finally understood what it was to lose one's heart.

His chest felt empty, hollowed out; he couldn't think, could barely function well enough to preserve an outward glamour of normalcy.

He couldn't let this—let her—go. Felt compelled to step far beyond what was wise and make one last push. . . .

Even if she didn't love him, he loved her.

He knew it, had always in some corner of his brain suspected it, but now there was no hiding from the truth. Not after last night, when he'd thought, been convinced beyond question, that she loved him—and he'd seized on the prospect, gloried, and rejoiced—and in doing so had finally recognized all he wanted of his life.

Had recognized, with an unshakable finality, that he had never felt and would never feel for any other woman what he felt for her. She was the only lady he would ever love.

And if in general love was deemed worth fighting for, then the chance to love was even more precious to a man like him.

Such thoughts, that understanding, drove him to hunt her down.

Luncheon, as usual, was taken with the entire household in the great hall. He and Heather sat apart, with the twins and Algaria between them. Neither Heather nor he made any effort to communicate in any way, not by word or glance; if the others found anything unusual in their mutual avoidance, no one gave any sign.

When the meal ended, and everyone rose and headed off in various directions to whatever tasks and chores awaited them, he followed Heather from the hall. He caught up with her in the shadowed alcove at the top of the stairs leading down to the dungeons.

Hearing his boot steps, she halted and faced him.

He was determined to keep this brief. "I'm about to ride out with Richard." During the meal, he'd heard her arranging with Algaria to process the herbs she'd gathered that morning. "Before I do, I wanted to state that I've had enough. Enough circling around our reality."

He couldn't stop his expression, already hard, from hardening even further; his face felt like graven stone. "I've given you time to grow accustomed to that reality—as much time as I can, as much as we can afford. As much as the situation allows us. Regardless, the facts haven't changed, and they dictate that we must wed." He held her stormy gaze. "You have to accept that, have to acknowledge that there's no choice, make up your mind to it, and then start planning to leave here for London. We can't hide here for forever."

Heather stared into his eyes, agate eyes that told her nothing—that showed her nothing beyond utterly determined, invincible implacability.

Her temper geysered; she opened her mouth on a scalding retort—

"Breckenridge!"

Richard, calling from the front hall.

They'd both turned their heads at the call.

She looked back at Breckenridge.

Just as he stepped away, met her gaze, and curtly nodded. "I'll find you when I get back. And we can start making the necessary decisions."

With that, he walked off.

Heather watched him stride down the corridor. Felt her fury fade.

Felt the cold emptiness within swell and grow.

And wondered where, in dealing with him, she had gone so terribly wrong.

Her heart had sunk so low that it had drowned.

It seemed she was finally seeing his true colors—his unswerving focus on getting his ring on her finger, love be damned.

Love—her "true affection"—was for him merely a route to his goal.

After he'd left, she'd come down to Catriona's workroom. Algaria had joined her, but only long enough to show her what to do with the wormwood, rue, and tansy she'd gathered that morning. Leaving her to bind the fronds in bunches, Algaria had hurried off to resume her oversight of the twins and their lessons.

In the cool, peaceful workroom, Heather methodically sorted and bound. Her gaze remained on her hands, her fingers deftly parting the delicate foliage before winding twine around the stems, but her mind was elsewhere, retreading her arguments, replaying conversations, trying to see, to re-examine it all in the desperate hope she'd missed something vital, or had misinterpreted . . . but no.

Underneath all their words, underlying all their actions, one fact remained unchallenged.

She loved him—and because she did, because she was the woman she was and he the man he was, she had to know beyond question or doubt that he loved her in return.

Yes, that need was an emotional one, one fed by both a fear and a dream.

The fear that if she accepted him without the surety of his love, of having it acknowledged and declared, then at some point, unbound by such a love, he would stray. That he would turn from her to one of the myriad ladies who were forever trying to lure him to their beds.

That fear was real enough, hard enough to counter, yet her

dream was even more an innate part of her, one she had no wish to deny. To her, marriage meant one thing—a partnership in which both parties were committed to, and therefore free to, love without restraint. Without reserve, without boundaries.

No such marriage could come about without both parties being openly and honestly committed to that ideal.

No marriage like that could ever be founded on the commitment of one party alone, with the other shying from the act.

The necessary investment had to come from both, or the marriage would never stand.

She'd clarified her thoughts, reaffirmed her decisions, when two hours later she heard Breckenridge's boots slowly, deliberately, descending the stairs.

She didn't look up as he loomed in the doorway, but continued neatly tying herbs.

Breckenridge ducked beneath the arch of the open doorway. Heather stood on the opposite side of a deal table, a welter of herby foliage spread before her.

She didn't lift her gaze from her hands. Gave no acknowledgment that she knew he was there, but of course she knew he was.

Halting, he, too, looked down at her hands, at the stems she was gathering and binding together.

This was, he knew, a risky gambit, a last desperate push to get their marriage that had to happen back on track, but he didn't know what else to do.

He glanced briefly at her face.

Didn't like the look of her closed expression, saw precious little to make him hope.

He'd rarely felt so helpless. So unsure.

Quelling a strong impulse to rake his hands through his hair, he sank both hands into his breeches' pockets, hauled in a huge breath. Let it out with, "So—when will we leave?"

The demand sounded a lot harsher than he'd intended.

She continued calmly working, pressing stem to stem. "I have no interest in when you leave. For myself, I've decided to remain here for the moment."

"Heather—"

"No—just listen. And please don't tell me what I can and can't do. You asked me to make up my mind, and I have—I've made up my mind that I will not marry you."

He stood there, absorbed the impact of her words, of the determination behind them, and felt a blade slide into his heart.

"However"—Heather laid aside the bunch she'd tied off, picked up more fronds, and tried one, last, desperate throw; men like him were possessive, at least about the women they loved—"you needn't fear any social repercussions. If later a marriage becomes necessary for me to do as I wish with my life, then as I am an heiress, well-connected, and passably attractive, I'm sure there'll be some gentleman ready and willing to overlook this adventure, especially as the family will no doubt have invented and spread some tale to account for my absence from town.

"So, you see, you may leave with a clear conscience." She paused, waited, but he said nothing. Drawing in a tight breath, she forced herself to continue, "There's no reason for you to stay longer—there's nothing to keep you here."

Silence fell.

Breckenridge felt chilled. Chilled to his marrow, frozen and numb.

Sightless, deaf, all that he was transfixed by the revelation that, if she had to marry, she'd rather marry any man but him.

That's what she'd just told him, in words impossible to misconstrue.

The knife slid deeper, and twisted.

The pain of it nearly brought him to his knees.

Breathing in—God, had he ever known such pain?—by main force he gathered the shredded remnants of his heart, of his pride. Clinging to the latter, he forced himself to stop thinking.

To stop dwelling on what he'd thought, on what he'd hoped and had barely dared dream . . .

He should be accustomed to women using him, engaging with him for fleeting pleasure without any true feeling involved; she hadn't treated him any worse than countless others before her. He couldn't fault her for that.

Couldn't fault her for not loving him as he loved her.

He had to get out of there before his control fractured.

Where had they been? Oh, yes. He'd had the bright notion to give her an ultimatum, and she'd responded.

Leaving him with only one way to go.

One road to follow. Alone.

"Very well." Even to his ears, his voice sounded distant, not just detached but disengaged, soulless. "If that's what you wish, so be it."

He told his feet to move. To his relief, they did. He could barely see as he walked to the doorway. Reaching it, he paused, then over his shoulder said, "I'll make arrangements to leave tomorrow."

Alone didn't need to be said.

Against all sense, despite all that had passed between them, he paused, waited, hoped, *prayed* that she would suddenly see her mistake, suddenly speak and reverse her decision . . .

"That would probably be best."

Hope died.

Dragging in a tight breath, he ducked under the arch and quietly started up the stairs.

Heather listened to his footsteps recede.

Wondered if she would ever feel warm again; she felt chilled to the core.

He was leaving—truly leaving. Going back to his life in the capital.

Leaving her there, alone and aching . . . as she'd wanted. That was for the best, wasn't it?

If she'd harbored any doubt that she loved him, immutably and ineradicably, she knew better now. Nothing but love was strong enough to evoke such icy, deadening pain.

But she knew all the arguments, knew it would never have worked, that there never truly had been any different option for her. For them.

She could still feel the tug, the witless but compelling impulse to rush after him and tell him she'd changed her mind, that she would marry him regardless . . . but no. If after their wedding he turned to another . . . that, she truly wouldn't be able to bear.

Looking down, she forced her fingers to bunch the last of the herbs. Felt bitterness at the back of her throat, the sting of tears in her eyes.

Told herself the tears, and the deadening chill inside, were a small price to pay to escape the devastation that would otherwise have come her way.

Loving him as she did to the depths of her soul, yet not being loved in return, if she'd acquiesced and allowed herself to be bound to him in marriage . . . when the inevitable happened, she might not have died, but she would have become as good as dead inside.

Despite the pain, despite any inner railing, despite all her rage and despair, she'd taken the right road; she knew it.

Better it end like this.

The afternoon was waning when, deep in the highlands, the laird rode into his castle bailey.

Alone he might be, yet he was glad to be home.

Swinging down from Hercules' back, he smiled and returned the cheery greeting of the young whelp who came running to take the big gelding's reins. He handed them over. "Give him a good rubdown and a helping of oats. He's done well carrying me over the miles. Give the saddle bags to Mulley."

"Aye, m'lord."

With a last fond stroke down Hercules' neck, he turned and crossed to the keep. Striding up the stone steps, he glanced up to the apex of the fluted arch rising above the massive, iron-studded door.

His family's crest, now his, stood out in sharp relief, carved upon a stone shield.

Honor above all.

The motto was barely legible now; he hoped that wasn't a portent.

Pushing open the heavy door, he crossed the threshold and felt the invisible weight of responsibility weigh on his shoulders again.

Not that he'd been in any danger of forgetting even the smallest tithe of that burden over the days he'd been away.

He heard his mother's footsteps rushing eagerly down from her tower. Halting just inside the great hall, he exchanged greetings and a quiet word with his steward, then she was there, striding swiftly up the hall, her black skirts flaring behind her.

"Well? Where is she?" She tried to peer around him, as if he might have left Heather Cynster trussed like a bundle in the foyer.

He started walking toward the dais at the far end of the hall. "She's not here, *but* you may well have got your wish."

He sincerely hoped not, but . . .

After confirming there truly was no captive hidden behind him, she whirled and swept after him. "What do you mean? What happened?"

Stepping onto the dais, he walked around and down the long oak table to the massive carved chair that sat midway along, facing the great hall. "I told you the men I'd hired to capture her had brought her as far as Gretna—that they were holding her there as I'd instructed." Pulling out the massive chair, he slumped into it, leaned back. Felt the familiar worn wood at his back, beneath his thighs. One of the things that told him he was home.

Halting two yards away, his mother frowned peevishly. "Yes, yes—that's why you went south. But what happened when you reached there?"

"By the time I got there, she'd escaped." He turned to smile gratefully at his housekeeper as she stepped onto the dais, a tray in her hands. "Thank you, Mrs. Mack—you've saved my life."

"Aye, well—you've been gone for over a week." Briskly, she set before him a silver tankard of ale, a bowl of rich stew, and a platter with half a loaf of coarse country bread. "You get that into you—it'll hold you until dinnertime, at least."

Already breaking the bread, he nodded. Stopped himself from asking after the boys; on his other side, his mother was barely restraining herself from screeching.

"Escaped?" she hissed the instant Mrs. Mack was out of easy earshot.

He nodded. Mumbled around a bite of bread, "Yes, but not alone. With a man." He didn't see any point in airing his view that said man had been a gentleman, if not a nobleman of similar station to himself.

His mother straightened. A gleam of pure malice lit her once fine eyes. "A man?" She turned the word over, eventually murmured, "So the silly chit might well be ruined anyway?"

He forced himself to nod. "Very possibly." With any luck, the silly chit was even now fronting some altar. "On top of that, by the time she escaped, she'd been in the kidnappers' hands, alone as far as anyone in London knows, for a good ten days. More than enough to irretrievably sully her reputation." He cocked a brow at his mother. "That's what you wanted, wasn't it? No real need to bring the girl up here, just as long as she suffers—isn't that what you want?"

"No!" Crossing her arms, she quite literally pouted. "I want to *watch* her suffer!" She glared at him. "Men! You never understand!"

She was in the right there. "Regardless, aside from viewing her disgrace and social ignominy in the flesh, with luck, you'll yet get all you wish for."

She snorted derisively. "There'll be no scandal. Her damn family will have covered up her absence."

"Possibly for a few days. But for well over a week? Difficult enough at any time, but during the Season? She'll have had engagements, and repeating the same excuse will have quickly worn thin. There'll have been questions, suspicions." He popped the last bit of bread, carrying the last of the stew's gravy, into his mouth. Chewed, swallowed, then looked down. "For all I—or you—know, she might well have vanished from the face of the earth by now."

He seriously doubted it; an image of the man who had escorted Heather Cynster onto Cynster lands hovered in his mind's eye. It seemed odd to be placing such faith in a stranger, let alone an Englishman, yet situations such as the one he faced made for strange bedfellows.

Pushing back his chair, he rose. Looked down at his mother, his expression as unencouraging as he could make it. "Regardless, until we hear for certain that she's not ruined, our bargain will remain in abeyance."

Stepping past her, he headed for his tower.

"Wait!" Hurrying after him, she gripped his sleeve. "You could go after one of the others." When he didn't slow, she skipped to keep up, gabbled, "Bring one of them here and I'll give you back the goblet. You want it back in your hands as soon as possible, don't you?"

He halted, looked down at her. "Madam—if it transpires I've already ruined one Cynster sister, I will consider our bargain fulfilled." He searched her dark eyes, then quietly, but no less forcefully, stated, "Unless and until we learn otherwise, I will not make a move on any other Cynster girl."

Barely managing not to curl his lip, he shook free of her hold, turned, and walked away.

As far as Heather Cynster was concerned, what would be would be. Meanwhile, he would use every hour of the necessary hiatus to scour the castle yet again for the goblet his mother had stolen away. Where the hell she'd hidden it . . . neither he nor his most trusted retainers had any clue. It had to be here somewhere, but the castle was massive; an eight-inch-tall, five-inch-wide, jewel-encrusted ceremonial goblet could have been concealed in a thousand different places.

Getting it back had to remain his paramount focus. If he didn't, he would lose the castle and all his lands—and all those dependent on him would lose everything. Their homes, their jobs, their heritage. They would be left truly destitute, and while he personally would have enough money to get by, he wouldn't be in any position to help them—and seeing them disperse, seeing them leave this glen and loch, would destroy him as much as it would destroy them.

The castle was his home. His roots were here, sunk deep in the rich highland soil. To lose castle, land, people . . . he might as well die trying to protect them, because losing them would be worse than any death.

Reaching his tower, he swung up the spiral stairs.

He was fairly certain that the only way he would avoid having to kidnap and attempt to ruin another Cynster girl was to find the damn goblet his mother was holding like Damocles' sword over his head.

Chapter Nineteen

The skies over the Vale were shading into pinks and the soft violets of encroaching dusk. Catriona stood just back from the west-facing window in her turret sitting room and, arms folded, watched Heather walk slowly away from the manor.

She walked as if she was tired, as if the day had dragged her down.

"Something's very wrong." Beside Catriona, Algaria watched, too, her face set in disapproving lines. "It was all going so well. What the devil did they do?"

"A moot point. Whatever it is, they've done it. The question is, what now?"

They'd spoken quietly, well aware of the pair of overly sharp ears attached to Lucilla and Marcus, playing knuckle-bones on the floor some yards behind them.

Far below, Heather walked past the stables and out along the track between the paddocks.

Algaria sighed. "It never ceases to amaze me that intelligent people can be such fools when it comes to love, at least while they're in the throes of it."

Catriona humphed, remembering her own throes, her own fears. She watched as Heather paused beside the high-railed paddock fence, then, still moving like an old woman, climbed up to perch on the top rail and look back at the manor. Catriona shook her head. "Regardless of whatever's happened between them, they must come around."

Algaria glanced at her. "You're sure? There's no mistake?"

"None. I wasn't *absolutely* sure at first, but I am now. They're fated for each other." She worried her lower lip. After a moment, added, "I wish I knew what to do."

"You don't know?"

"I haven't received any instructions—not yet."

Sitting on the rug ten paces behind the women, Lucilla and Marcus were engrossed in their game.

Marcus, seated comfortably cross-legged, took his turn, then held out the bones to his sister. When she didn't scoop them from his palm, he looked up, into her face, then softly sighed.

Laying the bones down between them, he propped his elbows on his knees and slumped his chin into his palms.

And waited.

Kneeling, sitting back on her ankles facing him, Lucilla held utterly still. She had a faraway, strangely distant look in her eyes. A look Marcus recognized.

He wasn't surprised when, a moment later, Lucilla blinked, snapped back into her usual vital state, then started to get up.

Tipping her head toward the door, she whispered, "Come on." With a careful glance at their mother's back, she added, "There's something we're supposed to do."

Marcus didn't argue. It wasn't his role to argue. After their mother, Lucilla would be the next Lady of the Vale. Even though he was slated to take up the mantle of Guardian of the Lady, he knew his place.

Without making a sound, he followed Lucilla from the room and silently shut the door.

Heather balanced on the top rail of the empty cattle pen and stared, unseeing, at the manor.

She felt wretched. Beaten down, disheartened in every sense of the word. She'd woken with such hope flooding her heart, an expectation that their joint future was assured and brilliantly bright.

Now . . . she felt dead and desolate inside.

What to do next? Were there any options?

Or was this truly the end?

He would leave, and she would remain here. They would part, and possibly never see each other again.

This time, it seemed, Catriona and the Lady had been wrong. Not even the necklace-charm had helped.

The thought of Catriona had her focusing on the manor. Hands spread to either side, lightly gripping the upper rail, she studied the fanciful gray stone building, honey tinted by the waning sunshine. It was a house filled with love, with an energy that was impossible to miss, a nurturing, caring atmosphere that embraced and infused all who lived within it.

That was the creation, the outcome, the outward expression of Richard and Catriona's love. A home filled with that sustaining glow, with laughter and a vibrant, vital sense of life. Of life continuing, past, present, and future.

Of family, and joys, and duties shared.

That—exactly that—was what she'd wanted to create with Breckenridge. They'd discussed it, yes, but she hadn't truly allowed the reality to take shape in her mind.

Now she had, now she had the manor as a solid example planted in front of her eyes, the resonance was too strong to be denied, as was the recognition, the realization that that future had always been her ultimate dream, a dream that had lived in her heart and her soul, that had always been so much a part of her she'd never bothered to examine it before, had never had reason to study it. Or acknowledge it.

She couldn't shut her eyes to it now.

If she let Breckenridge leave alone, if she let him go, let him walk out of her life, she would never have even another chance at realizing her dream.

Because her dream could only come true, could only be made real, with the man she loved.

Without him in it, her future would be unrelentingly bleak, devoid of love, lacking that vital, living spark.

It was tempting to simply wallow in despair, to let go

and sink into the mire of emotional gloom, yet somewhere deep in her mind she could hear—literally hear—a chiding chorus.

She could almost distinguish the voices: her aunt Helena, Lady Osbaldestone, her aunt Horatia, her mother, and at lower volume, all the rest.

Are you simply going to give up? Do you truly want your dream? If so, how much are you willing to risk to secure it? To sacrifice to secure it—your pride, for instance? Are you truly going to just let him go and so let the prospect of a golden future exactly as you've dreamed simply slip through your fingers?

Or are you going to fight for what you want?

In her mind's eye, she could see the shocked expressions, the ready-to-be-astonished-and-disappointed-if-she-answered-the-wrong-way looks that would accompany the questions. The firming of the chins that would go with the last.

For long moments, she sat on the rail, stared at the manor, and let her brain absorb that inner succor.

Gradually, her mind cleared.

All the distracting issues faded, slid away, until she felt bedrock beneath her mental feet.

Until she saw clearly, and saw her true path. The only path she could follow and remain true to herself, true to her dream, to the ambition that had sent her to Lady Herford's salon so many evenings ago.

That had been the start of it, and she hadn't yet reached the end of her road.

She couldn't—*could not*—give up at this point just because the way forward had become unbearably hard. She had to fight if she wanted to succeed.

The rose quartz pendant hanging between her breasts impinged on her senses.

Catriona had told her she'd have to risk her heart if she wanted to secure his. In her innocence, she'd thought that had meant she'd have to show her love for him before he would reciprocate. But that had been too easy, no real test.

She faced her real test now—to take her courage in both hands, return with him to London, accept his proposal, accept him and the possibility of his love, and then keep working, keep fighting, to lead him to love her as she loved him, to secure her envisaged golden future for them both.

That was her ultimate risk—the ultimate throw of the dice.

The ultimate committing of herself into the hands of fate.

Or, as the case might well be, of the Lady.

She blew out a breath. She felt far from sure of the hows and wheres, yet . . . inside, a steady resolve, a certainty that had risen from her depths, both buoyed and anchored her.

So, what next?

She was deep in cogitation, mentally evaluating several ways in which to couch her change of mind, when the sound of piping voices drew her gaze to the side of the manor.

To Lucilla and Marcus.

Emerging from the shadows of the manor's walls, both looked up, spotted her, and pointed.

And tugged forward the man whose hands they'd captured.

Breckenridge.

High-pitched voices chattering, the twins towed him toward her.

She stared, horrified by the thought that the twins had decided to play matchmaker and intended to haul Breckenridge to stand before her, then lecture them both . . . "Oh, no."

Yes, they needed to talk—she needed to tell him she'd changed her mind, needed to somehow find a way to bridge the yawning chasm that had opened between them, but to have a confrontation forced on them, along with an avid audience . . . oh, no, no, no.

But she could hardly leap down and run away.

The trio came on, Breckenridge clearly reluctant, but with little experience of children, let alone a pair like the twins, he clearly had no notion of how to escape.

Besides, Lucilla was prattling nonstop, giving her captive no chance to protest.

Lucilla and Marcus reached the opening to the track, about twenty yards away from where Heather sat. Abruptly dropping Breckenridge's hands, eyes shining, faces alight, the pair came running, laughing and waving, toward her.

Heather's gaze remained on Breckenridge—and his gaze was on her.

He slowed, then halted at the opening of the track. As if uncertain of his welcome.

That uncertainty was so far removed from his customary arrogance that it struck her to the heart.

He was hurting, too.

The twins were nearly upon her; she switched her gaze to them. The pair had their hands up, waving above their heads, apparently wanting to seize her hands.

Summoning a weak smile, she released her hold on the rail to either side. Balancing precariously—it would only be for a second—she held her hands out to them, one to each side.

They reached her. Two small palms struck each of hers.

Instinctively she'd shifted her weight back, expecting them to catch and pull, but neither did.

The unexpected impacts rocked her back.

To her utter amazement, she felt herself tipping.

She shrieked.

Arms wildly flailing, she toppled back off the rail.

Heard Breckenridge shout her name as she went down.

"*Oof!*" She landed in a heap on a cushion of green.

The ground beyond the fence was slightly lower than the track. Dragging in a breath, she blew hair from her face. An instant's thought confirmed she hadn't broken any bones, that the grass by the fence, less clipped by the animals, had been sufficiently thick to save her. She was shaken and winded, but not much else. She struggled up onto her elbows and saw two pale, horrified faces staring through the slats.

She managed a wobbly smile. "I'm not hurt."

The ground reverberated as Breckenridge raced up. Gathering her skirts, she got her feet under her, raised her voice, and said, "I'm all right."

Straightening, she glanced again at the twins' faces . . .

They weren't looking at her.

They were transfixed by something behind her, and looking increasingly terrified . . .

Nerves suddenly jumping, senses prickling, she slowly turned, and looked across the paddock—at the massive, shaggy-coated highland bull that, head ominously lowered, huge, sharp horns pointing her way, evil yellow eyes fixed balefully on her, was pawing the ground twenty paces away.

The monstrosity snorted violently.

Even as she registered the bunching of the bull's muscles, Breckenridge vaulted the fence and landed beside her. "*Quickly.*"

He grabbed her, hoisted her, and swung her over the top of the fence.

She stumbled as he released her but immediately whirled.

The bull had started his charge; the furious thuds of his heavy hooves racing toward the fence shook the ground.

Breckenridge flung one arm over the top railing.

She seized his sleeve with both hands and hauled. "Hurry! *Hurry!*"

He rose up one rung—

The bull struck.

The fence rocked, shuddered, bowed.

Breckenridge gasped, eyes going wide, blind with pain. . . .

Her gaze on his face, Heather lost her breath.

She glanced down and saw a blood-tipped horn protruding through the slats. "Oh, no."

With a hideous snort, the bull yanked and pulled back.

Breckenridge's eyes closed. He started to slump.

"*No!*" The bull was circling. Climbing halfway up the fence, Heather grabbed the back of Breckenridge's jacket, yanked desperately. "Come on! You *have* to get over."

With an horrendous effort, he gathered himself. His muscles were quivering as he managed to climb up another rung.

Hauling, tugging, Heather looked at the twins, standing with eyes wide and mouths open. "*Help me*!"

Marcus broke through the shock first. He came rushing up, climbed the fence on Breckeridge's other side, grabbed and hauled, too.

Then Lucilla was there, but rather than try to assist directly, she climbed up further down the fence, pointed an imperious finger at the bull, and started singing a strange little ditty.

Heather glanced at the bull—with immense relief saw the beast watching Lucilla, distracted and no longer about to charge. "Thank God. Or the Lady."

Breckenridge was rapidly losing strength. Even with Marcus's and her help, he'd only managed to reach the second rung down from the top of the fence—then he sagged, and tipped over it. She flung her arms around him, with Marcus battled to slow his descent, then he was lying in a sprawl on the thinly grassed track.

And she finally saw the jagged wound in his right side. "Oh, God."

Blood was pouring from the gaping tear. Falling to her knees, she slapped her hands over the gash, pressed hard. One glance at his face, at his pinched eyelids, at the white lines bracketing his mouth, told her he was still conscious.

She flung a glance at the twins. "Race to the house and get your mother and Algaria. Tell them what happened. Quickly!"

They'd turned before she'd uttered the final word. They pelted back along the track, then around the corner of the stable toward the manor's back door.

She refocused on Breckenridge, on the blood welling between her fingers. Her palms side by side barely covered the wound. She needed material to staunch the flow.

With no shawl, and no hands free to undo his cravat, she grabbed the loose side of his jacket, bundled it up, and pressed it down—then let go, leapt to her feet, stripped off her lawn petticoat, and shook it free as she fell back to her knees. She wadded the material, lifted aside his coat, and pressed the makeshift pad firmly over the wound.

Better. She leaned on the dressing and the bleeding slowed.

She glanced at his face. From the set of his lips, knew he was still conscious. Was it better if he remained so? Staring at his face, at the angles and planes now beloved, she felt a chill touch her soul.

He might die.

"Don't misunderstand, *but how dare you risk your life*? What the *devil* did you think, to leap over like that? You could have stayed safe on this side and *just helped me over*." Even to her ears, her tone bordered on the hysterical.

Beneath her fingers, the white lawn started to redden.

She sucked in a shaky breath. "How could you risk your life—your *life,* you idiot!" She leaned harder on the pad, dragged in another breath.

He coughed weakly, shifted his head.

"Don't you dare die on me!"

His lips twisted, but his eyes remained closed. "But if I die"—his words were a whisper—"you won't have to marry, me or anyone else. Even the most censorious in the ton will consider my death to be the end of the matter. You'll be free."

"Free?" Then his earlier words registered. *"If you die*? I told you—don't you dare! I won't let you—I forbid you to. How can I marry you if you die? And how the hell will I live if you aren't alive, too?" As the words left her mouth, half hysterical, all emotion, she realized they were the literal truth. Her life wouldn't be worth living if he wasn't there to share it. "What will I do with my life if you die?"

He softly snorted, apparently unimpressed by—or was it not registering?—her panic. "Marry some other poor sod, like you were planning to."

The words cut. *"You* are the only poor sod I'm planning to

marry." Her waspish response came on a rush of rising fear. She glanced around, but there was no one in sight. Help had yet to come running.

She looked back at him, readjusted the pressure on the slowly reddening pad. "I intend not only to marry you but to lead you by the nose for the rest of your days. It's the least I can do to repay you for this—for the shock to my nerves. I'll have you know I'd decided even before this little incident to reverse my decision and become your viscountess, and lead you *such* a merry dance through the ballrooms and drawing rooms that you'll be gray within two years."

He humphed softly, dismissively, but he was listening. Studying his face, she realized her nonsense was distracting him from the pain. She engaged her imagination and let her tongue run free. "I've decided I'll redecorate Baraclough in the French Imperial style—all that white and gilt and spindly legs, with all the chairs so delicate you won't dare sit down. And while we're on the subject of your—our—country home, I've had an idea about my carriage, the one you'll buy me as a wedding gift. . . ."

She rambled on, paying scant attention to her words, simply let them and all the images she'd dreamed of come tumbling out, painting a vibrant, fanciful, yet in many ways—all the ways that counted—accurate word picture of her hopes, her aspirations. Her vision of their life together.

When the well started to run dry, when her voice started to thicken with tears at the fear that they might no longer have a chance to enjoy all she'd described, she concluded with, "So you absolutely can't die now." Fear prodded; almost incensed, she blurted, "Not when I was about to back down and agree to return to London with you."

He moistened his lips. Whispered, "You were?"

"Yes! I was!" His fading voice tipped her toward panic. Her voice rose in reaction. "I can't *believe* you were so foolish as to risk your life like this! You didn't need to put yourself in danger to save me."

"Yes, I did." The words were firmer, bitten off through clenched teeth.

She caught his anger. Was anger good? Would temper help hold him to the world?

A frown drew down his black brows. "You can't be so damned foolish as to think I wouldn't—after protecting you through all this, seeing you safely all this way, watching over you all this time, what else was I going to do?"

She stared at him, at his face. Simply stared as the scales fell from her eyes. "Oh, my God," she whispered, the exclamation so quiet not even he would hear. She suddenly saw— saw it all—all that she'd simply taken for granted.

Men like him protected those they loved, selflessly, unswervingly, even unto death.

The realization rocked her. Pieces of the jigsaw of her understanding of him fell into place. He was hanging to consciousness by a thread. She had to be sure—and his shields, his defenses were at their weakest now.

Looking down at her hands, pressed over the nearly saturated pad, she hunted for the words, the right tone. Softly said, "My death, even my serious injury, would have freed you from any obligation to marry me. Society would have accepted that outcome, too."

He shifted, clearly in pain. She sucked in a breath— feeling his pain as her own—then he clamped the long fingers of his right hand about her wrist, held tight.

So tight she felt he was using her as an anchor to consciousness, to the world.

His tone, when he spoke, was harsh. "Oh, yes—after I'd expended so much effort keeping you safe all these years, safe even from me, I was suddenly going to stand by and let you be gored by some mangy bull." He snorted, soft, low. Weakly. He drew in a slow, shallow breath, lips thin with pain, but determined, went on, "You think I'd let you get injured when finally after all these long years I at last understand that the reason you've always made me itch is because you are the only woman I actually want to marry? And you think I would stand back and let you be harmed?"

A peevish frown crossed his face. "I ask you, is that likely? Is it even vaguely rational?"

He went on, his words increasingly slurred, his tongue tripping over some, his voice fading. She listened, strained to catch every word as he slid into semidelirium, into rambling, disjointed sentences that she drank in, held to her heart.

He gave her dreams back to her, reshaped and refined. "Not French Imperial—good, sound, English oak. You can use whatever colors you like, but no gilt—I forbid it."

Eventually he ventured further than she had. "And I want at least three children—not just an heir and a spare. At least three—more, if you're agreeable. We'll have to have two boys, of course—my evil ugly sisters will hound us to make good on that. But thereafter . . . as many girls as you like. . . . as long as they look like you. Or perhaps Cordelia—she's the handsomer of the two uglies."

He loved his sisters, his evil ugly sisters. Heather listened with tears in her eyes as his mind drifted and his voice gradually faded, weakened.

She'd finally got her declaration, not in anything like the words she'd expected, but in a stronger, impossible-to-doubt exposition.

He'd been her protector, unswerving, unflinching, always there; from a man like him, focused on a lady like her, such actions were tantamount to a declaration from the rooftops. The love she'd wanted him to admit to had been there all along, demonstrated daily right before her eyes, but she hadn't seen.

Hadn't seen because she'd been focusing elsewhere, and because, conditioned as she was to resisting the same style of possessive protectiveness from her brothers, from her cousins, she hadn't appreciated his, hadn't realized that that quality had to be an expression of his feelings for her.

Until now.

Until now that he'd all but given his life for hers.

He loved her—he'd always loved her. She saw that now, looking back down the years. He'd loved her from the time she'd fallen in love with him—the instant they'd laid eyes on each other at Michael and Caro's wedding in Hampshire four years ago.

He'd held aloof, held away—held her at bay, too— believing, wrongly, that he wasn't an appropriate husband for her.

In that, he'd been wrong, too.

She saw it all. And as the tears overflowed and tracked down her cheeks, she knew to her soul how right he was for her. Knew, embraced, and rejoiced.

And feared.

His voice had faded almost to nothing; she could no longer make sense of his words.

The fingers that had gripped her wrist so tightly were weakening.

She sniffed, glanced around. "Where the devil are they?"

At least the bleeding had slowed, grown sluggish, but in her estimation he'd lost far too much blood.

Drawing in a breath, holding it, clinging to her sanity and her strength, she leaned forward and brushed her lips across his. "Hush. Hold on to me, keep hold of me—never let go."

Her voice threatened to break. She sucked in a desperate breath, blinked hard, then went on, "They won't be long now. I want you to hang on, to stay with me. You have to hold on for me because I can't live without you."

She kept speaking, low and steady, willing him to live, yet she sensed him slipping further away.

She barely registered the rush of feet, the swirl of energy as the household descended, couldn't take her eyes from his face.

He slipped into unconsciousness as they neared.

Then Catriona, Algaria, Richard, and all the rest were

there, sweeping around them, taking charge, taking over, gently easing her aside.

It was Richard who closed his big hands about her shoulders and raised her, then drew her away. "Let them have at him."

She swallowed, nodded, but when Richard handed her over to Mrs. Broom, who gently suggested she come back to the house, she refused with a curt shake of her head. "I'll stay with him."

She wasn't going to let him out of her sight.

Catriona had brought supplies to bandage the wound before they risked lifting him. She and Algaria worked swiftly, cutting away his clothes, then cleaning the wound.

Heather breathed deeply, felt her composure, fragile though it was, firm. With a smile that was more a grimace, she thanked Mrs. Broom, then went forward to the still figure on the ground.

Halting at Catriona's side, she stated, "I need to help. Tell me what to do."

Both Algaria and Catriona glanced at her, sharp glances that stripped her face bare, then Catriona nodded. Indicated a set of unguent pots nearby. "The one with the blue lid. It'll only be temporary, but we need to make what stand we can against infection."

Heather picked up the pot, loosened the lid, and held it ready.

He'd saved her.

Now it was up to her to save him.

Chapter Twenty

The men of the household carried Breckenridge back to the house on a stretcher. The last of the light was fading from the sky as Heather followed them through the side door into the house. Catriona and Algaria had diverted to the herb garden, seeking extra ingredients for potions and tisanes. Mrs. Broom and Henderson had rushed ahead to prepare Breckenridge's bed.

Lamps were being lit throughout the house. As Heather crossed the front hall, someone handed her a small lantern. A footman appeared ahead of the stretcher, carrying a large lamp to light the bearers' way.

The main staircase was wide with a sweeping curve. After carefully negotiating the climb, the men turned toward the turret and Breckenridge's room on the next floor, only to find Mrs. Broom waiting to wave them to another door along the gallery.

"Ye'll never make it up the turret stairs, not without jiggling him something fearful. We've made up the bed in here instead."

The room they entered was a bed-cum-sitting room. Two maids were tugging sheets and fluffing pillows on a big four-poster bed. Henderson and a footman were feeding a blaze already roaring in the hearth.

Richard and the other three stretcher bearers carried Breckenridge to the side of the bed closest to the hearth. They laid the stretcher on the floor, then, under Richard's direction, with Mrs. Broom kneeling on the bed to help settle the patient, they carefully transferred Breckenridge's long and heavy body onto a plain cotton sheet spread over the covers and pillows.

As soon as Breckenridge was stretched out and settled, the other three men gathered the stretcher and left. Richard hovered by the side of the bed, looking down at Breckenridge.

Heather stood at the foot, her gaze locked on his face.

Then Catriona swept in, Algaria and three older women of the household behind her. Catriona came straight to the bed, circling to halt by Breckenridge's shoulder. Her hand briefly gripped Richard's, then she released him. "We'll handle this from here."

Heather felt Richard's gaze flick to her face, then he looked at his wife. "How bad is he? Should I send for Caro and Michael?"

Catriona studied Breckenridge, then held the back of one hand against his cheek. She hesitated, then drew breath and said, "He's very low. He might not die, but . . . yes, I think you should send for Caro."

"He also has two sisters—Constance and Cordelia." Heather's voice seemed to come from far away. "He . . . they're close. Caro will know how to contact them."

Richard's gaze rested on her face for a moment, then he nodded. "I'll send a rider to Michael immediately." With a nod to Catriona, he left her side. Reaching Heather, he paused, laid a hand on her shoulder, lightly gripped. "He's alive. While he is, there's hope."

Without taking her eyes from Breckenridge's still, pale face, she nodded.

Richard left.

Behind and about her the three women were setting bandages and bottles, pots and implements, on various surfaces. A footman appeared in the doorway carrying a brazier. Catriona saw him and pointed to the middle of the room. "Set it there."

Algaria paused by the bed, opposite Catriona, watching as Catriona checked Breckenridge's eyes. Algaria glanced at Heather, then came around the bed to halt at her side. "Go and wash your hands."

Heather frowned, looked down at her hands, and realized they were covered in dried blood.

"Go to your room, wash thoroughly, and change into something warm and comfortable." Algaria's tone was even, certain, and compassionate. "Then go to the kitchen and let Cook feed you. When you've done all that, you can come back and spell us. There's nothing we're about to do that we haven't done many times, nothing we need help with. There'll be nothing you can do to help him through the next hour or so, but after that . . . that's when you need to be here, when he might need you to be here. Best you're in as good a state as you can be to help him then."

Algaria had spoken slowly and steadily. Heather took in her words, could find no reason to argue. She drew in a tight breath, then nodded. "All right."

After one last, long look at the still figure on the bed, she turned and walked from the room.

She returned an hour later, washed, fed, and garbed in a soft, plain woolen gown a helpful maid had found for her, along with the knitted shawl she'd slung about her shoulders.

Refreshed in body she might be, but inside . . . she'd never felt so frozen, so full of icy dread.

Walking into the sickroom, she saw the three older women bundling up sheets, the remnants of Breckenridge's clothes, bloodied bandages, and basins of bloodied water. Despite their industry, their expressions remained serious. Hoisting their loads, they bustled out.

In the silence that fell, Heather approached the bed. Algaria was crouched before the fire, carefully setting more logs onto the blaze. The bedcurtains nearer the door and across half the bed's foot were drawn, the better to ward off drafts. Passing beyond their screen, she looked into the now shadowed bed.

Breckenridge lay on his back beneath the covers, stretched out straight, his arms by his sides. His face was pale, the elegant but severe lines set, unmoving. His lips were a thin line, showing no animation at all.

His eyes were closed, his long lashes black crescents stark against the white parchment of his skin. His dark locks had been pushed back from his forehead.

He looked like an effigy.

Catriona stood beside the bed, arms folded, her gaze on his face.

Eyes widening, Heather sent Catriona a suddenly fearful, pleading look.

"He's alive."

The relief nearly brought her to her knees.

Catriona hadn't looked up; she continued, "We've stopped the bleeding—you did well with that. We did the rest, and, Lady be blessed, the horn didn't damage anything vital."

"So he'll recover?"

Catriona hesitated, then said, "He shouldn't die from the wound itself. From that, he should recover well enough. Infection is the threat. We've done all we can for now. The poultices we've put on are the most powerful I know. We'll renew them twice a day, every time we change the bandages. But in fighting infection, it'll be his strength and his will that will turn the tide."

Finally raising her gaze, Catriona met Heather's eyes. "All we can do now is wait, and pray, and support him however we can."

Drawing in a deep breath, Heather nodded. "I'll be here."

Catriona studied her for a moment—another of her sharp, seeing-beneath-the-skin looks—then she relaxed her arms and walked around the bed, with a wave indicating that Heather should take her place by Breckenridge's head. "The bellpull is by the mantelpiece. Ring if he stirs, or if you need anything at all. Don't hesitate to ask for help."

"Or advice." Algaria rose from the fire. She, too, looked assessingly at Heather, then nodded as if saying she'd do. "One thing to remember—belief is the key. It's the one thing we can give them when they wake, when they stir, when in their delirium they're searching. We have to believe. We must believe. We must convince them we do. Only our absolute, unswerving belief will be strong enough to anchor them, to make them believe, too."

Heather looked into Algaria's eyes—eyes that were old, eyes that were wise. Was she talking of life, or love? Or both?

Perhaps in this case, life and love were one and the same.

Raising her head, Heather nodded. "I understand."

"Good." Turning to follow Catriona, who, after watching the exchange, had turned and was walking from the room, Algaria added, "One of us will check with you every few hours, in case there's any change, or if you need anything. He may not wake tonight, but as long as he continues to breathe, there's no reason to suppose all is not proceeding as it should."

Grateful for the reassurance, Heather watched Algaria follow Catriona from the room, watched the door close.

Then she looked at Breckenridge, lying so silent on the bed.

A straight-backed chair stood angled between the bed and the hearth. Drawing it to the bed, she sat, leaned her elbows on the covers, took one of his hands—so cold and lifeless— in hers, cradled it between her palms.

Willed him to live.

Ignoring the vast, chill emptiness inside, the devastating desolation hovering, she focused her mind, all her inner energy, on that one single goal.

He had to live.

Whatever it took, whatever she could do.

He was her all, her everything. She knew that now, believed that now—believed with her mind, her heart, and her soul, believed with every fibre of her being.

No matter what it took, she wasn't going to let him go.

* * *

He didn't wake. Not through that first long night, nor the day that followed.

Heather left the room, his bedside, only for minutes. Through the deep watches of the first night, she climbed onto the bed, and lay alongside him; she slept—napped—with one hand wrapped about one of his, just in case he woke.

He didn't even stir.

The next day dawned gray and chill, with a flurry of rain hitting the windows. Catriona and Algaria were in and out through most of the day, assessing his condition, changing the bandages and the poultice they were using to draw the infection.

Heather helped; between the three of them they could manage his weight, could shift him, strip him, wash and cleanse, then bandage him up once more.

She spoke little; there was little to say.

To her eyes, the wound was cleaner, yet still horrific, a hideous tear through his side. Having seen the damage, she redoubled her prayers to God, to the Lady, to any deity who might consent to listen, grateful for his survival thus far, even more desperate for his continuing life.

Catriona and Algaria exchanged observations in low murmurs; Heather didn't need to listen to know what they said. Their tones, their grave expressions, told her all she needed to know.

Breckenridge literally lay at death's door.

When night came again, he yet lay silent and still. The manor quieted; Catriona came to check on him one last time before seeking her bed. After examining him, she straightened, sighed. Then she laid a hand on Heather's shoulder, lightly gripped. "Have faith."

Releasing her, Catriona left.

Heather sat on the chair beside the bed, her gaze locked on his face. Unbidden, her fingers rose to touch the rose quartz pendant beneath her bodice.

Have faith. Believe.

She did.

She understood now what fate asked of her—to have the strength to hold on regardless. To acknowledge that, even if he died, even if he left her, she would still love him until the day she died.

Love didn't care. Love simply was.

Love was unconditional.

Love was for ever more.

She had faith in love. She believed in love.

She would love him in life and in death.

And if the chance came again she would convince him of that.

As the night closed around her, she closed her eyes and prayed.

His senses swam back to him, returned to him, yet not in the usual way. He felt . . . detached. Distanced. Still a part of reality, but as if a thin veil separated him from the earthly world.

He was floating.

Free of the pain that had gripped him for days.

Free of the body he'd inhabited for three and a half decades—the body lying, weak and wracked with agony, in the big bed.

That body—his body—was chilled to the bone.

He could see, but not with his eyes. He could feel, but he wasn't sure how or why. Which senses were telling him what he now knew, he could no longer discern.

The cold and the pain . . . they'd driven him out.

Out of his body, out into the night.

Out beyond the veil.

He could feel a tug, a gentle tempting encouraging him to just let go and float away, away from the world, from the pain and the cold and the devastating agony.

All he had to do was decide, just make up his mind and let

go, and his connection to the world would fade away and he would find blessed peace.

Blessed peace waited one last heartbeat away.

He—his body in the bed—drew a deeper, pain-wracked breath . . . and he thought of making that decision.

His last decision.

What reason did he have to live?

What was left to hold him to this world?

Even as the thought formed, the answers flooded in.

His father.

His two, dear, evil ugly sisters.

Heather.

He paused at that last, wondering why she was still in his list. She hadn't loved him, had told him to leave, to walk away . . . why, then, did his connection to her remain?

That connection . . . he could, in this odd state, almost feel it. Touch it, see it. Like a shining rope, stretched out yet strong, it glowed in his consciousness, vital and true, power-ful, alive . . . living.

Real.

He'd thought he was alone, lying cold, agony-wracked, and silenced in the big bed, but that shining rope . . . led somewhere. It was fixed somehow. It anchored him to the world, to life.

Another whisper from beyond shivered through him, beckoning, calling.

But now he'd seen what lived inside him, been dazzled by its beauty, he had to know—needed to know—before he took that last irrevocable step and turned his back on the wonder, on the joy.

On the incomparable beauty of love.

He opened his senses—not touch or sight, but whatever in this state passed for those—and immediately knew where the shining rope ended.

Heather was sitting by his bedside, but she had crossed her arms on the covers and laid her head down. One slim hand was nestled in his lax palm. Her hair was spread fanlike, a golden veil flung across the covers, gilt strands a delicate net across her cheek.

She was sleeping.

His immediate thought was that she couldn't be comfortable, that he should rise, lift her, and settle her in the bed . . .

He paused, thought.

Remembered she'd rejected him.

Remembered that he'd still risked his life—brought himself to this, to the edge of life—in order to save her.

If he lived, he would again.

His love for her was an intrinsic part of him, the strongest, most brilliant, and best part of him. He would no more wrench it, or her, from his heart than he would trade his soul . . . he would rather trade his soul than lose love, lose her.

Even if she wasn't his in the worldly, customary sense.

In every sense that mattered to him, she would always be his to guard, to protect.

To love.

He looked at her, studied her from his new distance, through the strange distortion of the veil.

She'd said she didn't care if he left . . . so why was she there?

Why was she . . . he broadened his senses and confirmed that it was only she . . . by his bedside, keeping vigil through the lonely night?

He focused on her again, saw, sensed, the tracks of the tears she'd shed.

Knew beyond question that she'd shed them for him.

Knew she cared.

Other words echoed in the distance of his mind; he focused, pulled them forward, remembered. Out by the bull pen, when his life had been draining from him and he'd felt so cold, she'd told him she'd changed her mind—she'd said she intended to marry him. They'd talked of their future life, of all the things they would do, would achieve.

The memories came rushing back.

She loved him.

The wonder of that distracted him. While he savored that new aspect of his shining reality, he floated back up to where he'd earlier been.

Hovering between life and death.

Once again, more insistent this time, he felt the tug, the summons to go. To let go of life and leave the world he knew.

Leave Heather. Leave their love.

He looked again—detached, dispassionate—at his body on the bed. The injuries were serious. Beneath the miasma induced by the herbs and potions they'd fed him, his corporeal self was writhing in agony. If he returned to that body, he would face days of searing agony, weeks of debilitating pain.

He switched his strange senses to Heather. Saw her as she truly was in that moment, vulnerable, lost, and unprotected. And it was her love for him, her acceptance of it, that left her so exposed. So emotionally unshielded.

If he left . . . who would hold her, shield her? Care for her, protect her?

Who would love her?

He couldn't leave. No matter the agony of staying, no matter the price, he couldn't walk away from her—not if there was any hope of staying, of remaining by her side.

The summons came again, more definite this time. He had to leave or stay—he had to make up his mind.

He didn't have to search to know what to do. He simply opened his consciousness, and within it said one word. "No."

And he was back in his body.

And the agony flayed him again.

"He's burning up." Heather looked up at Catriona. "What do we do?"

The worried look on Catriona's face did nothing to quell the fear coursing through her. After him being chilled, his skin cold to the touch through the first night and the next day, this morning, when she'd woken and studied Breckenridge's face, she'd seen a hint of color creeping into his cheeks. His hand had been warm in hers.

In her innocence and inexperience of serious injury, she'd thought that he was recovering. Talking quietly, telling him of all the things they would do once he got better, she'd waited eagerly for him to wake up.

Instead, a fever had built, and built, until now, in the late afternoon, it had reached the level of a raging conflagration, one that threatened to engulf and devour him from the inside out.

They'd gone from wiping his brow with iced water, to laying ice-water-dampened sheets over him, and constantly changing them, but nothing had worked to even stabilize his temperature.

It continued to climb.

Arms folded, Catriona stared down at him, then, as if she'd come to the conclusion of some inner debate, she nodded curtly. "An ice-bath. We've tried everything else to no avail, so it'll have to be that." She hesitated, then met Heather's eyes. "It's risky with that wound, but if we don't get his temperature down, we'll lose him regardless."

"Now?" was the only reply Heather made.

Catriona gave the orders. Within minutes Henderson arrived with two footmen carrying a large tin bath. Under Catriona's directions, they set it down on the other side of the room, away from the hearth even though they'd long ago doused the fire.

The first footman carrying two buckets of ice arrived five minutes later.

Algaria returned from the schoolroom and supervised. Richard came with Henderson and two other men. They stood ready to lift Breckenridge from the bed to the bath.

Catriona told them, "We'll need to lower him in, then lift him out again."

They fashioned a makeshift sling from a sheet. When Algaria deemed the ice slurry in the bath ready, the men shifted Breckenridge onto the sheet, lifted him in it, and lowered him into the bath.

Arms tightly folded, Heather watched, and shivered.

The instant the men stepped back, letting Breckenridge sink into the ice-and-water mix, she stepped to one side of the bath, went to her knees, and took one of his hands in hers.

On the other side of the bath, Catriona hovered close, watching. After a few minutes, Heather realized Catriona was watching Breckenridge's lips.

The instant they started to pale, Catriona said, "Out. Now."

Heather stepped back, and the men stepped in.

They lifted Breckenridge out, then laid him down, wrapped in the ice-cold sheet on a pallet of towels on the floor. Catriona and Algaria worked swiftly to replace his bandages with dry ones.

They had to dunk him twice more before midnight.

After the clocks throughout the manor tolled that hour, with Breckenridge once more lying on the bed covered only by the damp sheet, Heather sat on the chair by his side, his hand again in hers, and watched him sleep.

On the other side of the bed, seated in a rocker with a warm shawl wrapped about her, Catriona kept watch, too.

In the quiet, in the silence, Heather finally found courage to voice the question that had hovered in her mind all day. "Why hasn't he woken?"

Catriona, her gaze on Breckenridge, too, rocked, then softly said, "I think it's because of the amount of blood he lost. Not enough to kill, but enough to . . . make him hibernate might be nearest the truth. That, and the infection on top of it." Without taking her eyes from him, she went on, "The mind and body have ways of protecting themselves—the mind especially can send the body into this type of hibernating state, not true unconsciousness but a deep, deep sleep, so it can more effectively heal."

Raising a hand to resettle her shawl, Catriona flicked a

glance Heather's way. "I don't see him not waking as a bad sign—not yet. It might, in fact, be the opposite, an indication that his body is coping as it should and he's healing. The fever itself is a sign that his body is fighting the infection."

Heather nodded. The words were a comfort; she held them close.

Catriona reached out and laid her fingers on Breckenridge's wrist. After a moment, she sat back again. "His pulse is still steady. Not as strong as I'd like, but there's no hint it's weakening, and at the moment his temperature is good. However, fevers being as fevers are, I'd expect his to rise again before morning."

Settling in the chair, flicking the shawl across her shoulders, she caught Heather's gaze. "I suggest we take turns getting some sleep. One of us needs to be awake in case his temperature spikes—as I expect—or alternatively if it goes the other way and he starts to shiver." Closing her eyes, she wriggled down in the chair. "If he does start to shiver, or gets too hot again, wake me immediately."

"All right." Heather leaned on the bed, Breckenridge's hand between hers, and settled to watch him through the night.

After two hours, Catriona woke and insisted Heather needed to rest. Heather knew better than to argue; laying her head down on the bed, she closed her eyes.

Sometime later, Catriona shook her awake. Heather blinked, focused. It was still night. And under her palm, Breckenridge's hand was burning.

"We have to cool him down again." Catriona urged her up and to the side.

Heather stood and moved out of the way, blinking in surprise to find Richard and the other men back again. They'd already refilled the bath with fresh ice.

They repeated what was now a well-rehearsed process.

Once Breckenridge was back on the bed, his skin cold and damp, and Richard and the other men had retired once more, Heather sank back into the chair.

Standing opposite, Catriona took Breckenridge's pulse,

then she glanced at Heather. "I'm going to return to my own bed. His temperature shouldn't rise again before morning." Folding her arms, she frowned down at him. "If he starts to shiver, or does get too hot again, promise me you'll come and fetch me right away."

Heather nodded. "I promise."

Catriona turned away. "Try to nap if you can."

Heather sighed, took his hand once more, and settled to her vigil.

The days that followed were the darkest of her life. Although they didn't need the ice-bath again, Breckenridge's temperature remained erratic, spiking unpredictably—pricking her fears every time it did.

Then he grew restive, flinging off the covers, shifting in the bed enough to make himself groan.

As from the first, Heather rarely left him. Her reward came toward the end of the third day, when her voice, her words, noticeably soothed him.

Catriona, witnessing the event, humphed. "It's as I thought—he's not truly unconscious. He's in a healing state."

She seemed relieved, more assured, after that.

For her part, Heather couldn't take the same comfort— she wanted to see his eyes again, wanted to see recognition and understanding.

At the back of her mind was the unvoiced fear that after so many days "hibernating," when he returned he wouldn't remember. Her, or anything else.

To counter her fears, whenever she was alone with him she talked—of their past, of their present, of their future. She put no restraint on her tongue but let her heart dictate, let her love drive her.

More than anything else, it was those moments of letting their love shine between them that anchored her and gave her some respite.

Everyone in the household helped in their way. Cook sent

up trays regularly, and Algaria made sure she ate. Lucilla and Marcus, unusually subdued, crept in to see, to ask after Breckenridge, but didn't stay long. Richard often looked in and stayed to chat, to tell her bits and pieces of what was going on in the world outside.

But it was Catriona who was most often her support, especially through the long watches of the nights, even though, now that it seemed clear Breckenridge was improving, she slept in her own bed. She returned periodically to monitor Breckenridge's condition, to reassure Heather, and provide company and respite for a little while.

Toward the end of one such visit, with Heather seated in her customary place by the bed, Breckenridge's hand as always in hers, Catriona sat in the rocker on the opposite side of the bed and studied her with that look Heather thought of as seeing beneath the skin.

After a moment, Catriona asked, "So, have you and he settled your differences and agreed to share your future?"

Heather hadn't anticipated quite that question. *Your future.* Catriona made it sound as if they hadn't really had any option bar that one, as if a shared future was the only future either of them could have.

"Yes." Heather frowned. "At least . . . I believe we have." When Catriona arched her brows, she went on, "Before everyone rushed up, we talked, said things—both of us. But it was such a jumble, and at the end I don't know if he . . ." She drew in a breath. "I don't know how much he'll remember."

"Hmm. In that case, I would strongly suggest you make your position on that subject absolutely crystal clear the instant he wakes and is in any condition to take it in." Catriona held her gaze. "That's important, Heather. I don't normally tell people such things—we're not supposed to influence—but you and he are supposed to be together. But in order to reap the harvest that is waiting for you ahead, you must believe. To your heart and soul, you must believe in your ideal for it to happen. You have to let that belief guide you in everything—your actions, your speech, your very thoughts."

Catriona paused, then went on, her gaze steady on Heather's eyes, "I don't know why that's so vital, only that it is. For what's between you and he to be all that it could be, you must believe, so that he can believe, too."

Heather drank in the words, felt their truth resonate. Logic and reason, she'd learned, didn't always apply where love was concerned; perhaps faith—faith in love—was the only true touchstone.

Risky, perhaps, to have blind faith in an emotion, but she no longer had anything to lose. She nodded. "Yes. I will."

To her surprise, her reply seemed to ease Catriona, who visibly relaxed, almost ruefully smiled.

"Good." Rising, Catriona drew her shawl around her, then looked down at Breckenridge. "I don't expect you to have any trouble with him tonight. Sleep. He's not going to leave you." With that, she turned and walked to the door.

Heather watched her go, watched the door shut. Replayed their conversation, then, feeling more settled, crawled onto the bed by Breckenridge's side, laid her head down, and closed her eyes.

The days and nights had merged; she'd lost track of time.

The following afternoon, Heather allowed herself to be bullied into taking a relaxing bath. Into washing her hair, donning fresh clothes, refashioning her chignon. Eating a proper meal.

Feeling significantly refreshed, she returned to Breckenridge's bedside to relieve Algaria. Although the fever had abated and he seemed less wracked, he'd yet to awaken, but Catriona and Algaria expected he soon would.

She'd just settled on the straight-backed chair when she, and Algaria, at the door, heard the clatter of hooves and the rattle of wheels in the forecourt.

Algaria met her eyes. "Someone's come running."

Five minutes later, an elegantly slender lady, head crowned with a corona of fine, shimmery brown hair, swept into the room.

Heather smiled. "Caro." She got to her feet.

Caroline Anstruther-Wetherby came straight to the bed. Her gaze fixing on the still figure lying upon it, she circled to reach Heather, then switched her silver-blue gaze to her and wrapped her in a scented embrace. "My dear! We heard and came straightaway." Releasing Heather, Caro looked again at Breckenridge. "How is he?"

Heather paused, then said, "A lot better than he was."

Caro leaned down and took the limp hand Heather had been holding. She chafed it lightly, as if by touch she could tell Breckenridge that she was there, then laid it down and turned to Heather. "Tell me all."

"Tell us all."

Both Heather and Caro turned to see Michael Anstruther-Wetherby crossing the room toward them. It was through her marriage to Michael that Caro was connected to the Cynsters, Michael's sister, Honoria, being the Duchess of St. Ives, wife of Devil Cynster, the head of the Cynster clan, Richard's older brother and Heather's oldest cousin.

Michael, a tall, dark-haired, extremely well-connected gentleman deeply involved with politics, drew Heather in for a warm hug. He patted her shoulder as he released her. "I come charged to stand in place of your brothers and your father, let alone Devil and all the rest. As Caro was determined to come flying up here, and Breckenridge was apparently so low, we thought it better if the others contained their impatience and remained in London until we better understood the situation here."

Heather fleetingly closed her eyes in relief. "Thank you." The words were heartfelt. Dealing with her brothers' protectiveness just now would have required effort and tact she did not have to spare. Opening her eyes, she smiled at Michael; he was indeed a politician to his toes. "I'm truly grateful."

He smiled back. "I thought you would be. But the counter-side to that is that you must tell us all. From the start."

"Yes, all right." After one glance at Breckenridge confirmed he was still "asleep," she gestured to the sofa and chairs on the other side of the room.

Once they'd settled comfortably, she did as requested, started at the beginning—Lady Herford's house—and told them all.

She left nothing out but related their journey step by stage. Neither Michael nor Caro were slow-witted; they followed the puzzling, perplexing tale of her kidnap, her reasons for remaining and trying to learn more, and the difficulties she and Breckenridge had encountered in achieving her eventual escape, with commendable ease.

When she reached the point where they'd walked into the Vale and gained refuge at the manor, she paused, then raised her head and went on, "Breckenridge and I have been discussing our future, but I would prefer not to say anything more on that score until he wakes."

Caro and Michael exchanged a glance, one Heather couldn't read, then Caro nodded. "Quite right. But how did he get injured? Gored, Richard said?"

That was easier to answer. However, in doing so, in reliving the moments that had led to Breckenridge's wounding, Heather was struck—as she had been at the time, but had forgotten in the subsequent rush of events—by the oddity in the way the twins' hands had pushed at hers, rather than grabbed. What had the pair been about?

"So how has he been since then?" Caro asked.

Shaking free of the memory, she described the initial chill. "Catriona said it was deep shock. Then came the fever."

Glancing at the bed, Michael frowned. "He hasn't regained consciousness yet?"

Heather looked across the room, too. "Catriona says he's not unconscious, just in a very deep, healing sleep. The fever's come down, but it hasn't yet broken. She and Algaria think it soon will, and he'll wake after that."

"At least he was here when it happened, with expert hands close by." Caro rose. "If you like, I'll sit with you for a while. I've messages from your sisters and mother. We can chat while we watch over him."

"Yes, of course." Heather rose.

Michael rose, too. His and Caro's eyes met, and he smiled, first at Caro, then at Heather. "As I'm clearly not needed here, I'll go and find Richard."

With a salute, he headed for the door, leaving Heather to lead Caro back to the bed.

Back to her vigil by Breckenridge's side.

Later that night, Heather settled on the chair by Breckenridge's bed. Looking down at his face, features still unanimated, rather severe in repose, she thought of her hopes, of her lingering fears. Thought of all she'd seen, through the evening, of others' unions, others' shared lives.

Because she hadn't wanted to leave him unwatched, the others—Caro, Michael, Catriona, and Richard—had taken their evening meal there, in the sitting area on the other side of the room. There'd been lots of conversation, even some laughter; she'd hoped the sound might draw Breckenridge free of whatever held him to sleep, but he hadn't stirred.

His condition hadn't changed, but hers had clarified.

Growing up within her family, with marriages firmly based on love all around, she'd thought she'd known how such unions worked. Now, however, presumably because her desire to establish such a union, a working, sharing, caring partnership with him, had made her more aware, she'd seen more deeply, had been much more sensitive to the currents flowing between Michael and Caro, and between Richard and Catriona. The constant, effortless, most often unvoiced and unremarked flow of sharing, of giving and receiving.

She'd seen that usually the giving came first.

And it was offered without stipulation, without any assumption that the act would be reciprocated, even though, between couples who shared, it inevitably was.

She now understood that love, the giving of it, was paramount to everything else, that everything else was secondary to that unconditional giving.

Taking Breckenridge's hand in her own, she softly stated, "If you come back to me, regardless of whether you love me or not, I will marry you and love you unreservedly to the end of my days."

The saying of the words, the commitment made, changed things; she felt steady, stable, anchored.

She knew where she stood.

Understood now that even if she got nothing in return, her honoring of the love she'd been blessed to feel, to experience, would be the real measure of her success in this life.

Leaning forward, placing her elbows on the bed, clasping his hand between both of hers, she closed her eyes.

And prayed to God and the Lady—they were in Her Vale, after all.

"If you give me the chance to make a future with him, I will seize it and rejoice, and live that future to the best of my ability. I will be true to that vow, to him, and to the love I bear for him, forever and always. Amen."

Chapter Twenty-one

She woke to find dawn light, pearly silver tinged with pink, washing into the room. For a moment, she wondered what had woken her, then she glanced at Breckenridge—into his hazel eyes.

"You're awake!" She only just managed not to squeal. The joy leaping through her was near impossible to contain.

He smiled weakly. His lids drooped, fell. "I've been awake for some time, but didn't want to wake you."

His voice was little more than a whisper.

She realized it was the faint pressure of his fingers on hers that had drawn her from sleep. Those fingers, his hand, were no longer over-warm. Reaching out, she laid her fingers on his forehead. "Your temperature's normal—the fever's broken. *Thank God.*"

Retrieving her hand, refocusing on his face, she felt relief crash through her in a disorienting, almost overpowering wave. "You have to rest." That was imperative; she felt driven by flustered urgency to ensure he understood. "You're mending nicely. Now the crisis has passed, you'll get better day by day. Catriona says that with time, you'll be as good as new." Algaria had warned her to assure him of that.

He swallowed; eyes closed, he shifted his head in what she took to be a nod. "I'll rest in a minute. But first . . . did you mean what you said out there by the bull pen? That you truly want a future with me?"

407

"Yes." She clutched his hand more tightly between hers. "I meant every word."

His lips curved a fraction, then he sighed. Eyes still closed—she sensed he found his lids too heavy to lift—he murmured, "Good. Because I meant every word, too."

She smiled through sudden tears. "Even about our daughters being allowed to look like Cordelia?"

His smile grew more definite. "Said that aloud, did I? Yes, I meant even that, but for pity's sake don't tell her—she'll never let me hear the end of it, and Constance will have my head to boot."

His words were starting to slur again; he was slipping back into healing sleep.

Catriona's words, her warning, rang in Heather's head. She remembered her vow. Rising, she leaned over him; his hand still clasped between hers, she kissed him gently. "Go to sleep and get well, but before you do, I need to tell you this. I love you. I will until the end of my days. I don't expect you to love me back, but that doesn't matter anymore. You have my love regardless, and always will." She kissed him again, sensed he'd heard, but that he was stunned, surprised. He didn't respond.

She drew back. "And now you need to put your mind to getting better. We have a wedding to attend, after all."

She knew he heard that—his features softened, eased.

As he slid into sleep, he was, very gently, smiling.

Breckenridge finally returned to the land of the living just before noon. He opened his eyes and saw Algaria seated on the chair by the bed. She'd pushed it further back and was industriously knitting, but as if sensing his gaze, she looked up—looked at him in that unnerving way she and Catriona shared—then nodded.

"Welcome back." Laying aside her knitting, she stood. "Now, how are you feeling?"

To his surprise and irritation, he discovered he was as weak as a newborn kitten, and the gash in his side, although healing, was still capable of generating enough pain to stop him in his tracks.

But with the aid of Henderson he was able to rise, to attend to the inevitable call of nature, then take a bath. Afterward, he managed to keep upright long enough to shave, then Algaria rebandaged his side.

Catriona, who, summoned, had looked in earlier, returned with one of Richard's nightshirts.

"There's no sense in getting dressed," she informed him. "You won't be able to leave this room—won't be able to leave your bed for long—not until you regain your strength, and that's not going to happen overnight."

Having been laid low once before, he knew she was right. He held up a hand in surrender. "All right. I'll behave."

Nightshirt donned, he allowed Henderson to help him back into the freshly made bed. Catriona and Algaria were conferring on the other side of the room. Glancing at the door, he asked, "Where's Heather?"

Catriona looked at him. "She's sleeping. She's been by your side day and night through the last six days. Now that you're compos mentis again, I insisted she rest. I'll wake her for dinner, but not before."

He nodded absentmindedly. *Six days*? That couldn't be right.

"But as you're wide awake, I'll send Caro up to sit with you."

"Caro?" If Caro had reached here, then six days might well have passed.

"She and Michael arrived yesterday." Turning back to Algaria, Catriona exchanged a last comment, then headed for the door.

Algaria returned to pick up her knitting. "Caro won't be long—she's just finishing luncheon. I'll organize a tray and have it brought up to you. What would you like?"

He was famished but knew from experience he wouldn't be able to eat too much to begin with. Algaria approved his choice of broth and bread, and went off to arrange it.

Five minutes after the door closed behind her, it swung open again, and Caro glided in. Her pale blue gaze immediately fixed on his eyes. Then she smiled. "Thank heavens. You're all right."

He raised a hand and—weakly—gestured to the rocker. "Welcome to the sickroom. I understand I'm to be confined here for some time yet."

"Indeed." Coming forward, she swept up her skirts and sat, her bright eyes searching his face, her continuing smile stating she was happy with what she saw. "You're looking much improved, even from yesterday. Awake is a definite improvement over comatose."

Lips curving, he settled back on the pillows.

Caro, too, leaned back in the rocker. "I'll have you know that you should be abjectly grateful—by coming all this way myself, I've saved you from having to suffer the ministrations of your sisters. Both Constance and Cordelia were hot to set off the instant they heard—I had to exert my powers of persuasion to the fullest to restrain them."

"For which I most sincerely thank you." His smile was wry. "Much as I love them, they're overpowering, and, as you can see, I'm in no state at present to hold my own."

Caro's smile was understanding. "I promised to keep them informed and have duly sent reports south, so I believe you're not in imminent danger of having them descend on you."

"Hmm. Thinking back, I suspect you, and Michael, too, owe me for the last time. Then, you left me to my fate." Four years ago, he'd been shot while he and Michael had been trying to protect Caro.

She inclined her head. "That time we were in London—there was little we could do."

He humphed, but he was smiling.

410

After a moment of studying him, Caro said, "I'm pleased—very pleased—that you've finally made your choice. It's about time you came to your senses."

He arched a brow. "Even if it took a kidnapping to do it?"

She nodded sagely. "Even so." She paused, then more gently asked, "She's the right one for you, isn't she?"

He held her gaze, then nodded. "Yes. Definitely." He hesitated, then added, "I couldn't live without her."

Caro's smile widened until she was beaming. "Wonderful! That's just how it should be."

He wasn't so sure he needed to hear that; the sense of vulnerability and dependency took some getting used to; he wasn't yet sure he'd mastered the knack. "Sadly, it seems that whenever I get close to a prospective wedding, I end up wounded. With you and Michael, I got shot and nearly died. This time, with me and Heather, I got gored and nearly died. I suppose I should be happy that Constance and Cordelia are already married."

Caro laughed. "You probably escaped then because they're so much older than you—you were only a lad when they wed." She paused, head tilting as she studied him. Still smiling, she went on, "You're a protector, you know. That's what you are—that's what you do. And now you've found the lady you're supposed to protect for the rest of your life." Her smile deepened. "Once you marry her, you'll be safe."

He humphed, but continued to smile, and didn't attempt to argue.

Because she was right.

Heather was the lady he would protect for the rest of his life.

Five days later, he was up and about, but still largely confined to his room. Although he descended to the great hall to share meals with the household once more, Catriona and Algaria strongly discouraged any more extensive exercise.

411

As he was intent on regaining his customary rude health as soon as possible—so he and Heather could wed—he bit the bullet, held his tongue, and agreed to abide by their strictures.

Consequently, the meeting that had to be held between him, Richard, and Michael was conducted in the sitting area of his room. At least he was dressed; Caro had brought up trunks of both his and Heather's clothes. In a loose shirt and breeches, with one of his colorful silk robes donned over all, he sat comfortably sprawled on one end of the sofa, while Richard lounged on the other end and Michael sat in an armchair facing them both.

"Right." Michael met Breckenridge's eyes. "What exactly do we know about this blackguard?"

Breckenridge grimaced. "Sadly, not enough."

Richard stirred. "We do know that he's some Scottish laird. That much seems certain."

Breckenridge nodded. "He's a tall, black-haired, large, and well set-up Scotsman, pale, cold eyes his most distinctive feature, and he's at least a gentleman, almost certainly an aristocrat, and very likely a highland nobleman."

"And he arranged to have Heather kidnapped in London and conveyed to Gretna Green, there to be handed over to him." Michael's face was grim.

"Actually, no," Breckenridge said. "He arranged to have 'one of the Cynster sisters' kidnapped—he didn't distinguish between at least the three of them—and according to Heather, that's a highly pertinent fact."

Richard frowned. "Why pertinent?"

"Because while she and Eliza are significant heiresses, Angelica is not. And Heather couldn't tell whether Henrietta and young Mary were also possible targets."

Michael frowned. "So whatever his motive is, it's unlikely to be money."

Breckenridge nodded. "And considering how much blunt he invested in the kidnapping scheme—all the wages and costs involved—I think we must conclude that he isn't short of financial resources."

"Definitely not money, then." Richard caught Breckenridge's eyes. "I've been meaning to ask—do you think Gretna Green being nominated as the handover place was significant?"

Breckenridge grimaced. "It might have been—he might have intended to marry her as part of the plot—but equally it might have simply been convenient for some reason we don't know."

Richard nodded. "The man I sent to inquire in Gretna returned yesterday. No one there, including the magistrate, can add anything to the description we have. And Fletcher and Cobbins were freed by the laird—with plenty of bribes to go around—and they promptly disappeared, heading south at a good clip."

Breckenridge humphed. "I doubt we'd find them too easily. I'd wager they'll have been paid to go to ground. On top of that, I'm not sure they know any more than we now do—Heather did a fine job of milking them for everything they knew."

Michael nodded. "We have to assume this man is clever enough, and has the resources, to cover his tracks well. So where does that leave us?"

"With no real clue to his identity, and even less as to his motive." Expression grim, Breckenridge added, "And we shouldn't forget that he knew enough about the family to describe the girls, and also to avoid coming into the Vale. Once he saw us walk in, and learned this was Cynster land, he retreated."

All three fell silent, turning over all they knew.

Eventually, Richard said, "There's nothing more we can deduce. We have a general description that could fit any number of highland lairds, and enough evidence to discount money as the motive. He's clever, resourceful, and able, but beyond that, we know no more."

Breckenridge nodded. "The point we need to address is that there are two more Cynster sisters in London, possibly four, if Henrietta and Mary are targets, too. Having failed with Heather, will this mysterious laird attempt to seize one of them?"

"Until we understand what's behind this and nullify any threat, we need to consider that threat still extant." Michael met Breckenridge's, then Richard's, eyes. "Until we know otherwise, we need to treat this as a serious, ongoing situation."

Richard nodded. "I've already alerted Devil, but in general terms only."

"Caro and I will leave tomorrow," Michael said. "Our first stop in London will be Grosvenor Square, where I'll report all we've managed to glean to Devil. He'll make sure the other girls are protected and the rest of the family's on guard."

Richard winced. "I can see the battle lines forming. Us being on guard is not going to go over well with the young ladies in question."

Breckenridge shrugged. "Be covert about it, then. Hell— enlist Wolverstone. He'll know how to do it."

Richard shook his head. "A sound idea, but we can't. He— like me—has discovered his roots in the north. He's holed up in his castle in Northumbria, and none of the grandes dames, let alone anyone else, has yet succeeded in winkling him out, not this Season."

"He can still help," Breckenridge said. "And, Lord knows, there are plenty of his married colleagues about who'd be happy to assist."

Michael nodded. "That's true enough. I'll suggest it." He met the others' eyes. "And I'll make sure the gravity of the situation is made very clear. For whatever reason, the Cynster girls appear to be under siege."

Two nights later, Breckenridge lay on his back in his bed and stared up at the shadowy canopy.

Michael and Caro had left the day before, bearing with them news of his and Heather's impending betrothal, along with a notice he'd crafted for the *Gazette,* to which Heather had happily agreed.

All was well on that front.

He hadn't even had to utter the word he didn't want to say, swear the vow he hadn't wanted to swear.

Make the admission he hadn't wanted to make.

He'd been spared, by Heather, and for that he was inexpressibly grateful.

If Catriona hadn't extracted his promise that he wouldn't stir from his bed, from the room, until the next day, he would have been on his way to Heather's room to demonstrate how grateful he was.

The bandages that had wrapped his torso so restrictingly for the past weeks had been removed for good that evening. The stitches Catriona had set in his flesh were tiny, and her doctoring had proved exceptional; the scar was a short, puckered seam at the side of his waist, and he no longer felt any pain. Nevertheless, Catriona had insisted that he remain within the room until tomorrow morning; she wanted to examine how the exposed scar was faring before releasing him to the wider world.

But from tomorrow, he would be free. Free to walk the gardens, then the nearby land, regaining the strength in his legs. Free to ride after that. Free to engage in all sorts of other activities that the injury had denied him.

His mind, predictably, fixated on one particular activity. Clasping his hands behind his head, he stared, unseeing, upward, unable to keep his imagination from churning . . . which really didn't help at all. He'd given his word he wouldn't leave the room.

Beneath his satisfaction lurked a growing restlessness, one unlike any he'd experienced before. He was impatient. Impatient to get on with his life, to take Heather's hand and go forward into his—their—newly scripted future.

Perhaps not surprising. Since he'd regained his wits they'd spent countless hours discussing and planning. Joking and teasing often, yet steadily, element by element, refining their wishes and defining their marriage—their shared future life.

He knew he should sleep, that Catriona wouldn't be pleased if he greeted her hollow-eyed in the morning, but impatience and sexual hunger combined to keep him wide awake.

The door latch lifted; as he turned his head, he had a flash of déjà vu.

A flash that translated into solid reality as Heather slipped into the room.

She saw him looking, smiled, closed the door, and came to the bed.

As before, she was wearing her silk robe.

As before, she halted by the bed, tugged the sash free, and let the robe slide from her shoulders to the floor, revealing nothing but Heather—all pearly soft skin and mouthwatering curves—beneath.

He might have promised Catriona not to leave his bed—he hadn't said anything about someone joining him in it. His own smile wide, he unlaced his fingers and reached across to lift the covers; she beat him to it, quickly raising the sheets and slipping beneath.

But the instant he started to turn to face her, she pressed a hand to his shoulder. "No. You have to lie still, as you are, on your back."

"I do?"

She nodded, chin firm. "All the way through." As she spoke, she was sliding across beneath the sheet. Slipping one sleek thigh across his hips, she shifted and wriggled until she straddled him. The sensation of her skin touching, caressing his, the memories that evoked, poured like unadulterated ambrosia over his senses. The distraction momentarily swamped his wits. It was all he could do to keep his hands, greedy for the feel of her, at her waist, keep his suddenly slavering lust from slipping its leash and ravening.

Propping her elbows on his upper chest, she looked down into his face. And grinned. "Catriona said this should be perfectly all right as long as you remain flat on your back. You mustn't even try to sit up, or do anything else to put pressure on the stitches, but other than that . . ."

She dipped her head and kissed him, a long, languorous promise of pleasure. The necklace she'd taken to wearing hung down, the crystal pendant warm against his skin.

When she drew back to catch her breath, he had to ask, "You discussed this with Catriona?"

Her lips curved; they brushed his. "Not specifically, you and me and this—I simply asked what physical restrictions a man with a wound such as yours would face. She understood instantly what I meant."

He could imagine. "That, I suppose," he murmured, his lips following hers in a series of tempting little brushes, "explains why she's so keen to check my wound in the morning—to see if her handiwork has stood up to the strain."

"Mmm." Heather wasn't interested in talking. She set her lips to his and shut him up, ridiculously thrilled that she could. Thrilled, when he kissed her back, when he followed her lead into the dance, that she actually had that power, that he would indeed consent to let her script and direct, that he— the foremost rake in the ton—was willing to indulge her and follow where she led.

This was her time, her moment to reaffirm, wordlessly yet in a language they both understood, all she'd told him on that night long ago, before they'd somehow lost their way. Before they'd thought too much, spoken too much, perhaps expected too much of the other.

That was behind them now, all misunderstandings wiped away by his selfless act, her response, and his injury.

Her commitment to him, to them, was now much stronger, tried, tested, and forged through the trauma of nearly losing him.

As she pressed him back into the billows of the bed, let her hands, then her lips, whisper over his skin, she opened her heart and let all she felt, all she now knew, tumble out. Let it flow through her hands, her lips, through her limbs as she used them to caress him. Let her love infuse every act, because that was what this was all about. Loving him.

Loving him truly, with a whole and grateful heart.

Loving him with every breath she took, every touch, every yearning heartbeat.

With every scintilla of her soul.

When she raised up and took him in, when she sheathed him in her body and with passion and desire flaring, rode him, pleasured him, she paid homage to that reality and let it free, let it shine.

Let it fill her and overwhelm her.

Let it fill and overwhelm him.

Breckenridge gripped her hips, held her as she rode him, steady and sure and with such open devotion. Eyes nearly blind, all he could see, all he could sense, was her and the powerful currents raging through them. Driven by, carried on, the exquisite sensations she pressed on him, lavished on him.

As she loved him.

He felt the surge of emotions—hers and his—combining in a torrent powerful enough to sweep them both away.

And he was with her again, once again caught in that most giving of acts, that communion of souls. But this time he came to it willingly, wanting it not just at this time but for ever more.

Wanting the transcendent communion for what it was, with no ulterior motive.

As she threw back her head and he felt her body tighten, even as his body answered her call, he glimpsed what drove them—no purpose, no desire beyond one, beyond a deep and abiding, powerful and triumphant, exquisite and enduring love.

She reached for it, clung to it, and he was by her side.

Together they crested, touched and tasted the glory, savored it.

And let it fill them, let it swamp their senses, expand and swell until it shattered them, fragmented them, and flung them into the void.

Ecstasy rushed in and caught them, filled them, buoyed them.

Drowned them in a blissful sea of golden glory and satiation.

It left them at the last, washed up on some distant shore, wracked yet replete, safe in each other's arms.

Night closed her soothing wings over them.

Eventually, with gentle kisses and soothing murmurs, they disengaged. With the promise of that glorious, love-inspired future enshrined and shining in their hearts, in their minds, embedded in their souls, he closed his arms about her, and she held to him, and they slept.

"Catriona says my attack of measles would by now have run its course, so you and I are free to return to London whenever we wish." Her arm linked with Breckenridge's, Heather glanced up at him.

Lips curved, he shook his head in mock disbelief. "Measles. I'm amazed your mother consented to such a story."

Having been released from his room, and all further restrictions, by Catriona that morning, he and Heather were taking the air—blessed fresh air—in a slow stroll around the herb garden. Although he felt steady enough, he was grateful for Heather's support, the additional prop to his balance. His muscles would need a day or two to return to their usual reliable form.

"Mama and the others decided that, although your story of us coming up here to consider if we would suit away from the madding crowd explained our initial presence here, it didn't account well enough for such an extended stay." Meeting his eyes, she smiled. "You should be pleased—the story of you bringing me up here to recover, hidden away from the eyes of the ton, and then valiantly staying to keep me company through my convalescence, paints you in a distinctly romantic light."

He humphed. After a moment, added, "I suppose the distraction of measles will at least have ensured none of the gossipmongers caught any whiff of your abduction."

"Mama said they haven't, so all's well there." She glanced up at him again, a soft, confident smile in her eyes. "And the news of our engagement will wipe all other thoughts from their heads."

"True." He couldn't deny the surge of pure masculine satisfaction that filled him at the sight of that eminently feminine smile. When he'd dragged her out of Lady Herford's salon on that fateful night so many weeks ago, she'd been . . . like a chrysalis waiting to unfurl. Through her abduction and their journey, through the trials they'd faced since, she'd transformed into the beautiful, assured, scintillating lady who would be his viscountess.

His lover, his wife.

She tipped her head, eyes studying his face. "What is it?"

She'd grown so much . . . what about him?

He halted. Started to think, to evaluate. Stopped himself. Drawing in a breath, he turned to her, his hand sliding to caress hers. He looked into her eyes. "You've given me everything I need of you—thanks to you I have all my heart desires, all I thought I might never have. All I need for a wonderful, fulfilling future. And I nearly lost it all."

She held his gaze but was wise enough not to interrupt. If she had . . .

He drew breath and forged on, "Nearly dying clarified things. When you stand on the border between life and death, the truly important things are easy to discern. One of the things I saw and finally understood was that only fools and cowards leave the truth of love unsaid. Only the weak leave love unacknowledged."

Holding her gaze, all but lost in the shimmery blue of her eyes, he raised her hand to his lips, gently kissed. "So, my darling Heather, even though you already know it, let me put the truth—my truth—into words. I love you. With all my heart, to the depths of my soul. And I will love you forever, until the day I die."

Her smile lit his world. "Just as well." Happiness shone in her eyes. She pressed his fingers. "Because I plan to be with you, by your side, every day for the rest of your life, and in spirit far beyond. I'm yours for all eternity."

Smiling, he closed his hand about hers. "Mine to protect for our eternity."

Yes. Neither said the word, yet the sense of it vibrated in the air all around them.

A high-pitched giggle broke the spell, had them both looking along the path.

To Lucilla and Marcus, who slipped out from behind a raised bed and raced toward them.

Reaching them, laughing with delight, the pair whooped and circled.

Heather glanced to left and right, trying to keep the twins in sight, uncertain of what had them so excited. So exhilarated.

Almost as if they were reacting to the emotions coursing through her, and presumably Breckenridge. Her husband-to-be.

"You're getting married!" Lucilla crowed.

Catching Lucilla's eye as the pair slowed their circling dance, Heather nodded. "Yes, we are. And I rather think you two will have to come down to London to be flower girl and page boy."

Absolute delight broke across Lucilla's face. She looked at her brother. "See? I told you—the Lady *never* makes a mistake, and if you do what she tells you, you get a reward."

"I suppose." Marcus looked up at Breckenridge. "London will be fun." He switched his gaze to Lucilla. "Come on! Let's go and tell Mama and Papa."

The pair shot off, racing up the grassy path.

Along with Breckenridge, Heather stood and watched them go. Remembered . . .

"I've been meaning to ask," Breckenridge said, "just how you came to topple backward off that rail." He looked at her. "What with one thing and another, the point slipped my mind."

Heather met his gaze. "Mine, too."

He read her eyes, then, brows rising, looked in the direction in which the twins had gone. "Ah. Perhaps that's one of those questions that are better left unasked."

"It's certainly one of those better left unanswered." Sliding her hand from his and retaking his arm, she started them strolling again.

Breckenridge was quiet for a while, then he looked up at the manor and said, "Will you think it odd of me to suggest that we should, perhaps, leave the Vale and your sometimes unnerving relatives by marriage as soon as we possibly can?"

"How about tomorrow?" She glanced up at his face.

He caught her gaze. "Immediately after breakfast. It's too late to set out today."

She nodded. "Indeed." She looked ahead. "And besides, I have plans for tonight."

"Do you?"

"Of course." She met his gaze, her own filled with love and unexpected understanding. "The announcement you made a few minutes ago deserves an appropriate response, don't you think?"

He inclined his head. "Indubitably." After a moment, he added, "Who knows? With the right form of response, you might even induce me to utter the words again."

She laughed. "A challenge." She met his gaze. "A challenge we can wrestle with, wrestle over back and forth, for the rest of our days."

"Indeed." He held her loving gaze, raised her fingers to his lips. "For the rest of our days."

Epilogue

A week later, the laird who had arranged Heather Cynster's kidnapping walked into his great hall.

With more than an hour before the midday meal, he debated going to his office to fill the time. Instead, seeing his copy of yesterday's *Edinburgh Gazette* waiting on the sideboard, he picked up the news sheet, poured himself a tankard of ale from the pitcher left ready, and headed for his carver at the high table.

He was sitting, quietly perusing the latest news, when a shriek of fury rent the air. Luckily the sound was sufficiently distanced, muted by the solid stone walls, for him to ignore it. Idly he wondered what, this time, had displeased his mother, then, deciding he would no doubt hear soon enough, went back to the news sheet.

Sure enough, less than a minute later he heard her footsteps flying down her tower stairs. She burst into the great hall, saw him, and stormed onto the dais. Reaching his side, she slapped yesterday's *London Gazette* over the Edinburgh paper.

"She's not ruined!" She stabbed a finger at a notice in the social announcements column. Shrieked at the top of her voice, "The damned chit's not *ruined*—she's *engaged*! To Breckenridge!"

He picked up the London sheet, found and read the notice in question, the usual bland wording announcing the betrothal of Heather Cynster to Timothy Danvers, Viscount Breckenridge. Racking his memory for what, from his days in London, he recalled of Breckenridge, matching that with his recollection of the man who'd escorted Heather Cynster into the Vale . . . yes, Breckenridge could have been that man. The man who had so thoroughly disrupted his plans.

"Interesting," he murmured. And instantly regretted it.

"Interesting? *Interesting*? It's not interesting—its *infuriating*! It's—"

He shut his ears to his mother's diatribe. Consulted his own feelings instead. Revisited his impressions, what he'd sensed of the man—Breckenridge—and his relationship to the girl . . . would that he himself were so lucky. That being so, he couldn't find it in him to resent Breckenridge, to rail at his claiming the Cynster girl as his.

Reaching for his tankard, he sipped, silently toasting the pair. Good luck to them. They, at least, had escaped this nightmare.

"You!" His mother jabbed a fingernail into his upper arm, effectively jolting him back to his reality. She leaned close to hiss, "You were supposed to bring her here and make sure she was ruined. Ruined in the eyes of the entire ton. Instead, she's getting married to one of the most eligible noblemen in England! So you've failed with her, but you know my price. My nonnegotiable price. So what are you going to do about it?"

When he didn't rush to reply but instead raised his tankard and, gaze forward, took a long sip of ale, she leaned even closer to say, "Correct me if I'm wrong, *my dear*"—the endearment dripped with latent scorn and fury—"but for you, time is running out."

She was right, but he wasn't going to let her guess at the chill that gripped his innards at the thought of what was at stake. Keeping his posture relaxed, he almost languidly shrugged. "You'll just have to settle for one of her sisters. *One* of the Cynster sisters was our bargain, and either one of the others will do just as well to fulfill it."

He'd used every last hour while they'd waited to hear the fate of Heather Cynster to search, again, high and low, for the goblet his mother had stolen and hidden. The goblet he needed to save all he held dear. His mother had never been able to bend him to her will, any more than she'd been able to influence his father. But she'd learned of the goblet, and of its importance to him, and had seized her chance.

She now had an exquisitely honed weapon she could wield, and was intent on wielding, to get him to do as she wished.

Her wish, her obsession, was insane. He knew it.

He also knew he had no choice but to carry out her manic dictates.

Still . . . sipping his ale, he allowed himself to indulge the recurring fantasy of simply telling her to do her worst and be damned. . . .

A door deep in the keep slammed open. Two pairs of small feet came clattering over the flags.

Lifting his head, he set down his tankard as two tousle-headed young boys came rushing in, bringing the fresh air of the loch, the scent of pines and firs, and three water spaniels galloping in with them.

The boys saw him, and wide grins split their faces.

If they saw his mother standing beside him, they gave no sign as, with a cheer and a whoop, they raced up the great hall, clambered up onto the dais, and flung themselves at him.

He'd shifted his carver back enough to grab them, to tumble them in his arms, wrestle them about, then settle them in his lap.

They clung like monkeys, chattering nonstop, filling his ears with the highlights of their morning's excursion with his gamekeeper, Scanlon.

Their warmth wrapped about him, settled to his bones, dispelling the chill that dealing with his mother had evoked.

For her part, although she glared at the boys, furious at the interruption, and even more over his turning away from her to them, she knew better than to say a word against them. They were all he had left of a family he'd held dear. His cousin Mitchell had grown up alongside him, but Mitchell and his sweet wife Krista were now dead, and the boys, five and six years old, were all he had left of them. . . .

He drew in a deep breath. Struggled to harness the sudden rage that ripped through him—rage that the woman standing at his side should dare to threaten the boys, their future, and the future of every other soul under his care.

The dogs milled, whined, more attuned to his hidden emotions than the boys wriggling in his lap. One dog, the eldest, Gwarr, came to sit between him and his mother, dark eyes fixed on her, tongue lolling from between long jaws lined with strong white teeth.

His mother edged back a step, thin-lipped and tense.

He forced himself to look at her, the smile he'd summoned for the boys draining from his face. Keeping the anger, the sheer ire and fury she and her scheme provoked, from his voice—so the boys wouldn't sense it and be disturbed—he met her eyes and nonchalantly shrugged. "One of the Cynster sisters, brought here and thus effectively ruined—that was our bargain. I'll keep my end of it." He held her gaze. "And you'll keep yours."

Eyes narrowed, her face pinched, her expression, as always, sour, she held his gaze for a pregnant moment, then humphed, swung on her heel, and stalked off.

His fury drained from him.

Idly reaching out to stroke Gwarr's head, he turned back to the imps in his lap. Utterly trusting, their bright blue eyes looked out on the world with unalloyed hope and untarnished expectations.

He would give a great deal to ensure they had all the best in life he could give them.

Glancing at the large circular clock on the wall, he confirmed there was still half an hour before the meal. Summoning his broadest brogue, he looked down at the boys. "Shall we nae gae oot an' luk in on the horses, then?"

Later he could think about kidnapping Eliza Cynster.

First, he would remind himself of why he would.

Turn the page
for an excerpt from

In Pursuit of Eliza Cynster

Coming soon

from

Piatkus

J t really isn't fair." Elizabeth Marguerite Cynster, Eliza
to all, grumbled the complaint beneath her breath as
she stood alone, cloaked in the shadows of a massive
potted palm by the wall of her eldest cousin's ballroom.
The magnificent ducal ballroom was glittering and glowing,
playing host to the crème de la crème of the ton, bedecked
in their finest satins and silks, bejeweled and beringed, all
swept up in a near-rapturous outpouring of happiness and
unbridled delight.

As there were few among the ton likely to decline an
invitation to waltz at an event hosted by Honoria, Duchess
of St. Ives, and her powerful husband, Devil Cynster, Duke
of St. Ives, the huge room was packed.

The glow from the sparkling chandeliers sheened over
elaborately coiffed curls and winked and blinked from the
hearts of countless diamonds. Gowns in a range of brilliant
hues swirled as the ladies danced, creating a shifting sea
of vibrant plumage contrasting sharply with the regulation
black and white of their partners. Laughter and conversation blanketed the scene. A riot of perfumes filled the air. In
the background a small orchestra did its best with one of the
most popular waltzes.

Eliza watched as her elder sister, Heather, circled the
dance floor in the arms of her handsome husband-to-be, ex-

foremost rake of the ton, Timothy Danvers, Viscount Breckenridge. Even if the ball had not been thrown expressly to celebrate their betrothal, to formally announce it to the ton and the polite world, the besotted look in Breckenridge's eyes every time his gaze rested on Heather was more than enough to tell the tale. The ex-darling of the ton's ladies was now Heather's sworn protector and slave.

And Heather was his. The joy in her face, that lit her eyes, declared that to the world.

Despite her own less than happy state, much of it a direct outcome of the events leading to Heather's engagement, Eliza was sincerely, to her soul, happy for her sister.

They'd both spent years—literally *years*—searching for their respective heroes among the ton, through the drawing rooms and ballrooms in which young ladies such as they were expected to confine themselves in hunting for suitable, eligible parties. Yet neither Heather, Eliza, nor Angelica, their younger sister, had had any luck in locating the gentlemen fated to be their heroes. They had, logically, concluded that said heroes, the gentlemen for them, were not to be found within their proscribed orbit, so they had, also logically, decided to extend their search into those areas where the more elusive, yet still suitable and eligible, male members of the ton congregated.

The strategy had worked for their eldest female cousin Amanda, and, employed with a different twist, for her twin sister Amelia, as well.

And, albeit in a most unexpected way, the same approach had worked for Heather, too.

Clearly for Cynster females, success in finding their own true hero lay in boldly stepping beyond their accustomed circles.

Which was precisely what Eliza was set on doing *except* that, through the adventure that had befallen Heather within minutes of her taking her first step into that racier world—namely being kidnapped, rescued by Breckenridge, and then escaping in his company—a plot to target "the Cynster sisters" had been exposed.

Whether the targets were limited to Heather, Eliza, and Angelica, or included their younger cousins Henrietta and Mary, no one knew.

No one understood the motive behind the threat, not even what was eventually intended beyond being kidnapped and possibly taken to Scotland. As for who was behind it, no one had any real clue, but the upshot was that Eliza and the other three "Cynster sisters" as yet unbetrothed had been placed under constant guard. She hadn't been able to set toe outside her parents' house without one of her brothers, or if not them, one of her cousins—every bit as bad—appearing at her elbow.

And looming.

For her, taking even half a step outside the restrictive circles of the upper echelons of the ton was now impossible. If she tried, a large, male, brotherly or cousinly hand would close about her elbow and yank her unceremoniously back.

Such behavior on their part was, she had to admit, understandable, but . . . "For how long?" Their protective cordon had been in place for three weeks and showed no signs of relaxing. "I'm already twenty-four. If I don't find my hero this year, next year I'll be on the shelf."

Muttering to herself wasn't a habit, but the evening was drawing to a close and, as usual at such ton events, nothing had come of it for her. Which was why she was hugging the wall in the screening shadows of the huge palm; she was worn out with smiling and pretending she had any interest whatsoever in the very proper young gentlemen who, through the night, had vied for her attention.

As a well-dowered, well-bred, well-brought-up Cynster young lady she'd never been short of would-be Romeos. Sadly, she'd never felt the slightest inclination to play Juliet to any of them. Like Angelica, Eliza was convinced she would recognize her hero, if not in the instant she laid eyes on him—Angelica's theory—then at least once she'd spent a few hours in his company.

Heather, in contrast, had always been uncertain over recognizing her hero—but then she'd known Breckenridge, not well but more than by sight, for many years, and until their adventure, she hadn't realized he was the one for her. Heather had mentioned that their cousin-by-marriage, Catriona, who, being an earthly representative of the deity known in parts of Scotland as "The Lady," tended to "know" things, had suggested that Heather needed to "see" her hero clearly, which had proved very much to be the case.

Catriona had given Heather a necklace and pendant designed to assist a young lady in finding her true love—her hero; Catriona had said the necklace was supposed to be passed from Heather, to Eliza, to Angelica, then to Henrietta, and Mary, before ultimately returning to Scotland and Catriona's daughter, Lucilla.

Raising one hand, Eliza touched the fine chain interspersed with small amethyst beads that circled her neck; the rose quartz pendant depending from it was hidden in the valley between her breasts. The chain lay concealed beneath the delicate lace of the fashionable fichu and collar that filled the scooped neckline of her gold silk gown.

The chain was now hers, so where was the hero it was supposed to help her recognize?

Obviously not here. No gentleman with hero-potential had miraculously appeared. Not that she had expected one to, not here in the very heart of the upper echelons of tonnish society. Nevertheless, disappointment and dragging dejection bloomed.

Through finding her hero, Heather had—entirely unintentionally, but nevertheless effectively—stymied Eliza. Her hero did not exist within tonnish circles, but she could no longer step outside to hunt him down.

"What the devil am I to do?"

A footman drifting around the outskirts of the ballroom

with a silver salver balanced on one palm heard her and turned to peer into the shadows. Eliza barely glanced at him, but seeing her, his features relaxed and he stepped forward.

"Miss Eliza." Relief in his voice, the footman bowed and offered the salver. "A gentleman asked that this be delivered to you, miss. A good half hour ago, it must be now. We couldn't find you in the crowd."

Wondering which tedious gentleman was now sending her notes, Eliza reached for the folded parchment resting on the salver. "Thank you, Cameron." The footman was from her parents' household, seconded to the St. Ives' household to assist with the massive ball. "Who was it, do you know?"

"No, miss. It wasn't handed to me, but to one of the others. They passed it on."

"Thank you." Eliza nodded a dismissal.

With a brief bow, Cameron withdrew.

With no great expectations, Eliza unfolded the note. The writing was bold, a series of brash black strokes on the white paper.

Very masculine in style.

Tipping the sheet to catch the light, Eliza read:

Meet me in the back parlor, if you dare. No, we're not acquainted. I haven't signed this note because my name will mean nothing to you. We haven't been introduced, and there is no grande dame present who would be likely to oblige me. However, the fact I am here, attending this ball, speaks well enough to my antecedents and my social standing. And I know where the back parlor is.

I believe it is time we met face-to-face, if nothing else to discover if there is any further degree of association we might feel inclined to broach.

As I started this note, so I will end it: Meet me in the back parlor, if you dare.

I'll be waiting.

Eliza couldn't help but smile. How . . . impertinent. How daring. To send her such a note in her cousin's house, under the very noses of the grandes dames and all her family.

Yet whoever he was, he was patently there, in the house, and if he knew where the back parlor was . . .

She read the note again, debating, but there was no reason she could see why she shouldn't slip away to the back parlor and discover who had dared to send such a note.

Stepping out from her hiding place, she slipped swiftly, as unobtrusively as she could, around the still-crowded room. She felt certain the note writer was correct—she didn't know him; they'd never met. She didn't know any gentleman who would have thought to send such an outrageous summons to a private tryst inside St. Ives House.

Excitement, anticipation surged. Perhaps this was it—the moment when her hero would appear before her.

Stepping through a minor door, she walked quickly down a corridor, then turned down another, then another, increasingly dimly lit, steadily making her way to the rear corner of the huge mansion. Deep in the private areas, distant from the reception rooms and their noise, the back parlor gave onto the gardens at the rear of the house; Honoria often sat there of an afternoon, watching her children play on the lawns below the terrace.

Eliza finally reached the end of the last corridor. The parlor door stood before her. She didn't hesitate; turning the knob, she opened the door and walked in.

The lamps weren't lit, but moonlight poured through the windows and glass doors that gave onto the terrace. Glancing around and seeing no one, she closed the door and walked deeper into the room. Perhaps he was waiting in one of the armchairs facing the windows.

Nearing the chairs, she saw they were empty. She halted. Frowned. Had he given up and left? "Hello?" She started to turn. "Is there anyone—"

A faint rush of sound came from behind her.

She whirled—too late.

A hard arm snaked about her waist and jerked her back against a solid male body.

She opened her mouth—

A huge palm swooped and slapped a white cloth over her mouth and nose. And held it there.

She struggled, breathed in—the smell was sickly sweet, cloying. . . .

Her muscles went to water.

Even as she sagged, she fought to turn her head, but the heavy palm followed, keeping the horrid cloth over her mouth and nose. . . .

Until reality slid away and darkness engulfed her.